Praise for the Shiva Trilogy

'I wish many more would be inspired by Amish Tripathi...'

— Amitabh Bachchan, Indian actor and living legend

'It's a labour of love... Amish also humanizes his characters, something which most popular Indian writers fail miserably at.'

— Mint

'The Shiva Trilogy is a racy mytho-thriller with a masala twist, like *Amar Chitra Katha* on steroids.'

— Rashmi Bansal, bestselling author of
Stay Hungry Stay Foolish

'I was blown away with the world of Meluha and riveted by Amish's creation of it.'

— Karan Johar, renowned filmmaker

'Shiva rocks. Just how much Shiva rocks the imagination is made grandiosely obvious in *The Immortals of Meluha*. [...] Shiva's journey from cool dude [...] to Mahadev [...] is a reader's delight. [...] What really engages is the author's crafting of Shiva, with almost boy-worship joy.'

— The Times of India

www.authoramish.com

'The Immortals of Meluha [...] sees Lord Shiva and his intriguing life with a refreshing perspective. [...] Beautifully written creation. [...] Simply unputdownable for any lover of Indian history and mythology.'

– Society

'[...] a gripping tale that combines lots of action with deep yet accessible philosophy. Amish does not disappoint. [...] *The Secret of the Nagas* is furiously packed with action and intrigue and leaves the reader guessing.'

– Outlook

'The Secret of the Nagas is impressive in its conception... Tripathi is an excellent storyteller.'

– DNA

'Amish excels at describing action scenes, which are often a pleasure to read. The gore and raw emotion would make film maker Mel Gibson proud.'

– New Indian Express

'The author's grip is steady throughout the narrative ... The war has the readers' undivided attention, giving the Trilogy an end it deserves.'

– Mid-Day

The Secret of the Nagas

Book 2
of the
Shiva Trilogy

Amish

westland ltd

61, II Floor, Silverline Building, Alapakkam Main Road, Maduravoyal, Chennai 600095
93, I Floor, Sham Lal Road, Daryaganj, New Delhi 110002
www. westlandbooks.in

Published by westland ltd 2011

Amish Tripathi asserts the moral right to be identified as the author of this work.

This is a work of fiction. Names, characters, places and incidents are either the product of the author's imagination or are used fictitiously and any resemblance to any actual person living or dead, events and locales is entirely coincidental.

ISBN: 978-93-81626-34-4

Cover Design by Rashmi Pusalkar.
Photo of Lord Shiva by Chandan Kowli.

Inside book formatting and typesetting by Ram Das Lal
Printed at Thomson Press (India) Ltd.

www.authoramish.com

To Preeti & Neel...

Unlucky are those who search the seven
seas for paradise

Fortunate are those who experience the only
heaven
that truly exists, the heaven that lives in the
company
of our loved ones

I am truly fortunate

Satyam Shivam Sundaram
Shiva is truth. Shiva is beauty
Shiva is the masculine. Shiva is the feminine
Shiva is a Suryavanshi. Shiva is a Chandravanshi

Contents

Acknowledgements

The first book of the Shiva Trilogy, *The Immortals of Meluha*, was surprisingly well received. To be honest, I felt the pressure of trying to match up to the first book with *The Secret of the Nagas*. I don't know if I have succeeded. But I have had a great time bringing the second chapter in Shiva's grand adventure to you. I would like to take a minute to acknowledge those who made this journey possible for me.

Lord Shiva, my God, my Leader, my Saviour. I have been trying to decipher why He blessed an undeserving person like me with this beautiful story. I don't have an answer as yet.

My father-in-law & a devoted Shiva Bhakt, the late Dr Manoj Vyas, who passed away just a few months before the release of this book. A man I intensely admired, he continues to live in my heart.

Preeti, my wife. The bedrock of my life. My closest advisor. Not just the wind beneath my wings, but the wings themselves.

My family: Usha, Vinay, Bhavna, Himanshu, Meeta, Anish, Donetta, Ashish, Shernaz, Smita, Anuj, Ruta. For their untiring support and love. Bhavna needs an additional mention for helping me with the copy editing. As does Donetta for building and maintaining my first website.

Sharvani Pandit, my editor. Stubborn and fiercely committed to the Shiva Trilogy. It's an honour to work with her.

Rashmi Pusalkar, the designer of this book's cover. A fine artist, a magician. She is headstrong and always delivers.

Gautam Padmanabhan, Paul Vinay Kumar, Renuka Chatterjee, Satish Sundaram, Anushree Banerjee, Vipin Vijay, Manisha Sobhrajani and the fantastic team at Westland, my publishers. For their hard work, drive and supreme belief in the Shiva Trilogy.

Anuj Bahri, my agent. He has been a friend and has supported me when I needed it the most. And if I connect the dots of my serendipitous journey into writing, I must also thank Sandipan Deb, who introduced me to Anuj.

Chandan Kowli, the photographer for the cover. Talented & brilliant, he shot the required photograph perfectly. Chintan Sareen, for creating the snake in CG and Julien Dubois for assisting him. Prakesh Gor, for the make-up. Sagar Pusalkar, for the system work. They have truly created magic.

Sangram Surve, Shalini Iyer and the team at Think Why Not, the advertising & digital marketing agency for the book. It is a pleasure to work with these marketing geniuses.

Kawal Shoor and Yogesh Pradhan for their good advice during the formulation of the initial marketing plan. They helped me get my thoughts together on how the book should be marketed.

And last, but certainly not the least, you the reader. For accepting my first book with open arms. Your support has left me humbled. I hope I don't disappoint you with this second installment of the Shiva Trilogy. Everything that you may like in this book is the blessing of Lord Shiva. Everything that you don't like is due to my inability to do justice to that blessing.

The Shiva Trilogy

Shiva! The Mahadev. The God of Gods. Destroyer of Evil. Passionate lover. Fierce warrior. Consummate dancer. Charismatic leader. All-powerful, yet incorruptible. A quick wit, accompanied by an equally quick and fearsome temper.

Over the centuries, no foreigner who came to India – conqueror, merchant, scholar, ruler, traveller – believed that such a great man could possibly have existed in reality. They assumed that he must have been a mythical God, whose existence was possible only in the realms of human imagination. Unfortunately, this belief became our received wisdom.

But what if we are wrong? What if Lord Shiva was not a figment of a rich imagination, but a person of flesh and blood? Like you and me. A man who rose to become godlike because of his karma. That is the premise of the Shiva Trilogy, which interprets the rich mythological heritage of ancient India, blending fiction with historical fact.

This work is therefore a tribute to Lord Shiva and the lesson that his life is to us. A lesson lost in the depths of

time and ignorance. A lesson, that all of us can rise to be
better people. A lesson, that there exists a potential god
in every single human being. All we have to do is listen to
ourselves.

The Immortals of Meluha was the first book in the trilogy
that chronicles the journey of this extraordinary hero. You
are holding the second book, *The Secret of the Nagas*, in
your hands. One more book is to follow: *The Oath of the
Vayuputras.*

Note from the Author

The Secret of the Nagas is revealed from this page forth. This is the second book of the Shiva Trilogy and begins from the moment where its prequel, *The Immortals of Meluha*, ended. While I believe that you can enjoy this book by itself, perhaps, you may enjoy it more if you read *The Immortals of Meluha* first. In case you have already read *The Immortals of Meluha*, please ignore this message.

I hope you enjoy reading this book as much as I have loved writing it.

Also, there are many people from various different religions who write in to me, asking whether I believe that Lord Shiva is superior to other Gods. If I may, I would like to repeat my response here. There is a lovely Sanskrit line in the Rig Veda which captures the essence of my belief.

Ekam Sat Vipra Bahudha Vadanti.
Truth is one, though the sages know it as many.

God is one, though different religions approach Him differently.
Call Him Shiva, Vishnu, Allah, Jesus or any other form of
God that you believe in.
Our paths may be different. Our destination is the same.

Before the Beginning

The boy was running as fast as his feet could carry him, the frost-bitten toe sending shards of icy pain up his leg. The woman's plea kept ringing in his ears: 'Help me. Please help me!'

He refused to slow down, sprinting towards his village. And then, he was yanked effortlessly by a large hairy arm. He was dangling in the air, desperately trying to get a foothold. The boy could hear the monster's sickening laugh as he toyed with him. Then, the other grotesque arm spun him around and held him tight.

The boy was shocked into stillness. The body was that of the hairy monster, but the face was of the beautiful woman he had just fled away from moments ago. The mouth opened, but the sound that emanated was not a mellifluous feminine one, but a blood-curdling roar.

'You enjoyed this, didn't you? You enjoyed my distress at being tortured, didn't you? You ignored my pleas, didn't you? Now this face will haunt you for the rest of your life!'

Then a grotesque arm holding a short sword came up from nowhere and decapitated the gorgeous head.

'Noooooooo!' screamed the little boy, snapping out of his dream.

He looked around his straw bed, disoriented. It was late evening. A little bit of sunshine had made its way into the otherwise dark hut. A small fire was dying out near the door. It suddenly burst into flames with a fresh breath of oxygen as a person rushed into the tiny room.

'Shiva? What happened? Are you alright, my son?'

The boy looked up, completely bewildered. He felt his mother's hand wrap itself around him and pull his tired head down to her bosom. He heard her soothing voice, sympathetic and understanding. 'It's all right, my child. I am here. I am here.'

The boy felt the fear release from his taut body as his eyes shed long held back tears.

'What is it, my son? The same nightmare?'

The boy shook his head. The tears turned into an angrier deluge.

'It's not your fault. What could you have done, son? He was three times larger than you. A grown man.'

The boy didn't say anything, but stiffened. The mother continued to gently run her hand over his face, wiping the tears away. 'You would have been killed.'

The boy suddenly jerked back.

'THEN I SHOULD HAVE BEEN KILLED! I DESERVED IT!'

The mother was shocked into silence. He was a good son. He had never raised his voice at her before. Never. She quickly set this thought aside as she reached out to soothe his face. 'Don't say that again, Shiva. What would happen to me if you died?'

Shiva curled his small fist, banging it against his forehead. He kept at it till his mother pulled his fist away. An angry, reddish-black mark had formed right between his eyebrows.

The mother held his arms down again, pulling him towards her. Then she said something her son was not prepared to hear. 'Listen, my child! You yourself had said that she didn't fight back. She could have reached for his knife and stabbed him, couldn't she?'

The son didn't say anything. He just nodded.

'Do you know why she didn't do that?'

The boy looked up at his mother, curious.

'Because she was practical. She knew she would probably be killed if she fought back.'

Shiva continued to stare blankly at his mother.

'The sin was being committed against her. And yet, she did what she could to stay alive — not fight back.'

His eyes didn't waiver for one instant from his mother's face.

'Why is it wrong for you to be as pragmatic and want to stay alive?'

The boy started sobbing again as some sense of comfort seeped silently into him.

Chapter 1

The Strange Demon

'Sati!' screamed Shiva, as he rapidly drew his sword and started sprinting towards his wife, pulling his shield forward as he ran.

She'll run into a trap!

'Stop!' yelled Shiva, picking up his pace as he saw her dash into a cluster of trees alongside the road leading to the Ramjanmabhoomi temple in Ayodhya.

Sati was totally focused on chasing the retreating hooded Naga, her sword drawn and held far from her body, like a seasoned warrior with her prey in sight.

It took a few moments for Shiva to catch up with Sati, to ascertain that she was safe. As they continued to give chase, Shiva's focus shifted to the Naga. He was shocked.

How did that dog move so far ahead?

The Naga, showing surprising agility, was effortlessly navigating between the trees and undulating ground of the hillside, picking up pace. Shiva remembered battling with the Naga at the Brahma temple at Meru, when he had met Sati for the first time.

His slow leg movements at the Brahma temple were just a battle strategy.

Shiva flipped his shield, clipping it on to his back, to get room to run faster. Sati was keeping pace to his left. She suddenly made a grunting sound and pointed to the right, to a fork in the path that was coming up. Shiva nodded. They would split up and try to cut off the Naga from opposite ends on the narrow ridge ahead.

Shiva dashed to his right with a renewed burst of speed, sword at the ready. Sati stayed her course behind the Naga, running equally hard. The ground beneath Shiva's feet on the new path had evened out and he managed to cover the distance rapidly. He noticed that the Naga had pulled his shield into his right hand. The wrong hand for defence. Shiva frowned.

Quickly coming up to the Naga's right, with Sati still some distance away, Shiva reached with his left hand, drew a knife and flung it at the Naga's neck. A stunned Shiva then saw a magnificent manoeuvre that he hadn't imagined possible.

Without turning to look at the knife or even breaking a step, the Naga pulled his shield forward in the path of the knife. With the knife safely bouncing off the shield, the Naga effortlessly let the shield clip on to his back, maintaining his pace.

Shiva gaped in awe, his speed slackening.

He blocked the knife without even looking at it! Who the hell is this man?

Sati meanwhile had maintained her pace, edging closer to the Naga as Shiva ran in from the other trail onto the path that the Naga was on.

Seeing Sati cross the narrow ridge, Shiva picked up speed, closing in on his wife. Because of the steep angle of the sloping ridge, he could see the Naga further ahead, reaching the wall at the bottom of the hill. The wall protected the Ramjanmabhoomi temple at the base from animal attacks and trespassers. The height of the wall gave Shiva hope. There was no way the Naga could jump over it. He would have to climb, giving Sati and him the crucial seconds needed to catch up and mount an attack.

The Naga came to the same realisation as well. As he neared the wall, he pirouetted on his heels, hands reaching to his sides, drawing out two swords. The sword in his right hand was a traditional long sword, glinting in the evening sun. The one in his left, a short sword with a strange double blade mounted on a central pivot at the hilt. Shiva pulled his shield forward as he neared the Naga. Sati attacked the Naga from his right.

The Naga swung the long sword hard, forcing Sati to step back. With Sati on the back foot, the Naga swerved with his left hand, making Shiva duck to avoid a strike. As the Naga's sword swept safely away, Shiva jumped high and struck down from his height, a blow almost impossible to defend if the opponent is not holding a shield. The Naga, however, effortlessly stepped back, avoiding the strike, while thrusting forward with his short sword, putting Shiva on the back foot. The Neelkanth had to quickly swing his shield up to deflect the blow.

Sati again moved forward, her sword forcing the Naga back. Reaching behind with her left hand, she pulled out a knife and threw it. The Naga bent his head at the exact moment, letting the knife sail harmlessly into the wall. Shiva and Sati were yet to get a single strike on the Naga, but he was progressively being forced to retreat. It was a matter of time before he would be pinned against the wall.

By the Holy Lake, I finally have him.

And then, the Naga swung ferociously with his left hand. The sword was too short to reach Shiva and it appeared to be a wasted manoeuvre. Shiva pushed forward, confident he would strike the Naga on his torso. But the Naga swung back, this time his thumb pressing a lever on the pivot of the short sword. One of the twin blades suddenly extended beyond the length of the other, doubling the reach of the sword. The blade cut Shiva on his shoulder. Its poisoned edge sent a jolt of electricity through his body, immobilising him.

'Shiva!' screamed Sati, as she swung down on the sword in the Naga's right hand, hoping to knock the blade out. Moments before the impact, the Naga dropped his long sword, causing Sati to lurch, her sword slipping out of her hand as she struggled to regain her balance.

'No!' screamed Shiva, helpless on his back, unable to move.

He had noticed what Sati had forgotten. The knife Sati had flung at the Naga, when he had been discovered hiding behind a tree at the Ramjanmabhoomi temple, was tied to his right hand. The Naga swiped with his right hand at the falling Sati's abdomen. Sati realised her mistake too late.

But the Naga pulled his hand back at the last moment. What would have been a lethal blow turned into a surface wound, running a trickle of blood. The Naga jabbed Sati hard with his left elbow, breaking her nose and knocking her down.

With both his enemies immobilised, the Naga quickly flicked his long sword up with his right foot. He swung both his weapons into their scabbards, eyes still on Shiva and Sati. The Naga then jumped high, holding the top of the wall behind him with his hands.

'Sati!' screamed Shiva, rushing towards his wife as the poison released its stranglehold.

Sati was clutching her abdomen. The Naga frowned, for the wound was just a surface nick. Then his eyes flashed wide.

She is carrying a baby.

The Naga crunched his immense stomach, pulling his legs up in one smooth motion, soaring over the wall.

'Press tight!' shouted Shiva, expecting a deep gash.

Shiva breathed easy when he realised that it was a minor wound, though the blood loss and the knock on Sati's nose was causing him worry.

Sati looked up, blood running down her nose and her eyes ablaze with fury. She picked up her sword and growled, 'Get him!'

Shiva turned around, picking up his sword and pushing it into his scabbard as he reached the wall. He clambered quickly over. Sati tried to follow. Shiva landed on the other side on a crowded street. He saw the Naga at a far distance, still running hard.

Shiva started sprinting after the Naga. But he knew the battle was already lost. He was too far behind. He now hated the Naga more than ever. The tormentor of his wife! The killer of his brother! And yet, deep inside, he marvelled at the sheer brilliance of the Naga's martial skills.

The Naga was running towards a horse tied outside a shop. In an inconceivable movement, he leapt up high, his right hand stretched out. As the Naga landed smoothly on top of the horse, the knife in his right hand slickly cut the reins, freeing the tethered horse. The rearing of the startled horse had caused the reins to fly back. The

Naga effortlessly caught them in his left hand. Instantly, he kicked the horse, whispering in the animal's ear. The horse sprang swiftly to the Naga's words, breaking into a gallop.

A man came hurtling out of the shop, screaming loudly, 'Stop! Thief! That's my horse!'

The Naga, hearing the commotion, reached into the folds of his robe and threw something back with tremendous force while continuing to gallop away. The force of the blow caused the horseman to stagger, falling flat on his back.

'By the Holy Lake!' shouted Shiva, sprinting towards what he thought was a grievously injured man.

As he reached the horseman, he was surprised to see him get up slowly, rubbing his chest in pain, cursing loudly, 'May the fleas of a thousand dogs infest that bastard's armpits!'

'Are you all right?' asked Shiva, as he examined the man's chest.

The horseman looked at Shiva, scared into silence at seeing his blood–streaked body.

Shiva bent down to pick up the object that the Naga had thrown at the horseman. It was a pouch, made of the most glorious silk he had ever seen. Shiva opened the pouch tentatively, expecting a trap, but it contained coins. He pulled one out, surprised to see that it was made of gold. There were at least fifty coins. He turned in the direction that the Naga had ridden.

What kind of a demon is he? He steals the horse and then leaves enough gold to buy five more!

'Gold!' whispered the horseman softly as he snatched the pouch from Shiva. 'It's mine!'

Shiva didn't look up, still holding one coin, examining its markings. 'I need one.'

The horseman spoke gingerly, for he did not want to battle a man as powerful-looking as Shiva, 'But...'

Shiva snorted in disgust. He pulled out two gold coins from his own pouch and gave it to the horseman, who, thanking his stars for a truly lucky day, quickly escaped.

Shiva turned back and saw Sati resting against the wall, holding her head up, pressing her nose hard. He walked up to her.

'Are you all right?'

Sati nodded in response, dried blood smeared on her face. 'Yes. Your shoulder? It looks bad.'

'It looks worse than it feels. I'm fine. Don't worry.'

Sati looked in the direction that the Naga had ridden off. 'What did he throw at the horseman?'

'A pouch full of this,' said Shiva as he showed the coin to Sati.

'He threw gold coins?!'

Shiva nodded.

Sati frowned and shook her head. She took a closer look at the coin. It had the face of a strange man with a crown on his head. Strange, because unlike a Naga, he had no deformity.

'He looks like a king of some kind,' said Sati, wiping some blood off her mouth.

'But look at these odd markings,' said Shiva as he flipped the coin.

It had a small symbol of a horizontal crescent moon. But the bizarre part was the network of lines running across the coin. Two crooked lines joined in the middle in the shape of an irregular cone and then they broke up into a spidery network.

'I can understand the moon. But what do these lines symbolise?' asked Sati.

'I don't know,' admitted Shiva. But he did know one thing clearly. His gut instinct was unambiguous.

Find the Nagas. They are your path to discovering evil. Find the Nagas.

Sati could almost read her husband's mind. 'Let's get the distractions out of the way then?'

Shiva nodded at her. 'But first, let's get you to Ayurvati.'

'You need her more,' said Sati.

— ⵣ⚇ᚋ⏁⊕ —

'You have nothing to do with our fight?' asked a startled Daksha. 'I don't understand, My Lord. You led us to our greatest victory. Now we have to finish the job. The evil Chandravanshi way of life has to end and these people have to be brought to our pure Suryavanshi ways.'

'But, Your Highness,' said Shiva with polite firmness, shifting his bandaged shoulder slightly to relieve the soreness. 'I don't think they are evil. I understand now that my mission is different.'

Dilipa, sitting to the left of Daksha, was thrilled. Shiva's words were a balm to his soul. Sati and Parvateshwar, to

Shiva's right, were quiet. Nandi and Veerbhadra stood further away, on guard but listening in avidly. The only one as angry as Daksha was Bhagirath, the crown prince of Ayodhya.

'We don't need a certificate from a foreign barbarian to tell us what is obvious! We are not evil!' said Bhagirath.

'Quiet,' hissed Dilipa. 'You will not insult the Neelkanth.'

Turning towards Shiva with folded hands, Dilipa continued, 'Forgive my impetuous son, My Lord. He speaks before he thinks. You said your mission is different. How can Ayodhya help?'

Shiva stared at a visibly chafing Bhagirath before turning towards Dilipa. 'How do I find the Nagas?'

Startled and scared, Dilipa touched his Rudra pendant for protection as Daksha looked up sharply.

'My Lord, they are pure evil,' said Daksha. 'Why do you want to find them?'

'You have answered your own question, Your Highness,' said Shiva. He turned towards Dilipa. 'I don't believe you are allied with the Nagas. But there are some in your empire who are. I want to know how to reach those people.'

'My Lord,' said Dilipa, swallowing hard. 'It is rumoured that the King of Branga consorts with the dark forces. He would be able to answer your questions. But the entry of any foreign person, including us, is banned in that strange but very rich kingdom. Sometimes, I actually think the Brangas pay tribute to my empire only to keep us from entering their land, not because they are scared of being defeated by us in battle.'

'You have another king in your empire? How is that possible?' asked a surprised Shiva.

'We aren't like the obsessive Suryavanshis. We don't insist

on everyone following one single law. Every kingdom has the right to its own king, its own rules and its own way of life. They pay Ayodhya a tribute because we defeated them in battle through the great *Ashwamedh yagna.*'

'Horse sacrifice?'

'Yes, My Lord,' continued Dilipa. 'The sacrificial horse travels freely through any kingdom in the land. If a king stops the horse, we battle, defeat and annexe that territory. If they don't stop the horse, then the kingdom becomes our colony and pays us tribute, but is still allowed to have its own laws. So we are more like a confederacy of aligned kings rather than a fanatical empire like Meluha.'

'Mind your words, you impudent fool,' ranted Daksha. 'Your confederacy seems a lot like extortion to me. They pay you tribute because if they don't, you will attack their lands and plunder them. Where is the Royal Dharma in that? In Meluha, being an emperor does not just give you the right to receive tribute, but it also confers the responsibility to work for the good of all the empire's subjects.'

'And who decides what is good for your subjects? You? By what right? People should be allowed to do whatever they wish.'

'Then there will be chaos,' shouted Daksha. 'Your stupidity is even more apparent than your immoral values!'

'Enough!' asserted Shiva, struggling to tame his irritation. 'Will both your Highnesses please desist?'

Daksha looked at Shiva in surprised anger. Seeing a much more confident Shiva, not just accepting, but living his role as the Neelkanth. Daksha's heart sank. He knew that fulfilling his father's dream of a member of their family being Emperor of all India, and bringing the Suryavanshi way of life to all its citizens, was becoming increasingly remote. He could defeat the Swadweepans in battle due to his army's superior tactics and technology, but he did not have enough soldiers to control the conquered land. For that, he needed the faith that the Swadweepans had in the Neelkanth. If the Neelkanth didn't go along with his way of thinking, his plans were bound to fail.

'Why do you say that the Brangas are allied with the Nagas?' asked Shiva.

'I can't say for sure, My Lord,' said Dilipa. 'But I am going on the rumours that one has heard from traders in Kashi. It is the only kingdom in Swadweep that the Brangas deign to trade with. Furthermore, there are many refugees from Branga settled in Kashi.'

'Refugees?' asked Shiva. 'What are they fleeing from? You said Branga was a rich land.'

'There are rumours of a great plague that has struck Branga repeatedly. But I'm not quite certain. Very few people can be certain about what goes on in Branga! But the King of Kashi would certainly have better answers. Should I summon him here, My Lord?'

'No,' said Shiva, unsure whether this was another wild goose chase or whether the Brangas actually had something to do with the Nagas.

Sati suddenly piped up as a thought struck her and turned towards Dilipa. Her voice was nasal due to the bandage on her nose. 'Forgive me, Your Highness. But where exactly is Branga?'

'It is far to the East, Princess Sati, where our revered river Ganga meets their holy river which comes in from the northeast, Brahmaputra.'

Shiva started as he realised something. He turned to Sati, smiling. Sati smiled back.

They aren't lines! They are rivers!

Shiva reached into his pouch and pulled out the coin he had recovered from the Naga and showed it to Dilipa. 'Is this a Branga coin, Your Highness?'

'Yes, My Lord!' answered a surprised Dilipa. 'That is King Chandraketu on one side and a river map of their land on the other. But these coins are rare. The Brangas never send tribute in coins, only in gold ingots.'

Dilipa was about to ask where Shiva got the coin from, but was cut off by the Neelkanth.

'How quickly can we leave for Kashi?'

— ⟨symbols⟩ —

'Mmmm, this is good,' smiled Shiva, handing the chillum to Veerbhadra.

'I know,' smiled Veerbhadra. 'The grass is much better here than in Meluha. The Chandravanshis certainly know how to savour the finer things in life.'

Shiva smiled. The marijuana was working its magic on him. The two friends were on a small hill outside Ayodhya, enjoying the evening breeze. The view was stunning.

The gentle slope of the grassy hill descended into a sparsely forested plain, which ended in a sheer cliff at a far distance. The tempestuous Sarayu, which had cut through the cliff over many millennia, flowed down south, rumbling passionately. The sun setting gently beyond the horizon completed the dramatic beauty of the tranquil moment.

'I guess the Emperor of Meluha is finally happy,' smiled Veerbhadra, handing the chillum back to Shiva.

Shiva winked at Veerbhadra before taking a deep drag. He knew Daksha was unhappy about his changed stance on the Chandravanshis. And as he himself did not want any distractions while searching for the Nagas, he had hit upon an ingenious compromise to give Daksha a sense of victory and yet keep Dilipa happy as well.

Shiva had decreed that Daksha would henceforth be known as Emperor of India. His name would not only be taken first during prayers at the royal court at Devagiri, but also at Ayodhya. Dilipa, in turn, would be known as Emperor of Swadweep within the Chandravanshi areas, and the 'brother of the Emperor' in Meluha. His name would be taken after Daksha's in court prayers in both Devagiri and Ayodhya. Dilipa's kingdom would pay a nominal tribute of a hundred thousand gold coins to Meluha, which Daksha had pronounced would be donated to the Ramjanmabhoomi temple in Ayodhya.

Thus Daksha had at least one of his dreams fulfilled: Being Emperor of India. Content, Daksha had returned to Devagiri in triumph. The ever pragmatic Dilipa was delighted that despite losing the war with the Suryavanshis, for all practical purposes, he retained his empire and his independence.

'We leave for Kashi in a week?' asked Veerbhadra.

'Hmmm.'

'Good. I'm getting bored here.'

Shiva smiled handing the chillum back to Veerbhadra. 'This Bhagirath seems like a very interesting fellow.'

'Yes, he does.' Veerbhadra took a puff.

'What have you heard about him?'

'You know,' said Veerbhadra, 'Bhagirath was the one who had thought of taking that contingent of hundred thousand soldiers around our position at Dharmakhet.'

'The attack from the rear? That was brilliant. May have worked too, but for the valour of Drapaku.'

'It would certainly have worked if Bhagirath's orders had been followed to the T.'

'Really?' asked Shiva, smoking.

'I have heard Bhagirath wanted to take his army in the quiet of the night through a longer route that was further away from the main battleground. If he had done that, we would not have discovered the troop movement. Our delayed response would have ensured that we would have lost the war.'

'So what went wrong?'

'Apparently, the War Council didn't want to meet at night, when Bhagirath called them.'

'Why in the name of the holy lake wouldn't they meet urgently?'

'They were sleeping!'

'You're joking!'

'No, I'm not,' said Veerbhadra, shaking his head. 'And what is worse, when they did meet in the morning, they ordered Bhagirath to stick close to the valley between Dharmakhet and our position, helping us discover their movement.'

'Why the hell did the War Council make such a stupid decision?' asked a flabbergasted Shiva.

'Apparently, Bhagirath is not trusted by his father. And therefore, not by most Swadweepan kings or generals either. They believed he would have taken the soldiers, escaped to Ayodhya and declared himself Emperor.'

'That's ridiculous. Why does Dilipa not trust his own son?'

'Because he believes Bhagirath thinks he is a fool and a terrible emperor.'

'I'm sure Bhagirath doesn't actually think that!'

'Well, from what I've heard,' smiled Veerbhadra as he junked out the ash from the chillum, 'Bhagirath actually *does* think so of his father. And he's not far from wrong, is he?'

Shiva smiled.

'And then, to make matters worse,' continued Veerbhadra, 'the entire fiasco was blamed on Bhagirath. It was said that because he took a hundred thousand soldiers away, they lost the war.'

Shiva shook his head, saddened to see an intelligent man being rubbished by the idiots surrounding him. 'I think he is a capable person, whose wings have been clipped.'

The tranquil moment was suddenly shattered by a loud scream. Shiva and Veerbhadra looked up to see a rider galloping away, while his companion, lagging far behind, was screeching loudly: 'Help! Somebody help, Prince Bhagirath!'

Bhagirath had lost control of his speeding horse and was hurtling towards the cliff. A near certain death. Shiva jumped onto his horse and charged towards him with Veerbhadra in tow. It was a long distance, but the gentle slope helped Shiva and Veerbhadra make up the expanse quickly. Shiva rode in an arc to intercept Bhagirath's horse.

A few minutes later, Shiva was galloping along Bhagirath's path. He was impressed that Bhagirath seemed calm and focussed, despite facing a life threatening situation.

Bhagirath was pulling hard on his reins, trying to slow his horse down. But his action agitated the horse even further. It picked up more speed.

'Let the reins go!' shouted Shiva, over the loud rumble of the threateningly close Sarayu river.

'What?!' screamed Bhagirath. All his training told him letting the reins go was the stupidest thing to do when a horse was out of control.

'Trust me! Let it go!'

Bhagirath would later explain it to himself as fate guiding him towards the Neelkanth. At this moment, his instinct told him to forget his training and trust this barbarian from Tibet. Bhagirath let go. Much to his surprise, the horse immediately slackened.

Shiva rode in close. So close that he could almost whisper into the animal's ear. Then he began to sing a strange tune. The horse gradually started calming down, reducing its speed to a canter. The cliff was coming close. Very close.

'Shiva!' warned Veerbhadra. 'The cliff is a few hundred metres away!'

Shiva noted the warning, matching the pace of his horse with Bhagirath's. The prince kept his control, staying on the horse, while Shiva kept singing. Slowly but surely, Shiva was gaining control. It was just a few metres before the cliff that Bhagirath's horse finally came to a halt.

Bhagirath and Shiva immediately dismounted as Veerbhadra rode in.

'Damn!' said Veerbhadra, peering towards the cliff. 'That was too close!'

Shiva looked at Veerbhadra, before turning towards Bhagirath. 'Are you all right?'

Bhagirath kept staring at Shiva, before lowering his eyes in shame. 'I'm sorry for putting you through so much trouble.'

'No trouble at all.'

Bhagirath turned to his horse, hitting its face hard for embarrassing him.

'It's not the horse's fault!' shouted Shiva.

Bhagirath turned back to Shiva, frowning. Shiva walked towards Bhagirath's horse, gently cradling its face, almost like it was a child being punished unfairly. Then he carefully pulled its reins out, signalled to Bhagirath to come closer and showed him the nail buried in the leather close to the horse's mouth.

Bhagirath was shocked. The inference was obvious.

Shiva pulled the nail out, handing it to Bhagirath. 'Somebody doesn't like you, my friend.'

Meanwhile, Bhagirath's companion had caught up with them. 'My Prince! Are you all right?'

Bhagirath looked towards his companion. 'Yes I am.'

Shiva turned towards the man. 'Tell Emperor Dilipa his son is an exceptional rider. Tell him that the Neelkanth has yet to see a man with greater control over an animal, even when the odds were stacked so desperately against him. Tell him the Neelkanth requests the honour of Prince Bhagirath accompanying him to Kashi.'

Shiva knew that for Dilipa, this would not be a request but an order. This was probably the only way of keeping Bhagirath safe from the unknown threat to his life. The companion immediately went down on his knee. 'As you command, My Lord.'

Bhagirath stood dumbfounded. He had come across people who plotted against him, people who took credit for his ideas, people who sabotaged him. But this... This was unique. He turned to his companion. 'Leave us.'

The man immediately rode away.

'I have experienced such kindness from only one person up until now,' said Bhagirath, his eyes moist. 'And that is my sister, Anandmayi. But blood justifies her actions. I don't know how to react to your generosity, My Lord.'

'By not calling me Lord,' smiled Shiva.

'That is one order I would request you to allow me to refuse,' said Bhagirath, his hands folded in a respectful namaste. 'I will follow any other order you give. Even if it is to take my own life.'

'Now don't get so dramatic! I am not about to ask you to commit suicide right after having worked strenuously to save your life.'

Bhagirath smiled softly. 'What was it you sang to my horse, My Lord?'

'Sit with me over a chillum sometime and I will teach you.'

'It will be my honour to sit at your feet and learn, My Lord.'

'Don't sit at my feet, my friend. Sit beside me. The sound carries a little better there!'

Bhagirath smiled as Shiva patted him on the shoulder.

Chapter 2

Sailing Down the Sarayu

'Tell Princess Anandmayi,' said Parvateshwar to the Captain of the Women's Guard at Anandmayi's palace entrance, 'that General Parvateshwar is waiting outside.'

'She had told me she was expecting you, General,' said the Captain bowing low. 'May I request you to wait a moment while I go and check on her?'

As the Captain walked into Anandmayi's chamber, Parvateshwar turned around. Shiva had made him in-charge of the expedition to Kashi. Shiva knew if he left the organisation to one of Ayodhya's administrators, they would probably be debating the mode of transport for the next three years. Parvateshwar, with his typical Suryavanshi efficiency, had seen to the arrangements within a week. The contingent was to travel east down the Sarayu on royal boats, to the city of Magadh, where the river merged into the mighty Ganga. From there, they would turn west to sail up the Ganga to *Kashi, the city where the supreme light shines.*

Parvateshwar had been inundated with inane requests from some of the Ayodhya nobility who were taking the opportunity to travel with the Neelkanth. He did plan to honour some strange appeals, like one from a superstitious nobleman who wanted his boat to leave exactly thirty two minutes after the beginning of the third prahar. Others he had flatly refused, such as a request from another nobleman for his boat to be staffed only by women. The General was quite sure that Anandmayi must also have some special arrangements she wanted made.

Like carrying a ship hold of milk for her beauty baths!

The Captain was back shortly. 'You may go in, General.'

Parvateshwar marched in smartly, bowed his head, saluted as he must to royalty and spoke out loud, 'What is it you want, Princess?'

'You needn't be so coy, General. You can look up.'

Parvateshwar looked up. Anandmayi was lying on her stomach next to a picture window overlooking the royal gardens. Kanini, her masseuse, was working her magic on the princess' exotic and supple body. Anandmayi only had one piece of cloth draped loosely from her lower back to her upper thighs. The rest of her, a feast for his eyes.

'Beautiful view, isn't it?' asked Anandmayi.

Parvateshwar blushed a deep red, his head bowed, eyes turned away. To Anandmayi, he appeared to be like the rare cobra male that bows his head to its mate at the beginning of their mating dance, as though accepting the superiority of its partner.

'I'm sorry, Princess. I'm so sorry. I didn't mean to insult you.'

'Why should you apologise for looking at the royal gardens, General? It is allowed.'

Parvateshwar, a lifelong celibate, was mollified. It did not appear as though Anandmayi had misunderstood his intentions. He whispered in a soft voice, eyes on the floor, 'What can I do for you, Princess?'

'It's quite simple really. A little further south down the Sarayu is the spot where Lord Ram had stopped with his Guru Vishwamitra and brother Lakshman on his way to slay the demon Tadaka. It is the spot where Maharishi Vishwamitra taught Lord Ram the arts of Bal and Atibal, the fabled route to eternal good health and freedom from hunger and thirst. I would like to halt there and offer a puja to the Lord.'

Parvateshwar, pleased at her devotion to Lord Ram, smiled. 'Of course, we can stop there Princess. I will make the arrangements. Would you need any special provisions?'

'None whatsoever. An honest heart is all that is needed for a prayer to reach the Lord.'

Parvateshwar looked up for a brief moment, impressed. Anandmayi's eyes, however, seemed to be mocking him. He growled softly. 'Anything else, Princess?'

Anandmayi grimaced. She was not getting the reaction that she had desired. 'Nothing else, General.'

Parvateshwar saluted smartly and left the room.

Anandmayi kept staring at Parvateshwar's retreating form. She sighed loudly and shook her head.

— 人◍Ʊ♀⊕ —

'Gather around please,' said the Pandit, 'we will commence the puja.'

Shiva's contingent was at Bal-Atibal kund, where Guru Vishwamitra had taught Lord Ram his legendary skills.

The Neelkanth was unhappy that many of Ayodhya's nobility had inveigled their way into the voyage to Kashi.

What should have been a super-fast five ship convoy had turned into a lethargic fifty ship caravan. The straightforward Parvateshwar had found it difficult to deny the convoluted logic of the Chandravanshi nobility. Therefore, Shiva was delighted that Bhagirath had found an ingenious method to cut down the numbers. Craftily, he had suggested to one noble that he should rush to Kashi and set up a welcoming committee for the Neelkanth, and thus gain favour with the powerful Lord. Seeing one noble hustle away, many others had followed, in a mad dash to be the first to herald the arrival of the Neelkanth at Kashi. Within hours, the convoy had been reduced to the size that Shiva desired.

The puja platform had been set up some fifty metres from the riverbank. It was believed that anyone who conducted this prayer with full devotion would never be inflicted with disease. Shiva, Sati, Parvateshwar, Ayurvati, Bhagirath and Anandmayi sat in the innermost circle next to the Pandit. Others like Nandi, Veerbhadra, Drapaku, Krittika and the men of the joint Suryavanshi-Chandravanshi brigade sat a little further back. The earnest Brahmin was reciting Sanskrit shlokas in the exact same intonations that had been taught to him by his Guru.

Sati was uneasy. She had an uncomfortable feeling that someone was watching her. For some strange reason, she felt intense hatred directed at her. Along with that she also felt boundless love and profound sadness. Confused, she opened her eyes. She turned her head to her left. Every single person had his eyes closed, in accordance with the guidelines of this particular puja. She then turned to the right and started as she saw Shiva gazing directly at her. His eyes open wide, reflecting an outpouring of love, Shiva's face sported a slight smile.

Sati frowned at her husband, gesturing with her eyes that he should concentrate on his prayers. Shiva, however, pursed his lips together and blew her a kiss. A startled Sati frowned even more. Her Suryavanshi sensibilities felt offended at such frivolous behaviour, which she considered a violation of the code. Shiva pouted like a spoilt child, closed his eyes and turned towards the fire. Sati turned too, eyes closed, allowing herself a slight smile at the fact that she had been blessed with an adoring husband.

But she still felt she was being watched. Stared at intently. The last ship of the Neelkanth's convoy turned round

— 人◎U♀⊕ —

the bend in the Sarayu. With his enemies out of sight, the Naga emerged from the trees. He walked briskly to the place where the Brahmin had just conducted the puja. He was followed by the Queen of the Nagas and a hundred armed men. They stopped at a polite distance from the Naga, leaving him alone.

Karkotak, Prime Minister to the Queen of the Nagas, looked up at the sky, judging the time. Then he looked disconcertedly at the Naga in the distance. He wondered why the Lord of the People, as the Naga was referred to in his lands, was so interested in this particular puja. The Lord had far greater powers and knowledge. Some even considered him better than the Naga Queen.

'Your Highness,' said Karkotak to the Queen, 'do you think it advisable to emphasise to the Lord of the People the importance of returning home?'

'When I want your advice, Karkotak,' said the Queen in

a curt whisper, 'I will ask for it.'

Karkotak immediately retreated, terrified as always of his Queen's temper.

The Queen turned back towards the Naga, her mind considering Karkotak's words. She had to admit that her Prime Minister was right. The Nagas had to return to their capital quickly. There was little time to waste. The *Rajya Sabha*, the Naga *Royal Council* was to be held soon. The issue of medical support to the Brangas would come up again. She knew that the severe cost of that support was turning many Nagas against the alliance with the Brangas, especially the peace-loving ones who wanted to live their ostracised lives quietly, calling it a product of their bad karma. And without the alliance, her vengeance was impossible. More importantly, she could not desert the Brangas in their hour of need when they had been unflinchingly loyal to her.

On the other hand, she could not abandon her nephew, the Lord of the People. He was troubled; the presence of that vile woman had disturbed his usual calm demeanour. He was taking unnecessary risks. Like the idiotic attack on Sati and Shiva at the Ramjanmabhoomi temple. If he didn't want to kill her, why the hell did he put his own person in such grave peril? What if he had been killed? Or worse, caught alive? He had justified it later as an attempt to draw Sati out of Ayodhya, as capturing her within the city was impossible. For what it was worth, he had succeeded in drawing her out on a voyage to Kashi. But she was accompanied by her husband and a whole brigade. It was impossible to kidnap her.

The Queen saw her nephew move slightly. She stepped forward a little distance, motioning for Karkotak and the men to remain behind.

The Naga had taken out a knife from a newly built hold on his belt. It was the knife Sati had flung at him at the Ramjanmabhoomi temple. He looked at it longingly, letting the blade run up his thumb. Its sharp edge cut his skin lightly. He shook his head angrily, dug the knife hard into the sand and turned around to walk towards the Queen.

He stopped abruptly. Oddly hesitant.

The Queen, clearly out of her nephew's earshot, willed her thoughts in a quiet whisper. 'Let it go, my child. It's not worth it. Let it go.'

The Naga stood rooted to his spot. Indecision weighed heavy on him. The men in the distance were shocked to see their Lord in such a weak state. To the Queen's dismay, the Naga turned around and walked back to the spot where he had buried the knife. He picked it up carefully, held it reverentially to his forehead and put it back into his side hold.

The Queen snorted in disgust and turned around, signalling Karkotak to come forward. She knew she had no choice. She would have to leave her nephew with bodyguards, while she herself would ride out towards Panchavati, her capital.

'Portage charges? What rubbish!' bellowed Siamantak,

— ⟨symbols⟩ —

Ayodhya's Prime Minister. 'This ship belongs to the Emperor of Swadweep. It carries a very important individual, the most important in the land.'

Siamantak was in the pilot boat of Andhak, Port Minister of Magadh, who unlike typical Chandravanshis, was known to turn a blind eye to everything except the letter of the law. Siamantak turned to look nervously at the massive ship that carried the Neelkanth. Shiva was standing on the balustrade with Parvateshwar and Bhagirath. Siamantak was aware that Shiva wanted to stop at Magadh. He had expressed a desire to visit the Narsimha temple on the outskirts of the city. Siamantak did not want to disappoint the Neelkanth. However, if he paid portage charges for the ship, it would set a dangerous precedent. How could the Emperor's ship pay portage in his own empire? It would open a can of worms with all the river port kingdoms across the empire. The negotiations with Andhak were delicate.

'I don't care who the ship belongs to,' said Andhak. 'And I don't care if you have Lord Ram himself on that ship. The law is the law. Any ship that ports at Magadh has to pay portage. Why should Emperor Dilipa be worried about a small fee of one thousand gold coins?'

'It's not the money. It's the principle,' argued Siamantak.

'Precisely! It is the principle. So please pay up.'

Shiva was getting impatient. 'What the hell are they talking about for so long?'

'My Lord,' said Bhagirath. 'Andhak is the Port Minister. He must be insisting that the law of portage charges be followed. Siamantak cannot allow any ship owned by my father to pay portage. It is an insult to my father's fragile ego. Andhak is an idiot.'

'Why would you call a person who follows the law stupid?' frowned Parvateshwar. 'On the contrary, he should be respected.'

'Sometimes even circumstances should be looked at, General.'

'Prince Bhagirath, I can understand no circumstance

under which the letter of the law should be ignored.'

Shiva did not want to witness yet another argument between the Suryavanshi and Chandravanshi way of life. 'What kind of ruler is the King of Magadh?'

'King *Mahendra*?' asked Bhagirath.

'Doesn't that mean *the conqueror of the world?*'

'Yes, it does, My Lord. But he does not do justice to that name. Magadh was a great kingdom once. In fact, there was a time when it was the overlord kingdom of Swadweep and its kings were widely respected and honoured. But as it happens with many great kings, their unworthy descendants frittered away the wealth and power of their kingdoms. They have been trying hard to live up to Magadh's past glory, but have been spectacularly unsuccessful. We share a prickly relationship with them.'

'Really, why?'

'Well, Ayodhya was the kingdom that defeated them more than three hundred years ago to become the overlord of Swadweep. It was a glorious Ashwamedh Yagna, for this was a time when Ayodhya had still not fallen prey to the wooden kings who rule it today. As you can imagine, Magadh was not quite pleased about the loss of status and revenue from tributes.'

'Yes, but three hundred years is a long time to carry a grudge!'

Bhagirath smiled. 'Kshatriyas have long memories, My Lord. And they still suffer from their defeat to Ayodhya. Magadh could theoretically benefit from the fact that it is at the confluence of two rivers. It becomes the most convenient trading hub for merchants travelling on river ports on the Sarayu or the Ganga. This advantage was negated after they lost the Ashwamedh to us. A ceiling was imposed on their portage and trading hub charges. And then, our enmity received a fresh lease of life a hundred years back.'

'And how did that happen?'

'There is a kingdom to the west, up the Ganga, called Prayag. It had historically been in close alliance with Magadh. In fact the ruling families are very closely related.'

'And...'

'And when the Yamuna changed course from Meluha and started flowing into Swadweep, it met the Ganga at Prayag,' said Bhagirath.

'That would have made Prayag very important?' asked Shiva.

'Yes, My Lord. Just like Magadh, it became a crucial junction for river trade. And unlike Magadh, it was not bound by any treaty on its portage and trading charges. Any trader or kingdom wanting to settle or trade in the newly opened hinterlands of the Yamuna had to pay charges at Prayag. Its prosperity and power grew exponentially. There were even rumours that they were planning to support Magadh in an Ashwamedh Yagna to challenge Ayodhya's suzerainty. But when my great grandfather lost the battle to the Suryavanshis and a dam was built on the Yamuna to turn the flow towards Meluha, Prayag's importance fell again. They have blamed Ayodhya ever since. They actually believe we purposely lost the war to give them a devastating blow.'

'I see.'

'Yes,' said Bhagirath, shaking his head. 'But to be honest, we lost the war because my great grandfather employed terrible battle strategy.'

'So you people have hated each other forever?'

'Not forever, My Lord. There was a time when Ayodhya and Magadh were close allies.'

'So will you be welcome here?'

Bhagirath burst out laughing. 'Everyone knows I don't really represent Ayodhya. This is one place I will not be suspect. But King Mahendra is known to be highly suspicious. We should expect spies keeping a close tab on us all the time. He does that to every important visitor. Having said that, their spy network is not particularly efficient. I do not foresee any serious problems.'

'Will my blue neck open doors here?'

Bhagirath looked embarrassed. 'King Mahendra does not believe in anything my father believes in, My Lord. Since the Emperor of Ayodhya believes in the Neelkanth, the Magadh king will not.'

Their conversation was interrupted by Siamantak climbing up the ship ladder. He came up to the Neelkanth, saluted smartly and said, 'A deal has been struck, My Lord. We can disembark. But we will have to stay here for at least ten days.'

Shiva frowned.

'I have temporarily transferred the ownership of the ship to a palace guesthouse owner in Magadh, My Lord. We will stay in his guesthouse for ten days. He will pay the portage charges to Andhak from the guesthouse rent we pay. When we wish to leave, the ownership of the ship will be transferred back to King Dilipa. We have to stay for ten days so that the guesthouse owner can earn enough money for his own profit and for portage charges.'

Shiva gaped at Siamantak. He didn't know whether to laugh at this strangely convoluted compromise or be impressed at Siamantak's bureaucratic brilliance in achieving

Shiva's objective of visiting Magadh while upholding his Emperor's prestige. The portage charges would be paid, but technically not by Emperor Dilipa.

The Naga and his soldiers had been silently tracking the

— 𑀰𑀬𑀉𑀝𑀦𑀤 —

fleet carrying Shiva, Sati and their entourage. The Naga Queen, Prime Minister Karkotak and her bodyguards had left for Panchavati, the Naga capital. The smaller platoon allowed the Naga to maintain a punishing pace, staying abreast with the fast moving ships of Shiva's convoy.

They had wisely remained away from the banks. Far enough to not be visible to the boat look-outs but close enough to follow their paths. They had moved further inland to avoid Magadh and intended to move closer to the river once they had bypassed the city.

'A short distance more, My Lord,' said Vishwadyumna. 'Then we can move back towards the river.'

The Naga nodded.

Suddenly, the still of the forest was shattered by a loud scream. 'NOOOOO!'

The Naga immediately went down on his knees, giving Vishwadyumna rapid orders with hand signals. The entire platoon went down quickly and quietly, waiting for the danger to pass.

But trouble had just begun.

A woman screamed again. 'No! Please! Leave him!'

Vishwadyumna silently gestured to his soldiers to stay down. As far as he was concerned, there was only one course of action to take. Retrace their steps, take a wide arc around this area and move back towards the river. He turned towards his Lord, about to offer this suggestion. The Naga, however, was transfixed, eyes glued to a heartbreaking sight.

At a distance, partially hidden by the trees and underbrush, lay a tribal woman, frantically clutching a boy, no older than six or seven years. Two armed men, possibly Magadhan soldiers, were trying to pull the child away. The woman, showing astounding strength for her frail frame, was holding on to the child desperately.

'Dammit!' screamed the leader of the Magadhans. 'Push that woman off, you louts!'

In the wild and unsettled lands between the Ganga and Narmada lived scattered tribes of forest people. In the eyes of the civilised city folk living along the great rivers, these tribals were backward creatures because they insisted on living in harmony with nature. While most kingdoms ignored these forest tribes, others confiscated their lands at will as populations grew and need for farmlands increased. And a few particularly cruel ones preyed on these helpless groups for slave labour.

The Magadhan leader kicked the woman hard. 'You can get another son! But I need this boy! He will drive my bulls to victory! My father will finally stop his endless preening about winning every race for the last three years!'

The Naga looked at the Magadhan with barely concealed hate. Bull-racing was a craze in the Chandravanshi areas, subject to massive bets, royal interest and intrigue. Riders were needed to scream and agitate the animals to keep them running on course. At the same time, if the riders were too heavy, they would slow down the animal. Therefore, boys between the ages of six and eight were considered perfect. They would shriek out of fear and their weight was inconsequential. The children would be tied to the beasts. If the bull went down, the boy rider would be seriously injured or killed. Therefore, tribal children were often kidnapped to slave away as riders. Nobody important missed them if they died.

The Magadhan leader nodded to one of his men who drew his sword. He then looked at the woman. 'I am trying to be reasonable. Let your son go. Or I will have to hurt you.'

'No!'

The Magadhan soldier slashed his sword, cutting across the mother's right arm. Blood spurted across the child's face, making him bawl inconsolably.

The Naga was staring at the woman, his mouth open in awe. Her bloodied right arm hanging limply by her side, the woman still clung to her son, wrapping her left arm tightly around him.

Vishwadyumna shook his head. He could tell it was a matter of time before the woman would be killed. He turned towards his soldiers, giving hand signals to crawl back. He turned back towards his Lord. But the Naga was not there. He had moved swiftly forward, towards the mother. Vishwadyumna panicked and ran after his Lord, keeping his head low.

'Kill her!' ordered the Magadhan leader.

The Magadhan soldier raised his sword, ready to strike. Suddenly, the Naga broke out from the cover of the trees, his hand holding a knife high. Before the soldier knew what had happened, the knife struck his hand and his sword dropped harmlessly to the ground.

As the Magadhan soldier shrieked in agony, the Naga drew out two more knives. But he had failed to notice the platoon of Magadhan soldiers at the back. One had his bow at the ready, with an arrow strung. The soldier released it at the Naga. The arrow rammed into his left shoulder, slipping between his shoulder cap and torso armour, bursting through to the bone. The force of the blow caused the Naga to fall to the ground, the pain immobilising him.

Seeing their Lord down, the Naga's platoon ran in with a resounding yell.

'My Lord!' cried Vishwadyumna, as he tried to support the Naga back to his feet.

'Who the hell are you?' screamed the cruel Magadhan leader, retreating towards the safety of his platoon, before turning back to the Naga's men.

'Get out of here if you want to stay alive!' shouted one of the Naga's soldiers, livid at the injury to his Lord.

'Bangas!' yelled the Magadhan, recognising the accent. 'What in the name of Lord Indra are you scum doing here?'

'It's Branga! Not Banga!'

'Do I look like I care? Get out of my land!'

The Branga did not respond as he saw his Naga Lord getting up slowly, helped by Vishwadyumna. The Naga signalled Vishwadyumna to step back and tried to pull the arrow out of his shoulder. But it was buried too deep. He broke its shaft and threw it away.

The Magadhan pointed at the Naga menacingly. 'I am Ugrasen, the Prince of Magadh. This is my land. These people are my property. Get out of the way.'

The Naga did not respond to the royal brat.

He turned around to see one of the most magnificent sights he had ever seen. The mother lay almost unconscious behind his soldiers. Her eyes closing due to the tremendous loss of blood. Her body shivering desperately. Too terrified to even whimper.

And yet, she stubbornly refused to give up her son. Her left hand still wrapped tight around him. Her body protectively positioned in front of her child.

What a mother!

The Naga turned around. His eyes blazing with rage. His body tense. His fists clenched tight. He whispered in a voice that was eerily calm, 'You want to hurt a mother because she is protecting her child?'

Sheer menace dripped from that soft voice. It even managed to get through to a person lost in royal ego. But Ugrasen could not back down in front of his fawning courtiers. Some crazy Branga with an unseasonal holi mask was not going to deprive him of his prize catch. 'This is my kingdom. I can hurt whoever I want. So if you want to save your sorry hide, get out of here. You don't know the power of...'

'YOU WANT TO HURT A MOTHER BECAUSE SHE IS PROTECTING HER CHILD?'

Ugrasen fell silent as terror finally broke through his thick head. He turned to see his followers. They too felt the dread that the Naga's voice emanated.

A shocked Vishwadyumna stared at his Lord. He had never heard his Lord raise his voice so loud. Never. The Naga's breathing was heavy, going intermittently through gritted teeth. His body stiff with fury.

And then Vishwadyumna heard the Naga's breathing return slowly to normal. He knew it instantly. His Lord had made a decision.

The Naga reached to his side and drew his long sword.

Holding it away from his body. Ready for the charge. And then he whispered his orders. 'No mercy.'

'NO MERCY!' screamed the loyal Branga soldiers. They charged after their Lord. They fell upon the hapless Magadhans. There was no mercy.

Chapter 3

The Pandit of Magadh

It was early morning when Shiva left the guesthouse for the Narsimha temple. He was accompanied by Bhagirath, Drapaku, Siamantak, Nandi and Veerbhadra.

Magadh was a far smaller town than Ayodhya. Not having suffered due to commercial or military success and the resultant mass immigration, it remained a pretty town with leafy avenues. While it did not have the awesome organisation of Devagiri or the soaring architecture of Ayodhya, it was not bogged down by the boring standardisation of the Meluhan capital or the grand chaos of the Swadweepan capital.

It did not take Shiva and his entourage more than just half–an–hour to get across to the far side of the city where the magnificent Narsimha temple stood. Shiva entered the compound of the grand shrine. His men waited outside as per his instructions, but only after scoping the temple for suspects.

The temple was surrounded by a massive square garden, a style from Lord Rudra's land, far beyond the western borders of India. The garden had an ingeniously designed gargantuan fountain at its heart and rows of intricate waterways, flowerbeds and grass spread out from the centre in simple, yet stunning symmetry. At the far end stood the Narsimha temple. Built of pure white marble, it had a giant staircase leading up to its main platform, a spire that shot up at least seventy metres and had ornately carved statues of gods and goddesses all across its face. Shiva was sure this awe-inspiring and obviously expensive temple had been built at a time when Magadh had the resources of the entire Swadweep confederacy at its command.

He took off his sandals at the staircase, climbed up the steps and entered the main temple. At the far end was the main sanctum of the temple, with the statue of its god, Lord Narsimha, on a majestic throne. Lord Narsimha had lived many thousands of years ago, before even Lord Rudra's time. Shiva mused that if the Lord's idol was life size, then he must have been a powerful figure. He looked unnaturally tall, at least eight feet, with a musculature that would terrify even the demons. His hands were unusually brawny with long nails, making Shiva think that just the Lord's bare hands must have been a fearsome weapon.

But it was the Lord's face that stunned Shiva. His mouth was surrounded by lips that were large beyond imagination. His moustache hair did not flow down like most men, but came out in rigid tracks, like a cat's whiskers. His nose was abnormally large, with sharp eyes on either side. His hair sprayed out a fair distance, like a mane. It almost looked as though Lord Narsimha was a man with the head of a lion.

Had he been alive today, Lord Narsimha would have been considered a Naga by the Chandravanshis and hence feared, not revered. Don't they have any consistency?

'Consistency is the virtue of mules!'

Shiva looked up, surprised how someone had heard his thoughts.

A Vasudev Pandit emerged from behind the pillars. He was the shortest Pandit that Shiva had met so far; just a little over five feet. But in all other aspects, his appearance was like every other Vasudev, his hair snowy white and his face wizened with age. He was clad in a saffron *dhoti* and *angvastram*.

'How did you...'

'That is not important,' interrupted the Pandit, raising his hands, not finding it important to explain how he discerned Shiva's thoughts.

That conversation... another time... great Neelkanth.

Shiva could have sworn he heard the Pandit's voice in his head. The words were broken, like the voice was coming from a great distance. Very soft and not quite clear. But it was the Pandit's voice. Shiva frowned, for the Pandit's lips had not moved.

Oh Lord Vasudev... this foreigner's...impressive.

Shiva heard the Pandit's voice again. The Pandit was smiling slightly. He could tell that the Neelkanth could hear his thoughts.

'You're not going to explain, are you?' asked Shiva with a smile.

No. You're certainly... not ready... yet.

The Pandit's appearance may have been like other Vasudevs, but his character was clearly different. This Vasudev was straightforward to the point of being rude. But Shiva knew the apparent rudeness was not intended. It was just a reflection of the mercurial nature of this particular Pandit's character.

Maybe the Pandit was a Chandravanshi in another life.

'I'm a Vasudev,' said the Pandit. 'There is no other identity I carry today. I'm not a son. Or husband. Or father. And, I'm not a Chandravanshi. I am only a Vasudev.'

A man has many identities, Panditji.

The Pandit narrowed his eyes.

'Were you born a Vasudev?'

'Nobody is born a Vasudev, Lord Neelkanth. You earn it. There is a competitive examination, for which Suryavanshis or Chandravanshis can appear. If you pass, you cease to be anything else. You give up all other identities. You become a Vasudev.'

'But you were a Chandravanshi before you earned your right to be a Vasudev,' smiled Shiva, as though merely stating a fact.

The Pandit smiled, acknowledging Shiva's statement.

Shiva had many questions he wanted answered. But there was a most obvious one for this particular Vasudev.

'A few months back, the Vasudev Pandit at the Ramjanmabhoomi temple had told me that my task is not to destroy evil, but to find out what evil is,' said Shiva.

The Vasudev Pandit nodded.

'I'm still digesting that idea. So my question is not on that,' continued Shiva. 'My query is about something else he said. He had told me that the Suryavanshis represent the masculine life force and the Chandravanshis represent the feminine. What does this mean? Because I don't think it has anything to do with men and women.'

'You can't get more obvious than that, my friend! You're right, it has nothing to do with men and women. It has to do with the way of life of the Suryavanshis and Chandravanshis.'

'Way of life?'

— $\dagger \textcircled{0} \textchange{U} \dagger \oplus$ —

'Prince Ugrasen has been killed?' asked Bhagirath.

'Yes, Your Highness,' said Siamantak softly. 'The news is from a source I trust implicitly.'

'Lord Ram help us! This is all we need. King Mahendra will think Ayodhya arranged the assassination. And you know how vengeful he can get.'

'I hope that he doesn't think that, Your Highness,' said Siamantak, 'It's the last thing we need.'

'Their spies have been following us,' said Nandi. 'I'm sure they have a report of our whereabouts and movements since we have entered the city. We cannot be blamed.'

'No, Nandi,' said Bhagirath. 'King Mahendra can also think that we hired assassins to do his son in. By the way, where are the spies?'

'Two of them,' said Drapaku, pointing with his eyes in the direction of the spies. 'They are quite amateurish. That tree doesn't really hide them!'

Bhagirath smiled slightly.

'It could be Surapadman,' said Siamantak. 'Everyone in Swadweep is aware that the younger Magadh Prince is ruthless. He could have arranged the killing to claim the throne.'

'No,' said Bhagirath, narrowing his eyes. 'Surapadman is by far the more capable son of King Mahendra. For all his faults, the king of Magadh does respect capability, unlike some other rulers I know. Surapadman practically has the throne. He doesn't need to kill his brother for it.'

'But how come there is no public mourning as yet?' asked Drapaku.

'They're keeping the news secret,' said Siamantak. 'I don't know why.'

'Maybe to arrange a credible story to give at least some respectability to Ugrasen's memory,' said Bhagirath. 'That idiot was quite capable of stumbling upon his own sword!'

Siamantak nodded before turning towards Drapaku. 'Why does the Lord want to spend so much time in the temple alone? It's quite unorthodox.'

'That's because the Lord himself is quite unorthodox. But why are we keeping his identity secret in Magadh?'

'Not everyone who believes in the legend is a follower of the Neelkanth, Drapaku,' said Bhagirath. 'The present king of Magadh does not follow the Neelkanth. And the people here are loyal followers of the King. The Lord's identity is best kept undisclosed here.'

— ⋏◎ᚒ⼐⊕ —

'You know what makes humans special when compared to animals?' asked the Pandit.

'What?' asked Shiva.

'The fact that we work together. We collaborate to achieve combined goals. We pass on knowledge to each other, so every generation begins its journey from the shoulders of the previous generation and not from scratch.'

'I agree. But we are not the only ones who work in a pack. Other animals, like the elephants or lions, do it as well. But nobody does it on the scale that we do.'

'Yes, that's true. But it's not always about collaboration. It is sometimes about competition as well. It's not always about peace. Many times, it's also about war.'

Shiva smiled and nodded.

'So the key point is that we humans are nothing individually,' said the Pandit. 'Our power flows from all of us. From the way all of us live together.'

'Yes,' agreed Shiva.

'And if we have to live together, we must have a way of life, right?'

'Yes. Some method for all of us to collaborate or compete with each other.'

'Most people believe there are many hundred ways of life in the world,' said the Pandit. 'Every civilisation thinks that it is unique in some way.'

Shiva nodded in agreement.

'But if you actually distil the way people live, there are only two ways: The Masculine and the Feminine.'

'And what do these ways of life mean?'

'The masculine way of life is "life by laws". Laws that could be made by a great leader, perhaps a Vishnu like Lord Ram. Or laws that come down from a religious tradition. Or collective laws decreed by the people themselves. But the masculine way is very clear. Laws are unchangeable and they must be followed rigidly. There is no room for ambiguity. Life is predictable because the populace will always do what has been ordained. Meluha is a perfect example of such a way of life. It is obvious, therefore, why the people of this way of life live by the code of Truth, Duty and Honour. Since that's what they need to be successful in this system.'

'And the feminine?'

'The feminine way of life is "life by probabilities". There are no absolutes. No black or white. People don't act as per some preordained law, but based on probabilities of different outcomes perceived at that point of time. For example, they will follow a king who they think has a higher probability of remaining in power. The moment the probabilities change, their loyalties do as well. If there are laws in such a society, they are malleable. The same laws can be interpreted differently at different points of time. Change is the only constant. Feminine civilisations, like Swadweep, are comfortable with contradictions. And the code for success in such a system? Unmistakeably, Passion, Beauty and Freedom.'

'And no one way of life is better?'

'Obviously. Both types of civilisations must exist. Because they balance each other.'

'How?'

'You see, a masculine civilisation at its peak is honourable, consistent, reliable and spectacularly successful in an age suitable for its particular set of laws. There is order and society moves coherently in a preordained direction. Look at the Suryavanshis today. But when masculine civilisations decline, they cause horrible turmoil, becoming fanatical and rigid. They will attack those that are different, try to "convert" them to their "truth", which will lead to violence and chaos. This especially happens when an age changes. Change is difficult for the masculine. They will cling even more rigidly to their laws, even though those laws may be unsuitable for the new age. Masculine civilisations enforce order which is welcome when they are strong, but is suffocating when they decline. The Asuras, who were followers of the masculine way, had faced similar problems when their power started waning.'

'So when fanaticism causes rebellions born of frustration, the openness of the feminine brings a breath of fresh air.'

'Exactly. The feminine way incorporates all differences.

People of varying faiths and belief can coexist in peace. Nobody tries to enforce their own version of the truth. There is a celebration of diversity and freedom, which brings forth renewed creativity and vigour causing tremendous benefits to society. The Devas, who were followers of the feminine way, brought in all this when they defeated the Asuras. But as it happens with too much freedom, the feminine civilisations overreach into decadence, corruption and debauchery.'

'Then the people once again welcome the order of the masculine.'

'Yes. The feminine Deva way was in decline during Lord Ram's times. The country was corrupt, immoral and depraved. People clamoured for order and civility. Lord Ram ushered that in as he created a new masculine way of life. Very intelligently, to prevent unnecessary rebellions, he never decried the Deva way. He just called his rule a new way of life: the Suryavanshi path.'

'But can you really say the masculine and the feminine only exist at the level of civilisations?' asked Shiva. 'Doesn't it really exist within every man and woman? Doesn't everyone have a little bit of the Suryavanshi and a bit of the Chandravanshi within themselves? Their relative influence within the individual changing, depending upon the situations he faces?'

'Yes, you are right. But most people have a dominant trait. Either the masculine or the feminine.'

Shiva nodded.

'The reason why you need to know the two ways of life is because once you have discovered evil, you would have to tailor your message depending on which people you speak to. You will have to convince the Suryavanshis in one manner and the Chandravanshis in an altogether different manner in the battle against evil.'

'Why would I need to convince them? I don't think either the Suryavanshis or Chandravanshis lack in courage.'

'It has nothing to do with courage, my friend. Courage is only needed once the war begins. To begin with you need to persuade the people to embark upon the war against evil. You will need to influence them to give up their attachment to evil.'

'Attachment! To evil!' cried a flabbergasted Shiva. 'Why in the name of the holy lake would anyone be attached to evil?'

The Pandit smiled.

Shiva sighed. 'Now what? What's the explanation for stopping the conversation at this moment? I'm not ready? The time is not right?'

The Pandit laughed. 'I can't explain it to you right now, O Neelkanth. You would not understand. And when you discover evil, you would not need my explanation in order to understand. Jai Guru Vishwamitra. Jai Guru Vashisht.'

Chapter 4

The City Where the Supreme Light Shines

'Prince Surapadman?' asked a surprised Bhagirath. 'Here!'

'Yes, Your Highness,' said Siamantak, worried.

Bhagirath turned towards Shiva. The Neelkanth nodded.

The prince of Ayodhya turned towards Siamantak. 'Let Prince Surapadman in.'

Moments later a dashing figure marched in. Tall, well-built and swarthy, Surapadman sported a handle bar moustache smoothly oiled and curled up at the edges. His well-maintained hair was long and neatly arranged under an extravagant yet tasteful crown. He wore an ochre *dhoti* with a white *angvastram*, sober for a Chandravanshi royal. There were numerous battle scars on his body, a sign of pride on any Kshatriya.

He walked straight up to Shiva, went down on his haunches and touched the Neelkanth's feet with his head. 'My Lord, it is an honour to finally have your presence in India.'

A surprised Shiva had the presence of mind not to step back. That could easily have been seen as an insult.

He blessed Surapadman with a long life. '*Ayushman Bhav*, Prince. How did you know who I am?'

'Divine light cannot be kept secret, My Lord,' said Surapadman, turning towards Bhagirath with a knowing smile. 'No matter how strong a veil one puts on it.'

Bhagirath smiled and nodded at Surapadman.

'I heard about your brother,' said Shiva. 'Please accept my condolences.'

Surapadman didn't say anything to acknowledge the commiseration. He bowed politely and changed the subject. 'I would like to apologise to you for not receiving you with the ceremonial honour due to the long-awaited Neelkanth. But my father can be a little stubborn.'

'That's all right. I've not given anybody any reason to honour me just as yet. Why don't we talk about what you actually came here for, Surapadman?'

'My Lord, I suppose nothing remains a secret from you. My brother was killed a few days back while in the forest with some friends and his bodyguards. There is a belief that Ayodhya may have carried out this dastardly act.'

'I can assure you we didn't...,' started Bhagirath. Surapadman stretched out his hand, requesting for silence.

'I know that, Prince Bhagirath,' said Surapadman. 'I have a different theory about his murder.'

Surapadman reached into the pouch tied to his waist band and fished out a Branga gold coin. It was exactly similar to the gold coin that Shiva had recovered from the Naga *Lord of the People*.

'My Lord,' said Surapadman. 'This is something I found near my brother's body. I believe that you had recovered a gold coin from a Naga while you were in Ayodhya. Is this similar to that coin?'

Bhagirath stared at Surapadman with shock. He was wondering how Surapadman knew about the Neelkanth's discovery. Rumours about Surapadman building his own spy network must be true. A network independent of the outrageously incompetent Magadh intelligence services.

Shiva took the coin from Surapadman, staring at it hard, his body taut with anger. 'I don't suppose that filthy rat has been caught?'

Surapadman was surprised at Shiva's intense reaction. 'No, My Lord, regrettably not. I fear he may have escaped into the rat hole he emerged from.'

Shiva handed the coin back to Surapadman. He was quiet.

Surapadman turned towards Bhagirath. 'This is all the confirmation I needed, Prince. I will report to the King that my brother, Prince Ugrasen, died while valiantly defending Magadh from a Naga terrorist attack. I will also report that Ayodhya had nothing to do with this. I am sure even you don't want a pointless war between the two pillars of the Chandravanshi confederacy. Especially not now, when we have suffered such a grievous loss to the Suryavanshis.'

The last comment was a jibe. Ayodhya had lost face amongst Chandravanshis due to its leadership in the disastrous war against the Meluhans at Dharmakhet.

'Your words assuage a deep concern of mine, Prince Surapadman,' said Bhagirath. 'I assure you of Ayodhya's friendly intentions towards Magadh. And please allow me to officially convey Ayodhya's condolences on your brother's untimely death.'

Surapadman nodded politely. He turned towards Shiva again with a low bow. 'My Lord, I can see that you too have a bone to pick with the Nagas. I request you to call me to your service when the war with this particular demon is to be fought.'

Shiva looked at Surapadman with a surprised frown. The prince had not given an impression till now that he loved his brother or even sought vengeance.

'My Lord, whatever he may have been like,' said Surapadman, 'he was my brother. I must avenge his blood.'

'That Naga killed my brother as well, Prince Surapadman,' said Shiva, referring to Brahaspati, the Chief Scientist of Meluha, who was like a brother to him. 'I will call you to battle when the time is right.'

— 𑀓𑀐𑀉𑀙𑀓 —

Shiva's entourage left Magadh quietly. Unlike any other city that Shiva had been to, both in Meluha and Swadweep, there was no jamboree organised to see him off. His coming and going had been secret from most people in Magadh. Surapadman however had come to the Magadh port incognito to pay his respects to the Neelkanth before his departure.

The ships sailed in the standard Meluhan convoy formation with the main ship carrying the Neelkanth and his companions, surrounded on all four sides by a ship each. Regardless of which side an enemy cutter came from, they would have to fight through an entire battleship before reaching the Neelkanth's craft. A crucial role in this formation was played by the lead ship. It was the speed controller for the entire convoy. It had to sail slow enough to protect the Neelkanth's ship from the front, but be fast enough to afford enough space for Shiva's ship to slip through and escape if need be.

A Chandravanshi captain was in command of the lead ship and he was doing a spectacularly inept job. He was speeding at a maniacal pace, perhaps to show the prowess of his vessel. This kept opening up a breach between his lead boat and Shiva's vessel. Parvateshwar had to keep blowing the ship horn to alert the lead boat Captain and slow him down.

Tired of this inefficiency, Parvateshwar had decided to travel in the lead ship to teach a thing or two to the Chandravanshi captain about the basics of naval defence formations. Considering the task at hand, Parvateshwar was distressed that Anandmayi had, for some inexplicable reason, decided to also travel on the lead ship.

'So why are we so slow?' asked Anandmayi.

Parvateshwar turned from the balustrade at the fore of the ship. He had not seen her tip-toe to his side. She was standing with her back to the railing, her elbows resting on it lightly with one of her heels placed on the block at the bottom of the railing. Her posture had the effect of raising her already short *dhoti* a fair distance up her right leg and stretching her bosom out provocatively. Parvateshwar, uncomfortable for some reason he could not fathom, stepped back a bit.

'This is a naval defence formation, Princess,' laboured Parvateshwar, as if explaining complicated mathematics to a child unprepared to understand. 'It would take me a lifetime to explain it to you.'

'Are you asking me to spend a lifetime with you? You old devil, you.'

Parvateshwar turned red.

'Well,' continued Anandmayi, 'it will certainly not take me a lifetime to tell you something quite basic. Instead of trying to keep our lead boat agonisingly slow, simply tie a rope of approximately the right length from here to the main ship. Then have a soldier posted at the back who signals every time the rope touches the water, which would mean that the lead vessel is too slow and should speed up. And if the rope becomes taut, the soldier can relay a signal that the lead ship should slow down.'

Anandmayi slipped her hands into her hair to straighten them out. 'You'll make much better time and I will be able to get off these ridiculously small quarters into a more comfortable Kashi palace.'

Parvateshwar was struck by the ingenuity of her suggestion. 'That is brilliant! I will immediately have the captain execute these orders.'

Anandmayi reached out a delicate hand, catching hold of Parvateshwar and pulling him back. 'What's the hurry, Parva? A few minutes will make no difference. Talk to me for a while.'

Parvateshwar turned beet red at both the corruption of his name and Anandmayi's unyielding grip on his arm. He looked down at her hands.

Anandmayi frowned and pulled her hands back. 'They're not dirty, General.'

'That's not what I was implying, Princess.'

'Then what?' asked Anandmayi, her tone slightly harsher.

'I cannot touch a woman, Princess. Especially not you. I am sworn to lifelong celibacy.'

Anandmayi was aghast, staring as though Parvateshwar was an alien. 'Hold on! Are you saying you are a 180-year-old *virgin?!*'

Parvateshwar, chagrined at the completely inappropriate

conversation, turned around and stormed off. Anandmayi collapsed into a fit of giggles.

— ⚰ —

Vishwadyumna heard the soft footfalls. He immediately drew his sword, giving hand signals to his platoon to do likewise.

Their platoon had moved deeper into the forests south of Magadh after the skirmish with Prince Ugrasen and his platoon. The Naga had been injured seriously and was not in a position to travel far. They had travelled as fast as they could without risking the Naga's life, as the angry Magadhans scoured the land for the killers of their prince.

Vishwadyumna hoped the sounds he was hearing did not come from the Magadhans. His Lord was in no state to fight. Or flee.

'Put your sword down, you imbecile,' whispered a strong feminine voice. 'If I'd really wanted to kill you, I would have done it even before you drew your weapon.'

Vishwadyumna did not recognise the hoarse whisper. Perhaps, the tiredness of long travel or the cold of winter had roughened the voice. But he certainly recognised the tone. He immediately put his sword down and bowed his head.

The Queen of the Nagas emerged from the trees, leading her horse quietly. Behind her was her trusted Prime Minister, Karkotak, and fifty of her elite bodyguards.

'I asked you to do just one simple thing,' hissed the Queen. 'Can't you ensure the protection of your Lord? Is that so difficult to do?'

'My Lady,' whispered a nervous Vishwadyumna, 'the situation suddenly got out of...'

'Shut up!' glared the Queen, throwing the reins of her horse to one soldier, as she walked quickly towards the cloth tent at the centre of the clearing.

She entered the cramped tent and took off her mask. On a bed of hay lay her nephew, the Lord of the People. He was covered in bandages, his body limp and weak.

The Queen looked at her nephew with concerned eyes, her tone kind. 'Are we now in alliance with the tribals also?'

The Naga opened his eyes and smiled. He whispered weakly, 'No, Your Highness.'

'Then in the name of the Parmatma, why are you risking your own life to save one of the forest people? Why are you causing me so much grief? Don't I have enough on my plate already?'

'Forgive me, *Mausi*, but haven't I already taken care of your biggest source of tension?'

'Yes, you have. And that is the only reason why I have come all this way for you. You have earned the devotion of all the Nagas. But your karma is still not complete. There are many things you need to do. And stopping some royal brat from what you believe is wrong does not figure high on that list. This country is full of repulsive royals who abuse their people. Are we going to fight every single one?'

'It is not that simple, *Mausi*.'

'Yes, it is. The Magadh prince was doing something wrong. But it is not your duty to stop every person who does something wrong. You are not Lord Rudra.'

'He was trying to kidnap a boy for a bull race.'

The Queen sighed. 'It happens all over. It happens to

thousands of children. This bull fighting is an addictive disease. How many will you stop?'

'But he didn't just stop there,' whispered the Naga. 'He was about to kill the boy's mother, because she was trying to protect her child.'

The Queen stiffened. Quick anger rose within her.

'There aren't too many mothers like this,' whispered the Naga with rare emotion. 'They deserve protection.'

'Enough! How many times have I told you to forget this?'

The Queen rapidly put her mask back on her face and stormed out. Her men kept their heads bowed, terrified of her fearsome rage. 'Karkotak!'

'Yes, my lady.'

'We leave within the hour. We're going home. Make preparations.'

The Lord of the People was in no position to travel. Karkotak knew that. 'But, Your Highness...'

His words were cut short by a petrifying glare from the Queen.

— 人◎Ʊ♀⊕ —

It was just a little over three weeks when Shiva's convoy was closing in on *Kashi, the city where the supreme light shines.* The city had been settled along a voluptuous bend of the holy Ganga river as it took a leisurely northwards meander before flowing East again. If looked at from the sky, this meander gave the impression of a crescent moon, incidentally the royal insignia of the Chandravanshis. Therefore, in the eyes of the Swadweepans, Kashi was the most natural Chandravanshi city.

Kashi also had its own superstition. The city had been built only along the western banks of the river meander, leaving its eastern banks bare. It was believed that whoever built a house on the eastern side at Kashi would suffer a terrible fate. The royal family of Kashi had therefore bought all the land to the East, ensuring that nobody, even by mistake, would suffer the wrath of the gods.

As Shiva's ship was moving towards the legendary *Assi Ghat* or *Port of Eighty,* one of the main docking points of this thriving city, the crowd on the steps started beating their drums for the ceremonial welcome aarti.

'It's a beautiful city,' whispered Sati, running her hand over her protruding belly.

Shiva looked at her and smiled, taking her hand, kissing it gently and holding it close to his chest. 'For some reason, it feels like home. This is where our child should be born.'

Sati smiled back. 'Yes. This shall be the place.'

Even from afar, Bhagirath could make out the countenance of many Ayodhya nobles jostling with the Kashi aristocracy, striving to raise their welcome lamps while berating their aides to hold their family pennants higher. They wanted the Mahadev to notice and favour them. But the Neelkanth noticed something more unusual.

'Bhagirath,' said Shiva, turning to his left, 'this city has no fortifications. Why in the name of the Holy Lake do they have no protection?'

'Oh! That's a long story, My Lord,' said Bhagirath.

'I have all the time in the world. Tell me the entire tale, for this is one of the strangest sights I have seen in India.'

'Well, My Lord, the story starts at Assi Ghat, where we are about to dock.'

'Hmm.'

'This dock did not get its peculiar name because it has eighty steps. Neither did it get its name from the small Assi rivulet that flows close by. It got its name due to an execution that took place here. In fact, eighty executions in just one day.'

'Lord Ram be merciful,' said a flabbergasted Sati. 'Who were these unfortunate people?'

'They were not unfortunate, My Lady,' said Bhagirath. 'They were the worst criminals in history. Eighty members of the Asura royalty were put to death by Lord Rudra for war crimes. Many believe that it was not the exhausting battles between the Devas and Asuras that put an end to the evil Asura menace, but this sublime act of justice that Lord Rudra performed. Without their key leaders, the Asura insurrection against the Devas fizzled out.'

'And then?' asked Shiva, remembering what the Vasudev Pandit at Ayodhya had told him.

Who said the Asuras were evil?

'And then, something strange happened. Soon thereafter, Lord Rudra, the greatest and most fearsome warrior in history, abandoned all violence. He banned the use of *Daivi Astras* that had caused enormous casualties in the Deva-Asura war. Anyone who disobeyed this order would feel the wrath of Lord Rudra who said he would even break his vow of non-violence and destroy seven generations of the man who used any divine weapons.'

'I know of Lord Rudra's order on the *Daivi Astras*,' said Sati, as the Meluhans were also aware of the Mahadev's ban on *divine weapons*. 'But I didn't know the story behind it. What made him give this order?'

'I don't know, My Lady,' said Bhagirath.

I know, mused Shiva. *This must have been the moment when*

Lord Rudra realised the Asuras were not evil, just different. He must have been racked by guilt.

'But the story did not end there. Lord Rudra also said Assi Ghat and Kashi had become holy. He didn't explain why, but the people of that time assumed that it must be because this was the place that ended the war. Lord Rudra said there would be no further killing at Assi Ghat. Ever. That the place should be respected. That the spirits at Assi Ghat and Kashi would forgive the sins of even the most sinful and guide them to salvation if their dead body was cremated there.'

'Interesting,' said Sati.

'The Kashi kings, who were great followers of Lord Rudra, not only banned any executions or killing at Assi Ghat, they also threw it open for cremations for people from any kingdom, without prejudice of caste, creed or sex. Any person can find salvation here. Over time, the belief in Kashi being the gateway to a soul's deliverance gained ground and vast numbers of people started coming here to spend their final days. It was impossible for the small Assi Ghat to cater to such large numbers of the dead. So cremations were stopped at Assi and the city converted another massive ghat, called Manikarnika, into a giant crematorium.'

'But what does that have to do with there being no fort walls?' asked Shiva.

'The point is that if the most influential people in Swadweep came here at the time of their death, with the belief that this would be a place where their sins would be forgiven and they could attain salvation, very few would want Kashi to be destroyed or even be involved in the regular wars that raged in the confederacy. In addition,

Kashi kings took Lord Rudra's orders of nonviolence to what they believed was its logical conclusion. The royal family publicly swore that neither they, nor their descendants, would ever indulge in warfare. In fact, they foreswore any killing, except in the case of self-defence. To prove their commitment to their words, they actually tore down their fort ramparts and built an open ring road around the city. They then erected great temples all along the road, giving it an aura of spirituality.'

'Kashi wasn't attacked and conquered?'

'On the contrary, My Lord,' continued Bhagirath, 'their intense commitment to Lord Rudra's teachings almost made Kashi sacred. Nobody could attack this city, for it would be seen as an insult to Lord Rudra. It became a land of supreme peace and hence prosperity. Suppressed people from across the confederacy found solace here. Traders found that this was the safest place to base their business. Peace and nonalignment to any other kingdom in Swadweep has actually made Kashi an oasis of stability.'

'Is that why you find so many Brangas here?'

'Yes, My Lord. Where else would they be safe? Everybody is out of harm's way in Kashi. But the Brangas have tested even the famed Kashi patience and hospitality.'

'Really?'

'Apparently, they are very difficult to get along with. Kashi is a cosmopolitan city and nobody is forced to change their way of life. But the Brangas wanted their own area because they have certain special customs. The Kashi royal family advises its citizens that the Brangas have suffered a lot in their homeland and that Kashi denizens should be compassionate. But most people find that difficult. In fact, a few years back, it was rumoured that the situation came to such a pass that the king of Kashi was about to order the eviction of the Brangas.'

'And then what happened?' asked Shiva.

'Gold managed to do what good intentions couldn't. Branga is by far the richest land today. The king of Branga had apparently sent gold equivalent to ten years of Kashi's tax collections. And the eviction order was buried.'

'Why would the Branga king spend his own money to help people who have abandoned his country?'

'I don't know, My Lord. I think we can put that down as another strange characteristic of the Brangas.'

The ship docked softly at Assi Ghat and Shiva looked towards the multitudes gathered there to welcome him. Parvateshwar was already organising the place so that Shiva could alight. He saw Drapaku at a distance giving orders to Nandi and Veerbhadra. Bhagirath had already bounded down the gangway in search of the Kashi head of police. Sati tapped Shiva lightly. He turned to look at her and she gestured delicately with her eyes. Shiva looked in the direction she had indicated. In the distance, away from the melee, letting his nobles and the Ayodhya aristocracy hog the frontlines of the Neelkanth's welcome, under an understated royal umbrella, stood a sombre old man. Shiva joined his hands in a polite namaste and bowed slightly to Athithigva, the king of Kashi. Athithigva in turn bowed low in respect to the Neelkanth. Sati could not be sure from the distance, but it appeared as though the king had tears in his eyes.

Chapter 5

A Small Wrong?

'Mmm,' mumbled Shiva as Sati softly kissed him awake. He cupped her face gently. 'Are my eyes deceiving me or are you getting more beautiful every day?'

Sati smiled, running her hand along her belly. 'Stop flattering me so early in the morning!'

Shiva edged up on his elbows, kissing her again. 'So there is a fixed schedule for compliments now?'

Sati laughed again, slowly getting off the bed. 'Why don't you go wash? I have requested for breakfast to be served in our room.'

'Ahh! You are finally learning my ways!' Shiva always hated eating at the organised and civilised dining room gatherings that Sati liked.

As Shiva walked into the comfortable washroom attached to their chamber at the Kashi palace, Sati looked out. The famous ring road, also called the Sacred Avenue, was clearly visible. It was an awe-inspiring sight. Unlike the congested city of Kashi itself, the avenue was very broad, allowing even six carts to pass simultaneously. There was a breathtaking profusion of trees around the road, with probably all the species of flora from the Indian subcontinent represented. Beyond the trees lay the plethora of temples. The boulevard extended upto a roughly semi-circular distance of more than thirty kilometres and not one of the buildings built on its sides was anything but a place of worship. The Chandravanshis liked to say that almost every Indian god has a home on Kashi's Sacred Avenue. But of course, that belief was scarcely built on reality, considering that the Indians worshipped over thirty million gods. But one could safely state that practically all the popular gods had a temple dedicated to them on this holy pathway. And the most majestic temple of them all was dedicated, but of course, to the most admired of them all, the great Mahadev himself, Lord Rudra. It was this temple that Sati was staring at. It had been built close to the Brahma Ghat. Legend had it that the original plan for the temple, hatched by the Devas during the life of Lord Rudra himself, was to have it close to Assi Ghat, the scene of Lord Rudra's deliverance of justice. But the great Mahadev, the scourge of the Asuras, had ordered that no memorial to him must ever be built near Assi Ghat, with one of his most unfathomable lines — *'Not here. Anywhere else. But not here'.* No one had understood why. But at the same time, no one argued with the fearsome Lord Rudra.

'They call it the *Vishwanath* temple,' said Shiva, startling Sati with his sudden appearance. 'It means the *Lord of the World.*'

'He was a great man,' whispered Sati. 'A true God.'

'Yes,' agreed Shiva, *bowing to Lord Rudra.* '*Om Rudraiy namah.*'

'*Om Rudraiy namah.*'

'It was good of King Athithigva to leave us alone last night. We certainly needed the rest after the string of ceremonies at Assi Ghat.'

'Yes, he seems to be a good man. But I fear he will not be leaving you alone today. I could make out that he has a lot to talk to you about.'

Shiva laughed. 'But I do like his city. The more I see it, the more it feels like home.'

'Let's eat our breakfast,' said Sati. 'I think we have a long day ahead!'

— 𝍦⊙𝍦𝍦⊕ —

'*Especially not you*?' asked Kanini. 'He actually said that?'

'Those very words,' said Anandmayi. 'He said he cannot touch any woman. Especially not me!'

Kanini expertly massaged the rejuvenating oil into Anandmayi's scalp. 'That does make sense, Princess. There are only two women who can make a man break the vow of lifelong celibacy. Either the *apsara* Menaka or you.'

'Two?' Anandmayi had her eyebrows raised at being considered akin to the *celestial nymph*.

'My apologies,' chuckled Kanini. 'What is Menaka compared to you!'

Anandmayi laughed.

'But this is a far tougher challenge than Menaka's, Princess,' continued Kanini. 'Sage Vishwamitra had taken the vow late in his life. He had already experienced the pleasures of love. Menaka just had to remind him, not create the need. The General on the other hand is a virgin!'

'I know. But when something is so beautiful, achieving it cannot be easy, can it?'

Kanini narrowed her eyes. 'Don't lose your heart before you have won his, Princess.'

Anandmayi frowned. 'Of course I haven't!'

Kanini stared hard at Anandmayi and smiled. The Princess was obviously in love. She hoped Parvateshwar had the good sense to realise his good fortune in time.

— 人◎Ʇ↑⊕ —

'You have a beautiful capital, Your Highness,' said Shiva.

The sun had already covered a third of its daily journey. Shiva was sitting in King Athithigva's private chambers with Sati. Drapaku, Nandi and Veerbhadra stood guard at the door supporting the baton-wielding Kashi royal guard. It was a mystery to Drapaku how only batons could be used to protect a royal family. What if there was a serious attack? Meanwhile, Parvateshwar had set off on a tour with the Kashi police chief. He wanted to ensure that the path from the palace to the Kashi Vishwanath temple was well-protected for the Neelkanth's planned visit in the afternoon. It was expected that practically the entire city would be lining the Sacred Avenue to catch a glimpse of the Neelkanth, for only the nobility had been allowed to meet him at his arrival at Assi Ghat.

'Actually, this is your city, My Lord,' said Athithigva with a low bow.

Shiva frowned.

'Lord Rudra had spent most of his time in Kashi, calling it his adopted home,' explained Athithigva. 'After his departure to his birth land to the West, the Kashi royal family conducted a puja at Assi Ghat, effectively making Lord Rudra and his successors our true kings for eternity.

My family, while being different from the royal family that conducted that puja, honours the promise to this day. We only function as the caretakers of the birthright of Lord Rudra's successors.'

Shiva was getting increasingly uncomfortable.

'Now that Lord Rudra's successor is here, it is time for him to ascend the throne of Kashi,' continued Athithigva. 'It will be my honour to serve you, My Lord.'

Shiva almost choked on a combination of surprise and exasperation.

These people are all mad! Well intentioned, but mad!

'I have no intentions of becoming a King, Your Highness,' smiled Shiva. 'I certainly don't think of myself as worthy of being called Lord Rudra's successor. You are a good king and I suggest you continue to serve your people.'

'But, My Lord...'

'I have a few requests though, Your Highness,' interrupted Shiva. He did not want to continue the discussion on his royal antecedents.

'Anything, My Lord.'

'Firstly, my wife and I would like our child to be born here. May we impose on your hospitality for this duration?'

'My Lord, my entire palace is yours. Lady Sati and you can stay here for all time to come.'

Shiva smiled slightly. 'No, I don't think we will stay that long. Also, I want to meet the leader of the Brangas in your city.'

'His name is Divodas, My Lord. I will certainly summon him to your presence. Speaking to anyone else from that unfortunate tribe is useless. Divodas is the only one sensible or capable enough to interact with others. I believe he is out on a trading trip and should be returning by tonight. I'll ensure that he is called here at the earliest.'

'Wonderful.'

— ⅄Ⓦᴜ⅄⊕ —

'The crowd out there looks like it is slipping out of control, Drapaku,' pointed Parvateshwar.

Parvateshwar was with Bhagirath, Drapaku and Tratya, the Kashi police chief, upon a raised platform on the Sacred Avenue. It almost seemed like all of Kashi's 200,000 citizens had descended there to catch a glimpse of the Neelkanth. And the Kashi police appeared woefully ill-trained to manage the crowd. They were polite to a fault, which usually worked with the courteous Kashi citizens. But on an occasion like this, when every person was desperate to jump up front and touch the Lord, the firm hand of the Suryavanshis was called for.

'I'll take care of it, General,' said Drapaku as he bounded off the platform to issue instructions to Nandi waiting at the bottom.

'But he must not raise his hand,' said Tratya.

'He'll behave as required by the situation, Tratya,' said Parvateshwar, irritated.

Nandi, on hearing Drapaku's orders, was off with his platoon. Drapaku, using the hook on his amputated left hand, pulled himself back onto the platform with surprising agility.

'It's done, General,' said Drapaku. 'That crowd will be pushed back.'

Parvateshwar nodded and turned to look at Shiva and his party. Shiva, holding Sati's hand, walked slowly with a broad smile, acknowledging almost every single person who screamed out his name. Krittika, Sati's companion, paced slightly behind Sati while Athithigva, beaming with the commitment of a true devotee, marched silently, with his family and ministers in tow.

'Chief Tratya,' shouted a panicked Kashi policeman bounding up the platform.

Tratya looked down. 'Yes, Kaavas?'

'A riot is breaking out in the Branga quarter!'

'Tell me exactly what happened.'

'They have killed a peacock once again. But this time they were caught red-handed by some of their neighbours, who are swearing retribution for this sin.'

'I'm not surprised! I don't know why His Highness insists on keeping those uncivilised dolts in our city. It was only a matter of time before some citizens lost their patience and did something.'

'What happened?' asked Parvateshwar.

'It's the Brangas. They know that killing peacocks is banned in Kashi as they were Lord Rudra's favourite amongst the birds. There is a widespread belief that they sacrifice the bird in some bizarre ceremonies in their colony. Now they have been caught red-handed and are going to be taught a lesson.'

'Why don't you send some of your men there to break up the riot?'

Tratya looked at Parvateshwar strangely. 'You won't understand some things. We accept every community from India in Kashi. All of them live peacefully, making this great city their home. But the Brangas purposely want to infuriate every one of us. This riot is actually a bad path to a good end. Just let it happen.'

Parvateshwar was shocked at the words of the same police chief who had been propagating the virtues of non-violence just a while back. 'If they have committed a crime, they should be punished by your courts. Your citizens do not have the right to riot and hurt innocent people who may have had nothing to do with the killing of the bird.'

'It doesn't matter if some of them were innocent. It's a small price to pay if it rids the city of the Brangas and their evil ways. I cannot and will not do anything on this.'

'If you won't do anything, I will,' warned Parvateshwar.

Tratya looked at Parvateshwar in exasperation and turned back to look at the Neelkanth's entourage. Parvateshwar stared hard at Tratya. It took only a moment for him to make up his mind.

'Drapaku, you have the command,' said Parvateshwar. 'Make sure the crowd breaks as soon as the Lord is in the Vishwanath temple. Prince Bhagirath, will you accompany me? I would need some help as I don't know Chandravanshi customs.'

'It will be my honour, General,' said Bhagirath.

'This is not your job,' said Tratya, raising his voice for the first time in the day. 'You have no right to interfere in our internal affairs.'

'He has every right,' interjected Bhagirath, with the arrogance that only a royal can possess. 'Have you forgotten Lord Ram's words? Standing by and doing nothing while a sin is committed is as bad as committing the sin yourself. You should be thanking the General for doing your job.'

Parvateshwar and Bhagirath quickly stepped down from the platform along with Kaavas, ordered Veerbhadra to follow them with a hundred men and rushed towards the Branga quarters.

— ⚥◎ᛃᚦ⊕ —

'This is tough and tricky,' said Bhagirath.

They were in front of the Branga quarters. The legendary hoards of gold brought in by the refugees from the East had transformed this particularly congested part of the city into spacious residences. Brangas lived in a lavishly designed and intricately carved multi-storey building, the tallest in all of Kashi, save for the Vishwanath temple and the royal palaces. The building was surrounded on all sides by a large garden, strangely enough both lusciously landscaped and conservatively symmetrical, much like the one at the Narsimha temple in Magadh. A board at its entrance proudly proclaimed the loyalty of its residents: 'May Lord Rudra bless the most divine land of Branga.'

The city's congestion and confusion began immediately at the border of the fenced garden. Narrow paths led out into what were suburbs dominated by immigrants from Ayodhya, Magadh, Prayag and other parts of the Chandravanshi confederacy. A little known fact was that even some Meluhans, tired of the regimented life in their homeland and fearful of giving up their birth children at Maika, had found refuge in Kashi. They tolerated the chaos of the Chandravanshi ways for the pleasure of watching their children grow.

'I'm sure it's not just anger at their customs,' said Veerbhadra, taking in the stark difference in the lifestyles of the common folk of Kashi and the Brangas, 'Resentment about their wealth must also drive the hatred towards the Brangas.'

Bhagirath nodded before turning towards Parvateshwar, who was evaluating the situation. 'What do you think, General?'

From a perspective of defence, the location was a disaster. The Brangas were stuck between a rock and a hard place. They were surrounded on all four sides by a hostile population living in densely-populated areas along congested streets leading to the Branga quarters. Escape was out of the question. They would be easily mobbed in the narrow lanes. The garden gave them some measure of protection. Any mob attacking the Brangas would be exposed in that area for at least a minute till they reached the building itself.

The Brangas, perhaps always fearful of their status in Kashi, had stocked the roof of their building with a huge horde of rocks. Thrown from that height, the rocks were like missiles, capable of causing serious injury, possibly even death if it hit the right spot.

The Kashi mob, meanwhile, was releasing dogs, which the Brangas considered unclean, into the closed compound. They knew the Brangas would respond with stones to chase the animals back. Parvateshwar realised that in this battle of attrition, it was a matter of time before the Branga rocks ran out and they were susceptible to a full frontal attack. Outnumbered at more than a hundred to one, despite the fact that their enemies were armed with such laughable weapons as kitchen knives and washing clubs, the Brangas had little chance of survival.

'It doesn't look good for the Brangas,' said Parvateshwar. 'Can we reason with the Kashi mob?'

'I already tried, General,' said Bhagirath. 'They will not listen. They believe the Brangas can buy out the courts with their gold.'

'It's probably true,' mumbled the Kashi Captain Kaavas, quietly revealing his own leanings.

Bhagirath turned towards Kaavas, who immediately recoiled with fear, for Bhagirath's reputation was legendary in Kashi.

'You don't agree with the mob, do you?' asked Bhagirath.

Kaavas' face glowered, 'I detest the Brangas. They are dirty scoundrels who break every law, even as they throw their gold around.' Having said his piece, Kaavas seemed to calm down. He looked down and whispered. 'But is this the way they should be treated? Would Lord Rudra have done this? No, Your Highness.'

'Then find us a solution.'

Pointing to the angry Kashi citizens surrounding them, Kaavas said, 'This horde will not back off till the Brangas are punished in some form, Prince Bhagirath. How can we ensure that, while keeping the Brangas alive and safe? I don't know.'

'What if the Suryavanshis attack them?' asked Parvateshwar, shocked at the effective but borderline ethical solution that had entered his mind.

Bhagirath smiled immediately, for he could suspect where Parvateshwar was going. 'We'll use the batons of the Kashi police, not our weapons. We'll only injure, not kill.'

'Exactly,' said Parvateshwar. 'The mob will get its justice and back off. The Brangas will be injured, but alive. I know this is not entirely right. But sometimes, the only way to prevent a grave wrong is to commit a small wrong.

I will have to take full responsibility for this and answer to the Parmatma.'

Bhagirath smiled softly. Some Chandravanshi ways were entering Parvateshwar's psyche. It had not escaped his notice that his elder sister had been lavishing attention on the Meluhan General.

Parvateshwar turned to Kaavas. 'I will need a hundred batons.'

Bhagirath shot off with Kaavas towards the Sacred Avenue. They were back in no time. Parvateshwar had meanwhile spoken to the leaders of the Kashi mob, promising them justice if they dropped their weapons. They waited patiently for the Suryavanshis to deliver.

Parvateshwar gathered the Suryavanshis in front of him. 'Meluhans, do not use your swords. Use the batons. Limit the blows to their limbs, avoid their heads. Keep your shield rigidly in the tortoise formation. Rocks from that height can kill.'

The Suryavanshis stared at their General.

'This is the only way the Brangas can be saved,' continued Parvateshwar.

The Meluhans moved quickly into battle formation, with Parvateshwar, Bhagirath and Veerbhadra in the lead. Kaavas, who was unfamiliar with such tactics, was placed in the middle, where it was safest. As the soldiers marched into the Branga garden, there was a hailstorm of stones. Their shields kept them safe as they strode slowly but surely towards the building entrance.

The entrance itself was, naturally, narrower than the garden path. The tortoise formation would have to be broken here. Parvateshwar ordered a double file charge into the building, shields held left-right to prevent attacks from the sides. He had assumed the rocks could not be used within the building. A grave miscalculation.

— ⚚ ⊙ ℧ ⚛ ⊕ —

'What a statue,' whispered Sati, shuddering slightly at the awe-inspiring sight of Lord Rudra.

Shiva and Sati had just entered the massive Vishwanath temple.

The temple, built a little distance away from the Brahma Ghat, was an imposing structure. It wasn't just the gargantuan height of one hundred metres, but also the overwhelming simplicity of the edifice that inspired wonder. An open garden, built in the symmetrical style of Lord Rudra's native land, provided the entry from the Sacred Avenue to the temple. The red sandstone structure, almost the colour of blood, was startlingly sober. The giant platform, almost twenty metres in height, which soared from the farthest point of the garden, had absolutely no carvings or embellishments, unlike any other temple Shiva had seen so far. A hundred steps had been carved into the platform. Devotees, who reached atop the platform, would be stunned by the main temple spire, again of red sandstone, which soared an improbable eighty metres. Just like the platform, the main temple also had no carvings. There were a hundred square pillars to hold up the spire. Unlike other temples, the sanctum sanctorum was in the centre and not at the far end. Within the sanctum was the statue that drew devotees from across the land: The formidable Lord Rudra.

Legend had it that Lord Rudra mostly worked alone. He had no known friends whose stories could be immortalised in frescoes on the temple walls. There was no favourite devotee whose statue could be placed at his feet. The only partner Lord Rudra had, the only one he listened to, was Lady Mohini. Hence Krittika found it odd that her legendary beauty had not been rendered into an idol.

'How come Lady Mohini's statue is not here?' whispered Krittika to an aide of Athithigva.

'You know the stories of the Lord well,' replied the aide. 'Come.'

She led Krittika to the other side of the sanctum. To her surprise, Krittika discovered that the sanctum had another entrance from the back. Through that entrance a devotee would see an idol of Lady Mohini, rumoured to be the most gorgeous woman of all time, sitting on a throne. Her beautiful eyes were in an enchanting half stare. But Krittika noticed that in her hand, surreptitiously hidden at first view, was a knife. Mohini, ever capricious and deadly. Krittika smiled. It seemed fitting that the idols of Lady Mohini and Lord Rudra were back to back. They shared a complex relationship; partners but with vastly different outlooks.

Krittika bowed low to Lady Mohini. While some refused to honour her as *Vishnu*, Krittika was amongst the majority which believed that Lady Mohini deserved the title of *the Propagator of Good*.

On the other side of the sanctum, Shiva was staring at Lord Rudra's idol. The Lord was an imposing and impossibly muscled man. His hirsute chest sported a pendant. Upon closer examination, Shiva realised the pendant was a tiger claw. The Lord's shield had been laid at the side of his throne and while the sword too rested along the seat, the Lord's hand was close to the hilt. Clearly, the sculptor wanted to signify that while the most ferocious warrior in history had renounced violence, his weapons lay close at hand, ready to be used on anyone who dared to break his laws. The sculptor had faithfully recreated the proud battle scars that must have adorned Lord Rudra's body. One of the scars ran across his face from his right temple to his left cheek. The Lord also sported a long beard and moustache, many strands of which had been painstakingly curled with beads rolled into them.

'I have never seen anyone in India wear beads in their beard,' said Shiva to Athithigva.

'This is the way of the Lord's native people in Pariha, My Lord.'

'*Pariha*?'

'Yes, My Lord. The *land of fairies*. It lies beyond the western borders of India, beyond the Himalayas, our great mountains.'

Shiva turned back to the Lord's idol. The strongest feeling he had in the temple was fear. Was it wrong to feel like this about a God? Wasn't it always supposed to be love? Respect? Awe? Why fear?

Because sometimes, nothing clarifies and focuses the mind except fear. Lord Rudra needed to inspire fear to achieve his goals.

Shiva heard the voice in his head. It appeared to come from a distance, but it was unquestionably clear. He knew it was a Vasudev Pandit.

Where are you, Panditji?

Hidden from view, Lord Neelkanth. There are too many people around.

I need to talk to you.

All in good time, my friend. But if you can hear me, can't you hear the desperate call of your most principled follower?

Most principled follower?

The voice had gone silent. Shiva turned around, concerned.

Chapter 6

Even a Mountain Can Fall

'Take cover!' shouted Parvateshwar.

Bhagirath and he had entered the Branga building to be greeted by a volley of stones.

The building had a huge atrium at the entrance, with a sky light. It was a brilliant design that allowed natural sunlight and fresh air to come in unhindered. There was a cleverly constructed retractable ceiling to cover the atrium during the rains. At present, however, the atrium was like a valley of death for the Suryavanshis, surrounded as it was on all sides by balconies from where the Brangas rained stones upon them.

A sharp missile hit Parvateshwar on his left shoulder. He felt his collar bone snap. A furious Parvateshwar drew his baton high and bellowed, 'Har Har Mahadev!'

'Har Har Mahadev!' yelled the Suryavanshis.

They were gods! Mere stones wouldn't stop them. The Suryavanshis charged up the stairs, clubbing all who came in their path, including women. But even in their fury, they were mindful of Parvateshwar's instructions: No strikes on the head. They injured the Brangas, but killed none.

The Brangas started falling back, faced with the relentless

and disciplined Suryavanshi attack. Soon the Suryavanshis were charging up the building to the top. Parvateshwar found it strange that there appeared to be no leader. The Brangas were just a random mob, which was fighting heroically, but in a disastrously incompetent manner. By the time the Suryavanshis reached the top, practically all the Brangas were on the floor, writhing in agony. Injured, but alive.

It was then that Parvateshwar heard the noise. Even in the commotion of the numerous Brangas howling in pain, the horrifying din could not be missed. It sounded like hundreds of babies were howling desperately, as if their lives depended on it.

Parvateshwar had heard rumours of ghastly ritual sacrifices that the Brangas committed. Fearing the worst, he ran towards the room where the sound emanated from. The General broke open the door with one kick. He was sickened by what he saw.

The limp body of the decapitated peacock was held at a corner of the room, its blood being drained into a vessel. Around it were many women, each holding a baby writhing in pain. Some babies had blood on their mouths. A horror-struck Parvateshwar dropped his club and reached for his sword. There was a sudden blur to his left. Before he could react, he felt a sharp pain on his head. The world went black.

Bhagirath screamed, drawing his sword, as did the Suryavanshis. He was about to run his sword through the man who had clubbed Parvateshwar when a woman screamed: 'PLEASE DON'T!'

Bhagirath stopped. The woman was very obviously pregnant.

The Branga man was about to raise his club again. The woman screamed once more. 'NO!'

To Bhagirath's surprise, the man obeyed.

The other Branga women at the back were carrying on with their sickening ritual.

'Stop!' screamed Bhagirath.

The pregnant Branga woman fell at Bhagirath's feet. 'No, brave Prince. Don't stop us. I beg you.'

'High priestess, what are you doing?' asked the Branga man. 'Don't humiliate yourself!'

Bhagirath looked at the scene once again, and this was when the real inference dawned on him. He was stunned. The only children crying were the ones who did not have blood on their mouths. Their limbs were twisted in painful agony, as if a hideous force was squeezing their tiny bodies. The moment some of the peacock blood was poured into a baby's mouth, the child quietened down.

Bhagirath whispered in shock. 'What the hell...'

'Please,' pleaded the Branga high priestess. 'We need it for our babies. They will die without it. I beg you. Let us save them.'

Bhagirath stood silent. Bewildered.

'Your Highness,' said Veerbhadra. 'The General.'

Bhagirath immediately bent down to check on Parvateshwar. His heart was beating, but the pulse was weak.

'Suryavanshis, we need to carry the General to an *ayuralay*. Quickly! We don't have much time!'

Bearing their leader along, the Suryavanshis rushed out. Parvateshwar had to be taken to a *hospital*.

— ⚘◎⚐⚕⊕ —

Ayurvati came out of the operating room. Chandravanshi doctors simply did not have the knowledge to deal with Parvateshwar's injury. Ayurvati had been sent urgent summons.

Shiva and Sati immediately rose. Sati's heart sank on seeing the dejected look on Ayurvati's face.

'How soon will he be all right, Ayurvati?' asked Shiva.

Ayurvati took a deep breath. 'My Lord, the club hit the General at a most unfortunate spot, right on his temple. He is suffering severe internal haemorrhaging. The blood loss could be fatal.'

Shiva bit his lip.

'I...,' said Ayurvati.

'If anyone can save him, it is you Ayurvati,' said Shiva.

'There is nothing in the medical manuals for such a severe injury, My Lord. We could do brain surgery, but that cannot be performed while the patient is unconscious. In the surgery, we apply local pain relievers to allow the conscious patient to guide us with his actions. Taking this risk while Parvateshwar is unconscious could prove more dangerous than the injury itself.'

Sati's eyes were welling up.

'We cannot allow this to happen, Ayurvati,' said Shiva. 'We cannot!'

'I know, My Lord.'

'Then think of something. You are Ayurvati, the best doctor in the world!'

'I have only one solution in mind, My Lord,' said Ayurvati. 'But I don't even know if it would work.'

'The Somras?' asked Shiva.

'Do you agree?'

'Yes. Let's try it.'

Ayurvati rushed off to find her assistants.

Shiva turned towards Sati, worried. He knew how close Sati was to her *Pitratulya*. Her obvious misery would also impact their unborn child. 'He'll be all right. Trust me.'

— 🕉 —

'Where is the damn Somras?' asked an agitated Shiva.

'I'm sorry, My Lord,' said Athithigva. 'But we don't really have large quantities of the Somras. We don't keep any at the ayuralay.'

'It's coming, My Lord,' assured Ayurvati. 'I have sent Mastrak to my quarters for some.'

Shiva snorted in frustration and turned towards Parvateshwar's room. 'Hang on, my friend. We will save you. Hang on.'

Mastrak came in panting, holding a small wooden bottle. 'My lady!'

'You've prepared it correctly?'

'Yes, my lady.'

Ayurvati rushed into Parvateshwar's room.

— 🕉 —

Parvateshwar was lying on a bed in the far corner. Mastrak and Dhruvini, Ayurvati's assistants, sat at the bedside, rubbing the juice of neem leaves under his nails. There was a pumping apparatus attached to the General's nose in order to ease his breathing.

'The haemorrhaging has stopped, My Lord,' said Ayurvati. 'He is not getting worse.'

The vision of the apparatus attached to the General's

nose shook Shiva. To see a man such as Parvateshwar in this helpless state was too much for him. 'Then why is that apparatus required?'

'The bleeding has harmed the parts of his brain that control his breathing, My Lord,' said Ayurvati, in the calm manner she always willed herself into when faced with a medical crisis. 'Parvateshwar cannot breathe on his own. If we remove this apparatus, he will die.'

'Then why can't you repair his brain?'

'I told you, My Lord, a brain surgery cannot be done while the patient is unconscious. It is too risky. I may injure some other vital function with my instruments.'

'The Somras...'

'It has stopped the bleeding, My Lord. He is stable. But it doesn't appear to be healing his brain.'

'What do we do?'

Ayurvati remained silent. She didn't have an answer. At least an answer that was practical.

'There must be a way.'

'There is one remote possibility, My Lord,' said Ayurvati. 'The bark of the Sanjeevani tree. It is actually one of the ingredients in the Somras. A very diluted ingredient.'

'Then why don't we use that?'

'It is very unstable. The bark disintegrates very rapidly. It has to be taken from a live Sanjeevani tree and used within minutes.'

'Then find a...'

'It doesn't grow here, My Lord. It grows naturally in the foothills of the Himalayas. We have plantations in Meluha. But getting it could take months. By the time we return with the bark, it would have disintegrated.'

There has to be a way! Holy lake, please find me a way!

— ⋏◎꜓⪦⊕ —

'Your Highness,' said Nandi, who had been promoted from the rank of Captain.

'Yes, Major Nandi,' said Bhagirath.

'Can you come with me please?'

'Where?'

'It's important, Your Highness.'

Bhagirath thought it was odd that Nandi wanted him to leave the ayuralay at a time when Parvateshwar was fighting for his life. But he knew that Nandi was the Neelkanth's close friend. More importantly, he also knew that Nandi was a level-headed man. If he was asking him to go somewhere, it would be important.

Bhagirath followed.

— ⋏◎꜓⪦⊕ —

Bhagirath could not hide his surprise as Nandi took him to the Branga building.

'What is going on, Major?'

'You must meet him,' said Nandi.

'Who?'

'Me,' said a tall, dark man stepping out of the structure. His long hair was neatly oiled and tied in a knot. His eyes were doe-shaped, his cheekbones high. He had a clear complexion. His lanky frame was draped in a white starched *dhoti*, with a cream *angvastram* thrown over his shoulder. His face bore the look of a man who had seen too much sadness for one lifetime.

'Who are you?'

'I am Divodas. The chief of the Brangas here.'

Bhagirath gritted his teeth. 'The General saved all your sorry hides. And your men have brought him to the brink of death!'

'I know, Your Highness. My men thought the General would have stopped us from saving our children. It was a genuine mistake. Our most sincere apologies.'

'You think your apology is going to save his life?'

'It will not. I know that. He has saved my entire tribe from a certain death. He has saved my wife and unborn child. It is a debt that must be repaid.'

The mention of payment made Bhagirath even more livid. 'You think your filthy gold will get you out of this? Mark my words, if anything happens to the General, I will personally come here and kill every single one of you. Every single one!'

Divodas kept quiet. His face impassive.

'Your Highness,' said Nandi. 'Let us hear him out.'

Bhagirath grunted in an irritated manner.

'Gold means nothing, Your Highness,' said Divodas. 'We have tonnes of it back home. It still cannot buy us out of our suffering. Nothing is more important than life. Nothing. You realise the simplicity of that point only when you confront death every day.'

Bhagirath didn't say anything.

'General Parvateshwar is a brave and honourable man. For his sake, I will break the vow I took on the name of my ancestors. Even if it damns my soul forever.'

Bhagirath frowned.

'I am not supposed to share this medicine with anyone who is not Branga. But I will give it to you for the General.

Tell your doctor to apply it on his temple and nostrils. He will live.'

Bhagirath looked suspiciously at the small silk packet. 'What is this?'

'You don't need to know what it is, Your Highness. You just need to know one thing. It will save General Parvateshwar's life.'

— ≀◯⊍ϟ⊕ —

'What is this?'

Ayurvati was looking at the silk pouch Bhagirath had just handed over to her.

'That doesn't matter,' said Bhagirath. 'Just apply it on his temples and nostrils. It may save his life.'

Ayurvati frowned.

'Lady Ayurvati, what is the harm in trying?' asked Bhagirath.

Ayurvati opened the pouch to find a reddish-brown thick paste. She had never seen anything like it. She smelt the paste and immediately looked up at Bhagirath, stunned. 'Where did you get this?'

'That doesn't matter. Use it.'

Ayurvati kept staring at Bhagirath. She had a hundred questions running through her mind. But she had to do the most obvious thing first. She knew this paste would save Parvateshwar.

— ≀◯⊍ϟ⊕ —

Parvateshwar opened his eyes slowly, his breathing ragged.

'My friend,' whispered Shiva.

'My Lord,' whispered Parvateshwar, trying to get up.

'No! Don't!' said Shiva, gently making Parvateshwar lie back. 'You need to rest. You are strong-headed, but not that strong!'

Parvateshwar smiled wanly.

Shiva knew the question that would arise first in the General's mind. 'All the Brangas are safe. What you did was brilliant.'

'I don't know, My Lord. I will have to do penance. I have committed a sin.'

'What you did saved lives. There is no need for any penance.'

Parvateshwar sighed. His head still throbbed immensely. 'They had some ghastly ritual going on...'

'Don't think about it, my friend. Right now you need to relax. Ayurvati has ordered strictly that nobody is to disturb you. I will leave you alone. Try to catch some sleep.'

'Anandmayi!'

— 大◎ᄁᄼ⊗ —

Bhagirath tried to stop his sister. Anandmayi was rushing into the ayuralay chamber where Parvateshwar lay. She had been out of the city the whole day attending a music lesson at a nearby ashram. She ran into her brother's arms.

'Is he all right?'

'Yes,' said Bhagirath.

Anandmayi glowered. 'Who is the bastard who did this? I hope you killed that dog!'

'We will let Parvateshwar decide what to do.'

'I heard he was hit on the temple. That there was blood

haemorrhaging.'

'Yes.'

'Lord Agni be merciful. That can be fatal.'

'Yes. But some medicines from the Brangas have saved him.'

'Brangas? First they nearly kill him and then give medicines to save him? Is there no limit to their madness?'

'The medicine was given by their leader, Divodas. He arrived in Kashi a few hours back and heard about this incident. He seems like a good man.'

Anandmayi was not interested in the Branga leader. 'Has Parvateshwar woken up?'

'Yes. The Lord Neelkanth just met him. He has gone back to sleep. He is out of danger. Don't worry.'

Anandmayi nodded, her eyes moist.

'And, by the way,' said Bhagirath. 'I've also recovered from my injuries.'

Anandmayi burst out laughing. 'I'm sorry, my brother! I should have asked.'

Bhagirath made a dramatic pose. 'Nobody can hurt your brother. He's the greatest Chandravanshi warrior ever!'

'Nobody hurt you because you must have been hiding behind Parvateshwar!'

Bhagirath burst out laughing and reached out playfully to chuff his sister. Anandmayi pulled her younger brother into her arms.

'Go,' said Bhagirath. 'Looking at him may make you feel better.'

Anandmayi nodded. As she entered Parvateshwar's room, Ayurvati emerged from another chamber. 'Your Highness.'

'Yes, Lady Ayurvati,' said Bhagirath with a namaste.

'The Lord Neelkanth and I would like to talk to you. Could you come with me?'

'Of course.'

'Where did you get the medicine from, Bhagirath?' asked

— ☖◎☟♀⊕ —

Shiva.

Bhagirath was surprised at Shiva's tone. The Lord had always appeared kind. He now seemed cold. Angry.

'What is the matter, My Lord?' asked Bhagirath, worried.

'Answer my question, Prince. Where did you get the medicine from?'

'From the Brangas.'

Shiva stared hard into Bhagirath's eyes. Bhagirath could gauge the Neelkanth was struggling to believe his words.

'I'm not lying, My Lord,' said Bhagirath. 'And why would I? This medicine has saved the General's life.'

Shiva continued to stare.

'My Lord, what is the problem?'

'The problem, Your Highness,' said Ayurvati, 'is that this medicine is not available in the Sapt Sindhu. I could tell that it was made from the bark of the Sanjeevani tree. But the problem with any Sanjeevani medicine is that it deteriorates rapidly. It cannot be used unless freshly taken from a live tree. This medicine was stabilised. It was a paste. We could use it.'

'My apologies Lady Ayurvati, but I still do not understand the problem.'

'There is only one element, the crushed wood of another specific tree, which is capable of mixing with the Sanjeevani and stabilising it. That tree does not grow in the Sapt Sindhu.'

Bhagirath frowned.

'That tree only grows south of the Narmada river. In Naga territory.'

The prince of Ayodhya froze. He knew what the Neelkanth would be thinking. 'My Lord, I have nothing to do with the Nagas. I got this medicine from the Branga leader Divodas. I swear on Ayodhya. I swear on my beloved sister. I have nothing to do with the Nagas.'

Shiva continued to stare at Bhagirath. 'I want to meet Divodas.'

'My Lord, I swear I have nothing to do with the Nagas.'

'Get me Divodas within the next hour, Prince Bhagirath.'

Bhagirath's heart was beating madly. 'My Lord, please believe me...'

'We will talk about this later, Prince Bhagirath,' said Shiva. 'Please get Divodas.'

'I believe King Athithigva has already arranged for Divodas to have an audience with you tomorrow morning, My Lord.'

Shiva stared at Bhagirath, eyes narrowing a bit.

'I will arrange for Divodas to come here right away, My Lord,' said Bhagirath, rushing from the room.

Anandmayi sat silently on a chair next to Parvateshwar's

— ༈◍༙༕⊕ —

bed. The General was asleep, breathing slowly. The Princess ran her fingers slowly down Parvateshwar's powerful shoulder, arm and all the way to his fingers. The General's body seemed to shiver a bit.

Anandmayi laughed softly. 'For all your vows, you are a

man after all!'

As if driven by instinct, Parvateshwar withdrew his hand. He blabbered something in his sleep. The voice not clear enough to reach Anandmayi's ears. She leaned forward.

'I'll never break my vow... father. That is my... Dashrath promise. I will never break... my vow.'

A Dashrath promise, named after a vow that Lord Ram's father had once taken, was an open-ended word of honour that could never be broken. Anandmayi shook her head and sighed. Parvateshwar was repeating his vow of *brahmacharya*, or *eternal celibacy*, once again.

'I'll never break... my vow.'

Anandmayi smiled. 'We'll see.'

'My Lord,' said Divodas, immediately bending to touch

— 人◎ᴜ4⊗ —

the Neelkanth's feet.

'*Ayushman bhav*, Divodas,' said Shiva, blessing the man with *a long life*.

'Such an honour to meet you, My Lord. The dark days are over. You will solve all our problems. We can go home.'

'Go home? You still want to go back?'

'Branga is my soul, My Lord. I would never have left my homeland if it weren't for the plague.'

Shiva frowned, before coming to the point that concerned him. 'You are a good man, Divodas. You saved my friend's life. Even at your own cost.'

'It was a matter of honour, My Lord. I know all that happened. General Parvateshwar saved my tribe from certain death. We had to return the favour. And there was no cost to me.'

'That depends on you, my friend. Remember your code of honour when you answer this.'

Divodas frowned.

'How did you get the Naga medicine?' asked Shiva.

Divodas froze.

'Answer me, Divodas,' repeated Shiva gently.

'My Lord...'

'I know that medicine could only be made by the Nagas. The question, Divodas, is how you came by it.'

Divodas did not want to lie to the Neelkanth. Yet he was afraid of speaking the truth.

'Divodas, be truthful,' said Shiva. 'Nothing angers me more than lies. Speak the truth. I promise you that you will not be harmed. It is the Nagas I seek.'

'My Lord, I don't know if I can. My tribe needs the medicines every year. You saw the chaos that a few days of delay led to. They will die without it, My Lord.'

'Tell me where to find those scum and I give you my word, I will get you the medicines every year.'

'My Lord...'

'It is my word, Divodas. You will always have your medicine. Even if it's the only thing I do for the rest of my life. Nobody in your tribe will die for the lack of medicine.'

Divodas hesitated. Then his faith in the Neelkanth legend overcame his fear of the unknown. 'I have never met a Naga, My Lord. Many of us believe that they have put a curse on Branga. The plague peaks every year, without fail, during the summer. The only medicines that can save us are the ones the Nagas supply. King Chandraketu gives the Nagas untold amounts of gold and a large supply of men in return for the medicines.'

Shiva was stunned. 'You mean King Chandraketu is forced to deal with the Nagas? He is their hostage?'

'He is a virtuous king, My Lord. Even the few of us who have escaped and found refuge outside Branga are given gold by him to sustain ourselves. We go back to Branga every year to get the medicines.'

Shiva stayed silent.

Divodas had a smidgeon of moisture in his eyes. 'Our king is a great man, My Lord. He has made a deal with the devils and cursed his own soul, only to save the people of Branga.'

Shiva nodded slowly. 'Is the King the only one who deals with the Nagas?'

'From what I know, he and a few trusted advisors, My Lord. Nobody else.'

'Once my child is born, we will leave for Branga. I will need you to accompany me.'

'My Lord!' cried Divodas in shock. 'We cannot bring any non-Branga into our land. Our secrets must remain within our borders. My tribe's future is at stake. My land's future is at stake.'

'This is much bigger than you, your tribe or me. This is about India. We must find the Nagas.'

Divodas gazed at Shiva, torn and confused.

'I believe I can help, Divodas,' said Shiva. 'Is this a life worth leading? Desperately begging for the medicines every year? Not even knowing what ails your tribe? We have to solve this problem. I can do it. But not without your help.'

'My Lord...'

'Divodas, think. I have heard that peacock blood has

many other side-effects that are just as bad. What if you had not reached in time with the Naga medicines? What would have happened to your tribe? Your wife? Your unborn child? Don't you want this resolved once and for all?'

Divodas nodded slowly.

'Then take me to your kingdom. We will free your King and the land of Branga from the clutches of the Nagas.'

'Yes, My Lord.'

'I swear I have nothing to do with the Nagas, My Lord,'

— ⵊⵔⵓⵜⵝⵟ —

said Bhagirath, his head bowed.

Nandi, standing at the door of Shiva's chamber, was looking on sympathetically.

'I swear, My Lord, I would never go against you,' said Bhagirath. 'Never.'

'I know,' said Shiva. 'I think the presence of the medicine shook me. Nandi has already spoken to me. I know how you came by the medicine. My apologies that I doubted you.'

'My Lord,' cried Bhagirath. 'You don't need to apologise.'

'No Bhagirath. If I have made a mistake, I must apologise. I will not doubt you again.'

'My Lord...' said Bhagirath.

Shiva pulled Bhagirath close and embraced him.

'Thank you once again for gracing us with your presence,

— ⵊⵔⵓⵜⵝⵟ —

My Lord,' said Kanakhala, the Meluhan Prime Minister,

bowing down to touch the *great sage, Maharishi* Bhrigu's feet. 'I will take your leave.'

'*Ayushman Bhav*, my child,' said Bhrigu with a slight smile.

Kanakhala was astonished at the sudden appearance of the reclusive Maharishi in Devagiri, the capital city of Meluha. But her Emperor, Daksha, did not seem the least bit surprised. Kanakhala knew how the strict *Saptrishi Uttradhikari, a successor to the seven great sages,* liked to live. She had organised his chamber to be exactly like the Himalayan cave that was Bhrigu's home. No furniture except for a stone bed, on which Bhrigu was sitting presently. Cold water had been sprinkled on the floor and the walls to simulate the uncomfortable chilly and damp atmosphere of the mountains. Light had been restricted through the presence of thick curtains on all the windows. A bowl of fruit had been placed in the room; the only food for the sage for days. And most importantly, an idol of Lord Brahma had been installed on an indentation in the wall, at the north end of the chamber.

Bhrigu waited for Kanakhala to leave before turning to Daksha, speaking in a calm, mellifluous voice. 'Are you sure about this, Your Highness?'

Daksha was sitting on the floor, at Bhrigu's feet. 'Yes, My Lord. It is for my grandchild. I have never been surer of anything in the world.'

Bhrigu smiled slightly, but his eyes were unhappy. 'Your Highness, I have seen many kings forget their dharma in their love for their child. I hope your obsession with your daughter doesn't make you forget your duty to your nation.'

'No, My Lord. Sati is the most important person in the world to me. But I will not forget my duties towards the cause.'

'Good. That is the reason I supported you in becoming Emperor.'

'I know, My Lord. Nothing is more important than the cause. Nothing is more important than India.'

'You don't think your son-in-law is intelligent enough to start asking questions when he sees it?'

'No, My Lord. He loves my daughter. He loves India. He will not do anything to hurt the cause.'

'The Vasudevs have begun to influence him, Your Highness.'

Daksha looked shocked, at a loss for words. Bhrigu realised the futility of carrying on this conversation. Daksha was too simple-minded to understand the implications. He would have to fight for the cause by himself.

'Please go ahead then, if that is what you believe,' said Bhrigu. 'But you are not to answer any questions on where it came from. To anyone. Is that clear?'

Daksha nodded. He was still shocked by the statement Bhrigu had made about Shiva and the Vasudevs.

'Not even to your daughter, Your Highness,' said Bhrigu.

'Yes, My Lord.'

Bhrigu nodded. He breathed deeply. This was troubling. He would have to fight hard to save the legacy. It was imperative. He believed the very future of India was at stake.

'There is nothing to fear in any case, My Lord,' said Daksha, feigning a brilliance he didn't quite feel. 'Whatever may have happened with Brahaspati, the secret is safe. It will remain alive for centuries. India will continue to prosper and rule the world.'

'Brahaspati was a fool!' said Bhrigu, his voice rising.

'Even worse, maybe he was a traitor to the cause.'

Daksha kept quiet. As always, he was afraid of Bhrigu's temper.

Bhrigu calmed down. 'I can't believe I even considered giving my disciple Tara to him in marriage. The poor girl's life would have been destroyed.'

'Where is Tara, Your Highness? I hope she is safe and happy.'

'She is safe. I have kept her in the land of Lord Rudra. Some of them remain true to me. As for happiness...,' Bhrigu shook his head wearily.

'She still loves him?'

'Stupidly so. Even though he is no more.'

'No point in talking about Brahaspati,' said Daksha. 'Thank you so much for your permission, My Lord. From the deepest corner of my heart, thank you.'

Bhrigu nodded, bending lower and whispering, 'Remain careful, Your Highness. The war is not over. Don't think that you are the only one who can use the Neelkanth.'

Chapter 7

Birth Pangs

Shiva stood at the edge of the Dasashwamedh Ghat in a royal enclosure. On his side stood Their Highnesses Dilipa and Athithigva, with other key members of the nobility behind them. The citizens of Kashi stood away from the enclosure. They were not over excited. They had got used to the constant attention that came the way of their city since the Neelkanth had made it his temporary home.

It was a busy day for Kashi's diplomatic staff. Dilipa had arrived just that morning. The standard protocols for the Emperor of Swadweep had been followed, right down to the single white flag at the royal enclosure with the Chandravanshi crescent moon darned on it. Now, they were waiting for Daksha, the Emperor of India.

The protocol had been tricky. But they had finally decided to have a red Suryavanshi flag placed at the highest point of the enclosure. After all, the Lord Neelkanth had declared Daksha the Emperor of all of India. Bowing to the sensitivities of Dilipa, Kashi protocol officers had also placed a Chandravanshi flag in the enclosure at a slightly lower height as compared to the Suryavanshi flag.

Shiva, of course, did not really care about the ceremonies. He was more interested in the workers busy at the temporary shipyard across the river, where the Brangas, led by Divodas himself, had been furiously working away for the last three months. Given the superstition about not living on the eastern side of the Ganga's meander, it was naturally the safest place for the Brangas to do their job. They had been constructing special ships that could sail through the great Gates of Branga, massive barriers across the main river access to their land. Shiva couldn't imagine how barricades could be built in a river as broad as the Ganga. But Divodas had said that these special ships would be required. Shiva remembered telling a sceptical Athithigva, who had opposed this move of the Brangas: 'Just because you can't imagine it, doesn't mean it doesn't exist.' But Athithigva had refused the usage of the royal palace and grounds on the eastern bank as a shipyard. So the Brangas worked on a dangerous, recently dried stretch of the riverbank.

Divodas had begun work the very next day after promising the Neelkanth that he would accompany him to Branga.

Divodas has been true to his word. He is a good man.

The sound of Daksha's ship finally docking at the ghat brought Shiva back from his thoughts. He saw the rope pulley lowering the walkway. Daksha, without caring for royal protocol, immediately bounded onto the walkway and almost ran to Shiva. He bowed low and spoke breathlessly. 'Is it a boy, My Lord?'

Shiva stood up to welcome the Emperor of India, did a formal namaste and spoke with a smile. 'We still don't know Your Highness. She is not due till tomorrow.'

'Oh wonderful. I have not been late then! I was very scared that I would miss this joyous day.'

Shiva laughed out loud. It was difficult to say who was more excited — the father or the grandfather!

— 人◎Ⴑ � ⊛ —

'Such a delight to meet you again, Purvaka*ji*,' said Shiva, rising from his chair and bending down to touch the blind man's feet. The suffix *ji* was a form of respect.

Purvaka, Drapaku's blind father, was the same Vikarma whose blessings Shiva had sought at Kotdwaar in Meluha a few years ago. Kotdwaar residents had been stunned by the Neelkanth's public rejection of the Vikarma law. Leave alone finding the touch of a Vikarma polluting, Shiva had actually sought to be blessed by one.

Purvaka had come along in Emperor Daksha's convoy to Kashi. He immediately stepped back, as though sensing what Shiva was about to do. 'No, My Lord. You are the Neelkanth. How can I allow you to touch my feet?'

'Why not, Purvakaji?' asked Shiva

'But My Lord, how can you touch my father's feet?' said Drapaku. 'You are the Mahadev.'

'Isn't it my choice as to whose feet I touch?' asked Shiva.

Turning back to Purvaka, Shiva continued, 'You are elder to me. You cannot deny me the right to seek your blessings. So please do so quickly. My back is hurting from bending for so long.'

Purvaka laughed, placing his hand on Shiva's head. 'Nobody can refuse you, great one. *Ayushman bhav.*'

Shiva rose, satisfied with the *blessing for a long life*. 'So you intend to spend your time with your son now?'

'Yes, My Lord.'

'But we would be going on a dangerous voyage. Are you sure?'

'I was a warrior too once, My Lord. I still have the strength. I can kill any Naga who stands in front of me!'

Shiva smiled, turning towards Drapaku, his eyebrows raised. Drapaku smiled back, signalling with his hand that he would protect his father.

'My boy, don't think I cannot sense what you are saying,' said Purvaka. 'I may be blind, but you learnt to wield the sword holding my hands. I will protect myself. And, you as well.'

Both Shiva and Drapaku burst out laughing. Shiva was delighted to see that the diffident Purvaka he had met at Kotdwaar, a man who had suppressed his natural valour in a defeatist manner against the assaults of fate, was rediscovering his old fire.

'Forget about your son,' said Shiva, 'I would be delighted to have you as *my* bodyguard!'

— ⚲⚲⚲⚲⚲ —

'I am scared, Shiva.'

Sati was sitting on her bed in their chamber. Shiva had just entered the room with a plateful of food. Much to the horror of the royal cook, the Neelkanth had insisted on cooking for his wife himself.

Pretending to be hurt, Shiva said, 'My cooking isn't that bad!'

Sati burst out laughing. 'That's not what I meant!'

Shiva came closer and smiled. Setting the plate aside on the table, he caressed her face. 'I know. I have insisted on

Ayurvati overseeing the delivery. She is the best doctor in the world. Nothing will go wrong.'

'But what if this child too is stillborn? What if my past life's sins affect our poor child?'

'There are no past life sins, Sati! There is only this life. That is the only reality. Everything else is a theory. Believe the theory that gives you peace and reject the one that causes you pain. Why believe in a theory if it causes you unhappiness? You have done all you can to take care of your child and yourself. Now have faith.'

Sati kept quiet, her eyes still mirroring the foreboding she felt inside.

Shiva ran his hand along Sati's face again. 'My darling, trust me. Your worrying is not going to help. Just think positive and happy thoughts. That is the best you can do for our child. And leave the rest to fate. In any case, fate has ensured that you will lose your bet tomorrow.'

'What bet?'

'You can't wriggle out of it now!' said Shiva.

'Seriously, what bet?'

'That we will have a daughter.'

'I had forgotten about that,' smiled Sati. 'But I have a strong feeling it will be a son.'

'Nah!' laughed Shiva.

Sati laughed along and rested her face against Shiva's hand.

Shiva broke a piece of the roti, wrapped some vegetables in it and held out the morsel for Sati. 'Is the salt all right?'

— 人◎ᗷꝶ⊕ —

'Are there really past life sins?' asked Shiva.

The Neelkanth was in the Kashi Vishwanath temple. Seated in front of him was a Vasudev pandit. The setting sun shone through the spaces between the temple pillars. The red sandstone shone even brighter, creating an awe-inspiring atmosphere.

'What do you think?' asked the Vasudev.

'I don't believe anything till I've seen the proof. For anything without proof, I think we should believe the theory that gives us peace. It doesn't matter whether the theory is true or not.'

'That is a good strategy for a happy life, no doubt.'

Shiva waited for the pandit to say more. When he didn't, Shiva spoke again. 'You still haven't answered my question. Are there really past life sins that we suffer for in this life?'

'I didn't answer the question because I don't have the answer. But if people believe that sins of the past life can impact this life, won't they at least try to lead a better life this time around?'

Shiva smiled. *Are these people just talented wordsmiths or great philosophers?*

The Pandit smiled back. *Once again, I don't have the answer!*

Shiva burst out laughing. He had forgotten the Pandit could receive his thoughts and that he could, in turn, do the same with the Pandit's.

'How does this work? How is it that I can hear your thoughts?'

'It's a very simple science really. The science of radio waves.'

'This is not a theory?'

The Pandit smiled. 'This is certainly not a theory. This is a fact. Just like light, which helps you see, there are radio waves to help you hear. While all humans can easily use the properties of light to see, most don't know how to use radio waves to hear. We are dependent on sound waves to hear. Sound waves travel much slower through the air and for much shorter distances. Radio waves travel far and fast, just like light.'

Shiva remembered his uncle, who he always thought could hear his thoughts. In his youth, he had thought it was magic. Now he knew better, that there was a science behind it. 'That's interesting. Then why can't you create a machine to convert radio waves into sound waves?'

'Aah! That is a tough one. We haven't succeeded in that as yet. But we have succeeded in training our brains to pick up radio waves. It takes years of practice to do it. That's why we were shocked that you could do it without any training.'

'I got lucky, I guess.'

'There is no luck, great one. You were born special.'

Shiva frowned. 'I don't think so. In any case, how is it supposed to work? How do you pick up radio waves? Why can't I hear everyone's thoughts?'

'It takes effort to be able to even transmit your thoughts clearly as radio waves. Many people do it unconsciously, even without training. But picking up radio waves and hearing other people's thoughts? That is completely different. It is not easy. We have to stay within the range of powerful transmitters.'

'The temples?'

'You are exceptionally intelligent, O Neelkanth!' smiled the Pandit. 'Yes, the temples work as our transmitters. Therefore the temples we use have to have a height of at least fifty metres. This helps in catching radio waves from other Vasudevs and in turn transmitting my thoughts to them as well.'

You mean other Vasudevs are hearing us all the time, Panditji?

Yes. Whoever chooses to hear our conversation. And very few Vasudevs would choose not to hear the saviour of our times, great Neelkanth.

Shiva frowned. If what the Pandit was saying was true, then he could speak to any Vasudev Pandit at any of their temples across India right now. *Then tell me this O Vasudev of the Magadh temple, what did you mean by saying that people are attached to evil?*

Shiva heard a loud laugh. It appeared to be coming from a distance. The Vasudev Pandit of the Narsimha temple at Magadh. *You are too smart, Lord Neelkanth.*

Shiva smiled. *I would prefer answers to flattery, great Vasudev.* Silence.

Then Shiva heard the voice from Magadh clearly. *I really liked your speech at the Dharmakhet war. Har Har Mahadev. All of us are Mahadevs. There is a god in every single one of us. What a beautiful thought.*

What does that have to do with my question? I asked why people should be attached to evil.

It does. It very profoundly does. There is a god in every single one of us. What is the obvious corollary?

That it is the responsibility of every single one of us to discover the god within.

No, my friend. That is the moral. I asked what the corollary was.

I don't understand, Panditji.

Everything needs balance, Neelkanth. The masculine needs the feminine. The energy requires the mass. So think! Har Har Mahadev. What is the corollary? What balances this statement?

Shiva frowned. A thought occurred to him. He didn't like it.

The Vasudev of Ayodhya urged Shiva. *Don't stop your*

thoughts, my friend. Free flow is the only way to discover the truth.

Shiva grimaced. *But this cannot be true.*

Truth doesn't have to be liked. It only has to be spoken. Speak it out. The truth may hurt you, but it will set you free.

But I can't believe this.

The truth doesn't ask for belief. It just exists. Let me hear what you think. There is a god in every single one of us. What is the obvious corollary?

There is evil in every single one of us.

Exactly. There is a god in every single one of us. And there is evil in every single one of us. The true battle between good and evil is fought within.

And the great evil connects itself to the evil within us. Is that why people get attached to it?

I believe that when you discover the great evil of our times, you will not need any explanation about how it attaches itself so deeply to us.

Shiva stared at the Pandit in front of him. The conversation had shaken him. His task was not just to discover evil. That would probably be easy. How would he get people to give up their attachment to evil?

'You don't have to find all the answers now, my friend,' said the Kashi Vasudev.

Shiva smiled weakly, uneasy. Then he heard the distant voice of someone he didn't recognise. A commanding voice, a voice that appeared to be used to being powerful. Strong, yet calm.

The medicine...

'Of course,' said the Kashi Pandit, as he got up quickly. He was back in no time, with a small silk pouch.

Shiva frowned.

'Apply this on your wife's belly, my friend,' said the

Kashi Pandit. 'Your child will be born healthy and strong.'

'What is this?'

'Its identity doesn't matter. What matters is that it will work.'

Shiva opened the pouch. There was a thick reddish-brown paste inside. *Thank you. If this ensures my child's safety, I will be forever grateful to you.*

The voice that Shiva had not recognised, the one that had ordered the Kashi Vasudev, spoke. *You don't need to be grateful, Lord Neelkanth. It is our duty, and honour, to be of any assistance to you. Jai Guru Vishwamitra. Jai Guru Vashisht.*

— ⚹ —

Shiva was at the window. From the height of the palace walls, he could see the congested city and beyond that the wide Sacred Avenue. On its edge, close to the Brahma Ghat stood the mighty Vishwanath temple. Shiva was staring at it, his hands clasped together in prayer.

Lord Rudra, take care of my child. Please. Let nothing go wrong.

He turned around as he heard a soft cough.

The most important people in India were waiting with bated breath for news of Sati and Shiva's child. Daksha was fidgeting nervously, deeply afraid.

He is truly concerned about Sati. Whatever else he may or may not be, he is a devoted father.

An impassive Veerini was holding Daksha's hand. Emperor Dilipa sat quietly, watching his children, Bhagirath and Anandmayi, who were in an animated, but soft conversation.

Dilipa kept staring at Bhagirath...

Parvateshwar, who had recovered completely from his

injuries in the past three months, stood strong at a corner of the chamber. King Athithigva paced up and down the room, upset that his own doctors had not been given the honour to deliver the Neelkanth's first-born. But Shiva was not about to take chances. Only Ayurvati would do.

Shiva turned around. He saw Nandi standing near the wall and gestured with his eyes.

'Yes, My Lord?' asked Nandi, coming up to Shiva.

'I feel so helpless, Nandi. I'm nervous.'

'Give me a moment, My Lord.'

Nandi rushed out of the chamber. He was back with Veerbhadra.

Both friends went up to the window.

'This one is good!' said Veerbhadra.

'Really?' asked Shiva.

Veerbhadra lit the chillum and gave it to Shiva, who took a deep puff.

'Hmmm...,' whispered Shiva.

'Yes?'

'I'm still nervous!'

Veerbhadra started laughing. 'What do you hope it will be?'

'A girl.'

'A girl? Sure? A girl can't be a warrior.'

'What nonsense! Look at Sati.'

Veerbhadra nodded. 'Fair point. And the name?'

'Krittika.'

'Krittika! You don't have to do this for me my friend.'

'I'm not doing it for you, you fool!' said Shiva. 'If I wanted to do that, I would name my daughter Bhadra! I am doing it for Krittika and Sati. Krittika has been a rock of support in my wife's life. I want to celebrate that.'

Veerbhadra smiled. 'She is a good woman, isn't she?'

'That she is. You have done well.'

'Hey, she hasn't done so badly either. I'm not that terrible a husband!'

'Actually, she could have done better!'

Bhadra playfully slapped Shiva on his wrist, as both friends shared a quiet laugh. Shiva handed the chillum back to Veerbhadra.

Suddenly, the door to the inner chamber opened. Ayurvati rushed out to Shiva. 'It's a boy, My Lord! A strong, handsome, powerful boy!'

Shiva picked up Ayurvati in his arms and swung her around, laughing heartily. 'A boy will also do!'

Setting an embarrassed Ayurvati back on the ground, Shiva rushed into the inner chamber. Ayurvati stopped everyone else from entering. Sati was on the bed. Two nurses were hovering close by. Krittika was sitting on a chair next to Sati, holding her hand. The most beautiful baby that Shiva had ever seen was next to Sati. He had been wrapped tight in a small white cloth and was sleeping soundly.

Sati smiled softly. 'It's a boy. Looks like I won, darling!'

'That's true,' whispered Shiva, scared of touching his son. 'But I haven't lost anything!'

Sati laughed, but immediately quietened down. The stitches hurt. 'What do we call him? We certainly cannot call him Krittika.'

'Yes, that is out of the question,' smiled Sati's handmaiden. 'Krittika is a woman's name.'

'But I still want him named after you, Krittika,' said Shiva.

'I agree,' said Sati. 'But what can that name be?'

Shiva thought for a moment. 'I know! We'll call him Kartik.'

Chapter 8

The Mating Dance

Daksha rushed into the room as soon as he was allowed, followed closely by Veerini.

'Father,' whispered Sati. 'Your first grandchild...'

Daksha didn't answer. He gently picked up Kartik and much to Sati's irritation, unfastened the white cloth that had bound the baby tightly, letting it fall back to the bed. Daksha held up Kartik, turning him around, admiring every aspect of his grandson. Tears were flowing furiously down the eyes of the Emperor of India. 'He's beautiful. He's just so beautiful.'

Startled, Kartik woke up and immediately began crying. It was the loud, lusty cry of a strong baby! Sati reached out for her son. Daksha, however, handed the baby over to a beaming Veerini. To Sati's surprise, Kartik immediately calmed down in Veerini's arms. The Queen placed Kartik on the white cloth and swaddled him again. Then she placed him in Sati's arms, his tiny head resting on her shoulders. Kartik gurgled and went back to sleep.

Daksha's tears had seemed to develop a life of their own. He embraced Shiva tightly. 'I'm the happiest man in all of history, My Lord! The happiest ever!'

Shiva patted the Emperor lightly on his back, smiling slightly. 'I know, Your Highness.'

Daksha stepped back and wiped his eyes. 'Everything is all right. You, Lord Neelkanth, have purified all that went wrong with my family. Everything is all right once again.'

Veerini stared at Daksha, her eyes narrowed, her breathing ragged. She gritted her teeth, but kept her silence.

— ⵣⵔⵓⵜⵗⵛ —

Bhagirath was walking back from the riverbank after checking on the progress of the ships being built by Divodas' men. As it was late, he had sent his bodyguards home. After all, this was Kashi, the city where everyone sought refuge. The city of peace.

The streets were deathly quiet. So silent that he clearly heard a soft crunch behind him.

The Prince of Ayodhya continued walking, appearing nonchalant. His hand on the hilt of his blade, ears focussed. The soft tread was gaining ground. A sword was drawn softly. Bhagirath spun around suddenly, drew his knife and flung it, piercing his assailant through his stomach. The blow was enough to paralyse his attacker. He would be in excruciating pain, but not dead.

Through the corner of his eye, Bhagirath saw another movement. He reached for his other knife. But the new threat crashed against a wall, a short sword buried in his chest. Dead.

Bhagirath turned to see Nandi to the left. 'Anyone else?' he whispered.

Nandi shook his head.

Bhagirath rushed to the first assailant. Shaking him from the shoulders, Bhagirath asked, 'Who sent you?'

The assassin remained mute.

Bhagirath twisted the knife in the man's stomach.

'Who?'

The man's mouth suddenly started frothing. The rat had eaten his poison. He died within seconds.

'Dammit!' said a frustrated Bhagirath.

Nandi looked at the Prince of Ayodhya, alert for any new threat, sword drawn.

Bhagirath shook his head and rose. 'Thank you, Nandi. Lucky that you were around.'

'It wasn't luck, Your Highness,' said Nandi softly. 'The Neelkanth has asked me to follow you for the duration of your father's visit. I honestly thought the Lord was over-reacting. No father would make an attempt on his child's life. I guess I was wrong.'

Bhagirath shook his head. 'It's not my father. At least not directly.'

'Not directly? What do you mean?'

'He doesn't have the guts. But he makes it well–known that I am not in his favour. That obviously encourages rival claimants to the throne, people who travel in his court. All they have to do is take me out of the equation. Make it appear as if I died in an accident.'

'This,' said Nandi, pointing to the dead assassins, 'wouldn't look like an accident.'

'I know. It just means that they're getting desperate.'

'Why?'

'My father's health is not good. I think they feel that they don't have time. If he dies while I am alive, I will be crowned king.'

Nandi shook his head.

Bhagirath patted Nandi. 'I'm in your debt, my friend. Forever grateful. As long as I live.'

Nandi smiled. 'And you will live a long life, Your Highness. Nothing will happen to you as long as I am around. I will stand between you and any man who dares to attack you. And there is a lot of me to cover you with!'

Bhagirath smiled at Nandi's attempt at humour on his elephantine girth.

— 𑀊𑀓𑀼𑀖𑀫 —

'Did you get any names? Who sent them?'

'I don't know, My Lord,' said Bhagirath. 'They died before I could get any answers.'

Shiva sighed. 'The dead bodies?'

'Handed over to the Kashi police,' said Bhagirath. 'But I don't expect that they will be able to gather any leads.'

'Hmm,' said Shiva.

'For the second time, I owe you my life, My Lord.'

'You owe me nothing,' said Shiva, before turning towards Nandi. 'Thank you, my friend. It is you who deserves credit.'

Nandi bowed low. 'It's my honour to serve you, My Lord.'

Shiva turned back to Bhagirath. 'What are you going to tell Anandmayi?'

Bhagirath frowned. 'Nothing. I don't want her getting troubled unnecessarily. I am fine. There is no need for anyone to know.'

'Why?'

'Because I am sure that father will not even try to

investigate this attack. Other nobles will see this as a sign of his tacit acceptance of a more aggressive attack on me rather than difficult-to-organise "accidents". Letting this news become public will only encourage rival claimants further.'

'Are there so many nobles after you?'

'Half the court is related to my father, My Lord. All of them think that they have a right to the throne.'

Shiva breathed deeply. 'Never stay alone while your father's here. And you are coming with me on the voyage to Branga, far away from here.'

Bhagirath nodded.

Shiva patted Bhagirath on his shoulder. 'Make sure that you don't get yourself killed. You are important to me.'

Bhagirath smiled. 'I will try to remain alive for you, My Lord!'

Shiva laughed softly. So did Nandi.

— ⸻ 人◎Ｕ♀⊕ ⸻ —

'Your Highness, I don't think it is wise for you to give away so much Somras powder,' said Shiva.

Shiva and Daksha were in Shiva's quarters. It had been a week since Kartik's birth. Sati and Kartik were sleeping in the next room, with Krittika and a bevy of nurses in close attendance. Shiva was shocked at the large amount of Somras powder Daksha had got with him as a present for Kartik. Daksha wanted Kartik to start taking the Somras from birth, every day, so that he would grow to be a strong, powerful warrior. He had got enough powder to last until Kartik's eighteenth birthday!

'My Lord,' said Daksha, 'it's not fair for you to tell a

doting grandfather what he can or cannot give his first grandchild.'

'But My Lord, with the destruction of Mount Mandar, you must be running short on Somras supplies. I don't think it is right for so much to be given to my son, when your entire country could use the blessings of the Somras.'

'Let me worry about that, My Lord. Please don't say no.'

Shiva gave up. 'How are the plans to rebuild Mount Mandar coming along?'

'It's taking too long,' said Daksha, waving his hand dismissively. 'Let's forget about that. This is such a happy event. I have a grandchild. A whole, complete, handsome grandchild who will grow up to be the Emperor of India!'

— 𝙰⊙ᴜ𝟺⊛ —

The citizens of Kashi customarily celebrated the birth of a child with music and dance after exactly seven days of its birth. Shiva decided to honour the traditions of his hosts.

The Neelkanth was sitting on a throne in the dance theatre. Next to him, on the throne meant for the Queen of Kashi, sat Sati, cradling a sleeping Kartik in her arms. Daksha and Dilipa had the seat of honoured guests next to Shiva and Sati. The royal family of Kashi sat beyond them. It was unorthodox for the King of the kingdom to occupy such a low place in the seating protocol. But Athithigva did not mind.

Sati bent towards Shiva and whispered, 'You danced marvellously. As always!'

'You noticed?' teased Shiva.

Earlier in the evening, Shiva had insisted on opening the

celebrations with his own performance. The audience could not believe their good fortune at seeing the Neelkanth himself dance. And they applauded his fabulous dancing skills with a five-minute long standing ovation. The dance was one of his best ever. And the audience was moved to raptures. But Shiva had noticed, much to his chagrin, that Sati was distracted during his performance. She had been troubled since the time Shiva had told her of the Somras powder brought by Daksha.

'Of course, I did,' smiled Sati. 'I'm just troubled that father is giving away so much Somras. It's not right. It is for all of Meluha. Kartik should not get any special treatment just because he is a royal. This is against Lord Ram's principles.'

'Then, speak to your father.'

'I will. At the right time.'

'Good. For now, however, look at Anandmayi when she dances. She may not be as forgiving as me.'

Sati smiled and rested her head on Shiva's shoulders as she turned to look at the stage just in time to see Anandmayi walk onto it. She was wearing a shockingly tiny *dhoti* and a tight blouse, leaving very little to the imagination. Sati raised her eyebrow and looked at Shiva. Shiva was smiling.

'It's the right costume for this dance,' said Shiva.

Sati nodded and turned towards the stage again. Shiva sidled a glance at Parvateshwar and smiled. The General's face was an impenetrable mask. His Suryavanshi training had kicked in, but the man's clenched jaw and tick near his brow betrayed that he was far from unmoved.

Anandmayi bent low to touch the stage with her forehead, seeking blessings and inspiration for her performance. The Chandravanshis in the front row leaned forward to get a better view of the ample cleavage that was revealed. If it had been any other dancer, the audience would probably have been whistling by now. But this was the Princess of Swadweep. So, they just kept ogling silently at her.

Then another dancer walked onstage: Uttanka. The progeny of a famed Magadhan brigadier, Uttanka's military career was cut short by an injury which left him with a severe hump on his right shoulder. Like most people frustrated with their lot in life, he too had sought refuge in Kashi, where he discovered the beauty of dance. But the same injury which had stumped his military career held back his dancing career as well. His shoulder movements were restricted, keeping him from becoming a truly great performer. There were whispers that Anandmayi, a true Chandravanshi whose heart automatically reached out towards the weak, had felt pity for Uttanka and hence had agreed to partner him.

But there was also a feeling that this sympathy was misplaced. Uttanka would probably be humiliated on stage. They were expected to perform a complex dance which encaptured the enticement of the legendary sage Vishwamitra by the celestial nymph Menaka. Would Uttanka be equal to the task?

Anandmayi, unmindful of such speculation, bowed towards Uttanka. He bowed back. Then, they stepped close to each other. Far closer than the standard position for commencing this dance. Probably a necessary adjustment as Uttanka's arm could not extend very far. Shiva turned once again towards Parvateshwar. He had narrowed his eyes a bit and seemed to be holding his breath.

Is he jealous?

The Princess of Ayodhya had choreographed their dance

well, having changed the ancient rules of this particular act, in order to suit Uttanka's restricted arm movements. But the changes also ensured that the two of them danced very close to each other throughout the performance, creating an air of intense sensuality. The audience first watched in shock, their jaws open. How could a former soldier be allowed to hold Princess Anandmayi so close? But then they were pulled in by the sheer quality of the act. Nobody had seen the dance of Vishwamitra and Menaka in such a blatantly passionate form before.

As the piece ended, the audience stood up, applauding wildly and whistling. It had been a truly remarkable performance. Anandmayi bowed low and then pointed at Uttanka, graciously giving the credit to the physically-challenged former soldier. Uttanka beamed at the appreciation he received, finding meaning in his life, perhaps for the first time.

Parvateshwar was the only one present who wasn't clapping.

— ⋏◎⊍⇂⊕ —

Next day, Parvateshwar was sparring with Purvaka within the temporary military training grounds that had been constructed in the Kashi royal palace. The former brigadier was rediscovering his seemingly lost fearsome powers. Despite the lack of sight, Purvaka could sense Parvateshwar's actions with his keen hearing and was responding brilliantly, dodging when necessary, jabbing when possible.

Parvateshwar was delighted.

Calling a halt, Parvateshwar turned towards Drapaku

and nodded. He then turned towards Purvaka and executed the formal Meluhan salute, with a slight bow of his head. Purvaka too beat his chest with his fist and bent low, far lower than Parvateshwar had bowed. He respected Parvateshwar's legendary prowess.

'It will be my honour to include you in the Suryavanshi brigade travelling with the Neelkanth, Brigadier Purvaka,' said Parvateshwar.

Purvaka smiled. This was the first time he had been called Brigadier in decades. 'The honour is all mine, General. And thank you for not shafting me into the Chandravanshi brigade. I don't think I could tolerate their inefficiency!'

Bhagirath, standing at one end of the room, could not stop himself from laughing. 'We'll see who works harder for the Neelkanth, Purvaka! Don't forget, you are in Chandravanshi territory now. Battles are fought differently here.'

Purvaka did not respond. His training forbade him from talking back to a royal. He nodded.

Just then, Anandmayi entered the room. Bhagirath smiled and glanced at Parvateshwar, before looking back at her. She was in a bright, harlequin-green blouse and short *dhoti*, a colour so loud that only a woman of Anandmayi's beauty and chutzpah could have carried it off. He suspected that Anandmayi's need to gain Parvatshwar's attention was making her become more brazen by the day. He had never seen his sister quite this way and wasn't sure whether to have a chat with her or to draw Parvateshwar out and ask him about his intentions.

Waving to her brother, Anandmayi marched straight up to Parvateshwar, Uttanka at her heels. She came uncomfortably close to Parvateshwar, forcing him to step back. 'How is my favourite Meluhan General doing?' she asked, arching her brows after giving him the once over.

'We don't have different kingdoms within Meluha, Your Highness. We have only one army,' said Parvateshwar.

Anandmayi frowned.

'It means that there is no need to play favourites since there is only one Meluhan General.'

'I agree. There is only one Parvateshwar...'

Parvateshwar turned red. Drapaku grimaced with distaste.

'Is there anything I can do for you, Princess?' Parvateshwar wanted to quickly find a way to end this conversation.

'I thought you'd never ask,' smiled Anandmayi, pointing towards Uttanka. 'This young man here is a refugee from Magadh. His name is Uttanka. He always wanted to be a warrior. But a riding accident left him with an injured shoulder. The idiotic, apparently merit-obsessed, Prince Surapadman dismissed him. Like most unhappy souls, he found his way to Kashi. I'm sure you saw him dance yesterday. He dances brilliantly. I want you to include him in the Neelkanth's brigade.'

'As a dancer?' asked a flabbergasted Parvateshwar.

'Do you like being deliberately stupid or is this just an act?'

Parvateshwar frowned.

'Obviously not as a dancer,' shrugged an exasperated Anandmayi. 'As a soldier.'

Parvateshwar turned towards Uttanka. Feet spread. Arms close to his side weapons. Ready for battle. Uttanka had obviously been trained well. Then Parvateshwar's eyes settled on Uttanka's shoulders. The hump caused by the injury restricted his right arm's movements. 'You will not be able to battle a taller man.'

'I will die before retreating, My Lord,' said Uttanka.

'I have no use for soldiers who die,' said Parvateshwar. 'I need soldiers who will kill and live. Why don't you stick to dancing?'

'Are you saying that dancers cannot be warriors?' butted in Anandmayi.

Parvateshwar glared. The Neelkanth was a celebrated dancer and a fearsome warrior. He turned around, picked up two wooden swords and shields, throwing one pair to Uttanka. He held up his sword, adjusted his shield and gestured to the Magadhan to get into position.

'You're going to fight him?' asked a shocked Anandmayi. She knew Uttanka would be no match for Parvateshwar. 'What is wrong with you? Why can't he just come along...'

Anandmayi stopped as Bhagirath touched her arm. He pulled her back. Purvaka and Drapaku too stepped back.

'You still have a choice, soldier,' said Parvateshwar. 'Walk away.'

'I'd rather be carried out, My Lord,' said Uttanka.

Parvateshwar narrowed his eyes. He liked the man's spirit. But he had to test his ability now. For spirit without ability usually led to a gruesome death on the battlefield.

Parvateshwar moved slowly, waiting for Uttanka to charge. But the man kept still. Parvateshwar realised that the Magadhan was being defensive. Uttanka's shoulder injury prevented a high arm assault that would be required to attack a taller man like Parvateshwar.

The General charged. It was an unorthodox assault.

He struck only from above, keeping his shield upfront at medium height. Uttanka had to keep stepping back, holding his shield high with his left hand to defend against the powerful blows. If he could have raised his right arm high, he would have struck Parvateshwar's exposed head and shoulder. But he couldn't. So he kept jabbing back at chest height. Parvateshwar easily parried the blows with his shield. Slowly, but surely, Parvateshwar kept pushing Uttanka back towards the wall. It was a matter of time before he would have no place to retreat.

Anandmayi, while happy at what she thought was the Meluhan General's jealousy, was also worried about Uttanka. 'Why can't he show some compassion?'

Bhagirath turned to his sister. 'Parvateshwar is doing the right thing. An enemy will show no quarter in battle.'

Just then Uttanka's back hit the wall. His shield bobbed. Parvateshwar immediately swung from the right and hit Uttanka hard on his chest.

'That would be a death blow with a real sword,' whispered Parvateshwar.

Uttanka nodded. He did not try to rub his obviously hurting chest.

Parvateshwar walked calmly back to the centre of the room and called out loudly. 'Once more?'

Uttanka trudged back into position. Parvateshwar attacked once more. Again with the same result.

Seeing Uttanka in pain, Anandmayi hissed. She was about to step forward, but Bhagirath held her back. He too was worried. But he knew he couldn't step in. That would be an insult to the General and the foolishly brave soldier who was trying to combat him.

'Why did you bring that man here?' asked Bhagirath.

'Uttanka dances beautifully. I thought it would be fun to have him along on the voyage to Branga.'

Bhagirath turned towards his sister with narrowed eyes. 'That is not the whole truth. I know what you are doing. And it's not fair.'

'Everything's fair in love and war, Bhagirath. But I certainly don't want Uttanka getting hurt.'

'Then you shouldn't have brought him here!'

Parvateshwar was back in the centre. 'Again?'

Uttanka lumbered back. He was evidently in pain, his face revealing his increasing rage and frustration. Parvateshwar, on the other hand, was worried. He was afraid that he would end up breaking the soldier's ribs if they had one more joust. But he had to stop this foolhardiness. If this was a real battle, Uttanka would have already been killed twice over.

He charged at Uttanka again. To his surprise, Uttanka stepped to the side, letting Parvateshwar move forward with his momentum. Then Uttanka turned and charged as an aggressor. He swung to the left, letting his shield come down, leaving his flank open. Parvateshwar pushed his sword forward. Uttanka turned right to avoid the blow and in the same motion rolled his right arm in a swing, letting the momentum carry the sword higher than his injured shoulder would normally have allowed. He struck Parvateshwar on his neck. A kill strike, if it had been a real blade and not a practice weapon.

Parvateshwar stood stunned. How had Uttanka managed to do that?

Uttanka himself looked shocked. He had never managed to strike that high after his injury. Never.

Parvateshwar's face broke into a slight smile. Uttanka

had given up being defensive, turned into an aggressor, and won.

'Give up your attachment to your shield,' said Parvateshwar. 'When you attack hard, you do have the ability to kill.'

Uttanka, still panting hard, smiled slowly.

'Welcome to the Meluhan army, brave soldier.'

Uttanka immediately dropped his sword and fell at Parvateshwar's feet, his eyes moist.

Parvateshwar pulled Uttanka up. 'You are a Meluhan soldier now. And my soldiers don't cry. Conduct yourself in the manner befitting a Meluhan military man.'

Bhagirath sighed in relief and turned towards Anandmayi. 'You were lucky this time.'

Anandmayi nodded slowly. But her heart was already racing a few steps ahead. What really impressed Parvateshwar was military prowess. Anandmayi developed a new plan to ensnare her General.

— 人◎ᵾᛇ⊕ —

'Shiva is right, father,' said Sati. 'You can't give away so much Somras. Meluha needs it.'

It had been ten days since Kartik's birth. Emperor Dilipa and his entourage had left for Ayodhya. Shiva had gone to the banks of the Ganga to supervise the ship building. Daksha and Veerini were sitting in Sati's private chambers as the proud mother gently rocked Kartik's crib.

Veerini looked at Daksha, but did not say anything.

'Let Meluha be my concern, my child,' said Daksha. 'You worry your pretty little head only with Kartik.'

Sati hated being spoken to in such a patronising manner.

'Father, of course I am thinking about Kartik. I am his mother. But I cannot forget our duties to Meluha.'

'My child,' smiled Daksha. 'Meluha is safe. Safer than it has ever been. I don't think you need to doubt my abilities to care for my people.'

'Father, I'm not doubting your abilities. Or your commitment. All I'm saying is that I feel it's wrong for Kartik to receive such a large share of Somras that rightly belongs to the people of Meluha. I am sure there is an immense shortage of the Somras after the destruction of Mount Mandar. Why give so much to my son? Just because he is the Emperor's grandson? This is against Lord Ram's rules.'

Daksha laughed out loud. 'My darling daughter, nowhere do Lord Ram's rules say that an emperor cannot give Somras powder to his grandchild.'

'Of course the exact words will not be there, father,' argued Sati, irritated. 'And it is not about the exact words. It is the principles that Lord Ram had set up. An emperor must always put his people above his family. We are not following that principle.'

'What do you mean we are not following that principle?' asked Daksha, sounding angry. 'Are you calling me a law-breaker?'

'Father, please keep your voice low. Kartik will wake up. And if you are favouring Kartik over the common Meluhans, then yes, you are breaking Lord Ram's laws.'

Veerini cringed. 'Please...'

Ignoring Veerini's plea, Daksha ranted. 'I am not breaking Lord Ram's laws!'

'Yes, you are,' said Sati. 'Are you saying you have enough Somras for the Suryavanshis? That Kartik is not benefiting at the cost of another less fortunate Meluhan? Unless you promise me that, this Somras powder will just lie waste. I will not let anyone give it to Kartik.'

'You will hurt your own son?' asked Daksha, turning briefly to glance at his sleeping grandson, before glaring at Sati.

'Kartik is my son. He will not like to benefit at the cost of others. Because I will teach him what *raj dharma* is.'

His own daughter accusing him of not following his *royal duties?* Daksha exploded. 'I HAVE TAKEN CARE OF MY RAJ DHARMA!'

Kartik woke with a start and Sati reached out for him instinctively. His mother's familiar fragrance calmed him instantly. Sati turned and glared at her father.

'I didn't want to tell you this,' said Daksha, 'but since you are bent on hurting Kartik's interests, listen. Another Somras manufacturing facility exists. Maharishi Bhrigu ordered me to build it secretly many years ago. It was a back-up for Mount Mandar. We kept it secret because there are traitors in our midst.'

Sati stared at her father in shock. Veerini was holding her head.

'So my beloved child,' said a sarcastic Daksha. 'I have followed my raj dharma. There is enough Somras for all of Meluha for centuries to come. Now give the drink of the gods to Kartik every day till he turns eighteen. He will go down in history as the greatest man ever.'

Sati didn't say anything. She still appeared shocked by the news of the secret Somras manufacturing facility. There were hundreds of questions running through her head.

'Did you hear me?' asked Daksha. 'You will give the Somras to Kartik every day. Every day!'

Sati nodded.

— ⚕ —

Shiva was standing on the dried river bed where the Brangas had made their temporary workshop. Five ships were being constructed. Shiva, who had seen some massive ships being built at Karachapa, the Meluhan sea port, was amazed at the radically different design of the Branga ships. So was Parvateshwar.

They walked together around the great wooden stands on which the ships rested. The size and structure of the ships was vastly superior to the standard Swadweepan vessels. They were almost the size of Meluhan crafts. But the difference was at the bottom of the hull. Below the waterline, the hull had been thinned out to a ridiculously narrow range and it went down flat for a good two or three metres.

'What is the point of this, Parvateshwar?' asked Shiva.

'I don't know, My Lord,' said Parvateshwar. 'It is the strangest design I have ever seen.'

'You think it helps the ship cut through the water faster?'

'I'm not sure. But shouldn't this extension make the ship less stable?'

'The coating on it should make it heavy,' said Shiva as he touched the metal plates that had been hammered into the wood. 'Is this that strange new metal your people have discovered recently?'

'Yes, My Lord. It does look like iron.'

'In that case its heaviness probably increases stability.'

'But the heaviness would also slow down the ship.'

'That's true.'

'I wonder what these strange grooves are for?' asked Parvateshwar, running his hand over a deep furrow which ran all along the metal plates on the hull extension.

'Or these hooks for that matter,' said Shiva as he looked up at the many large hooks on the hull, around two metres above the furrow.

Just then Divodas, accompanied by Ayurvati, joined them. Working in the sun for double shifts was tiring out the Brangas. Divodas had requested Shiva for Ayurvati's help. Ayurvati was only too delighted to have her team prepare some ayurvedic energy infusions for the Brangas.

'My Lord,' said Divodas, smiling. 'Lady Ayurvati is a genius. Drinking her medicines is like getting a shot of pure energy. My worker's efforts have doubled over the last few days.'

An embarrassed Ayurvati turned red. 'No, no, it's nothing.'

'What is it with you Suryavanshis?' asked Divodas. 'Why can't you take a compliment properly?'

Shiva and Ayurvati laughed out loud. Parvateshwar did not find it funny. 'Lord Ram said humility is the mark of a great person. If we forget our humility, we insult Lord Ram.'

'Parvateshwar, I don't think Divodas was suggesting anything that would hurt Lord Ram,' said Ayurvati. 'We all respect the Lord. I think Divodas was only suggesting we enjoy the better aspects of our life a little more uninhibitedly. Nothing wrong with that.'

'Well,' said Shiva, changing the topic, 'what I'm more interested in is this strange extension at the bottom of the ship. First of all, it must have been very difficult to design. You would have to get the weight and dimensions exactly right or else the ship would keel over. So I must compliment your engineers.'

'I have no problems with accepting compliments, My Lord,' smiled Divodas. 'My engineers are brilliant!'

Shiva grinned. 'That they are. But what is the purpose of this extension? What does it do?'

'It opens locks, My Lord.'

'What?'

'It is a key. You will see how it works when we reach the gates of Branga.'

Shiva frowned.

'Any ship without this can never enter Branga. It will be crushed.'

'The gates on the mighty Ganga?' asked Parvateshwar. 'I had thought that was a myth. I can't imagine how a gate could be built across a river of this size and flow.'

Divodas smiled. 'You need legendary engineers to build reality out of myth. And we have no shortage of such men in Branga!'

'So how does that gate work?' asked Shiva.

'It will be much better if you see it, My Lord,' said Divodas. 'Awesome structures like that cannot be described. They can only be seen.'

Just then, a woman holding a one-month old baby came up. It was the Branga high priestess. The same one who had stopped Bhagirath's attack at the Branga building.

Shiva looked at the child and smiled. 'What a lovely baby!'

'That's my daughter, My Lord,' said Divodas. 'And this is Yashini, my wife.'

Yashini bent down to touch Shiva's feet and then placed her daughter there. Shiva immediately bent down and picked up the child. 'What's her name?'

'Devayani, My Lord,' said Yashini.

Shiva smiled. 'She's been named after the daughter of Shukra, the teacher?'

Yashini nodded. 'Yes, My Lord.'

'It's a beautiful name. I'm sure she will teach the world great knowledge as she grows up,' said Shiva, as he handed the baby back to Yashini.

'Dreaming for our children's careers is too ambitious for us Brangas, My Lord,' said Yashini. 'All we can hope for is that they live to see their future.'

Shiva nodded in sympathy. 'I will not stop till I change this, Yashini.'

'Thank you, My Lord,' said Divodas. 'I know you will succeed. We do not care for our own lives. But we have to save our children. We will be forever grateful to you when you succeed.'

'But Divodas,' interrupted Ayurvati. 'Even the Lord is grateful to you.'

Both Shiva and Divodas turned towards Ayurvati. Surprised.

'Why?' asked Divodas.

'Your medicine saved Kartik's life,' explained Ayurvati.

'What are you talking about?'

'Well, many a times, within the womb, the umbilical cord gets wrapped around the baby's neck. In some of these cases, the baby cannot survive the journey of birthing. It suffocates and dies. I'm not sure since I wasn't there, but I think that is what may have happened with Princess Sati's first child as well. Kartik had the umbilical cord wrapped around his neck. But this time, I applied your medicine on Princess Sati's belly. It somehow permeated the womb and gave Kartik the strength to survive those few crucial moments till he slipped out. Your medicine saved his life.'

'What medicine?' asked Divodas.

'The Naga medicine,' said Ayurvati, frowning. 'I recognised the paste as soon as I smelt it. And only you could have given it, right?'

'But I didn't!'

'You didn't?' asked a shocked Ayurvati, turning to Shiva. 'Then... Where did you get the medicine from, My Lord?'

Shiva was stunned. Like someone had cruelly destroyed one of his most precious memories.

'My Lord? What is it?' asked Ayurvati.

Shiva, looking furious, abruptly turned around. 'Nandi! Bhadra! Come with me.'

'My Lord, where are you going?' asked Parvateshwar.

But Shiva was already walking away. Followed by Nandi, Veerbhadra and their platoon.

— 🜨 ☉ ♉ ♄ ⊕ —

'PANDITJI!'

Shiva was in the Kashi Vishwanath temple. As ordered, Nandi and Veerbhadra waited outside, along with their platoon.

'PANDITJI!'

Where the hell is he?

And then Shiva realised he didn't need to shout. All he needed to do was transmit his thoughts. *Vasudevs! Are any of you listening?*

No answer. Shiva's anger rose another notch.

I know you can hear me! Will one of you have the guts to speak?

Still no answer.

Where did you get the Naga medicine from?

Absolute silence.

Explain yourself! What relationship do you and the Nagas have? How deep does this go?

No Vasudev responded.

By the holy lake, answer me! Or I add your name to the enemies of Good!

Shiva didn't hear a word. He turned towards the idol of Lord Rudra. For some strange reason, it didn't appear as fearsome as he remembered. It seemed peaceful. Serene. Almost like it was trying to tell Shiva something.

Shiva turned around and screamed one last time. 'VASUDEVS! ANSWER ME NOW OR I ASSUME THE WORST!'

Hearing no answer, Shiva stormed out of the temple.

Chapter 9

What is Your Karma?

'What happened, Shiva?'

The little boy turned around to find his uncle standing behind him. The boy quickly wiped his eyes, for tears were a sign of weakness in Guna men. The uncle smiled. He sat down next to Shiva and put his arm around his diminutive shoulder.

They rested in silence for a while, letting the waters of the Mansarovar lake lap their feet. It was cold. But they didn't mind.

'What ails you, my child?' asked the uncle.

Shiva looked up. He had always wondered how a fierce warrior like his uncle always sported such a calm, understanding smile.

'Mother told me that I shouldn't feel guilty about...'

The words stopped as tears choked Shiva. He could feel his brow throbbing once again.

'About that poor woman?' asked the uncle.

The boy nodded.

'And, what do you think?'

'I don't know what to think anymore.'

'Yes, you do. Listen to your heart. What do you think?'

Shiva's little hands kept fidgeting with his tiger skin skirt. 'Mother thinks I couldn't have helped her. That I am too small, too young, too powerless. I would have achieved nothing. Instead *of helping her, I would probably have just got myself injured.'*

'That's probably true. But does that matter?'

The little boy looked up, his eyes narrowed, tears welling up.
'No.'

The uncle smiled. 'Think about it. If you had tried to help her,
there is a chance that she would still have suffered. But there is also
a chance, however small, that she may have escaped. But if you
didn't even try, there was no chance for her. Was there?'

Shiva nodded.

'What else did your mother tell you?'

'That the woman didn't even try to fight back.'

'Yes, that may be true.'

'And mother says that if the woman didn't try to fight, why
would it be wrong for me to do the same?'

'That is an important point. The sin was being committed against
her. And yet she was accepting it.'

They kept quiet for some time, staring at the setting sun.

'So, even if the woman didn't fight back,' said the uncle. 'What
do you think you should have done?'

'I...'

'Yes?'

'I think it doesn't matter if the woman didn't fight to protect
herself. No matter what, I should have fought for her.'

'Why?'

Shiva looked up. 'Do you also think I should have been pragmatic?
That it wasn't wrong to run away?'

'What I think doesn't matter. I want to hear your interpretation.
Why do you think it was wrong for you to run away?'

Shiva looked down, fidgeting with his skirt. His brow was
throbbing madly. 'Because it feels wrong to me.'

The uncle smiled. 'That is the answer. It feels wrong, because
what you did was against your karma. You don't have to live with

the woman's karma. What she did was her choice. You have to live with your own karma.'

Shiva looked up.

'It is your karma to fight evil. It doesn't matter if the people that evil is being committed against don't fight back. It doesn't matter if the entire world chooses to look the other way. Always remember this. You don't live with the consequences of other people's karma. You live with the consequences of your own.'

Shiva nodded slightly.

'Does that hurt?' asked the uncle, pointing at the blackish-red blotch on Shiva's brow, right between his eyes.

Shiva pressed it hard. The pressure provided some relief. 'No. But it burns. It burns a lot.'

'Especially when you are upset?'

Shiva nodded.

The uncle reached into his coat and pulled out a small pouch. 'This is a very precious medicine. I have carried it for a long time. And I feel you are the correct person to receive it.'

Shiva took the pouch. Opening it, he found a reddish-brown thick paste inside. 'Will it make the burning go away?'

The uncle smiled. 'It'll set you on the path of your destiny.'

Shiva frowned. Confused.

Pointing towards the gargantuan Himalayas extending beyond the Mansarovar, the uncle continued. 'My child, your destiny is much larger than these massive mountains. But in order to realise it, you will have to cross these very same massive mountains.'

The uncle didn't feel the need to explain any more. He took some of the reddish-brown paste and applied it on Shiva's brow, in a neat vertical line, up from between his eyes to his hair line. Shiva felt immediate relief as his brow cooled down. Then the uncle applied some paste around Shiva's throat. He took the remaining portion of the medicine and placed it in Shiva's right palm. Then he cut *his finger lightly and dropped a little bit of blood into the paste, whispering, 'We will never forget your command, Lord Rudra. This is the blood oath of a Vayuputra.'*

Shiva looked at his uncle and then down at his palm, which cradled the strange reddish-brown paste mixed with his uncle's blood.

'Put it at the back of your mouth,' said the uncle. 'But don't swallow it. Massage it with your tongue till it gets absorbed.'

Shiva did that.

'Now you are ready. Let fate choose the time.'

Shiva didn't understand. But he felt the relief the medicine gave. 'Do you have any more of this medicine?'

'I have given you all that I have, my child.'

— ⚇⚇⚇⚇⚇ —

'The Vasudevs had the Naga medicine?' asked a shocked Sati.

She had intended to speak to Shiva about the disturbing conversation with her father in the morning. She was still stunned that a back-up manufacturing facility for the Somras existed and that no one knew about it. But that was immediately forgotten on seeing Shiva's enraged face.

'I have been misled. They are probably in alliance with the Nagas! Can't you trust anyone in this country?'

Something within Sati told her that the Vasudevs couldn't be evil. It didn't add up. 'Shiva, are you probably jumping to...'

'Jumping? Jumping to conclusions?' glared Shiva. 'You know what Ayurvati said. That medicine could only be made in Naga lands. We know how the Brangas got it. They are being blackmailed. What is the explanation for the Vasudevs? They needed the Nagas to build their temples?'

Sati kept quiet.

Shiva walked up to the window and stared hard at the Vishwanath temple. For some strange reason, he could hear his inner voice repeating the same thought. *Stay calm. Don't jump to conclusions.*

Shiva shook his head.

'I'm sure the Vasudevs would have assumed that you would figure out where the medicine came from,' said Sati. 'So there can be only two explanations as to why the Vasudevs gave it to you.'

Shiva turned around.

'Either they are stupid. Or they think the safe birth of your son is so important that they are willing to risk your anger.'

Shiva frowned.

'From what I have gathered from you, I don't think they are stupid,' said Sati. 'That leaves us with only one choice. They think that if anything happened to our son, you would be so devastated that it would harm their cause against evil.'

Shiva chose silence.

— 🜨 —

The Naga Lord of the People sat on his chair in his personal chambers, right next to the window. He could hear the songs of the choir that paraded the streets of Panchavati at this time of the evening, once a week. The Queen had wanted to ban the sad songs they sang. She despised them as defeatist. But the Naga *Rajya Sabha*, the elected *Royal Council*, had voted against her move, allowing the songs to continue.

The song triggered powerful emotions in the Naga, but he held them within.

You were my world, my God, my creator,

And yet, you abandoned me.

I didn't seek you, you called me,

And yet, you abandoned me.

I honoured you, lived by your rules, coloured myself in your colours,

And yet, you abandoned me.

You hurt me, you deserted me, you failed in your duties,

And yet, I am the monster.

Tell me Lord, what can I...

'Disgusting song,' said the Queen, interrupting the Naga's thoughts. 'Shows our weakness and our attachments!'

'*Mausi*,' said the Naga as he rose. 'I didn't hear you come in.'

'How could you? These nauseating songs drown out the world. Drown out any positive thought.'

'Vengeance is not a positive thought, Your Highness,' smiled the Naga. 'Also the choir does sing happy songs as well.'

The Queen waved her hand. 'I have something more important to discuss.'

'Yes, *Mausi*.'

The Queen took a deep breath. 'Did you meet the Vasudevs?'

The Naga narrowed his eyes. He was surprised that it had taken the Queen so long to find out. 'Yes.'

'Why?' asked the Queen, barely restraining her temper.

'Your Highness, I believe we can use their help.'

'They will never support us. They may not be our enemies. But they will never be our friends!'

'I disagree. I think we have a common enemy. They will come to our side.'

'Nonsense! The Vasudevs are fanatic purveyors of an ancient legend. Some foreigner with a blue throat is not going to save this country!'

'But another foreigner with a beaded beard saved this country once, didn't he?'

'Don't compare this tribal to the great Lord Rudra. This country is probably fated for destruction. All India has given us is pain and sorrow. Why should we care?'

'Because whatever it may be, it is our country too.'

The Queen grunted angrily. 'Tell me the real reason why you gave them our medicine. You know it is in short supply. We have to send the annual quota to the Brangas. I am not breaking my word. They are the only decent people in this wretched land. The only ones who don't want to kill us all.'

'The quota of the Brangas will not be affected, Your Highness. I have only given my personal share.'

'In the holy name of Bhoomidevi, why? Have you suddenly started believing in the Neelkanth too?'

'What I believe doesn't matter, Your Highness. What matters is that the people of India believe.'

The Queen stared hard at the Naga. 'That is not the real reason.'

'It is.'

'DON'T LIE TO ME!'

The Naga kept quiet.

'You did it for that vile woman,' stated the Queen.

The Naga was disturbed, but his voice remained calm. 'No. And at least you shouldn't speak of her that way, Your Highness.'

'Why not?'

'Because besides me, you are the only one who knows the truth.'

'Sometimes I wish I didn't!'

'It's too late for that now.'

The Queen sniggered. 'It's true that the gods don't give all abilities to one person. You truly are your own worst enemy.'

— ⋏◍�⋔⌖ —

Daksha was sitting on the ground. He had been shocked at the unscheduled appearance of Maharishi Bhrigu in Devagiri. The Emperor of Meluha had not sought an audience with the sage.

Bhrigu looked down hard at Daksha, deeply unhappy. 'You disobeyed a direct command, Your Highness.'

Daksha remained quiet, head bowed low. *How did the Maharishi get to know? Only Sati, Veerini and I had been in on the conversation. Is Veerini spying on me? Why is everyone against me? Why me?*

Bhrigu stared at Daksha, reading his thoughts. The sage always knew that Daksha was weak. But the Emperor had never dared disobey a direct order. Furthermore, Bhrigu didn't really give that many orders. He was concerned about only one thing. On all other matters, he let Daksha do whatever he liked.

'You have been made Emperor for a reason,' said Bhrigu. 'Please don't make me question my judgement.'

Daksha kept quiet, scared.

Bhrigu bent down and turned Daksha's face up. 'Did you also tell her the location, Your Highness?'

Daksha whispered softly. 'No, My Lord. I swear.'

'Don't lie to me!'

'I swear, My Lord.'

Bhrigu read Daksha's thoughts. He was satisfied.

'You are not to mention this to anyone. Is that clear?'

Daksha remained silent.

'Your Highness,' said Bhrigu, his voice louder. 'Is that clear?'

'Yes, My Lord,' said a scared Daksha, holding Bhrigu's feet.

— 人◎Ⴓ⊹⊕ —

Shiva stood at the Assi Ghat. The sails of the five gleaming Branga ships had been folded in all but one of the ships. On the ship anchored closest to port, the sails had been pulled up, creating a grand sight, much to the appreciative glances of the people present.

'They look good, Divodas,' said Shiva.

'Thank you, My Lord.'

'I can't believe that your tribe built all this in just nine months.'

'We Brangas can do anything, My Lord.'

Shiva smiled.

Athithigva, standing next to Shiva, spoke up. 'Divodas, are you sure the ships will sail? This ship here has all its sails open and the winds are strong. And yet, it doesn't seem to be shaking the ship at all.'

Clearly the king did not know much about sailing.

'That is a very good point, Your Highness,' said Divodas. 'But the ship is not moving because we don't want it sailing off without us. The sails have been aligned such that they are directly against the wind. Can you see the main sail fluttering dramatically?'

Athithigva nodded.

'That means that the sail is laughing at us since it's not catching any wind.'

Shiva smiled. 'Laughing?'

'That's the term we use when the sail has been set wrong and is fluttering, My Lord,' said Divodas.

'Well,' said Shiva. 'I'll be serious then. We leave in three days for Branga. Make all the preparations.'

— ⁂ —

Sati was staring at the Ganga from her chamber window. She could see a small entourage of boats carrying King Athithigva across the river to his palace on the eastern banks.

Why does he keep going there? Why does he only take his family?

'What are you thinking, Sati?'

Shiva was standing behind her. She embraced him. 'I'm going to miss you.'

He pulled her face up, kissed her and smiled. 'That's not what you were thinking.'

Sati patted him lightly on his chest. 'You can read my mind as well?'

'I wish I could.'

'I wasn't thinking anything serious. Just wondering why King Athithigva goes to the Eastern palace so often. Even more oddly, he only takes his family there.'

'Yes, even I've noticed that. I'm sure he has some good reason. There is the superstition of the eastern banks being inauspicious, right?'

Sati shrugged. 'Is it fixed? You're leaving in three days?'

'Yes.'

'How long do you think you'll be gone?'

'I don't know. Hopefully, not too long.'

'I wish I could come.'

'I know. But Kartik is simply not old enough for a voyage like this.'

Sati looked at Kartik sleeping on his bed. He had grown so fast that he didn't fit in his crib any more. 'He looks more and more like you.'

Shiva smiled. 'It's been just six months, but he looks like a two–year–old!'

Sati had to take Shiva's word for it. Being a Meluhan who did not live in Maika, she had never seen a child younger than sixteen years of age.

'Maybe it's the blessings of the Somras,' said Sati.

'Possible. Ayurvati was surprised that he didn't fall sick the first time he took the Somras.'

'That was surprising. But maybe that's simply because he is a special boy!'

'That he is. I've never seen a baby who could walk at six months.'

Sati smiled. 'He will make us proud.'

'I'm sure he will.'

Sati looked up and kissed Shiva again. 'Just find a path to the Nagas and come back to me soon.'

'I certainly will, my love.'

— 𝕏◎ᘮ♀⊕ —

The ships had been provisioned. They did not intend to wait at any port along the way. Speed was of the essence.

Much to the mortification of Parvateshwar, a joint brigade of Suryavanshis and Chandravanshis had been created. It was difficult to carry more men in the five ships. But the saving grace was that the overall command remained with Drapaku.

Shiva looked at the ships from the steps of the Assi Ghat. Drapaku, as the commander, was on the lead craft, accompanied by his father Purvaka. The key companions of the Neelkanth were stationed on the main vessel, which would sail in the safest zone, surrounded by the other four boats. Parvateshwar, Bhagirath, Anandmayi, Ayurvati, Nandi and Veerbhadra, all stood at the balustrade of this ship. Shiva was surprised to find Uttanka too on the main ship.

Anandmayi must have insisted. If there is one woman who can entice Parvateshwar into breaking his vow of celibacy, it is her.

'My Lord,' said Athithigva, interrupting Shiva's thoughts.

The King of Kashi bent down to touch the Neelkanth's feet.

Shiva touched Athithigva's head gently. '*Ayushman Bhav.*'

With folded hands, Athithigva whispered, 'I beg you to return to Kashi quickly, My Lord. We are orphans without you.'

'You don't need me, Your Highness. You don't really need anyone else. Have faith in the one person that loves you the most: Yourself.'

Shiva turned towards a moist-eyed Sati, who was holding Kartik's hand as he stood by her side, wobbling slightly due to the strong winds.

Kartik pointed up at Shiva and said, 'Ba-ba.'

Shiva smiled and picked Kartik up. 'Ba-ba will be back soon, Kartik. Don't give your mother too much trouble.'

Kartik pulled Shiva's hair and repeated. 'Ba-ba.'

Shiva smiled even more broadly and kissed Kartik on his forehead. Then he held Kartik to his side and stepped forward to embrace Sati. Some Suryavanshi habits were too hard to break. Sati embraced Shiva lightly, for she was embarrassed of such public displays of affection. Shiva didn't let go. Sati's love for Shiva conquered her Suryavanshi reserve. She looked up and kissed Shiva. 'Come back soon.'

'I will.'

Chapter 10

The Gates of Branga

The waters were rising fast, flooding the small boat.

Shiva tried desperately to control the vessel, fighting the raging river with his oars, labouring to reach his friend.

Brahaspati was struggling. Suddenly his eyes opened wide in surprise. What seemed like a rope came out of nowhere and bound itself to his legs. He started getting pulled in rapidly.

'Shiva! Help! Please help me!'

Shiva was rowing hard. Desperately so. 'Hold on! I'm coming!'

Suddenly a massive three headed snake rose from the river. Shiva noticed the rope around Brahaspati slithering up and around him, crushing him ruthlessly. It was the serpent!

'Nooooo!'

Shiva woke up with a start. He looked around in a daze. His brow was throbbing hard, his throat intolerably cold. Everyone was asleep. He could feel the ground beneath him sway as the ship rocked gently, in tune with the Ganga waters. He walked up to the porthole of his cabin, letting the gentle breeze slow his heart rate down.

He curled his fist and rested it against the ship wall. 'I will get him, Brahaspati. That snake will pay.'

— 𑀟𑀋𝔘𝟜⊕ —

It had been two weeks since Shiva's entourage had left Kashi. Making good time since they were sailing downriver, they had just crossed the city of Magadh.

'We should be reaching Branga in another three weeks, My Lord,' said Parvateshwar.

Shiva, who was staring upriver, towards Kashi, turned around with a smile. 'Did you speak to Divodas?'

'Yes.'

'Where is he right now?'

'At the mast head, My Lord, trimming his sails to the prevailing wind. Obviously, he too wants to get to Branga quickly.'

Shiva looked at Parvateshwar. 'No, I don't think so. I think he yearns to play his role in my quest and then get back to his wife and daughter. He really misses them.'

'As you miss Sati and Kartik, My Lord.'

Shiva smiled and nodded, both of them leaning against the ship rail, looking at the tranquil Ganga. A school of dolphins emerged from the river and flew up into the air. Falling gracefully back into the waters, they jumped up once again, continuing this handsome dance, in graceful symphony. Shiva loved looking at the dolphins. They always seemed happy and carefree. 'Carefree fish in a capricious river! Poetic, isn't it?'

Parvateshwar smiled. 'Yes, My Lord.'

'Speaking of carefree and capricious, where is Anandmayi?'

'I think the Princess is with Uttanka, My Lord. She keeps going to the practice room with him. Perhaps they are perfecting some other dance moves.'

'Hmm.'

Parvateshwar kept looking at the river.

'She does dance well, doesn't she?' asked Shiva.

'Yes, My Lord.'

'Exceptionally well, actually.'

'That would be a fair comment to make, My Lord.'

'What do you think of Uttanka's dancing skills?'

Parvateshwar looked at Shiva and then towards the river once again. 'I think there is scope for improvement, My Lord. But I'm sure Princess Anandmayi will teach him well.'

Shiva smiled at Parvateshwar and shook his head. 'Yes, I'm sure she will.'

— ⵊ◎Ʊ⇞⊕ —

'The Neelkanth and his entourage left for Branga a month back, Your Highness,' said the Naga Lord of the People to the Queen.

They were sitting in her private chambers.

'Good to see you focus once again. I'll send a warning message to King Chandraketu.'

The Naga nodded. He was about to say something more, but kept silent. Instead, he looked out of the window. From this position in Panchavati, he could see the calm Godavari river in the distance.

'And?' asked the Queen.

'I'd like your permission to go to Kashi.'

'Why? Do you want to open trade relations with them?' asked the Queen, highly tickled.

'She did not go with the Neelkanth.'

The Queen stiffened.

'Please, Your Highness. This is important to me.'

'What do you hope to achieve, my child?' asked the Queen. 'This is a foolhardy quest.'

'I want answers.'

'What difference will that make?'

'It will give me peace.'

The Queen sighed. 'This quest will be your downfall.'

'It will complete me, Your Highness.'

'You are forgetting that you have duties towards your own people.'

'I first have a duty unto myself, *Mausi*.'

The Queen shook her head. 'Wait till the Rajya Sabha is over. I need you here to ensure that the motion to support the Brangas is not defeated. After that you can go.'

The Naga bent low and touched the Queen's feet. 'Thank you, *Mausi*.'

'But you will not go alone. I don't trust you to take care of yourself. I will come with you.'

The Naga smiled softly. 'Thank you.'

— 𑀊𑀐𑀉𑀖𑀙 —

Shiva's entourage was just a week's distance from the gates of Branga. The ships had maintained a punishing schedule. Parvateshwar and Divodas had taken a clipper to the lead boat in order to confer with Drapaku about the protocol on reaching the gates. Parvateshwar made it very clear that the Lord Neelkanth did not want any bloodshed. Divodas was to complete the negotiations necessary in order to enter the restricted Branga territory. He felt it would be impossible to enter without showing the Neelkanth, for the Brangas too believed in the legend. Parvateshwar advised him to try and enter without having to resort to that.

Divodas was left with Drapaku so they could plan the

flag display as well, while Parvateshwar returned to the central vessel. He wanted to take the Lord Mahadev's advice on how he would like the Branga border guards handled. Parvateshwar did not want to let his guard down and yet, given the delicacy of the mission, it was imperative that the Brangas did not view the five ship fleet as a threat.

His rowers tied the cutter to the main ship and he climbed up to the aft section. He was taken aback to see Anandmayi there. She had her back to him. Six knives in her hand. The standard target board at the wall had been removed and the expert board, much smaller in size, had been hung up there. Bhagirath and Uttanka were standing a short distance away.

Uttanka turned towards Anandmayi. 'Remember what I've taught you, Princess. No breaks. A continuous shower of knives.'

Anandmayi rolled her eyes. 'Yeeesss Guruji. I heard you the first time. I'm not deaf.'

'I'm sorry, Your Highness.'

'Now stand aside.'

Uttanka moved away.

Parvateshwar standing at the back was dumbfounded by what he saw. Anandmayi was standing correctly. Like a trained warrior. With her feet slightly spread in a stable posture. Her right hand relaxed to her side. The left hand holding the six knives from the hilt, positioned close to her right shoulder. Her breathing, light and calm. Perfect.

Then she raised her right hand. And in a dramatically rapid action, pulled the first knife from her left hand and threw. Almost simultaneously, she reached for the second knife and released it. And then the third, fourth, fifth and sixth.

Anandmayi's movements were so flawless that Parvateshwar did not even see the target. He stood there admiring her action. His mouth open in awe. Then he heard Uttanka and Bhagirath applauding. He turned towards the board. Every knife had hit dead centre. Perfect.

'By the great Lord Ram!' marvelled Parvateshwar.

Anandmayi turned with a broad smile. 'Parva! When did you get here?'

Parvateshwar, meanwhile, had found something else to admire. He was staring at Anandmayi's bare legs. Or so it seemed.

Anandmayi shifted her weight, relaxing her hips to the side saucily. 'See something you like, Parva?'

Parvateshwar whispered softly, pointing with a bit of wonder at the scabbard hanging by Anandmayi's waist. 'That is a long sword.'

Anandmayi's face fell. 'You really know how to sweep a woman back onto her feet, don't you?'

'Sorry?' asked Parvateshwar.

Anandmayi just shook her head.

'But that is a long sword,' said Parvateshwar. 'When did you learn to wield that?'

Wielding a sword that was significantly longer than a warrior's arm length was a rare skill. Difficult to master. But those who mastered it, dramatically improved their chances of a kill.

Bhagirath and Uttanka had now walked up close.

Bhagirath answered, 'Uttanka has been teaching her for the last month, General. She is a quick student.'

Parvateshwar turned back to Anandmayi, bowed his head slightly. 'It would be my honour to duel with you, Princess.'

Anandmayi raised her eyebrows. 'You want to duel with me? What the hell do you think you're trying to prove?'

'I'm not trying to prove anything, Your Highness,' said Parvateshwar, surprised at Anandmayi's belligerence. 'It would just be a pleasure to duel with you and test your skills.'

'*Test* my skills? You think that's why I'm learning the art of warfare? So that you can test me and prove yourself superior? I already know you're better. Don't exert yourself.'

Parvateshwar breathed deeply, trying to control his rising temper. 'My lady, that's not what I was trying to imply. I was just...'

Anandmayi interrupted him. 'For a sharp man, you can be remarkably stupid sometimes, General. I just don't know what I was thinking.'

Bhagirath tried to step in. 'Umm listen, I don't think there is a need to...'

But Anandmayi had already turned and stormed off.

— ⚹◎🜛♄⊕ —

The sun had just risen over the Ganga, tinting it a stunning orange. Sati was standing at her chamber window, looking down at the river. Kartik was playing in the back with Krittika. Sati turned to look at her friend and son. She smiled.

Krittika is almost like a second mother to Kartik. My son is so lucky.

Sati turned back towards the river. She noticed a movement. Peering harder, she saw what was going on and frowned. Emperor Athithigva was off again to his mystery palace. Apparently, for yet another puja for the future of Kashi. She found this odd.

The entire city of Kashi was celebrating *Rakshabandhan* that day. A day when each sister *tied a thread on her brother's wrist, seeking his protection in times of distress.* This festival was celebrated in Meluha as well. The only difference in Swadweep was that the sisters also demanded gifts from their brothers. And the brothers had no choice but to oblige.

Shouldn't he be spending his time in Kashi? In Meluha, women would come to tie a rakhi to the local governor. And, it was his duty to offer protection. This had been clearly established by Lord Ram. Why is King Athithigva not following this tradition and is instead going to his other palace? And why in Lord Ram's name is he carrying so many things? Are they part of some ritual to rid the eastern banks of bad fate? Or are they gifts?

'What are you thinking, Your Highness?'

Sati turned around to find Krittika staring at her. 'I must find an answer to the mystery of this Eastern palace.'

'But nobody is allowed in there. You know that. The king even made some strange excuses to not take the Neelkanth there.'

'I know. But something is not right. And why is the King taking so many gifts there today?'

'I don't know, Your Highness.'

Sati turned towards Krittika. 'I'm going there.'

Krittika stared at Sati in alarm. 'My Lady, you cannot. There are lookouts at the palace heights. It is surrounded by walls. They will see any boat approaching.'

'That's why I intend to swim across.'

Krittika was now in panic. The Ganga was too broad to swim across. 'My Lady...'

'I've been planning this for weeks, Krittika. I've practised many times. There's a sand bank in the middle of the river where I can rest, unseen.'

'But how will you enter the palace?'

'I can hazard a guess about the structural layout from the terrace of our chamber. The Eastern palace is guarded heavily only at the entrance. I have also noticed that guards are not allowed into the main palace. There is a water drain at the far end of the palace. I can swim in through it, without leaving anyone the wiser.'

'But...'

'I'm going. Take care of Kartik. If all goes well, I will be back by nightfall.'

— 人◎Ⴒᚴ⊕ —

The ships turned the last meander of the Ganga to emerge a short distance from the legendary gates of Branga.

'By the Holy Lake!' whispered Shiva in awe.

Even the Meluhans, used to their own renowned engineering skills and celebrated monuments, were dumbstruck.

The gates gleamed in the midday sun, having been built almost entirely of the newly discovered metal, iron. The barrier was spread across the river, and it extended additionally into fort walls along the banks which ran a further hundred kilometres inland. This was to prevent anyone from dismantling a smaller ship, carrying it across land and then reassembling it on the other side. There were no roads at the Branga border. The Ganga was the only way in. And anyone stupid enough to go deep into the jungle would probably be killed by wild animals and disease before meeting any Branga man.

The barrier's base was a cage built of iron, which allowed the waters of the mighty Ganga to flow through, but prevented any person or large fish from swimming through underwater. The barrier had, oddly enough, five open spaces in between, to allow five ships to sail through simultaneously. It seemed odd at first sight because it appeared that a fast cutter could just race through the gap before any Branga could attack it.

'That seems bizarre,' said Bhagirath. 'Why build a barrier and then leave openings through it?'

'Those aren't openings, Bhagirath,' said Shiva. 'They are traps.'

Shiva pointed at a Branga ship that had just entered the gates. At the beginning of the opening was a deep pool of water with a base made of water-proofed teak, into which the ship had sailed in. There was a cleverly designed pump system that allowed the waters of the Ganga to come into the pool. This raised the ship to the correct height. And then, they saw the fearsome magic of the gates of Branga. Two thick iron platforms rapidly extended from both sides of the pool onto the ship, fitting onto the groove on the extended iron base at the bottom of the hull. The platform had rollers on its edge which fit snugly within the channel of the iron base of the ship.

Shiva looked at Parvateshwar. 'So that's why Divodas built the base at the bottom of our hulls.'

Parvateshwar nodded in awe. 'The platforms extended with such rapid force. If we didn't have the iron base at the bottom, it would just crush the hull of our ship.'

Iron chains were being fitted onto the hooks on the hull

of the ship. The chains were then attached to a strange looking machine which appeared to be like a medley of pulleys.

'But what animal did they use to make the platform move so fast?' asked Bhagirath. 'This force is beyond any animal's capability. Even a herd of elephants!'

Shiva pointed to the Branga ship. The pulleys had started moving with rapid force, extending the chains, pulling the vessel forward. The rollers on the platform permitted the ship to move with minimum friction, allowing it to maintain its amazing speed.

'My God!' whispered Bhagirath again. 'Look at that! What animal can make the pulleys move so quickly?'

'It's a machine,' said Shiva. 'Divodas had told me about some accumulator machines, which store the energy of various animals over hours and then release them in seconds.'

Bhagirath frowned.

'Look,' said Shiva.

A massive cylinder of rock was coming down rapidly. Next to it was another similar cylinder, being slowly pushed up by pulleys, as twenty bulls, yoked to the machine, gradually went around it in circles.

'The bulls are charging the machine with hours of labour,' said Shiva. 'The massive rock is locked at a height. When the platform is to be extended or a ship pulled, they remove the lock on the rock. It comes crashing down, the momentum releasing a tremendous force that propels the platforms.'

'By the great Lord Indra,' said Bhagirath. 'A simple design. But so brilliant!'

Shiva nodded. He turned towards the Branga office at the entry gates.

Their ships had anchored close to the gates. Divodas had already stepped off to negotiate with the Branga Officer in-charge.

— 𑀖𑀖𑀖𑀖𑀖𑀖 —

'Why are you back so soon? You have enough medicines for a year.'

Divodas was shocked at the manner in which Major Uma was speaking. She was always strict, but never rude. He had been delighted that she had been posted at the gates. Though he hadn't met her in years, they had been friends a long time back. He had thought he could use his friendship with her to gain easy passage into Branga.

'What is the matter, Uma?' asked Divodas.

'It is Major Uma. I am on duty.'

'I'm sorry Major. I meant no disrespect.'

'I can't let you go back unless you give me a good reason.'

'Why would I need a reason to enter my own country?'

'This is not your country anymore. You chose to abandon it. Kashi is your land. Go back there.'

'Major Uma, you know I had no choice. You know the risks to the life of my child in Branga.'

'You think those who live in Branga don't? You think we don't love our children? Yet we choose to live in our own land. You suffer the consequences of your choice.'

Divodas realised this was getting nowhere. 'I have to meet the King on a matter of national importance.'

Uma narrowed her eyes. 'Really? I guess the King has some important business dealings with Kashi, right?'

Divodas breathed in deeply. 'Major Uma, it is very important that I meet the King. You must trust me.'

'Unless you are carrying the Queen of the Nagas herself on one of your ships, I can't see anything important enough to let you through!'

'I'm carrying someone far more important than the Queen of the Nagas.'

'Kashi has really improved your sense of humour, Divodas,' sneered Uma. 'I suggest you turn back and shine your supreme light somewhere else.'

The snide pun on Kashi's name convinced Divodas that he was facing a changed Uma. An angry and bitter Uma, incapable of listening to reason. He had no choice. He had to get the Neelkanth. He knew Uma used to believe in the legend.

'I'll come back with the person who is more important than the Queen of the Nagas herself,' said Divodas, turning to leave.

— 𑀓𑀰𑀶𑀟𑀤𑀓 —

The small cutter had just docked at the Branga office. Divodas alit first. Followed by Shiva, Parvateshwar, Bhagirath, Drapaku and Purvaka.

Uma, standing outside her office, sighed. 'You really don't give up, do you?'

'This is very important, Major Uma,' said Divodas.

Uma recognised Bhagirath. 'Is this the person? You think I should break the rules for the Prince of Ayodhya?'

'He is the Prince of Swadweep, Major Uma. Don't forget that. We send tribute to Ayodhya.'

'So you are more loyal to Ayodhya as well now? How many times will you abandon Branga?'

'Major, in the name of Ayodhya, I respectfully ask you

to let us pass,' said Bhagirath, trying hard not to lose his temper. He knew the Neelkanth did not want any bloodshed.

'Our terms of the Ashwamedh treaty were very clear, Prince. We send you a tribute annually. And Ayodhya never enters Branga. We have maintained our part of the agreement. The orders to me are to help you maintain your part of the bargain.'

Shiva stepped forward. 'If I may...'

Uma was at the end of her patience. She stepped forward and pushed Shiva. 'Get out of here.'

'UMA!' Divodas pulled out his sword.

Bhagirath, Parvateshwar, Drapaku and Purvaka too drew out their swords instantly.

'I will kill your entire family for this blasphemy,' swore Drapaku.

'Wait!' said Shiva, his arms spread wide, stopping his men.

Shiva turned towards Uma. She was staring at him, shocked. The *angvastram* that he had wrapped around his body for warmth had come undone, revealing his *neel kanth,* the prophesied blue throat. The Branga soldiers around Uma immediately went down on their knees, heads bowed in respect, tears flooding their eyes. Uma continued to stare, her mouth half open.

Shiva cleared his throat. 'I really need to pass through, Major Uma. May I request your cooperation?'

Uma's face turned mottled red. 'Where the hell have you been?'

Shiva frowned.

Uma bent forward, tears in her eyes, banging her small fists on Shiva's well-honed chest. 'Where the hell have you been? We have been waiting! We have been suffering! Where the hell have you been?'

Shiva tried to hold Uma, to comfort her. But she sank down holding Shiva's leg, wailing. 'Where the hell have you been?'

A concerned Divodas turned to another Branga friend also posted at the border. His friend whispered, 'Last month, Major Uma lost her only child to the plague. Her husband and she had conceived after years of trying. She was devastated.'

Divodas looked at Uma with empathy, understanding her angst. He couldn't even begin to imagine what would happen to him if he lost his baby.

Shiva, who had heard the entire conversation, squatted. He cradled Uma in the shelter of his arms, as though trying to give her his strength.

'Why didn't you come earlier?' Uma kept crying, inconsolable.

Chapter 11

The Mystery of the Eastern Palace

Sati was resting on the sandbank in the middle of the Ganga. She kept low to avoid being seen from the Eastern palace. Her brown clothes, an effective camouflage.

She kept her breathing steady, rejuvenating her tired muscles. Reaching back, she again checked the hold on her sword and shield. It was secure on her back. She didn't want it slipping out into the Ganga, leaving her defenceless when she entered the palace.

Reaching to her side, she pulled out a small pouch. She ate the fruit inside quickly. Once done, she tucked the empty pouch back. Then slipped quietly back into the Ganga.

A little while later Sati crept gradually onto the eastern banks. Far from the well guarded ghats of the palace, where the King's boats had been anchored, was a concealed drain. It was impossible to see from anywhere in Kashi or the Ganga. But the elevation of the palace that was Sati's quarters for the duration of her visit to the city, the only building of that height in Kashi, allowed her to chance upon it. She crept slowly into the foliage, suspecting the channel was behind it.

She quietly slipped into the drain, swimming with powerful strokes towards the palace. The drain was surprisingly clean. Not too many people in the palace perhaps. Closer to the palace wall, the drain disappeared underground. Sati dived underwater. Metal bars protected the drain opening near the palace premises. Sati pulled out a file from her pouch and started cutting away at the bar. She only went up for air when her lungs started burning for oxygen. She dived back and continued filing the rusty, old metal bars. With only five trips up for air, Sati was able to cut through two of the rods, space enough for her to slip through.

Sati emerged along the western wall of the palace to find herself in a breathtaking garden. The area was completely deserted. Perhaps nobody expected an intruder from this end. While the ground was covered with lush green grass, flowers and trees appeared to have been allowed to go wild, giving the garden the appearance of a barely restrained forest. Picturesque and natural.

Sati hurried through the garden, careful not to step on any dried twigs. She reached a side entrance and walked in.

The eeriness of the palace was starting to get her. There was no sound. No servants toiling away. No sounds of royalty making merry. No sounds of birds in the garden. Nothing. It was like she had stepped into a vacuum.

She hurried through the corridors. Not finding anyone to obstruct or challenge her, she went through the luxurious palace, which looked like it had never been lived in!

Suddenly she heard the soft sounds of laughter. She crept in that direction.

The corridor opened into the main courtyard. Sati hid
behind a pillar. She could see King Athithigva sitting in
the centre on a throne. Standing next to him were his wife
and son. Three ancient-looking attendants, who Sati had
never seen before, stood next to them, holding puja thalis
with all the necessary accoutrements for a rakhi ceremony,
including the sacred thread itself.

Why is he getting his rakhi tied here?

And then, a woman stepped forward.

Sati's breathing stopped in horror.

Naga!

— ⟨symbols⟩ —

The entire crew on all five ships was crowded on the
port and starboard side, watching the operation with awe
and wonder. Shiva's men were completely astounded by the
Branga gates. They had seen the platform close in on their
ship with frightening force. Then the hooks were secured
to the chains. The Brangas, after the go-ahead from the
respective ship captains, began towing the fleet.

Shiva was standing aft, looking at the office at the
gate entrance.

Every Branga not working on the gate machinery was
on his knees, paying obeisance to the Neelkanth. But Shiva
was staring at a broken woman curled up against the wall
in a foetal position. She was still crying.

Shiva had tears in his eyes. He knew Uma believed that
fate had cheated her daughter. She believed that if the
Neelkanth had arrived a month earlier, her child would
still be alive. But the Neelkanth himself was not so sure.

What could I have done?

He continued to stare at Uma.

Holy Lake, give me strength. I will fight this plague.

The ground staff got the signal. They released the accumulator machines and the pulleys began turning, moving the ship rapidly forward.

Seeing the vision of Uma retreating swiftly, Shiva whispered, 'I'm sorry.'

— ⚡⚙☂⚘✵ —

Sati was stunned. A Naga woman with the King of Kashi!

The Naga woman was actually two women in one body. The body was one from the chest down. But there were two sets of shoulders, fused to each other at the chest, each with a single arm dangling in either direction. The Naga had two heads.

One body, two arms, four shoulders and two heads. Lord Ram, what evil is this?

Sati realised quickly that each head was fighting for control over their common body. One head seemed docile, wanting to come forward to tie the rakhi on the King's extended arm. The other head, playful and mischievous, intent on playing pranks on her brother, was pulling back.

'Maya!' said Athithigva. 'Stop playing pranks and tie the rakhi on my wrist.'

The mischievous head laughed and commanded the body to come forward, to fulfil her brother's wish. Athithigva proudly displayed his rakhi to his wife and son. Then he took some sweets from the plates held by the attendants and gave them to his sister. The attendant then came forward with a sword. Athithigva looked at the mischievous sister and gave the sword to her. 'Practice well. You are really improving!'

The attendant then gave a *Veena*, a stringed musical instrument to the King. Athithigva turned to the other sister and gave the instrument to her. 'I love to hear you play.'

The arms seemed to be in a quandary as to which gift to hold.

'Now don't you squabble over the gifts dear sisters. I mean for you to share them sensibly.'

Just then one of the attendants noticed Sati. She screamed out loud.

Sati immediately drew her sword. Maya did as well. But the heads hadn't come to a consensus. She seemed to be hesitating. Ultimately, the docile head won. She ran behind her brother. Athithigva's wife and son stood rooted to their spot.

Athithigva however was staring hard at Sati, eyes defiant, arm protectively drawn around his sister.

'Your Highness,' said Sati. 'What is the meaning of this?'

'I'm only getting a rakhi tied by my sister, My Lady,' said Athithigva.

'You are sheltering a Naga. You are hiding this from your people. This is wrong.'

'She is my sister, My Lady.'

'But she is a Naga!'

'I don't care. All I know is that she is my sister. I am sworn to protect her.'

'But she should be in the Naga territory.'

'Why should she be with those monsters?'

'Lord Rudra would not have allowed this.'

'Lord Rudra said judge a person by his karma, not his appearance.'

Sati kept quiet, troubled.

Maya suddenly stepped forward. The aggressive personality had come up front. The docile one seemed to be struggling to pull the body back.

'Let me go!' screamed the aggressive one.

The docile head capitulated. Maya moved forward and dropped her sword, not wanting to convey any threat.

'Why do you hate us?' said the Naga's aggressive head.

Sati stood dumbfounded. 'I don't hate you... I was just talking about the rules to be followed...'

'Really? So rules made thousands of years back, in a different land, by people who don't know us or our circumstances, will govern every aspect of our life?'

Sati kept silent.

'You think that is how Lord Ram would have liked it?'

'Lord Ram ordered his followers to obey the rules.'

'He also said rules are not an end in itself. They are made to create a just and stable society. But what if the rules themselves cause injustice? Then how do you follow Lord Ram? By following those rules or breaking them?'

Sati didn't have an answer.

'Brother has spoken a lot about the Lord Neelkanth and you,' said Maya. 'Aren't you supposed to be a Vikarma?'

Sati stiffened. 'I followed those rules as long as they were active.'

'And why was the Vikarma law changed?'

'Shiva didn't change it for me!'

'Believe what you want. But the change in the law helped you as well, right?'

Sati kept quiet, disturbed.

Maya continued. 'I have heard many tales about the Neelkanth. I'll tell you why he changed it. The Vikarma law may have made sense a thousand years back. But in this day and age, it was unfair. It was just a tool to oppress people one doesn't understand.'

Sati was about to say something, but kept quiet.

'And who is more misunderstood today than a person with a deformity? Call us Naga. Call us a monster. Throw us to the South of the Narmada, where our presence will not trouble your lily white lives.'

'So what you are saying is that all Nagas are paragons of virtue?'

'We don't know! And we don't care! Why should we answer for the Nagas? Just because we were born deformed? Will you answer for any Suryavanshi who breaks the law?'

Sati kept silent.

'Isn't it punishment enough that we live alone in this god forsaken palace, with only three servants for company? That the only excitement in our lives is the periodic visits of our brother? How much more do you want to punish us? And will you kindly explain what we are being punished for?'

The docile personality suddenly seemed to assert herself and Maya abruptly moved back, hiding behind Athithigva.

Athithigva bent low. 'Please, Lady Sati. I beg you. Please don't tell anyone.'

Sati remained quiet.

'She's my sister,' pleaded Athithigva. 'My father made me swear on his deathbed that I would protect her. I cannot break my pledge.'

Sati looked at Maya and then at Athithigva. For the first time in her life, she was confronted with the viewpoint of a Naga. And she could see the unfairness that they faced.

'I love her,' said Athithigva. 'Please.'

'I promise to keep quiet.'

'Will you swear in the name of Lord Ram, My Lady?'

Sati frowned. 'I am a Suryavanshi, Your Highness. We don't break our promises. And everything that we do is in the name of Lord Ram.'

— 𑀓𑀁𑀝𑀤𑀫 —

As soon as the ships were through the gates, Drapaku ordered the sails up full mast. He directed the other ships to quickly fall into formation.

They had just gone a short distance when they beheld the mighty Brahmaputra flowing down to marshal with the Ganga, and together form probably one of the largest fresh water bodies in the world.

'By the great Lord *Varun*,' said Drapaku in awe, remembering the *God of water and seas*. 'That river is almost as big as an ocean!'

'Yes,' said Divodas proudly.

Turning to Purvaka, Drapaku said, 'I wish you could see this, father. I have never seen a river so massive!'

'I can see through your eyes, my son.'

'Brahmaputra is the largest river in India, Brigadier,' said Divodas. 'The only one with a masculine name.'

Drapaku thought about it for a moment. 'You are right. I never thought of that. Every other river in India has a feminine name. Even the great Ganga that we sail on.'

'Yes. We believe the Brahmaputra and Ganga are the father and mother of the Branga.'

Purvaka started. 'Of course! That must be the source of the names of your main river and your kingdom. The *Bra*hmaputra and Ga*nga* conjugate to create *Branga!*'

'Interesting point, father,' said Drapaku. He then turned to Divodas. 'Is that true?'

'Yes.'

The ships set sail, down the Branga river, to the capital city of the kingdom, *Brangaridai*, literally, *the heart of Branga.*

— ⚕ ⊚ Ʊ ⚲ ⊕ —

Parvateshwar was standing alone at the stern, watching the lead boat. The system that Anandmayi had suggested, of tying a line from the lead boat to the central boat, was being followed. The General still marvelled at the brilliant simplicity of this idea.

'General.'

Parvateshwar turned around to find Anandmayi standing behind him. Due to the cold, she had wrapped a long *angvastram* around her.

'Your Highness,' said Parvateshwar. 'I'm sorry, I didn't hear you come.'

'It's all right,' said Anandmayi with a slight smile. 'I have soft feet.'

Parvateshwar nodded, about to say something, but he hesitated.

'What is it, General?'

'Your Highness,' said Parvateshwar. 'I meant no insult when I asked you to duel with me. In Meluha, it is a form of fellowship.'

'Fellowship! You make our relationship sound so boring, General.'

Parvateshwar kept silent.

'Well, if you have called me a friend,' said Anandmayi, 'perhaps you can answer a question.'

'Of course.'

'Why did you take the vow of lifelong celibacy?'

'That is a long story, Your Highness.'

'I have all the time in the world to hear you.'

'More than two hundred and fifty years ago, noblemen in Meluha voted for a change in Lord Ram's laws.'

'What is wrong with that? I thought Lord Ram had said his laws can be changed for the purpose of justice.'

'Yes, he did. But this particular change did not serve justice. You know about our Maika system of child management, right?'

'Yes,' said Anandmayi. How a mother could be expected to surrender her child without any hope of seeing him ever again was something she did not understand. But she didn't want to get into an argument with Parvateshwar. 'So what change was made in it?'

'The Maika system was relaxed so that the children of nobility would not be surrendered into the common pool. They would continue to be tracked separately and returned to their birth parents when they turned sixteen.'

'What about the children of common people?'

'They were not a part of this relaxation.'

'That's not fair.'

'That's exactly what my grandfather, Lord Satyadhwaj, thought. Nothing wrong with the relaxation itself. But one of Lord Ram's unchangeable rules was that the law should apply equally to everyone. You cannot have separate sets of rules for the nobility and the masses. That is wrong.'

'I agree. But didn't your grandfather oppose this change?'

'He did. But he was the only one opposing it. So the change still went through.'

'That is sad.'

'To protest against this corruption of Lord Ram's way, my grandfather vowed that neither he nor any of his adopted Maika descendants would ever have birth children.'

Anandmayi wondered who gave Lord Satyadhwaj the right to make a decision for all his descendants in perpetuity! But she didn't say anything.

Parvateshwar, chest puffed up in pride, said, 'And I honour that vow to this day.'

Anandmayi sighed and turned towards the riverbank, watching the dense forest. Parvateshwar too turned to look at the Branga river, heavily laden with silt, flowing sluggishly on.

'It's strange how life works,' said Anandmayi, without turning towards Parvateshwar. 'A good man rebelled against an injustice in a foreign land more than two hundred and fifty years ago. Today, that very rebellion is causing me injustice...'

Parvateshwar turned to glance at Anandmayi. He stared hard at her beautiful face, a soft smile on his lips. Then he shook his head and turned back towards the river.

Chapter 12

The Heart of Branga

The Branga river carried too much water and silt to remain whole for long. It rapidly broke up into multiple distributaries, which spread their bounty across the land of Branga before disgorging themselves into the Eastern Sea, creating what was probably the largest river delta on earth. It was rumoured that the land was so fertile with the flood-delivered silt and so bountiful in water that the farmers did not have to labour for their crops. All they had to do was fling the seeds and the rich soil did the rest!

Brangaridai lay on the main distributary of the Branga river, the Padma.

Shiva's fleet closed in on Brangaridai a little over two weeks after crossing the gates of Branga. They had sailed through lands that were prosperous and wealthy. But there was an air of death, of pathos, which hung heavy.

The walls of Brangaridai spread over an area of a thousand hectares, almost the size of Devagiri. While the city of Devagiri had been built on three platforms, Brangaridai spread itself on naturally higher ground, around a kilometre inland from the Padma, as a safeguard against floods. Surrounded by high walls, the capital stayed true to the Chandravanshi disdain for any long term planning. The roads were laid out in a haphazard manner and not in the grid form of the Meluhan cities. But the streets were still broad and tree-lined. Vast quantities of Branga wealth ensured that their buildings were superbly built and maintained, while their temples were lofty and grand. A large number of public monuments had been constructed over the centuries: stadia for performances, halls for celebrations, exquisite gardens and public baths. Despite their superb condition, these public buildings were rarely used. The repeated bouts of the plague ensured that the Brangas saw death every day. There was very little zest left for life.

The river port off the city had multiple levels to allow for the vastly varying depth of the Padma at different times of the year. At this time of the year, the peak of winter, the Padma was at its medium flow. Shiva and his entourage disembarked on the fifth level of the port. Shiva saw Parvateshwar, Drapaku, Purvaka and Divodas waiting for him on the comfortable concourse at this port level.

'It's a massive port, Purvaka ji,' said Shiva.

'I can sense it, My Lord,' smiled Purvaka. 'I think these Brangas may probably have the capability to be as efficient as the Meluhans.'

'I don't think they care about efficiency, father,' said Drapaku. 'I sense that the bigger challenge for them is to simply stay alive.'

Just then a short, rotund Branga man, wearing an impossibly large array of gold jewellery, came rushing down the steps. He saw Parvateshwar and went down on his knees, bringing his head down to his feet. 'My Lord, you have come! You have come! We are saved!'

Parvateshwar bent down to pick up the man sternly. 'I am not the Neelkanth.'

The Branga man looked up, confused.

Parvateshwar pointed towards Shiva. 'Bow down to the true Lord.'

The man rushed towards Shiva's feet. 'My apologies, My Lord. Please don't punish Branga for my terrible mistake.'

'Get up, my friend,' smiled Shiva. 'How could you recognise me when you had never seen me before?'

The Branga stood up, tears flooding his eyes. 'Such humility, despite so much power. It could only be you, the great Mahadev.'

'Don't embarrass me. What is your name?'

'I am Bappiraj, Prime Minister of Branga, My Lord. We have set up the welcoming party for you at ground level, where King Chandraketu awaits.'

'Please take me to your king.'

— 𑀓𑀡𑀝𑀢𑀧 —

Bappiraj proudly climbed the last step to the ground level, followed by Shiva. Bhagirath, Parvateshwar, Anandmayi, Ayurvati, Divodas, Drapaku, Purvaka, Nandi and Veerbhadra followed.

As soon as Shiva ascended, loud conch shells were blown by a posse of pandits. A large herd of elephants, decked in fine gold ornaments, standing a little further away, trumpeted loud enough to startle Purvaka. The splendidly-carved stone pavilion at the ground level had been sheathed in gold plates to honour the Mahadev. It seemed as though almost the entire population — 400,000 citizens — of Brangaridai had gathered to receive the

Neelkanth. At the head was the poignant figure of King Chandraketu.

He was a man of medium height, with a bronzed complexion, high cheekbones and doe-eyes. King Chandraketu's black hair was long like most Indians and had been neatly oiled and curled. He didn't have the muscular physique one expected of a Kshatriya. His lanky frame was clothed in a simple cream *dhoti* and *angvastram*. Despite ruling a kingdom with legendary hordes of gold and fabulous wealth, Chandraketu did not have a smidgeon of gold on his body. His eyes had the look of a defeated man, struggling against fate.

Chandraketu went down on his knees, his head touching the ground and his hands spread forward, as did every other Branga present.

'*Ayushman bhav*, Your Highness,' said Shiva, blessing King Chandraketu *with a long life*.

Chandraketu looked up, still on his knees, his hands folded in a namaste, copious tears rolling down his eyes. 'I know I will live long now, My Lord. And so will every Branga. For you have come!'

— ⵣⵔⵓⵣⵔ —

'We must stop this senseless war,' said Vasuki, looking around the Naga Rajya Sabha. Many heads nodded in agreement. He was the descendant of one of the celebrated kings of the Nagas in the past. His lineage earned him respect.

'But the war is over,' said the Queen. 'Mount Mandar has been destroyed. The secret is with us.'

'Then why are we sending the medicine to the Brangas?'

asked Nishad. 'We don't need them anymore. Helping them only gives reasons to our enemies to keep hostilities alive.'

'Is that how Nagas will work from now on?' asked the Queen. 'Abandoning a friend when not needed?'

Suparna, whose face seemed to resemble that of a bird, spoke up. 'I agree with the Queen. The Brangas were and are our allies. They are the only ones who supported us. We must help them.'

'But we are Nagas,' said Astik. 'We have been punished for the sins of our previous births. We must accept our fate and live out our lives in penance. And we should advice the same to the Brangas.'

The Queen bit her lip. Karkotak looked at her intensely. He knew his Queen hated this defeatist attitude. But he also knew what Astik said was the majority opinion.

'I agree,' said Iravat, before looking at Suparna. 'And I wouldn't expect the people of Garuda to understand that. They are hungry for war all the time.'

That comment hurt. The people of Garuda, or Nagas with the face of birds, had been the enemies of the rest of the Nagas for long. They used to live in the fabled city of Nagapur, far to the east of Panchavati, but still within the Dandak forest. The great Lord of the People had brokered peace many years back and Suparna, their present leader, had joined the Rajya Sabha as a trusted aide of the Queen. Her people now lived in Panchavati.

The Queen spoke firmly. 'That is uncalled for, Lord Iravat. Please don't forget Lady Suparna has brought the people of Garuda into the joint Naga family. We are all siblings now. Anyone who insults Lady Suparna shall incur my wrath.'

Iravat immediately backtracked. The Queen's anger was legendary.

Karkotak looked around with concern. Iravat had withdrawn but the discussion was going nowhere. Would they be able to continue sending the medicines to the Brangas as the Queen had promised? He looked at the Lord of the People, who rose to speak.

'Lords and Ladies of the Sabha, please excuse me for the impertinence of speaking amongst you.'

Everybody turned to the Lord of the People. While he was the youngest member of the Rajya Sabha, he was also the most respected.

'We are looking at this the wrong way. This is not about the war or our allies. This is about being true to the principles of Bhoomidevi.'

Everybody frowned. Bhoomidevi, a mysterious non-Naga lady who had come from the North in the ancient past and established the present way of life of the Nagas, was respected and honoured as a goddess. To question Bhoomidevi's principles was sacrilegious.

'One of her clear guidelines was that a Naga must repay in turn for everything that he receives. This is the only way to clear our karma of sins.'

Most Rajya Sabha members frowned. They didn't understand where the Lord of the People was going with this. The Queen, Karkotak and Suparna, however, smiled softly.

'I would encourage you to look inside your pouches and see how many gold coins in there have the stamp of King Chandraketu. At least three quarters of the gold in our kingdom has come from Branga. They have sent it as allied support. But let us recognise it for what it really is: Advance payment for the medicine.'

The Queen smiled at her nephew. It was his idea to tell King Chandraketu not to send plain gold ingots but coins bearing his stamp, to remind the Nagas of what they received from the Brangas.

'By my simple calculations, we have received enough gold to supply medicines for the next thirty years. If we are to honour Bhoomidevi's principles, I say we have no choice but to keep supplying the medicines to them.'

The Rajya Sabha had no choice. How could they question Bhoomidevi's guidelines?

The motion was passed.

— � symbols —

'My Lord, how do we stop the plague?' asked Chandraketu.

Shiva, Chandraketu, Bhagirath, Parvateshwar, Divodas and Bappiraj were in the king's private chambers in the Brangaridai palace.

'The route will be through the Nagas, Your Highness,' said Shiva. 'I believe they are the cause of the troubles of India. And, your plague. I know that you know where they live. I need to find them.'

Chandraketu stiffened, his melancholic eyes shutting for a bit. He then turned to Bappiraj. 'Please excuse us for a little while, Prime Minister.'

Bappiraj tried to argue. 'But, Your Highness...'

The King narrowed his eyes and continued to stare at his Prime Minister. Bappiraj immediately left the chambers.

Chandraketu went to a side wall, took off a ring from his forefinger and pressed it into an indentation. A small box sprang out of the wall with a soft click. The king picked up a parchment from it and walked back towards Shiva.

'My Lord,' said Chandraketu. 'This is a letter I received from the Queen of the Nagas just a few days back.'

Shiva scowled softly.

'I beg you to hear it with an open mind, My Lord,' said Chandraketu, before lifting the parchment and reading aloud. '*My friend Chandraketu. My apologies for the delay in the delivery of this year's supply of the medicines. The troubles with my Rajya Sabha continue. But whatever the situation, the medicines will be delivered soon. That is my word. Also, I have been informed that a charlatan claiming to be the Neelkanth is coming to your kingdom. I believe he wants to find a way to our land. All that he has to offer you are promises. What you get from us is our medicine. What do you think will keep your people alive? Choose wisely.*'

Chandraketu looked up at Shiva. 'It has the seal of the Naga Queen.'

Shiva did not have an answer.

Divodas spoke up. 'But, Your Highness, I think that the Nagas have cast this spell on us. The plague is their creation. Fight it we must. But to battle it properly, we have to attack the source. Panchavati, the city of the Nagas.'

'Divodas, even if I agree with you, we cannot forget that what keeps us alive is their medicine. Until the plague is stopped we cannot survive without the Nagas.'

'But they are your enemies, Your Highness,' said Bhagirath. 'How can you not seek vengeance for the plague they have wrought upon you?'

'I'm fighting everyday to keep my people alive, Prince Bhagirath. Vengeance is a luxury I cannot afford.'

'It's not about vengeance. It is about justice,' said Parvateshwar.

'No General,' said Chandraketu. 'It is not about

vengeance or justice. It is only about one thing: Keeping my people alive. I am not a fool. I do know that if I give you the route to Panchavati, the Lord will attack it with a massive army. The Nagas will be destroyed. Along with them, their medicine too, thus demolishing the only means to Branga's survival. Unless you can guarantee me another supply source, I cannot tell you where Panchavati lies.'

Shiva stared hard at Chandraketu. Though he didn't like what he was hearing, he knew what the Branga King said was right. He had no choice.

Chandraketu folded his hands together, as though pleading, 'My Lord, you are my leader, my God, my saviour. I believe in your legend. I know you will set everything right. However, while my people may forget the details, I remember the tales of Lord Rudra. I remember that legends take time to fulfil their promise. And time is the only thing my people don't have.'

Shiva sighed. 'You are right, Your Highness. I cannot guarantee supply of the medicines right now. And until I can, I have no right to demand this sacrifice of you.'

Divodas started to say something, but Shiva silenced him with a wave.

'I will take your leave, Your Highness,' said Shiva. 'I need to think.'

Chandraketu fell at Shiva's feet. 'Please don't be angry with me, My Lord. I have no choice.'

Shiva pulled Chandraketu up to his feet. 'I know.'

As Shiva turned to leave, his eyes fell upon the Naga Queen's letter. He stiffened as he saw the seal at the bottom. It was an Aum symbol. But not the standard one. At the meeting point of the top and bottom curve of the Aum were two serpent heads. The third curve, surging out to the East, ended in a sharp serpent head, with its fork tongue struck out threateningly.

Shiva growled softly, 'Is this the Naga Queen's seal?'

'Yes, My Lord,' said Chandraketu.

'Can any Naga man use this seal?'

'No, My Lord. Only the Queen can use it.'

'Tell me the truth. Does any man use this seal?'

'No, My Lord. Nobody.'

'That is not true, Your Highness.'

'My Lord from what I know...' Suddenly Chandraketu stopped. 'Of course, the Lord of the People also uses this seal. He is the only one in the history of the Nagas, besides the ruler, who has been allowed to do so.'

Shiva snarled. 'The Lord of the People? What is his name?'

'I don't know, My Lord.'

Shiva narrowed his eyes.

'I swear on my people, My Lord,' said Chandraketu. 'I don't know. All I know is that his formal title is the Lord of the People.'

— 𑀧𑀦𑀝𑀱𑀟 —

'My Lord,' said Bhagirath. 'We have to insist with King Chandraketu.'

Bhagirath, Parvateshwar and Divodas were sitting in Shiva's private chambers in the Brangaridai palace.

'I agree, My Lord,' said Divodas.

'No,' said Shiva. 'Chandraketu has a point. We have to guarantee the supply of the Naga medicine before we attack Panchavati.'

'But that is impossible, My Lord,' said Parvateshwar. 'Only the Nagas have the medicine. The only way we can get the medicine is if we control the Naga territories. And how can we attack and control the Naga territories if the Branga king does not tell us where Panchavati is?'

Shiva turned to Divodas. 'There must be another way to get the Naga medicine.'

'There is a very bizarre one, My Lord,' said Divodas.

'What?'

'But it's the worst possible way, My Lord.'

'Let me be the judge of that. What is the way?'

'There is a bandit in the forests beyond the Madhumati river.'

'Madhumati?'

'Also a distributary of the Branga, My Lord. To our West.'

'I see.'

'It is rumoured that this bandit knows how to make the Naga medicine. Apparently, he does it with the help of a secret plant he sources from beyond the Mahanadi river, which lies to the South–west.'

'So why doesn't this bandit sell it? After all a bandit should be interested in money.'

'He is a strange bandit, My Lord. It is rumoured that he was born a Brahmin, but has long given up the path of knowledge for violence. Most of us believe he has serious psychological problems. He refuses to make money. He has a pathological hatred for Kshatriyas and kills any warrior who ventures into his territory, even if the poor Kshatriya had just lost his way. And, he refuses to share the Naga medicine with anyone, even for untold amounts of gold, using it only for his gang of criminals.'

Shiva frowned. 'How bizarre.'

'He is a monster, My Lord. Even worse than the Nagas. It is rumoured that he even beheaded his own mother.'

'My God!'

'Yes, My Lord. How do you reason with a madman like that?'

'Is there any other way to get to the Naga medicine?'

'I don't think so.'

'Then our choice is made. We must capture that bandit.'

'What is the name of this bandit, Divodas?' asked Bhagirath.

'Parshuram.'

'Parshuram!' cried Parvateshwar in shock. 'That is the name of the sixth Lord Vishnu who lived thousands of years ago.'

'I know, General,' said Divodas. 'But trust me. This bandit does not have any of the qualities of the great sixth Lord Vishnu.'

Chapter 13

Man-eaters of Icchawar

'Maharishi Bhrigu! Here?' asked a surprised Dilipa.

All the nobles in India knew that Bhrigu was the *raj guru*, the *royal sage* of Meluha and strongly backed the Suryavanshi royalty. His sudden appearance in Ayodhya, therefore, had Dilipa bewildered. But it was also a rare honour, for Bhrigu had never ever visited Dilipa's capital before.

'Yes, My Lord,' said the Swadweepan Prime Minister, Siamantak.

Dilipa immediately rushed to the chambers Siamantak had housed the great sage in. Bhrigu's room, as expected, had been kept cold, severe and damp, just like his Himalayan abode.

Dilipa immediately fell at Bhrigu's feet. 'My Lord Bhrigu, in my city, my palace. What an honour!'

Bhrigu smiled, speaking softly, 'The honour is mine, great Emperor. You are the light of India.'

Dilipa raised his eyebrows, even more surprised. 'What can I do for you, Guruji?'

Bhrigu stared hard at Dilipa. 'I personally need nothing, Your Highness. Everything in the world is *maya*, an *illusion*.

The ultimate truth one has to realise is that we actually need nothing. Because to possess an illusion is as good as possessing nothing.'

Dilipa smiled, not quite understanding what Bhrigu said, but too terrified of disagreeing with the powerful Brahmin.

'How is your health now?' asked Bhrigu.

Dilipa wiped his lips with a damp cotton cloth, absorbing the medicine his royal doctor had applied on it. The Emperor of Swadweep had coughed some blood the previous morning. His doctors had told him that he had but a few months to live. 'Nothing is a secret from you, My Lord.'

Bhrigu nodded, not saying anything.

Dilipa smiled bravely. 'I have no regrets, My Lord. I have lived a full life. I am content.'

'True. How is your son, by the way?'

Dilipa narrowed his eyes. There was no point in lying. This was Maharishi Bhrigu, considered by many to be a *Saptrishi Uttradhikari*, a *successor to the seven sages*. 'Looks like he will not have to kill me. Fate will do his work for him. Anyway, who can fight destiny?'

Bhrigu bent forward. 'Fate controls only the weak, Your Highness. The strong mould the providence they want.'

Dilipa frowned. 'What are you saying, Guruji?'

'How long would you like to live?'

'Is it in my hands?'

'No. In mine.'

Dilipa laughed softly. 'The Somras will have no impact, My Lord. I have smuggled in large amounts from Meluha. I have found out the hard way that it cannot cure diseases.'

'The Somras was the greatest invention of the Saptrishis, Your Highness. But it wasn't the only one.'

'You mean to say that...'

'Yes.'

Dilipa edged back. Breathing quicker. 'And, in return?'

'Just remember your debt.'

'If you give me this blessing, Guruji, I will be forever indebted to you.'

'Not to me,' said Bhrigu. 'Remain indebted to India. And, I shall remind you when the time comes for you to serve your country.'

Dilipa nodded.

— ⚲⦾⨄⚶⊕ —

A few days later, a single ship bearing Shiva, Bhagirath, Parvateshwar, Anandmayi, Divodas, Drapaku, Purvaka, Nandi and Veerbhadra set off up the Padma. With them were around five hundred men, half the brigade that had set off from Kashi. Only the Suryavanshis. Shiva needed disciplined warriors to take on the fearsome bandit and his gang. He suspected that too large an army might hinder his attempt at drawing the brigand out. Four vessels and the five hundred Chandravanshis had been left behind to savour Brangaridai hospitality.

Of course, Ayurvati was also on the ship. Her medical skills were certainly needed, especially since Divodas had warned of a bloody confrontation.

After a few days of sailing, the ship reached the part of the Branga river where the Madhumati broke off. They swept down the Madhumati, the western-most edge of the Branga country and its most sparsely populated areas. The land became more wild, with dense forests on both banks.

'A perfect place for a bandit,' said Shiva.

'Yes, My Lord,' nodded Drapaku. 'This land is close enough to civilisation to mount raids. And yet, dense and impenetrable enough to hide quickly. I can imagine why the Brangas have had trouble arresting this man.'

'We need him alive, Drapaku. We need the conduit to the Naga medicine.'

'I know, My Lord. General Parvateshwar has already issued those instructions to us.'

Shiva nodded. The dolphins were dancing upon the waters. Birds chirped in the dense sundari trees. A large tiger lounged lazily along one bank. It was a picturesque scene of natural bounty, every animal enjoying the gifts of the Brahmaputra and Ganga.

'It is a beautiful land, My Lord,' said Drapaku.

Shiva didn't answer. He continued to stare hard at the banks.

'My Lord,' said Drapaku. 'Did you see something?'

'We're being watched. I can feel it. We're being watched.'

— 人◎ᠸ�Ϟ⊕ —

Ever since her trespass into the Eastern palace, Sati's relationship with Athithigva had deepened considerably, almost to a filial level. Shared secrets have a way of creating bonds. Sati had remained true to her word, not whispering to a soul about Maya. Not even to Krittika.

Athithigva routinely sought Sati's advice on matters of state, however inconsequential. Sati's counsel was always wise, bringing some order and control to the Chandravanshi penchant for unbridled freedom and chaos.

The problem this time around, however, was a knotty one.

'How can just three lions cause so much chaos?' asked Sati.

Athithigva had just told her about the most recent plea for help from the villagers of Icchawar. They had been living under a mortal threat of man-eating lions for many months. Representations had been coming to Kashi for a long time. Kashi had in turn requested Ayodhya, as the overlord of Swadweep, to come to its aid. Chandravanshi bureaucrats had so far been arguing over the terms of the Ashwamedh treaty; the main stalemate being on how the vow of protection made by Ayodhya did not cover animal attacks. Kashi, of course, had no warrior of note to lead them against even a few lions.

'What do we do, My Lady?'

'But you had sent a platoon of Kashi police a month back, right?'

'Yes, My Lady,' said Athithigva. 'They tried their best, having devised a brilliant plan to trap the lions, using the villagers to create commotion with their drums in order to drive the lions to a well-covered ditch with giant spikes in it. But to their surprise, most of the lions seemed to have escaped and attacked a school where the village children had been huddled for safe-keeping.'

Sati suppressed a gasp of shock.

Athithigva, with tears in his eyes, whispered, 'Five children were killed.'

'Lord Ram be merciful,' whispered Sati.

'The beasts didn't even drag the children's bodies away. Maybe they wanted vengeance for the single lion killed when he fell into the trap.'

'They are not humans, Your Highness,' said Sati, irritated. 'They do not feel anger or the need for vengeance. Animals kill for only two reasons: hunger or self-defence.'

But why would they kill and then leave the bodies there?

'Is there more to this than meets the eye?' asked Sati.

'I don't know, My Lady. I'm not sure.'

'Where are your men?'

'They are still in Icchawar. But the villagers are preventing them from mounting any more traps. They are saying that their own lives are in greater danger when the lions are lured. They want my police to venture into the jungle and hunt the lions down.'

'Which they don't want to do?'

'It's not that they don't want to, My Lady. They don't know *how* to. They're citizens of Kashi. We don't hunt.'

Sati sighed.

'But they are willing to fight,' said Athithigva.

'I'll go,' said Sati.

'Of course not, My Lady,' said Athithigva. 'That's not what I wanted from you. I only wanted you to send word to Emperor Dilipa for help. He cannot refuse you.'

'That would take forever, Your Highness. I know how the Swadweepan bureaucracy works. And your people will keep dying. I'll go. Assign two platoons of the Kashi police to travel with me.'

Sixty soldiers, forty travelling with me and another twenty already in Icchawar. That should do.

Athithigva did not want Sati to venture into the forest. He had come to love her as his sister. 'My Lady, I can't bear to see anything...'

'Nothing will happen to me,' interrupted Sati. 'Now assign two Kashi platoons. Sixty men ought to be enough against two lions. I want the joint platoon led by that man who helped General Parvateshwar protect the Brangas. His name was Kaavas, right?'

Athithigva nodded. 'My Lady, please don't think I'm unsure about your abilities... But you are like a sister to me. I cannot allow you to put yourself in danger like this. I don't think you should go.'

'And I think I must go. Innocents are being killed. Lord Ram would not allow me to stay here. Either I can leave Kashi alone, or with forty soldiers. Which option would you prefer?'

— 人◎∪�⊕ —

The ship was sailing slowly along the Madhumati. There had been no attack from Parshuram. No devil boats to set Shiva's ship on fire. No arrows to injure the lookouts. Nothing.

Parvateshwar and Anandmayi were standing against the balustrade at the stern of the ship, staring at the reflection of the sun rising gently in the sluggish Madhumati.

'The Lord is right,' said Parvateshwar. 'They are watching us. I can feel it. It irritates me.'

'Really?' smiled Anandmayi. 'I have had people staring at me all my life. It's never irritated me!'

Parvateshwar turned to Anandmayi as if trying to explain his point. Then, as he understood the pun, he smiled.

'By Lord Indra!' exclaimed Anandmayi. 'I got you to smile! What an achievement!'

Parvateshwar smiled even more broadly. 'Yes, well, I was only talking about why the bandits were not attacking...'

'Now don't spoil the moment,' said Anandmayi. She slapped Parvateshwar's wrist with the back of her hand. 'You know you look very nice when you smile. You should do so more often.'

Parvateshwar blushed.

'And you look even better when you blush,' laughed Anandmayi.

Parvateshwar blushed even deeper. 'Your Highness...'

'Anandmayi.'

'Sorry?'

'Call me Anandmayi.'

'How can I?'

'Very simple. Just say Anandmayi.'

Parvateshwar kept quiet.

'Why can't you call me Anandmayi?'

'I can't, Your Highness. It is not correct.'

Anandmayi sighed. 'Tell me Parvateshwar. Who exactly defines what is correct?'

Parvateshwar frowned. 'Lord Ram's laws.'

'And, what was Lord Ram's fundamental law on punishment for a crime?'

'Not even one innocent man should be punished. Not even one criminal must get away.'

'Then you are breaking his laws.'

Parvateshwar frowned. 'How so?'

'By punishing an innocent person for a crime she didn't commit.'

Parvateshwar continued to frown.

'Many noblemen committed a crime by breaking Lord Ram's law two hundred and fifty years ago. They got away with the crime. Nobody punished them. And, look at me. I had nothing to do with that crime. I wasn't even born then. And yet, you are punishing me today for it.'

'I am not punishing you, Your Highness. How can I?'

'Yes, you are. You know you are. I know how you feel. I

am not blind. Don't pretend to be deliberately stupid. It's insulting.'

'Your Highness...'

'What would Lord Ram have told you to do?' interrupted Anandmayi.

Parvateshwar clenched his fist. He looked down, sighing deeply. 'Anandmayi. Please understand. Even if I want to, I can't...'

Just then Drapaku marched up. 'My Lord, the Lord Neelkanth requests your presence.'

Parvateshwar stood rooted to his spot. Still staring at Anandmayi.

'My Lord...,' repeated Drapaku.

Parvateshwar whispered. 'Forgive me, Your Highness. I will speak with you later.'

The Meluhan General turned and marched away, followed by Drapaku.

Anandmayi hissed at Drapaku's retreating form. 'Impeccable timing!'

— ᝐⵔꭍⵏ⊕ —

'Do you have to go, My Lady?' asked Krittika, gently rocking a sleeping Kartik.

Sati looked at Krittika, bemused. 'There are innocents dying, Krittika. Do I have a choice?'

Krittika nodded before looking at Kartik.

'My son will understand,' said Sati. 'He would do the same. I am a Kshatriya. It is my dharma to protect the weak. Dharma comes before anything else.'

Krittika took a deep breath and whispered, 'I agree, My Lady.'

Sati gently ran her hand across Kartik's face. 'I need you to take good care of him. He is my life. I have never known the pleasures of motherhood. I never imagined there would be another person I would love as deeply as I love Shiva. But in such a short span of time, Kartik...'

Krittika looked at Sati with a smile, touching the Princess' hand. 'I will take care of him. He's my life as well.'

The Naga Lord of the People was kneeling in the cold

— 大◎Ｕ♀⊕ —

waters of the Chambal river. He scooped some water in the palm of his hands and allowed it to pour slowly, mumbling quietly. He then brushed his hands across his face.

The Queen, kneeling next to him, raised an eyebrow. 'A prayer?'

'I don't know if prayers will help. I don't think anybody up there is really interested in me.'

The Queen smiled and looked back at the river.

'But there are times when you wouldn't mind the help of the Almighty,' whispered the Naga.

The Queen turned towards him and nodded. Getting up slowly, she put the mask back on her face. 'I've received a report that she has left Kashi and is riding towards Icchawar.'

The Naga breathed deeply. He rose slowly and put the mask back on his face.

'She rides with only forty soldiers.'

The Naga's breathing picked up pace. At a distance, Vishwadyumna was sitting quietly with a hundred Branga soldiers. This could be the moment. Capturing her in a teeming city of two hundred thousand was well nigh impossible. The remoteness of Icchawar improved the odds dramatically. And they finally had the advantage of numbers. The Naga slowly brought his breathing back to normal. Trying to keep his voice calm, he whispered, 'That is good news.'

The Queen smiled and patted the Naga gently on his shoulder. 'Don't be nervous, my child. You are not alone. I am with you. Every step of the way.'

The Naga nodded. His eyes narrowed.

It was just the beginning of the second prahar when

— 人◎Ⅳↄ⊕ —

Sati rode into Icchawar at the head of her platoon, with Kaavas by her side. She was shocked to see a massive pyre at the far end of the village. She rode hard, followed by her men.

A man rushed up, breathless and panic-stricken, waving. 'Please leave! Please leave!'

Sati ignored him and kept riding up to the giant pyre.

'You cannot ignore me! I am the Headman of Icchawar!'

Sati noticed the faces of the villagers. Every single one had terror writ large on his face.

'Things have only gotten worse since you people came!' shouted the Headman.

Sati noticed the Brahmin who had just finished the puja at the pyre, praying for the safety of the departed souls. He was the only one who seemed to be in control.

Sati rode up to him. 'Where are the Kashi soldiers?'

The Brahmin pointed at the giant pyre. 'In there.'

'All twenty of them?' asked a stunned Sati.

The Brahmin nodded. 'They were killed by the lions last

night. Just like our villagers here, your soldiers didn't know what they were doing.'

Sati looked around the pyre. It was an open area, a little outside the village, which opened straight into the forest. To the far left were some blankets and the remnants of a camp fire. There was blood all over that area.

'Did they sleep here?' asked Sati in horror.

The Brahmin nodded.

'This is a suicide zone with man-eating lions around! Why in Lord Ram's name did they sleep here at night?'

The Brahmin looked at the Headman.

'It was their decision!' said the Headman defensively.

'Don't lie,' said the Brahmin. 'It wasn't solely their decision.'

'Don't you dare call me a liar, Suryaksh!' said the Headman. 'I told them their presence in any house only attracts the lions and leads to deaths. The decision to not stay in any house was their own!'

'You actually think the lions are interested only in the soldiers?' asked Suryaksh. 'You are wrong.'

Sati had stopped listening. She was surveying the area where the Kashi soldiers had been killed. Despite the immense amounts of blood and gore, she could clearly make out the tracks of some lions and maybe lionesses. There were at least seven distinct marks. The information they had was clearly wrong. She turned around and growled. 'How many lions are here?'

'Two,' said the Headman. 'We've never seen more than two lions. The third lion was killed in a trap.'

Sati ignored him and looked at Suryaksh. The Brahmin responded, 'Judging from the tracks, at least five to seven.'

Sati nodded. Suryaksh was the only one who appeared

to know what he was talking about. Turning towards the village, Sati told Suryaksh, 'Come with me.'

Seven. That means five lionesses at least. A standard pride. But counting the one that died, there were three lions in this pride? That is strange. There is usually just one adult male in a pride. Something isn't right!

'He is smarter than we have been told,' said Shiva.

— ⸸⍟ᛟ♀⊕ —

'Every ruse we have tried for weeks has failed.'

The sun was directly overhead. The ship was anchored close to a beach. Due to the heavy silt it carried, which settled and turned into natural dams, the Madhumati kept changing course all the time. The result was that there were many recently formed sandbanks along the current course of the river. These were areas clear of vegetation, which afforded enough open space for a fierce battle to be fought. Shiva had held the ship close to one such beach, firing arrows into the trees, hoping Parshuram would be goaded into coming out in the open. The plan had not succeeded so far.

'Yes, My Lord,' agreed Parvateshwar. 'He will not be provoked into attacking out of blind hatred.'

Shiva stared hard at the river bank.

'I think it is the ship,' said Parvateshwar.

'Yes, he cannot judge how many men we have.'

Parvateshwar agreed. 'My Lord, we have to take more risks to lure him out.'

'I have a plan,' Shiva whispered softly. 'Further ahead is another beach. I plan to go ashore with a hundred men. Once I've taken the soldiers deep inside the forest, the ship should turn back, giving Parshuram the impression that there is dissension in the ranks. That the vessel is deserting us and departing for Branga. I'll continue into the jungle and flush him out onto the beach. When I have him there, I'll send out a fire arrow as a signal.'

'Then Bhagirath can quickly get the ship over there, pull down the cutters and land on the beach with four hundred men, overwhelming them. Just two key things to remember, My Lord. They must be with their backs to the river. So that they can't escape when the cutters arrive. And of course, the ship must not depend only on the sails, but rowers as well. Speed will be of the essence.'

Shiva smiled. 'Exactly. Just one more thing. It will not be us on the beach. Only me. I need you on the ship.'

'My Lord!' cried Parvateshwar. 'I cannot let you take that risk.'

'Parvateshwar, I will lure the bastard out. But I need you watching my back. If the cutters don't come on time, we will be slaughtered. We will be trying to capture, not kill. He will show no such restraint.'

'But My Lord...' said Parvateshwar.

'I have decided, Parvateshwar. I need you on the ship. I can trust only you. Tomorrow is the day.'

'This is where we'll camp,' said Sati, pointing to the

— ⋏◉⎁⚛⊕ —

school building, the only unoccupied structure in Icchawar. It had no doors and could not be barricaded against the lions. But it had a terrace, with one defendable flight of stairs leading up.

It was halfway through the third prahar. Nightfall,

the favourite time for lions to attack, was just a few hours away. The villagers had all retired and barricaded themselves inside their homes. The massacre of the Kashi soldiers the night before had shaken all of them. Perhaps the Headman was right they thought. The presence of the Kashi soldiers was bad luck.

The Headman walked behind Sati, trailed by Suryaksh. 'You must leave. The presence of the foreigners is angering the spirits.'

Sati ignored him and turned to Kaavas. 'Station our men on the terrace. Pull the horses up as well.'

Kaavas nodded and rushed to carry out the orders.

The Headman continued, 'Look, they were only killing animals earlier. Now they're killing humans as well. All because of your soldiers. Just leave and the spirits will be calmed.'

Sati turned towards the Headman. 'They have tasted human blood. There is no escape. Either you abandon the village or we have to stay here and protect you till all the lions are killed. My advice is you gather all the villagers and we leave tomorrow morning.'

'We cannot abandon our motherland!'

'I will not allow you to condemn your people to death. I will leave tomorrow and I am taking your people as well. What you do for yourself is up to you.'

'My people are not going to desert Icchawar. Never!'

Suryaksh spoke up. 'If the villagers had listened to me, we would have left a long time back! And this suffering would never have happened.'

'If you were half the priest your father was,' snapped the Headman, 'you would have conjured up a puja to calm the spirits and drive the lions away.'

'Pujas will not drive them away, you fool! Can't you smell

it? The lions have marked this land. They think our village is their territory. There are only two options now. Fight or flee. We obviously don't want to fight. We have to flee.'

'Enough!' said Sati, irritated. 'No wonder the lions got the better of you. Go home. We'll meet tomorrow.'

Sati walked up the steps of the school. She was happy to note a large pile of kindling half-way up the steps. She jumped over it and continued climbing. As she entered the terrace, she saw a massive pile of firewood to the left.

She turned toward Kaavas. 'Enough to last the night?'

'Yes, My Lady.'

Sati scanned the forest and whispered, 'Light the fire on the staircase as soon as the sun goes down.'

She stared up ahead to see a goat tied at the spot where the lions had killed the Kashi soldiers. It was a clear shot from her elevated position. She anticipated that she would be able to fire arrows upon at least a few lions. Hoping the bait would work, Sati settled down on the terrace and waited.

Chapter 14

The Battle of Madhumati

Shiva, Parvateshwar, Bhagirath, Drapaku and Divodas were seated aft on the ship. The moon was absent, cloaking the entire area in darkness. The quietness of the jungle, except for the incessant beating of crickets, automatically made them speak softly.

'The problem is how do we make him believe that there is a rebellion and he has to fight only one hundred men, not the entire crew,' whispered Shiva.

'His spies would be watching us all the time,' murmured Divodas. 'It has to be a believable act. We can't let our guard down for even a minute.'

Shiva suddenly started. Motioning with his hands for everyone to keep talking, he slowly rose and crawled to the rail of the ship, picking his bow quietly, stealthily placing an arrow. And then, quick as lightening, he rose above the railing and shot the arrow. There was a loud scream of pain as one of the brigand's men, swimming towards the ship, was hit.

'COME OUT YOU COWARD!' yelled Shiva. 'FIGHT LIKE A MAN!'

There was commotion in the jungle as animals shrieked at

the sudden disturbance. Birds fluttered loudly. Hyenas howled, tigers roared, deer bleated. There was some splashing in the river. Someone possibly trying to rescue an injured comrade. Shiva thought he heard the sound of foliage breaking as someone or something broke through and retreated.

As his followers rushed up, Shiva whispered, 'It wasn't a kill wound. We need Parshuram alive. Remember. It makes our task tougher. But we need him alive.'

And then they heard a strong voice from the jungle. 'WHY DON'T YOU GET OUT OF THE SHIP, YOU SPINELESS WIMP? AND I'LL SHOW YOU HOW A MAN FIGHTS!'

Shiva smiled. 'This is going to be interesting.'

— 人◎U➞⊕ —

Sati woke up with a start. Not due to some sudden noise. But because the noise had stopped.

She looked towards the left. The flames were burning strong. Two men with swords drawn were at the top of the stairs, supervising the fire.

'More wood,' whispered Sati.

One of the soldiers immediately crept to the stack of firewood and dropped some more onto the raging fire in the middle of the staircase. Meanwhile, Sati tiptoed to the parapet. The goat had been bleating desperately all night. But no more.

She looked gingerly over the railing. The night had thrown a pitch-black shroud all around. But the flames of the school fire spread a bit of glow. The goat was still there. It wasn't standing anymore. Its hind legs had collapsed. And it was shivering desperately.

'Are they here, My Lady?' asked Kaavas, crawling quietly to Sati.

'Yes,' whispered Sati.

They heard a soft, deep roar. A sound which would terrorise any living creature in the jungle. Kaavas quickly woke the rest of the platoon, who drew their swords and crawled to the doorway at the end of the staircase, to defend the one passage from where the lions could charge up. Sati kept staring at the goat. Then she heard the sound of something being dragged softly.

She strained her eyes. One. Two. Three. Four. It wasn't their full pride. The fourth lion seemed to be dragging something.

'Oh Lord,' whispered Sati in horror.

The body being dragged was that of Suryaksh, the village Brahmin. His hand was moving a little. He was still alive. But barely so.

The largest lion, obviously the leader of the pack, came into full view. It was abnormally massive. The largest Sati had ever seen. And yet the mane was not dense. It was clearly an adolescent. Not more than a year old perhaps.

Then a troubling thought struck Sati. She stared at the lead animal's skin. It had the stripes of a tiger. It wasn't an adolescent at all! She gasped in shock. 'Liger!'

'What?' whispered Kaavas.

'A rare animal. The offspring of a lion and a tigress. It grows almost twice as big as its parents. And has many times their ferocity.'

The liger sauntered up to the goat. The goat's front legs too buckled, as it collapsed onto the ground in terror, waiting for its imminent death. But the liger didn't strike out. He just walked around the goat, whipping it with his tail. He was toying with the bait.

The lion dragging Suryaksh dropped the body and bent to bite into the Brahmin's leg. Suryaksh should have screamed in pain. But his neck was bleeding profusely. He simply didn't have the strength. The liger suddenly growled at the lion who was chewing Suryaksh's leg. The lion growled back, but retreated. The liger clearly didn't want Suryaksh eaten just as yet.

The liger is a recent leader. The other lion still seems to have the strength to at least protest.

Followed by the lionesses, the liger walked back to the goat, lifted his hind leg and urinated around the area, marking his territory again. Then he roared. Loud and strong.

The message was clear. This was his territory. Anyone in it was fair game.

Sati reached silently for her bow. The aggression of the pride would be cut if the liger was dead. She softly loaded an arrow and aimed. Unfortunately, just as she released the arrow, the liger stumbled on Suryaksh's body. The arrow flew past him and rammed deep into the eye of the lioness behind. She snarled in pain and ran into the forest. So did the others. But the liger turned around, baring his teeth ferociously at this intrusion, growling. He reached out with his paw and struck Suryaksh hard across the face. A fatal blow. Sati reloaded and fired again. This one hit the liger on his shoulder. The liger roared and retreated.

'The lioness will be dead soon,' said Sati.

'But the liger will come back,' said Kaavas. 'Angrier than ever. We better leave tomorrow with the villagers.'

Sati nodded.

— ⚹⦶∪⋔⊕ —

The sun had just broken through the night.

'You must leave. You have no choice,' said Sati. She couldn't believe she had to argue with the villagers about what was blatantly obvious.

It was the beginning of the second prahar. They were standing next to the pyre consuming Suryaksh's body. Sadly, there was nobody to say prayers for his brave soul.

'They will not come back,' said one villager. 'What the Headman says is right. The lions will not come back.'

'What nonsense!' argued Sati. 'The liger has marked his territory. You either kill him or leave this place. There is no third option. He cannot let you have a free run in this land. He will lose control over his pride.'

A village woman stepped up to argue. 'The spirits have been partially appeased by the blood of Suryaksh. At the most we will have to make one more sacrifice and they will leave.'

'One more sacrifice?' asked a flabbergasted Sati.

'Yes,' said the headman. 'The village cleaner is willing to sacrifice himself and his family for the good of the rest of the village.'

Sati turned to see a thin, wiry little man, who also had the onerous task of collecting firewood and cremating the dead over the last few days. Behind him stood his equally puny wife, with a look of utter determination on her face. Holding onto her *dhoti* were two little children, no older than two or three, wearing nothing but torn loincloths, unaware of the fate chosen for them by their parents.

Sati turned towards the Headman, fists clenched. 'You are sacrificing this poor man and his family because he is the most powerless! This is wrong!'

'No, My Lady,' said the cleaner. 'This is my choice. My fate. I have been born low in this birth because of my past life karma. My family and I will sacrifice ourselves willingly for the good of the village. The Almighty will see our good deed and bless us in our next birth.'

'I admire your bravery,' said Sati. 'But this will not stop the lions. They will not stop till all of you are either driven out or killed.'

'Our blood will satisfy them, My Lady. The headman has told me so. I am sure of this.'

Sati stared hard at the cleaner. Blind superstition can never be won over by logic. She looked down at his children. They were poking each other and laughing uproariously. They suddenly stopped and looked up at her. Surprised. Wondering why this foreign woman was staring at them.

I can't let this happen.

'I will stay here. I will stay till every lion has been killed. But you will not sacrifice yourself. Or your family. Is that clear?'

The cleaner stared at Sati, confused at what to him seemed a strange suggestion. Sati turned towards Kaavas. He immediately started leading the soldiers back to the school. Some of them were arguing, clearly unhappy at this turn of events.

— 𑀆𑀑𑀝𑀪𑀔 —

The spies of Parshuram, high in the trees, were watching

attentively. Shiva and Bhagirath were on the deck. They appeared to be arguing. Three cutters, lowered from the ship onto the Madhumati, were bobbing gently.

Finally, Shiva made an angry gesture and started climbing down onto his cutter, which had Drapaku, Nandi, Veerbhadra and thirty soldiers. He looked at two more cutters behind them, full of soldiers. Shiva gave a signal and they started rowing towards the bank.

The ship on the other hand appeared to be preparing to pull anchor.

One spy looked at the other with a smile. 'A hundred soldiers. Let's go tell Lord Parshuram.'

— ⚔ ◎ � ⚙ —

The rich waters of the Madhumati and the fertile soil of Branga had conspired to grow a jungle of ferocious density. Shiva looked up at the sky. A little bit of sunshine pierced through the dense foliage. The direction of the rays told Shiva that the sun had already begun its downward journey.

His platoon had hacked through the almost impenetrable forest for a good eight hours, tracking the movements of the brigand. Shiva had broken for lunch two hours earlier. Though physically satiated, his soldiers were getting restless, waiting for action. Parshuram seemed to be avoiding battle even here.

Suddenly Shiva raised his hand. The platoon halted. Drapaku slipped up to Shiva and whispered, 'What is it, My Lord?'

Shiva pointed with his eyes and whispered, 'This territory has been marked.'

Drapaku stared, confused.

'See the cut on this bush,' said Shiva.

Drapaku stared harder. 'They have passed through here. This route has been hacked.'

'No,' said Shiva, looking ahead, 'This hasn't been hacked to walk through. It has been cut from the right side to make us think they have walked through here. There is a trap straight ahead.'

'Are you sure, My Lord?' asked Drapaku, noticing Shiva reach slowly for his bow.

Shiva suddenly turned around, pulling an arrow simultaneously and loading it onto his bow. He fired it immediately onto the top of one of the trees. There was a loud noise as an injured man came crashing down.

'This way!' said Shiva, running hard to the right.

The soldiers followed, desperately keeping pace with their charging Lord. They ran hard for what must have been a few minutes. Shiva suddenly emerged onto a beach. And stopped dead.

Standing in front, at a distance of around one hundred metres, was Parshuram with his gang. There were at least one hundred men, an equal match for the Suryavanshis. Shiva's soldiers kept running out of the jungle in a single file and started getting into formation quickly on the beach.

'I'll wait!' said Parshuram sarcastically, his gaze locked onto Shiva. 'Get your men into position.'

Shiva stared right back. Parshuram was a powerful man. Though a little shorter than Shiva, he was ridiculously muscled. His shoulders spread wide, his barrel chest heaving. In his left hand was a mighty bow, much too big for any man. But clearly, his powerful arms had enough strength to pull the string clean. On his back was a quiver full of arrows. But slung the other way was the weapon that had made him famous. The weapon he used to decapitate his hapless victims. His battleaxe. He wore a simple saffron *dhoti*, but no armour. In a sign of his Brahmin antecedents, Parshuram's head was shaved clean except for a neat tuft of hair tied at the back and a *janau* thread tied loosely down from his left shoulder across his torso to his right. His face bore a long, mighty beard.

Shiva looked to his side, waiting for all his soldiers to get into line. He sniffed.

What is that?

It seemed like the paraffin used by the Meluhans to light their prahar lamps. He looked down. The sand was clean. His men were safe. Shiva drew his sword and bellowed. 'Surrender now, Parshuram. And you shall get justice.'

Parshuram burst into laughter. 'Justice?! In this wretched land?'

Shiva turned his eyes to his sides. His men were in position. Ready. 'You can either bow your head towards justice. Or you can feel its flames bear down on you! What do you want?'

Parshuram sniggered and nodded at one of his men. The man raised an arrow, touched it to a flame, and shot the burning arrow high into the air, way beyond the range of the Suryavanshis.

What the hell?

Shiva lost sight of the arrow in the light of the sun for a moment. It landed quite some distance behind Shiva's men, and immediately set off the paraffin lying there. The flames spread quickly, making an impenetrable border. The Suryavanshis were trapped on the beach. No retreat was possible.

'You're wasting your arrows, you idiot!' shouted Shiva. 'Nobody is retreating from here!'

Parshuram smiled. 'I am going to enjoy killing you.'

To Shiva's surprise, Parshuram's archer turned around, lit another arrow and shot it towards the river.

Shit!

Parshuram's men had tied thin canoes, touching each other, across the bend of the river arching the beach. Full of large quantities of paraffin, these boats immediately burst into flames as the fiery arrow hit one of them. The massive blaze made it appear like the entire river was on fire. The inferno reached high, making it almost impossible for Parvateshwar's back-up cutters to row through.

Parshuram looked towards Shiva with a chilling sneer. 'Let's keep our merriment to ourselves, shall we?'

Shiva turned and nodded at Drapaku, who immediately passed an order. An arrow shot up high into the sky and burst into blue flames. Parvateshwar had been summoned. But Shiva didn't see how the Meluhan General would be able to get through the wall of fire on the Madhumati. Small cutters couldn't slip through. And the ship itself could not come so close to the banks as it would run aground.

Nobody's coming. We have to finish this ourselves.

'This is your last chance, barbarian!' screamed Shiva, pointing forward with his sword.

Parshuram dropped his bow. So did every archer at his command, drawing their *anga* weapons out. Parshuram pulled his battleaxe out. He clearly wanted brutal close combat. 'No, Brangan! It was your last chance. I'm going to make your end slow and painful.'

Shiva dropped his bow and drew his shield forward.

And spoke to his soldiers. 'On guard! Go for their sword arms. Injure, don't kill. We want them alive.'

The Suryavanshis pulled their shields forward and drew their swords. And waited.

Parshuram charged. Followed by his vicious horde.

The bandits ran into Shiva's men with surprising speed and agility, Parshuram racing in the lead. He had no shield to protect himself. His heavy battleaxe required both arms to wield. He was charging straight at Shiva. However, Drapaku swung to his left and charged. The bandit was momentarily surprised by Drapaku's charge. He swerved back to avoid the sword and with the same smooth motion, brought his battleaxe up in a brutal swing. Drapaku pushed out the shield fixed on the hook on his amputated left hand to defend himself. The formidable axe severed through a part of the hide-covered bronze shield. A stunned Drapaku swung his shield back, bringing his sword down, glancing a swerving Parshuram's left shoulder.

Meanwhile Shiva pirouetted smartly to avoid a vicious stab from one of the bandits, pushing the sword away with his shield. As the bandit lost balance, Shiva swung his sword down in a smooth arc, severing his enemy's sword arm from the elbow. The thug fell down. Incapacitated, but alive. Shiva immediately turned and pulled his sword up to deflect a strike from another man.

Nandi, pulling his sword out from the right shoulder of an enemy, pushed him down with his shield, hoping the brigand would remain down and surrender. To Nandi's surprise and admiration, the bandit dropped his shield, smoothly transferring his sword to his uninjured left hand, and jumped into the fray again. Nandi pulled his shield forward to prevent the sword strike and pushed his sword in once again into the injured right shoulder of the thug, shouting over the din, 'Surrender, you fool!'

Veerbhadra, however, was not having much luck keeping his enemies alive. He had already killed two and was trying desperately to avoid killing a very determined third. Ignoring his injured sword arm, the bandit had picked up his sword with his left hand. An exasperated Veerbhadra swung down hard with his shield on the brigand's head, hoping to knock the man out. The thug arched his shoulder, taking the blow on it while swinging his sword in a brutal cut at Veerbhadra. The sword slashed Veerbhadra across his torso. Enraged, he thrust his sword straight at the exposed flank of the bandit, driving the blade through his heart.

'Dammit!' screamed a frustrated Veerbhadra. 'Why didn't you just surrender?'

In another corner of the battlefield, Shiva swung his shield sideward at the outlaw he was combating. The brigand swung his head back, getting a slash across his face but preventing a knockout blow.

Shiva was now getting worried. Too many people were getting killed, mostly on Parshuram's side. He wanted them alive. Or the secret of the Naga medicine would be lost. Then he heard a loud sound. It was Parvateshwar's conch shell.

They're coming!

Brutally stabbing his enemy, Shiva also rammed his shield onto the bandit's head again, this time successfully knocking him cold. Then he looked up and smiled.

The massive Suryavanshi ship burst through the flaming canoes, running aground onto the beach, its hull cracking.

The flames on the Madhumati were high for a cutter, but not high enough for a large ship. Parshuram had banked on the idea that the Suryavanshis would not ground their ship as this would mean that they would have no way of returning to Branga. He had, however, miscalculated the determination of the Suryavanshi troops as well as the valour of their General, Parvateshwar.

The ship rammed through many of Parshuram's men, killing them instantly.

Parvateshwar, standing at the bow, jumped down as soon as the ship hit the sandbank. The rope tied around his waist broke his fall from the great height. As he swung close to the ground, Parvateshwar slashed his sword above him, cutting the rope neatly and landing free. Four hundred Suryavanshis followed their General into battle.

Drapaku had been momentarily distracted by the sight of the ship. As he swung his sword at Parshuram's axe, he failed to notice the bandit pull out a knife from behind. Parshuram brought up his left hand in a smooth action, thrusting the knife into Drapaku's neck. Pain immobilised the Suryavanshi Brigadier momentarily. Parshuram rammed the knife in brutally, right up to the hilt. Drapaku staggered back, bravely retaining his hold on his sword.

Meanwhile, the Suryavanshis, outnumbering Parshuram's men five times over, were rapidly taking control of the situation. Many brigands were surrendering, finally seeing the futility of their situation.

At the centre of the battle, Parshuram released the knife from a tottering Drapaku's neck. He gripped his battleaxe with both hands, pulled back and swung viciously. The axe rammed hard into Drapaku's torso, smashing through his hide and bronze armour. It struck deep, breaking through skin and flesh, right down to the bone. The mighty Suryavanshi Brigadier fell to the ground. Parshuram tried to pull the axe away, but it was stuck. He yanked hard. Ripping Drapaku's chest, the axe finally came out. Much to Parshuram's admiration, the Suryavanshi was still alive. The Brigadier tried to raise his drastically weakened sword arm, still attempting to fight.

Parshuram stepped forward and pinned Drapaku's arm down. He could feel the weakened motions of the Brigadier's limb. Attempts by a dying man to not give up the fight, the sword still held tight. Parshuram was awed. He had never needed more than one clear blow with his battleaxe to kill his opponents. His soldiers were rapidly losing the battle, but he didn't seem to notice. His eyes were transfixed upon the magnificent man dying at his feet.

Parshuram bowed his head slightly and whispered, 'It is an honour to slay you.'

The brigand raised his axe, ready for the decapitation strike. At the same instant, Anandmayi flung her knife from a distance. It pierced straight through Parshuram's left hand, causing the axe to fall safely away. Bhagirath, with the help of Divodas and two Suryavanshi soldiers, wrestled Parshuram to the ground without any further injury to the bandit.

Shiva and Parvateshwar ran to Drapaku. He was bleeding profusely, barely alive.

Shiva turned back and shouted, 'Get Ayurvati! Quickly!'

— ⵣⵙⵝⵃⵯ —

The sun still had a few hours of life left. Sati was on the school terrace, supervising the making of improvised bows and arrows. The Kashi soldiers were simply incapable of taking on the lions from close quarters. Neither were they skilled at shooting arrows. Sati was hoping that as long as they fired some in the general direction, the arrows might find their mark.

Sati double-checked the pile of wood near the staircase. The soldiers had replenished the stock and it appeared as though they would be able to last the night without running out.

She hoped to kill some members of the pride from the safety of the terrace. If fortune favoured her, she hoped to kill the liger and finish the key source of the menace. A few days of watch thereafter might solve the problem once and for all. After all, there were only seven animals. Not a very large pride.

She looked up at the sky, praying softly that nothing would go wrong.

Chapter 15

The Lord of the People

The sun was rapidly descending into the horizon, the twilit sky a vibrant ochre. The Suryavanshi camp was a hub of feverish activity.

Bhagirath was supervising the key task of the securing of the prisoners. Using bronze chains from the ship, Parshuram's men had been tied up, hand and foot, and forced to squat in a line in the centre of the sandbank. The chains had been hammered into stakes deep in the ground. As if that wasn't enough, another chain ran through their anklets, effectively binding them to each other. The Suryavanshi soldiers were stationed all around the prisoners. They would maintain a constant vigil. Escape was impossible for Parshuram and his men.

Divodas walked up to Bhagirath. 'Your Highness, I've inspected the ship.'

'And?'

'It will take at least six months to repair.'

Bhagirath cursed. 'How the hell do we get back?'

At the other end of the beach, ayuralay tents had been set up. Ayurvati and her medical unit were working desperately to save as many as they could, both the Suryavanshis and the bandits. They would succeed with most. But Ayurvati was presently in a tent where there was no hope.

Shiva was on his knees, holding Drapaku's hand. Ayurvati knew nothing could be done. The injuries were too deep. She stood at the back, with Nandi and Parvateshwar. Drapaku's father, Purvaka, was kneeling on the other side, looking lost once again.

Drapaku kept opening his mouth, trying to say something.

Shiva bent forward. 'What is it, my friend?'

Drapaku couldn't speak. Blood continued to ooze from his mouth. He turned towards his father and then back to Shiva. The movement caused his heart to spurt, spilling some more blood out of his gaping chest onto the sheet covering him.

Shiva, his eyes moist, whispered, 'I will take care of him, Drapaku. I will take care of him.'

A long breath escaped Drapaku. He had heard what he needed to. And he let himself die, at peace finally.

A gasp escaped Purvaka's lips. His head collapsed on his son's shoulders, his body shaking. Shiva reached out and touched Purvaka gently on his shoulders. Purvaka looked up, his forehead covered with his son's brave blood, tears flowing furiously. He looked at Shiva, devastated. The proud, confident Purvaka was gone. It was the same broken man that had met Shiva at Kotdwaar in Meluha. His only reason to stay alive had been brutally hacked away.

Shiva's heart sank. He couldn't bear to look at this Purvaka. And then, rage entered his heart. Pure, furious rage!

Shiva rose.

To Parvateshwar's surprise, Nandi lunged forward, grabbing Shiva. 'No, My Lord! This is wrong.'

Shiva angrily pushed Nandi aside and stormed out. He began running to where Parshuram had been tied up.

Nandi was running behind, still screaming. 'No, My Lord! He's a prisoner. This is wrong.'

Shiva was running even harder. As he came close to where Parshuram had been tied, he drew out his sword.

Bhagirath standing at the other end of the line screamed out. 'No, My Lord! We need him alive!'

But Shiva was frenzied, screaming, racing quickly towards Parshuram, his sword high, ready to behead the bandit.

Parshuram continued to stare blankly, not a hint of fear on his face. And then he shut his eyes and shouted the words he wanted to die with. 'Jai Guru Vishwamitra! Jai Guru Vashisht!'

A stunned Shiva stopped in his tracks. Paralysed.

Not feeling the sword strike on his neck, Parshuram opened his eyes and stared at Shiva, confused.

The sword slipped from Shiva's hands. 'Vasudev?'

Parshuram looked as shocked as Shiva. He finally got a good look at Shiva's throat, deliberately covered by a cravat. Realisation dawned. 'Oh Lord! What have I done? Neelkanth! Lord Neelkanth!'

Parshuram brought his head down towards Shiva's feet, tears flooding his eyes. 'Forgive me, Lord. Forgive me. I didn't know it was you.'

Shiva just stood there. Paralysed.

— ᛉⵔᚢᚯ⊕ —

A half-asleep Sati heard the throaty roars. She immediately became alert.

They're here.

She turned towards the doorway. The fire was burning strong. Two soldiers were sitting guard.

'Kaavas, they're here. Wake everyone up.'

Sati crept up to the terrace railing. She couldn't see any lion as yet. The moon had a bit of strength tonight. She wasn't dependant only on the fire.

Then she saw the liger emerge from the tree line. The arrow Sati had shot was still buried in his shoulder, its shaft broken. It made him drag his front foot marginally.

'There's another male lion,' whispered Kaavas, pointing.

Sati nodded. She drew her bow forward. But before she could shoot, the sight in front of her stunned her.

Numerous lionesses were pouring out from behind the liger. The pride was far larger than the seven animals she had assumed there would be. She continued to watch in horror as more and more animals emerged. One lioness after another, till there were nearly thirty of them on display.

Lord Ram be merciful!

After the attack the previous night, the liger had brought his whole army to combat the threat. And it was a massive pride.

This explains the three male lions. The liger has actually taken over and merged three prides into one.

Sati slunk back and turned around. She couldn't shoot so many lionesses. She looked around her. There was pure terror in the eyes of the Kashi soldiers.

She pointed to the doorway. 'Two more men there. And more wood into the fire.'

The Kashi soldiers rushed to obey. Sati's brain was whirring, but no idea struck her. That's when she heard it.

She immediately turned around and crept to the railing, hearing the sound clearer. Two children were crying. Howling desperately for their lives.

Sati opened her eyes wide in panic.

Please... No...

The village cleaner and his wife were walking determinedly towards the lions. They wore saffron, to signify their sacrifice, their final journey. The children, naked to the elements, were held one each by their parents. They were bawling frantically.

The liger turned towards the couple and growled.

Sati drew her sword. 'Noooo!'

'No, My lady!' screamed Kaavas.

But Sati had already jumped over onto the ground. She charged towards the lions, sword held high.

The lions turned towards her, surprised, forgetting about the cleaner and his family. Then the liger registered Sati. He roared loudly. And, his pride charged.

The Kashi soldiers jumped onto the ground after Sati, inspired by the sheer bravery displayed by their leader. But inspiration is no substitute for skill.

Sati swung as she neared a massive lioness, turning smoothly with the movement, slicing through the nose and eye of the beast. As the lioness retreated, howling, Sati turned in the same smooth motion to attack a lion in front of her. Another lioness charged her from the right. A brave Kashi soldier jumped in front. The lioness grabbed the unfortunate soldier from his throat, shaking him like a rag doll. The soldier, however, had managed to lodge his sword deep into the lioness' chest. As he died, so did the lioness. Kaavas was frantically battling a lioness that had sunk her teeth into his leg, gouging his flesh. He was swinging down with his sword, hitting her on her shoulder again and again with ineffective strikes.

The Kashi men were fighting desperately. Bravely. But it was clearly a matter of time before they would be overwhelmed. They didn't have the training or the skill to battle this well coordinated pride. Sati knew it was but a matter of time before they would succumb.

Lord Ram, let me die with honour!

Then, a resounding yell rose above the mayhem. A hundred soldiers broke through the tree-line, rushing into the melee. One of them was blowing a conch shell. The fierce call of a Naga attack!

A stunned Sati continued fighting the lioness in front of her, but her thoughts were distracted, wondering why these soldiers had come to the village, to their aid.

The tide of the battle turned immediately. The new soldiers, clearly more skilled than their Kashi counterparts, charged at the lions viciously.

Sati killed the lioness in front of her and turned to see numerous lion carcasses around her. She perceived a movement to her left. The liger had sprung high at her. From nowhere, a massive hooded figure emerged. He caught hold of the liger and flung the animal off. The liger's claws struck at the hooded figure, tearing deep through his shoulder. As the liger regained balance and swung to face this new threat, the hooded figure stood protectively in front of Sati, his sword drawn.

Sati looked at the back of her fearless protector.

Who is this man?

The hooded figure charged at the liger. Just then another lioness charged at Sati. She bent low and struck her sword up brutally through the lioness' chest, deep into the beast's heart. The lioness fell on Sati, dead. She tried to push the lioness off, her head turned to the right. She could see the hooded figure battling the gargantuan liger on his own. Then she screamed, 'Watch out!'

Another lioness charged from the right towards the hooded figure, grabbing his leg viciously. The hooded figure fell but not before stabbing deep through the eyes of the lioness mauling his leg. The liger jumped once again on the hooded figure.

'No!' screamed Sati, desperately trying to push the lioness off her.

Then she saw various soldiers rushing at the liger, swinging their swords at the same time. The liger, overwhelmed, turned and ran. Only three of the pride of thirty beasts were able to escape. The rest lay on the village grounds, dead. Along with them were the bodies of ten brave Kashi soldiers.

A soldier came to assist Sati, pushing the lioness' carcass off her. She immediately got up and ran towards the hooded figure, who was being helped to his feet.

Then she stopped. Stunned.

The hooded figure's mask had slipped off.

Naga!

The Naga's forehead was ridiculously broad, his eyes placed on the side, almost facing different directions. His nose was abnormally long, stretching out like the trunk of an elephant. Two buck teeth struck out of the mouth, one of them broken. The legacy of an old injury, perhaps. The ears were floppy and large, shaking of their own accord. It almost seemed like the head of an elephant had been placed on the body of this unfortunate soul.

The Naga was standing with his fists clenched tight,

fingers boring into his palms. He had dreamt of this moment for ages. Emotions were raging through his soul. Anger. Betrayal. Fear. Love.

'Ugly, aren't I?' whispered the Naga, his eyes wet, teeth gritted.

'What? No!' cried Sati, controlling her shock at seeing a Naga. How could she insult the man who had saved her life? 'I'm sorry. It's just that I...'

'Is that why you abandoned me?' whispered the Naga, ignoring what Sati had said. His body was shaking, his fists clenched tight.

'What?'

'Is that why you abandoned me?' Soft tears were rolling down the Naga's cheeks. 'Because you couldn't even bear to look at me?'

Sati stared at the Naga, confused. 'Who are you?'

'Stop playing innocent, you daddy's spoilt little girl!' shrieked a strong feminine voice from behind.

Sati turned and gasped.

Standing a little to her left was the Naga Queen. Her entire torso had an exoskeleton covering it, hard as bone. There were small balls of bone which ran from her shoulders down to her stomach, almost like a garland of skulls. On top of her shoulders were two small extra appendages, serving as a third and fourth arm. One was holding a knife, clearly itching to fling it at Sati. But it was the face that disturbed Sati the most. The colour was jet black, but the Naga Queen's face was almost an exact replica of Sati's.

'Who are you people?' asked a stunned Sati.

'Let me put this phony out of her misery, my child.' The Naga Queen's hand holding the knife was shaking.

'She will never acknowledge the truth. She is just like her treacherous father!'

'No, *Mausi.*'

Sati turned to the Naga again, before returning her gaze to the Naga Queen. 'Who are you?'

'Bullshit! You expect me to believe that you don't know?!'

Sati continued to stare at the Naga Queen, confused.

'*Mausi...,*' whispered the Naga. He was on his knees, crying desperately.

'My child!' cried the Naga Queen as she sprinted towards him. She tried to hand him her knife. 'Kill her! Kill her! That is the only way to find peace!'

The Naga was trembling, shaking his head, tears streaking down his face. Vishwadyumna and the Brangas were holding the Kashi soldiers at a distance.

Sati asked once again. 'Who are you people?'

'I've had enough of this!' screamed the Naga Queen, raising the knife.

'No *Mausi,*' whispered the Naga through his tears. 'She doesn't know. She doesn't know.'

Sati stared at the Naga Queen. 'I swear I don't know. Who are you?'

The Naga Queen shut her eyes, took a deep breath and spoke with all the sarcasm at her command. 'Then listen, oh exalted Princess. I am your twin sister, Kali. The one whom your two-faced father abandoned!'

Sati stared at Kali, mouth half-open, too shocked to react.

I have a sister?

'And this sad soul,' said Kali, pointing at the *Lord of the People,* 'is the son you abandoned, *Ganesh.*'

Sati gasped in shock.

My son is alive?

She stared at Ganesh.

My son!

Angry tears were flooding down Ganesh's face. His body was shaking with misery.

My son...

Sati's heart was crying in pain.

But... but father said my son was stillborn.

She continued to stare.

I was lied to.

Sati held her breath. She stared at her twin sister. An exact replica of her. A visible proof of the relationship. She turned to Ganesh.

'My son is alive?'

Ganesh looked up, tears still rolling down his eyes.

'My son is alive,' whispered Sati, tears spilling from her eyes.

Sati stumbled towards the kneeling Ganesh. She went down on her knees, holding his face. 'My son is alive...'

She cradled his head. 'I didn't know, my child. I swear. I didn't know.'

Ganesh didn't raise his arms.

'My child,' whispered Sati, pulling Ganesh's head down, kissing his forehead, holding him tight. 'I'll never let you go. Never.'

Ganesh's tears broke out in a stronger flood. He wrapped his arms around his mother and whispered that most magical of words. '*Maa...*'

Sati started crying again. 'My son. My son.'

Ganesh cried like the sheltered little child he had always

wanted to be. He was safe. Safe at last. Safe in his loving mother's arms.

— 𝄞⏀Ʊ⇞⊕ —

Parshuram was biding time.

The water holds of the Branga ship had been destroyed when it grounded. The Suryavanshis had no choice but to drink the Madhumati water. Divodas had insisted the water be boiled first. But Parshuram knew that people drinking Madhumati water for the first time would be knocked out for a few hours if they didn't have the antidote beforehand.

He waited patiently for the water to take effect. He had a task to carry out.

As the camp slept, Parshuram set to work. He found the weak link in his chain and banged it lightly with a stone till it broke. His lieutenant next to him expected to be set free. But Parshuram hammered the chain back into the stake.

'Nobody escapes. Is that clear? Anyone who dares to will be hunted down by me.'

The lieutenant frowned, thoroughly confused, but did not dare question his fearsome chieftain. Parshuram turned towards the kitchen area of the beach. His battleaxe gleamed in the moonlight. He knew what he had to do.

It had to be done. He had no choice.

Chapter 16

Opposites Attract

The fire was raging.

Shiva had never seen flames so high near the Mansarovar Lake. The howling winds, the open space, the might of the Gunas, his tribe, simply didn't allow any fire to last too long.

He looked around. His village was deserted. Not a soul in sight. The flames were licking at the walls of his hamlet.

He turned towards the lake. 'Holy Lake, where are my people? Have the Pakratis taken them hostage?'

'S-H-I-V-A! HELP ME!'

Shiva turned around to find a bloodied Brahaspati racing out of the village gates, through the massive inferno. He was being followed by a giant hooded figure, his sword drawn, his gait menacing in its extreme control.

Shiva pulled Brahaspati behind him, drew his sword and waited for the hooded Naga to come closer. When within shouting distance, Shiva screamed, 'You will never get him. Not as long as I live!'

The Naga's mask seemed to develop a life of its own. It smirked. 'I've already got him.'

Shiva spun around. There were three massive snakes behind him. One was dragging Brahaspati's limp body away, punctured by numerous massive bites. The other two stood guard, spewing fire from their mouths, preventing Shiva from moving closer. Shiva watched in helpless rage as they dragged Brahaspati towards the Naga. A furious Shiva turned towards the Naga.

'Lord Rudra be merciful!' whispered Shiva.

A severely bleeding Drapaku was kneeling next to the Naga. Defeated, forlorn, waiting to be killed.

Next to Drapaku, down on her knees was a woman. Streaks of blood ran down her arms. Her billowing hair covered her downcast face. And then the wind cleared. She looked up.

It was her. The woman he couldn't save. The woman he hadn't saved. The woman he hadn't even attempted to save. 'HELP! PLEASE HELP ME!'

'Don't you dare!' screamed Shiva, pointing menacingly at the Naga.

The Naga calmly raised his sword and without a second's hesitation, beheaded the woman.

Shiva woke up in cold sweat, his brow burning again. He looked around the darkness of his small tent, hearing the soft sounds of the Madhumati lapping the shores. He looked at his hand, the serpent Aum bracelet was in it. He cursed out loud, threw the bracelet onto the ground and lay back on the bed. His head felt heavy. Very heavy.

— ⵣⵔⵏⵉⵁ —

The Madhumati flowed quietly that night. Parshuram looked up. The moonlight gave just enough visibility for him to do his task.

He checked the temperature on the flat griddle heating up on the small fire. Scalding. It had to be. The flesh would have to be seared shut quickly. Otherwise the bleeding would not stop. He went back to sharpening the axe.

He tested the sharpness of the blade once again. Razor sharp. It would afford a clean strike. He looked back. There was nobody there.

He threw away his cloak and took a deep breath.

'Lord Rudra, give me strength.'

He curled up his left hand. The sinning hand that had dared to murder the Neelkanth's favourite. He held the outcrop of a tree stump. Held it tight. Giving himself purchase to pull his shoulder back.

The trunk had been used earlier to behead many of his enemies. The blood of those unfortunate victims had left deep red marks on the wood. Now his blood would mix with theirs.

He reached out with his right hand and picked up the battleaxe, raising it high.

Parshuram looked up one last time and took a deep breath. 'Forgive me, My Lord.'

The battleaxe hummed through the air as it swung down sharply. It sliced through perfectly, cutting the hand clean.

— 𑀕𑀰𑀝𑀦𑀅 —

'How in the name of the holy lake did he escape?' shouted Shiva. 'What were you doing?'

Parvateshwar and Bhagirath were looking down. The Lord had justifiable reasons to be angry. They were in his tent. It was the last hour of the first prahar. The sun had just risen. And with that had come to light Parshuram's disappearance.

Shiva was distracted by commotion outside. He rushed out to find Divodas and a few other soldiers pointing their sword at Parshuram. He was staggering towards Shiva, staring at him. Nobody else.

Shiva held his left hand out, telling his men to let Parshuram through. For some reason, he didn't feel the need to reach for his sword. Parshuram had his cloak wrapped tightly around himself. Bhagirath stepped up to check Parshuram for weapons. But Shiva called out loudly. 'It's alright, Bhagirath. Let him come.'

Parshuram stumbled towards Shiva, obviously weak, eyes drooping. There was a massive blood stain on his cloak. Shiva narrowed his eyes.

Parshuram collapsed on his knees in front of Shiva.

'Where had you gone?'

Parshuram looked up, his eyes melancholic. 'I... penance... My Lord...'

Shiva frowned.

The bandit dropped his cloak and with his right hand, placed his severed left one at Shiva's feet. 'This hand... sinned... My Lord. Forgive me...'

Shiva gasped in horror.

Parshuram collapsed. Unconscious.

— 人◎Ʊ♀⊕ —

Ayurvati had tended to Parshuram's wound. She had cauterised it once again in order to prevent any chance of infection. Juice of neem leaves had been rubbed into the open flesh. A dressing of neem leaves had been created and wound tight around the severed arm.

She looked up at Shiva. 'This fool is lucky the axe was sharp and clean. The blood loss and infection from a wound like this can be fatal.'

'I don't think the cleanliness or sharpness was an

accident,' whispered Bhagirath. 'He made it so. He knew what he was doing.'

Parvateshwar continued to stare at Parshuram, stunned. *Who is this strange man?*

Shiva had not uttered a word so far. He just kept looking at Parshuram, his face devoid of any expression. His eyes narrowed hard.

'What do we do with him, My Lord?' asked Parvateshwar.

'We use him,' suggested Bhagirath. 'Our ship will take up to six months to repair. We can't stay here for that long. I say we carry Parshuram in one of our cutters to the closest Branga outpost and hand him over. We'll use the leverage of handing over the most wanted criminal in Branga to wrangle a ship from them. They'll force the medicine out of him and we get our path to the Nagas.'

Shiva didn't say anything. He continued to stare at Parshuram.

Parvateshwar didn't like Bhagirath's solution. But he also knew it was the most practical thing to do. He looked at Shiva. 'My Lord?'

'We're not handing him over to the Brangas,' said Shiva.

'My Lord?' cried Bhagirath, shocked.

Shiva looked at Bhagirath. 'We're not.'

'But My Lord, how do we get to the Nagas? We have sworn to get the medicines to the Brangas.'

'Parshuram will give us the medicines. I'll ask him when he is conscious.'

'But, My Lord,' continued Bhagirath. 'He's a criminal. He will not help unless he is coerced. I admit he has made a sacrifice. But we need a ship to get out of here.'

'I know.'

Bhagirath continued to stare at Shiva. Then he turned

towards Parvateshwar. The Meluhan General gestured to the Ayodhya Prince to be quiet.

But Bhagirath would have none of it. What the Neelkanth was suggesting was not practical. 'Please forgive me for saying it again, My Lord. But the only practical way to get a ship is by letting the Brangas get their hands on him. And that's not the only reason to do so. Parshuram is a criminal, a mass murderer. Why shouldn't we surrender him to suffer the righteous Branga justice?'

'Because I said so.'

Saying this, Shiva walked out. Bhagirath kept staring at Parvateshwar, not saying a word.

Parshuram's eyes opened slightly. He smiled faintly. And then went back to sleep.

— ⋏◎⎊⚲⊕ —

As the second prahar came to a close, the sun shone brightly, right over head.

The Branga and Kashi soldiers had been hard at work, with Vishwadyumna having taken charge. Kaavas didn't seem to mind following orders from the capable Branga. The Branga travelling doctor had tended to all the wounded. They were all on the road to recovery. The dead had been cremated in the Icchawar village ground. While nobody expected the few remaining lionesses and the liger to return back to the village, for abundant precaution, the soldiers had dug ditches around the village. Temporary quarters had been erected for both Branga as well as Kashi soldiers in the school building. The villagers had been commandeered to arrange the food supplies.

The villagers, though rejoicing at the decimation of the

pride, stayed warily at a distance, carrying out the tasks assigned to them by Vishwadyumna. Their mortal fear of the Nagas, despite the fact that their lives had just been saved by them, kept them suppressed.

The cleaner's children, however, seemed to delight in playing with Kali. They pulled her hair, jumped on her and laughed uproariously every time she pretended to get angry.

'Children!' spoke their mother sternly. They turned and ran towards her, holding on to her *dhoti*. The cleaner's wife spoke to Kali. 'My apologies for this, Your Highness. They will not disturb you.'

In the presence of an adult Kali's demeanour became serious once again. She merely nodded wordlessly.

She turned to her right to find Ganesh sleeping with his head on Sati's lap, his face a picture of bliss. His wounds had been dressed. The doctor was especially worried about the mutilation caused by the lioness on Ganesh's leg. It had been cleaned and bandaged tight.

Sati looked up at Kali and smiled. She held her sister's hand.

Kali smiled softly. 'I've never seen him sleep so peacefully.'

Sati smiled and lovingly ran her hand along Ganesh's face. 'I must thank you for taking care of him for so long.'

'It was my duty.'

'Yes, but not everyone honours their duty. Thank you.'

'Actually, it was my pleasure as well!'

Sati smiled. 'I can't imagine how tough life must have been for you. I will make it up to you. I promise.'

Kali frowned slightly, but kept quiet.

Sati looked up once again as a thought struck her. 'You

had said something about father. Are you sure? He is weak. But he loves his family dearly. I can't imagine him consciously hurting any of us.'

Kali's face hardened. Suddenly, they were disturbed by a noise from Ganesh. Sati looked down at her son.

Ganesh was pouting. 'I'm hungry!'

Sati raised her eyebrows and burst out laughing. She kissed Ganesh gently on his forehead. 'Let me see what I can rustle up.'

As Sati walked away, Kali turned to Ganesh, about to scold him for his behaviour. But Ganesh himself was up in a flash. 'You will not tell her, *Mausi*.'

'What?' asked Kali.

'You will not tell her.'

'She's not stupid, you know. She will figure it out.'

'That she may. But she will not find out from you.'

'She deserves the truth. Why shouldn't she know?'

'Because some truths can only cause pain, *Mausi*. They're best left buried.'

— ⚊ 𑀓 ⚊ —

'My Lord,' whispered Parshuram.

Shiva, Parvateshwar and Bhagirath were huddled together around him in the tiny tent. It was the last hour of the third prahar. The sun was sinking into the horizon, turning the sludgy Madhumati waters orange-brown. Divodas and his team had already started working on repairing the ship. It was a daunting task.

'What is it, Parshuram?' asked Shiva. 'Why did you want to meet me?'

Parshuram closed his eyes, gathering strength. 'I will

have one of my people give the secrets of the Naga medicine to the Brangas, My Lord. We will help them. We will take them to Mount Mahendra in Kaling from where we get the stabilising agent for the medicine.'

Shiva smiled. 'Thank you.'

'You don't need to thank me, My Lord. This is what you want. Doing your bidding is my honour.'

Shiva nodded.

'You also need a ship,' said Parshuram.

Bhagirath perked up.

'I have a large ship of my own,' said Parshuram, before turning to Parvateshwar. 'Give me some of your men, brave General. I will tell them where it is. They can sail it here and we can leave.'

A surprised Parvateshwar smiled, looking at Shiva.

Shiva nodded. The bandit looked tired. Shiva bent down, touching Parshuram on his shoulder. 'You need to rest. We can talk later.'

'One more thing, My Lord,' said Parshuram, insistent. 'The Brangas are only a conduit.'

Shiva frowned.

'Your ultimate goal is to find the Nagas.'

Shiva narrowed his eyes.

'I know where they live,' said Parshuram.

Shiva's eyes widened in surprise.

'I know my way through the Dandak forests, My Lord,' continued Parshuram. 'I know where the Naga city is. I will tell you how to get there.'

Shiva patted Parshuram's shoulder. 'Thank you.'

'But I have one condition, My Lord.'

Shiva frowned.

'Take me with you,' whispered Parshuram.

Shiva raised his eyebrows, surprised. 'But why...'

'Following you is my life's duty. Please let me give my wretched life at least a little bit of meaning.'

Shiva nodded. 'It will be my honour to travel with you, Parshuram.'

— ⚲ —

It had been three days since the battle of Madhumati. Parvateshwar's men had located Parshuram's ship. It was even bigger than the one they had travelled in. Clearly a Branga ship, it even had hull extensions to allow passage through the gates of Branga. The ship must have been captured by Parshuram's men from one of the unfortunate Branga Kshatriya bands sent to arrest or kill him.

All the soldiers had boarded the ship. Parshuram's men were not prisoners anymore. They had been allotted comfortable quarters of the same order as the Suryavanshi soldiers who had beaten them.

Shiva had personally seen to the comfort of both Purvaka and Parshuram. Ayurvati had stationed her assistant Mastrak alongside Parshuram, who was still extremely weak from tremendous blood loss.

The ship was sailing comfortably up the Madhumati. When they would reach the Branga river, a fast cutter with one of Parshuram's men would be sent to guide King Chandraketu in finding the alternative source of the Naga medicine. The man would also inform the rest of Shiva's men at Brangaridai to leave immediately and rejoin the brigade at the point where the Madhumati broke away from the Branga.

The brigade would then sail back to Kashi. Shiva was

desperate to meet Sati and Kartik. He had been missing his family. After that he planned to raise an army and quickly turn South to find the Nagas.

Shiva was standing at the head of the ship, smoking some marijuana with Veerbhadra. Nandi stood next to them. They stared into the swirling waters of the Madhumati.

'This expedition went better than expected, My Lord,' said Nandi.

'That it did,' smiled Shiva, pointing at the chillum. 'Unfortunately, the celebration isn't quite up to the mark.'

Veerbhadra smiled. 'Let me get to Kashi. They really know how to roll good grass there.'

Shiva laughed aloud. So did Nandi. Shiva offered the chillum to Nandi but the Meluhan Major declined. Shiva shrugged and took another drag, before passing the chillum back to Veerbhadra.

Shiva was distracted as he saw Parvateshwar come up to them, hesitate and turn back.

'I wonder what he wants to talk about now,' asked Shiva, frowning.

'It's obvious, isn't it?' smiled Veerbhadra.

Nandi looked down and smiled, not saying a word.

'Why don't you two idiots excuse me for a minute?' smiled Shiva, as he walked away from his friends.

Parvateshwar was standing at a distance, deep in thought.

'General? A word, General.'

Parvateshwar immediately turned around and saluted. 'Your command, My Lord.'

'Not a command, Parvateshwar. Just a request.'

Parvateshwar frowned.

'In the name of the Holy Lake,' said Shiva. 'For once, listen to your heart.'

'My Lord?'

'You know what I am saying. She loves you. You love her. What else is there to think about?'

Parvateshwar turned beet red. 'Has it been that obvious?'

'Obvious to everyone, General!'

'But My Lord, this is wrong.'

'How? Why? You think Lord Ram purposely designed laws for you to be unhappy?'

'But my grandfather's vow...'

'You have honoured it for long enough. Trust me, even he would want you to stop now.'

Parvateshwar looked down, not saying anything.

'I remember hearing that one of Lord Ram's commandments was that laws are not important. What is important is justice. If the purpose of justice is served by breaking a law, then break it.'

'Lord Ram said that?' asked Parvateshwar, surprised.

'I'm sure he must have,' smiled Shiva. 'He never wanted his followers to be unhappy. You are not hurting anyone else by being with Anandmayi. You are not hurting the protest begun by your grandfather. You have served that purpose quite enough. Now let your heart serve another purpose.'

'Are you sure, My Lord?'

'I've never been surer of anything else in my life. In the name of Lord Ram, go to her!'

Shiva slapped Parvateshwar hard on his back.

Parvateshwar had been thinking about this for long. Shiva's words only helped him gather his dwindling courage. He saluted Shiva and turned. A man on a mission. Ready to take the plunge.

— ⸙⃝ᚹ♀⊕ —

Anandmayi was leaning against the railing astern of the ship, enjoying the strong evening breeze.

'Your Highness?'

Anandmayi spun around, surprised to find Parvateshwar there, looking sheepish. The Princess of Ayodhya was about to open her mouth, when he corrected himself.

'I meant Anandmayi,' whispered Parvateshwar.

Anandmayi stood up in surprise.

'Yes, General? You wanted something?' asked Anandmayi, her heart racing.

'Ummm... Anandmayi... I was thinking...'

'Yes?'

'Well, it's like this... It's about what we were talking about...'

Anandmayi was aglow, smiling from deep within her heart. 'Yes, General?'

'Ummm... I never thought I would face this day. So... Ummm...'

Anandmayi nodded, keeping quiet, letting him take his time. She could figure out exactly what Parvateshwar wanted to say. But she also knew that it would be very difficult for the Meluhan General.

'My vows and Suryavanshi laws have been the bedrock of my life,' said Parvateshwar. 'Unquestionable and unchanging. My destiny, the destination of my life and my role in it, has so far been clearly defined. This predictability is comforting. Rather, *had been* comforting, for many decades.'

Anandmayi nodded, silent.

'But,' said Parvateshwar, 'the last few years have turned my world upside down. First came the Lord, a living man that I could look up to. A person beyond the laws. I thought this would be the biggest change my simple heart had been forced to handle.'

Anandmayi continued to nod. Trying her best not to frown or laugh, touched to see this proud man baring his heart in what she thought was one of the most wooden attempts at courtship in history. But she was wise enough to know that her Parva had to say his piece or he would never be comfortable with himself or in the life she hoped he was choosing to make with her.

'But then... most unexpectedly, I also found a woman that I could look up to, could admire and adore. I have reached a crossroads in my life, where my destination is a blur. I do not know where my life is going. The road ahead is unclear. But to my surprise, I find that I am happy with that. Happy, as long as you walk this road with me...'

Anandmayi remained silent. Smiling. Tears in her eyes. He had really pulled it together at the end.

'It'll be one hell of a great journey.'

Anandmayi lunged forward and kissed Parvateshwar hard. A deep, passionate kiss. Parvateshwar stood stunned, his hands to his side, taking in a pleasure he hadn't ever imagined. After what seemed like a lifetime, Anandmayi stepped back, her eyes a seductive half-stare. Parvateshwar staggered, his mouth half open. Not even sure how to react.

'Lord Ram be merciful,' the General whispered.

Anandmayi stepped closer to Parvateshwar, running her hand across his face. 'You have no idea what you have been missing.'

Parvateshwar just continued to stare at her, dumbfounded.

Anandmayi held Parvateshwar's hand and pulled him away. 'Come with me.'

— ⵏ◍ⵎ⳦⊕ —

It had been a week since the battle with the liger. The few surviving lionesses and the liger had not come back. They were still licking their wounds. The villagers of Icchawar were using the moments of peace to start tilling their lands, preparing for the seasonal crops. It was a time of unexpected joy and relief.

The Chandravanshi soldiers were recovering. Ganesh's wounds were too deep. He still limped from the severe mauling his leg had taken. But he knew it was only a matter of time before he would be alright. He had to start preparing for the inevitable.

'*Maa*,' whispered Ganesh.

Sati looked at Ganesh, covering the dish she was cooking with a plate. She had spent the previous week listening to Kali share stories of Ganesh's childhood, sharing in his joys and sorrows, understanding her child's personality and character, right down to his favourite dishes. And she was satiating his stomach and soul with what she had learnt. 'What is it, my son?'

Kali had just stepped up close as requested by Ganesh.

'I think we have to start preparing to leave. I should be strong enough to travel in another week.'

'I know. The food I've been giving you has some rejuvenating herbs. They're giving you strength.'

Ganesh knelt and held his mother's hand. 'I know.'

Sati patted her son's face lightly.

Ganesh took a deep breath. 'I know you cannot come

to Panchavati. It will pollute you. I will come to visit you regularly in Kashi. I will come in secret.'

'What are you talking about?'

'I have also sworn the Kashi soldiers to an oath of silence, on pain of a gruesome death,' grinned Ganesh. 'They're terrified of us Nagas. They will not dare break this oath! The secret of my relationship with you will not be revealed.'

'Ganesh, what in Lord Ram's name are you talking about?'

'I will not embarrass you. Your acceptance of me is enough for my soul.'

'How can you embarrass me? You are my pride and joy.'

'*Maa...*' smiled Ganesh.

Sati held her son's face. 'You're not going anywhere.'

Ganesh frowned.

'You are staying with me.'

'*Maa*!' said Ganesh, horrified.

'What?'

'How can I? What will your society say?'

'I don't care.'

'But your husband...'

'He is your father,' said Sati firmly. 'Speak of him with respect.'

'I meant no disrespect, *Maa*. But he will not accept me. You know that. I am a Naga.'

'You are my son. You are his son. He will accept you. You don't know the size of your father's heart. The entire world can live in it.'

'But Sati...,' said Kali, trying to intervene.

'No arguments, Kali,' said Sati. 'Both of you are coming to Kashi. We travel when you are strong enough to do so.'

Kali stared at Sati, at a loss for words.

'You are my sister. I don't care what society says. If they accept me, they will accept you. If they reject you, I leave this society too.'

Kali smiled slightly, teary eyed. 'I was very wrong about you, *didi*.'

It was the first time Kali had called Sati her *elder sister*. Sati smiled and embraced Kali.

Chapter 17

The Curse of Honour

It had been ten days since the battle of the Madhumati. The ship carrying the now reconciled enemies — the Suryavanshis and Parshuram's men — was anchored where the Madhumati broke off from the Branga. They were waiting for their comrades to sail upriver from Brangaridai and join them.

A Branga Pandit had been called aboard to preside over Parvateshwar and Anandmayi's wedding. Bhagirath desired to conduct the ceremony at Ayodhya with regal pomp and grandeur befitting a princess. But Anandmayi would have none of it. She did not want to take any chances. Parvateshwar had taken his own sweet time to say yes and she wanted to have their relationship iron-tight 'as soon as humanly possible.' As Shiva had blessed the couple, all arguments about the hastiness of the ceremony had come to an end.

Shiva was standing at the ship railing, smoking with Veerbhadra.

'My Lord!'

Shiva turned around.

'By the Holy Lake! What are you doing, Parshuram?' asked a horrified Shiva. 'You should be resting.'

'I'm bored, My Lord.'

'But you were up for a long time yesterday for the wedding. Two days of continuous activity will be a bit too much. What does Ayurvati have to say?'

'I will go back in a little while, My Lord,' said Parshuram. 'Let me stand next to you for some time. It soothes me.'

Shiva raised an eyebrow. 'I'm not special. It's all in your mind.'

'I disagree, My Lord. But even if what you're saying is true, I'm sure you will find it in your heart to let me indulge my mind if it doesn't hurt anyone.'

Shiva burst out laughing. 'You're quite good with words for a...'

Shiva suddenly stopped.

'For a bandit,' grinned Parshuram.

'I meant no insult. I apologise.'

'Why apologise, My Lord? It is the truth. I was a bandit.'

Veerbhadra had become increasingly fascinated with this strange bandit. Intelligent, disturbed and ferociously devoted to Shiva. He spoke up, changing the topic, 'You were delighted about General Parvateshwar and Princess Anandmayi's wedding. I found that interesting.'

'Well, they are completely different,' said Parshuram. 'In terms of personality, thought, belief and region. Actually, pretty much everything. They are polar opposites. Extremes of the Chandravanshi and Suryavanshi thought processes. Traditionally, they should be enemies. Yet they found love in each other. I like stories like that. Reminds me of my parents.'

Shiva frowned. He remembered the terrible rumour he had heard about Parshuram beheading his own mother. 'Your parents?'

'Yes, My Lord. My father, Jamadagni, was a Brahmin, a scholarly man. My mother, Renuka, was from a Kshatriya clan. Rulers who were vassals of the Brangas.'

'So how did they get married?' smiled Shiva.

'Due to my mother,' smiled Parshuram. 'She was a very strong woman. My parents were in love. But it was her strength of character and determination that propelled their love to its logical conclusion.'

Shiva smiled.

'She worked at his *gurukul*. That in itself was against the norm in her clan.'

'How is working in *a school* a rebellion?'

'Because in her clan it was prohibited for women to go out and work.'

'They couldn't work? Why? I know that some clans have rules that do not allow women on the battlefield. Even the Gunas had that rule. But why against work in general?'

'Because my mother's clan was amongst the stupidest on the planet,' said Parshuram. 'My mother's people believed a woman should remain at home. That she shouldn't meet "strange" men.'

'What rubbish!' said Shiva.

'Absolutely. In any case, like I said, my mother was wilful. And, also her father's darling. So she convinced him to allow her to work at my father's gurukul.'

Shiva smiled.

'Of course, my mother had her own agenda,' said Parshuram, 'She was desperately in love. She needed time to convince my father to give up his vows and marry her.'

'Give up vows?'

'My father was a Vasudev Brahmin. And a Vasudev

Brahmin cannot marry. Other castes within the Vasudevs can, but not Brahmins.'

'There are non-Brahmins amongst the Vasudevs?'

'Of course. But Brahmins steer the community. To ensure that they remain true to the cause of the Vasudevs, they have to give up all earthly attachments like wealth, love and family. Therefore, one of their vows is that of lifelong celibacy.'

Shiva frowned. *What is this obsession among the Indians about giving up earthly attachments? How, in the Holy Lake's name, can that guarantee that you will evolve into a better human being?*

'So,' continued Parshuram, his eyes crinkling, 'my mother finally convinced my father to break the rules. He was in love with her, but she gave him the courage to give up his Vasudev vows so he could spend his life with her. Even more, she also convinced her own father to bless their relationship. Like I said, when she wanted something, she made it happen. My parents got married and had five sons. I was the youngest.'

Shiva looked at Parshuram. 'You are really proud of your mother, aren't you?'

'Oh yes. She was quite a woman!'

'Then why did you...'

Shiva stopped talking. *I shouldn't have said that.*

Parshuram became serious. 'Why did I... behead her?'

'You don't have to speak about it. I cannot even imagine the pain.'

Parshuram took a deep breath, sliding down to sit on the deck. Shiva sat on his haunches, touching Parshuram on his shoulder. Veerbhadra stood, staring directly into Parshuram's pain-ridden eyes.

'You don't need to say anything, Parshuram,' said Shiva.

Parshuram closed his eyes, right hand over his heart. He chanted repeatedly, *bowing to Lord Rudra* in his prayer. '*Om Rudraiy namah. Om Rudraiy namah.*'

Shiva watched the Brahmin warrior quietly.

'I have never spoken about it with anyone, My Lord,' said Parshuram. 'It was the trigger that set my life on the path it has taken.'

Shiva reached out and touched Parshuram's shoulder again.

'But I must tell you. If there is one person who can heal me, it is you. I had just completed my studies. And like my father, I too wanted to be a Vasudev. He didn't want me to. He didn't want any of his sons to become Vasudevs. He had been expelled from their tribe when he had chosen to marry my mother. He didn't want any of us to suffer his fate in the future.'

Veerbhadra sat down as well, all ears for Parshuram's story.

'But I had my mother's doggedness in me. Unlike my brothers, I was determined. I thought I would enter the tribe of Vasudevs as a Kshatriya, as this way, I wouldn't be bound by their detachment vows. I trained as a warrior. My father sent a letter to Ujjain, the Vasudev capital, to a few elders who still sympathised with him and requested them to consider my application. When the day finally arrived, I departed to the closest Vasudev temple for my examination.'

What did this have to do with his mother?

'What I didn't know when I left was that my grandfather had died. He was the only one holding back my mother's barbarian horde of a family. The moment his influence was gone, they decided to do what they had always wanted to do. Honour kill.'

'Honour kill?'

Parshuram looked at Shiva. 'When the people in the clan believe a woman in their community has insulted the honour of her family, the clan has the right to kill that woman and everyone else with her to avenge their loss of face.'

Shiva just stared, stunned.

What honour can there be in this barbarism?

'The men of my mother's family, her own brothers and uncles, attacked my father's gurukul.'

Parshuram stopped talking. A long-held back tear escaped from his eyes.

'They...' Parshuram held his breath and then found the strength to continue. 'They killed my brothers, all my father's students. They tied my mother to a tree and forced her to watch as they tortured my father for an entire day, doing unspeakable horrors. Then, they beheaded him.'

Veerbhadra squirmed, unable to comprehend such insanity, such evil.

'But they didn't kill my mother. They told her that they wanted her to live, to relive that day again and again. That she had to serve as an example to the other women so that they would never dare bring dishonour to their families. I returned to find my father's gurukul destroyed. My mother was sitting outside our house, holding my father's severed head in her lap. She looked like her soul had been burnt alive. Her eyes wide, blank. A shadow of the woman she had been, broken and brutalised.'

Parshuram stopped talking and turned to look at the river. This was the first time he was talking about his mother since that terrible day. 'She looked at me as though I was a stranger. And then she said words that would haunt me forever. She said: "Your father died because of me. It is my sin. I want to die like him."'

Shiva's mouth fell open in shock, his heart going out to the unfortunate Brahmin.

'At first I didn't understand. And then she commanded: "Behead me!" I didn't know what to do. I hesitated. Then she said once again: "I am your mother. I am ordering you. Behead me."'

Shiva pressed Parshuram's shoulder.

'I had no choice. My mother was catatonic. Without my father's love, she was nothing but an empty shell. As I picked up my axe to carry out her order, she looked straight into my eyes: "Avenge your father. He was the finest man that God ever created. Avenge him. Kill every single one of them! Every single one!"'

Parshuram fell silent. Shiva and Veerbhadra were too stunned to react. The only sounds were those of the somnolent waves of the Madhumati breaking gently against the ship.

'I did as she said. I beheaded her,' said Parshuram, taking a deep breath and wiping his tears. Then his eyes lit in remembered anger as he spoke through gritted teeth. 'And then I hunted down every single one of those bastards. I beheaded every single one of them. Every single one. The Vasudevs expelled me. I had killed people without the permission of their tribe, they said. Without a fair trial, they said. I had committed a wrong, they said. Did I, My Lord?'

Shiva looked straight into Parshuram's eyes, his heart heavy. He could feel the Brahmin's intense pain. He knew that Lord Ram would have probably acted as the Vasudevs had. The great Suryavanshi would have wanted the criminals to be punished but only after a fair trial. However, he also knew that if anyone had dared to do this to his own family, he would have burnt down their entire world. 'No. You didn't do anything wrong. What you did was in accordance with justice.'

Parshuram sighed as a dam burst.

What I did was just.

Shiva held Parshuram's shoulder. Parshuram covered his eyes with his hand, sniffing. At long last he shook his head slightly and looked up. 'The Branga king sent bands of Kshatriyas to arrest me. To apparently bring me to justice for annihilating his most important vassals. Twenty–one times they sent brigades to catch me. And twenty–one times I beat them. Finally they stopped.'

'But how did you fight the Brangas alone?' asked Veerbhadra.

'I wasn't alone. Some angels knew of the injustice I had suffered. They brought me to this haven, introduced me to the few unfortunate, ostracised brigands who lived here. I could build my own army. They gave me medicines so that I could survive despite the unclean waters here and food till I had established my people in the forests. They gave me weapons to fight the Brangas. And all this without any expectations from me. The battles with Brangaridai were also brought to an end because they finally threatened the Branga king. And King Chandraketu could not refuse them. They are the best people amongst us all. Angels who fight for the oppressed.'

Shiva frowned. 'Who?'

'The Nagas,' replied Parshuram.

'What?!'

'Yes, My Lord. That is why you are looking for them,

right? If you want to find Evil, you must make the Good your ally, right?'

'What are you talking about?'

'They never kill innocents. They fight for justice, despite the injustices they endure. They help the oppressed whenever and wherever they can. They truly are the best amongst us all.'

Shiva stared hard at Parshuram, not saying a word. Completely staggered.

'You are looking for their secret, aren't you?' asked Parshuram.

'What secret?'

'I don't know. But I have heard that the secret of the Nagas has a deep connection to Evil. Isn't that why you are searching for them?'

Shiva didn't answer. He was looking into the horizon, deep in thought.

— 人◎ᚊᚵ⊕ —

It had been two weeks since the battle with the liger's pride. All the injured soldiers were well on the path to recovery. But Ganesh's wounded leg had still not completely healed.

Sati had been supervising the building of some defences at the Icchawar village perimeter as a precaution against future animal attacks. She returned to the camp to see Kali changing the dressing on Ganesh's wound.

Both Kali and Ganesh, perhaps encouraged by Sati's complete acceptance of their appearance, had not worn their masks for the last two weeks. The Chandravanshi soldiers, however, still averted their eyes in dread when they saw them.

Kali had just finished applying the neem bandage. She patted Ganesh on his head and rose to walk towards the fire at one corner of the clearing. Sati saw the gesture and smiled. She turned to instruct Kaavas to carry on with his work and walked up to Kali.

'How is his wound?'

'It'll take another week, *didi*. The healing process has slowed down since last week.'

Sati grimaced, unhappy. 'The poor child lost a lot of blood and flesh.'

'Don't worry,' said Kali. 'He is very strong. He will recover.'

Sati smiled. Kali threw the bandage into the fire. The paste on the bandage, having drawn out much of the infection, burned a deep blue.

Sati looked up at Kali, took a deep breath and asked what had been troubling her since they had met. 'Why?'

Kali frowned.

'You are good people. I've seen the way you treat Ganesh and your men. You are tough, but fair. Then why did you do all those terrible things?'

Kali held her breath. She looked up at the sky and shook her head. 'Think again, *didi*. We have not done anything wrong.'

'Kali, you and Ganesh may not have personally done anything wrong. But your people committed grave crimes. They killed innocents.'

'My people work according to my orders, *didi*. If you want to blame them, then you cannot absolve me. Think once again. No innocents were killed in our attacks.'

'I'm sorry Kali, but that is not true. You attacked non-combatants. I have been thinking for some time. I agree that the Nagas are treated unfairly. The way Meluha treats Naga babies is unjust. But that doesn't mean every Meluhan, even if he personally hasn't done anything to hurt you, is your enemy.'

'*Didi*, you think we would attack people just because they were a part of a system which humiliated and wounded us? That is wrong. We never attacked anyone who hasn't directly harmed us.'

'You did. Your people attacked temples. They attacked innocents. They killed vulnerable Brahmins.'

'No. In every attack, we would let all the people except the temple Brahmins leave. Everyone. No innocents were killed. Ever.'

'But you did kill temple Brahmins. They're not warriors. They're innocent.'

'I disagree.'

'Why?'

'Because they directly hurt our people.'

'What? How? What wrong did the temple Brahmins do to you?'

'I'll tell you.'

— ⋏⦾Ⴚⵥ⊗ —

Shiva's caravan of ships was anchored at Vaishali, a pretty city on the Ganga river and an immediate neighbour of Branga. It had been three weeks since Shiva had allied with Parshuram. Vaishali had a massive Vishnu temple dedicated to the legendary fish god, Lord Matsya. Shiva was deeply disturbed by what Parshuram had said about the Nagas. He wanted to speak with a Vasudev, one who was other than the ostracised Vasudev Brahmin-Kshatriya on board. Time and space had dimmed his anger towards the tribe.

The temple was very close to the city's harbour. A massive crowd, including the King, had been waiting to receive him, but Shiva had requested that he be allowed to meet them later. He headed straight for the Matsya temple. It was a little taller than seventy metres, comfortably above the minimum height needed for the Vasudevs to transmit radio waves.

The temple was on the banks of the Ganga. Usually temples would have had most of the space outside dedicated to landscaped gardens or grand enclosures. This temple was different. The land outside was dominated by intricate water bodies. Water from the Ganga had been routed into a system of elaborate canals around the main temple. And these canals made some of the most ethereal designs that Shiva had ever seen. It formed a map of ancient India at a time when sea-levels were a lot lower. It told the story of Lord Manu and how he had led his band of followers out of his devastated homeland, the Sangamtamil. Despite his urgency to meet the Vasudevs, Shiva held back, enthralled by the breathtaking designs. At long last, he tore his eyes away and walked up the steps to the main temple. Crowds hung outside, waiting quietly in accordance with their Neelkanth's request.

Shiva looked at the sanctum sanctorum at the far corner of the temple. It was far bigger than in any other temple he had seen so far. Probably to accommodate the enormous statue of its reigning God. On a raised platform lay Lord Matsya, a giant fish, who had helped bring Manu and his band of refugees from Sangamtamil to safety. Manu, the founder of the Vedic civilisation, had made it clear in his guidelines to his descendants that Lord Matsya must always be respected and worshipped as the first Lord Vishnu. If any of them were alive, it was due to the benefaction of the great Lord Matsya.

Lord Matsya looks so much like the dolphins I've seen in the rivers here. Only He is much larger.

Shiva bowed down and paid his respects to the Lord. He said a quick prayer and then sat down against one of the pillars. And then he thought out loud.

Vasudevs? Are you here?

Nobody responded. No one from the temple came to see him.

Is there no Vasudev here?

Absolute silence.

Is this not a Vasudev temple? Have I come to the wrong place?

Shiva heard nothing except the gentle tinkle of the fountains in the temple compound.

Damn!

Shiva realised that maybe he had made a mistake. This temple probably wasn't a Vasudev outpost. His thoughts went back to the advice Sati had given to him.

Maybe what Sati said is right. Maybe the Vasudevs were trying to help me. They did help! I would have been devastated if anything had happened to Kartik.

A calm clear voice rang out loud in his head. *Your wife is wise, great Mahadev. It is rare to find such beauty and wisdom in one person.*

Shiva looked up and around quickly. There was nobody. The voice was from one of the other Vasudev temples. He recognised it. It was the one that had commanded the Kashi Vasudev to give him the Naga medicine. *Are you the leader, Panditji?*

No, my friend. You are. I am but your follower. And I bring the Vasudevs with me.

Where are you? Ujjain?

There was silence.

What is your name, Panditji?

I am Gopal. I am the Chief Guide of the Vasudevs. I bear the key task that Lord Ram had set us: Assisting you in your karma.

I need your advice, Panditji.

As you wish, great Neelkanth. What do you want to talk about?

— ⵣ◍ⵗⴹ⊕ —

Sati, Kali, Ganesh and the Branga-Kashi soldiers were marching towards Kashi. Loud conversation amongst them disturbed the silence of the forest.

Vishwadyumna turned to Ganesh. 'My Lord, don't you find the forest oddly silent?'

Ganesh raised his eyebrows, for the soldiers were creating quite a racket. 'You think our men should be talking even louder?!'

'No, My Lord. We are loud enough! It is the rest of the forest that I'm talking about. It is too quiet.'

Ganesh tilted his head. Vishwadyumna was right. Not a single animal or bird sound. He looked around. His instincts told him that something was wrong. He stared hard into the woods. Then, shaking his head, he looked ahead and goaded his horse into moving faster.

A short distance away, an injured animal, massive in his proportions, with his wounds partially healed, crept slowly forward. The shaft of a broken arrow, buried deep in his shoulder, caused the liger to limp a little. Two lionesses followed him silently.

Chapter 18

The Function of Evil

This country is very confusing.

Gopal thought softly: *Why would you say that, my friend?*

The Nagas are obviously the people who are evil, right? Almost everyone seems to agree. And yet, the Nagas helped a man in need, in the interests of justice. That's not how evil is supposed to be.

A good point, great Neelkanth.

Considering the mistake I've already made, I'm not about to attack anyone till I'm sure.

A wise decision.

So do you also think the Nagas may not be evil?

How can I answer that, my friend? I do not have the wisdom to find that answer. I am not the Neelkanth.

Shiva smiled. *But you do have an opinion, don't you?*

Shiva waited for Gopal to speak. When the Vasudev Pandit didn't, Shiva smiled even more broadly, giving up this discussion. Suddenly a disturbing thought struck him. *Please don't tell me the Nagas also believe in the legend of the Neelkanth.*

Gopal remained silent for a moment.

Shiva repeated, frowning. *Panditji? Please answer me. Do the Nagas also believe in the Neelkanth legend?*

As far as I know, great Mahadev, most of them do not believe in the Neelkanth. But do you think that would make them evil?

Shiva shook his head. *No, of course not.*

Silence for some time.

Shiva breathed deeply. *So what is the blessed answer? I have travelled through all of India. Met practically all the tribes except the Nagas. And if none are evil, maybe Evil hasn't arisen. Maybe I'm not required.*

Are you sure it is only people who can be Evil, my friend? There may be attachment to Evil within some. There may be a small part of Evil within them. But could the great Evil, the one that awaits the Neelkanth, exist beyond mere humans?

Shiva frowned. *I don't understand.*

Can Evil be too big to be concentrated within just a few men?

Shiva remained silent.

Lord Manu had said it's not people who are evil. True Evil exists beyond them. It attracts people. It causes confusion amongst its enemies. But Evil in itself is too big to be confined to just a few.

Shiva frowned. *You make it sound like Evil is a power as strong as Good. That it doesn't work by itself, but uses people as its medium. These people, maybe even good people, find purpose in serving Evil. How can it be destroyed if it serves a purpose?*

That is an interesting thought, O Neelkanth, that Evil serves a purpose.

What purpose? The purpose of destruction? Why would the universe plan that?

Let's look at it another way. Do you believe there is nothing random in the universe? That everything exists for a reason. That everything serves a purpose.

Yes. If anything appears random, it only means that we haven't discovered its purpose just as yet.

So why does Evil exist? Why can't it be destroyed once and for all? Even when it is apparently destroyed, it rises once again. Maybe after much time has elapsed, perhaps in another form, but Evil does rise and will keep rising again and again. Why?

Shiva narrowed his eyes, absorbing Gopal's words. *Because even Evil serves a purpose...*

That is what Lord Manu believed. And the institution of the Mahadev acts as the balance, the control for that purpose. To take Evil out of the equation at the correct time.

Take it out of the equation? asked a surprised Shiva.

Yes. That is what Lord Manu said. It was just a line in his commandments. He said that the destroyers of Evil would understand what he means. My understanding of it is that Evil cannot and should not be destroyed completely. That it needs to be taken out of the equation at the right time, the time when it rises to cause total annihilation. Do you think he said that because the same Evil may serve the purpose of Good in another time?

I came here for answers, my friend. You are only throwing more questions at me.

Gopal laughed softly. *I'm sorry my friend. Our job is to give you the clues that we know. We are not supposed to interfere in your judgement. For that could lead to the triumph of Evil.*

I have heard that Lord Manu said Good and Evil are two sides of the same coin?

Yes, he did say so. They are two sides of the same coin. He didn't explain any further.

Strange. That doesn't make sense.

Gopal smiled. *It does sound strange. But I know you will make sense of it when the time is right.*

Shiva was silent for some time. He looked out across the temple pillars. In the distance, he could see the people of Vaishali outside the gates, waiting patiently for their Neelkanth. Shiva stared hard, then turned back towards the idol of Lord Matsya. *Gopal, my friend, what is the Evil that Lord Rudra took out of the equation. I know the Asuras were not evil. So what Evil did he destroy?*

You know the answer.

No, I don't.

Yes, you do. Think about it, Lord Neelkanth. What is the enduring legacy of Lord Rudra?

Shiva smiled. The answer was obvious. *Thank you, Panditji. I think we've spoken enough for today.*

May I offer my opinion on your first question?

Shiva was surprised. *About the Nagas?*

Yes.

Of course! Please.

It is obvious that you feel drawn to the Nagas. That you feel that your path to Evil lies through them.

Yes.

That can be due to two reasons. Either Evil exists at the end of that path.

Or?

Or Evil has caused its greatest destruction on that path.

Shiva took a deep breath. *You mean the Nagas may be the ones who suffered the most at the hands of Evil?*

Maybe.

Shiva leaned back against the pillar. He closed his eyes. *Maybe the Nagas deserve a hearing. Maybe everyone else has been unfair to them. Maybe they deserve the benefit of the doubt. But one of them has to answer to me. One of them awaits justice for Brahaspati's assassination.*

Gopal knew who Shiva was thinking about. He kept quiet.

— ⚘◎ᘁᛉ⊕ —

Sati stood in front of Athithigva in his private chambers. Standing next to her were Kali and Ganesh. The stunned King of Kashi did not know how to react.

Sati had returned from Icchawar that morning with twenty-seven lion skins, proof of the destruction of the man-eating pride. Special prayers had been intoned at the Vishwanath temple for the brave Kashi soldiers who had died there. Kaavas had been promoted to the rank of Major. The courage of the Branga platoon had also been acknowledged. The Brangas of Kashi would be exempt from taxes for the next three months. But this specific problem was particularly knotty for Athithigva. He did not know how to react to the presence of the two Nagas beside Sati. He dare not expel the relatives of the wife of the Neelkanth from his city. At the same time, he couldn't allow them to live openly in Kashi. His people would consider it a crime against the laws of Karma. Superstitions about the Nagas ran deep.

'My Lady,' said Athithigva carefully. 'How can we allow this?'

Kali was staring at Athithigva, livid at the humiliation being meted out to her, a Queen in her own right. She touched Sati's arm. '*Didi*, forget this...'

Sati just shook her head. 'Lord Athithigva, Kashi is a shining light of tolerance within India. It accepts all Indians, no matter what their faith or way of life. Isn't rejecting some noble and valiant people, just because they are Nagas, going against the very reasons that make your city a beacon for the downtrodden and marginalised?'

Athithigva looked down. 'But, My Lady, my people...'

'Your Highness, should you give in to your people's biases? Or instead, lead them onto a better path?'

The Kashi king remained silent, wavering.

'Please do not forget, Your Highness, that if the Kashi platoon has returned and the villagers of Icchawar are alive today, it is due to the bravery of Kali, Ganesh and their men. We would all have been killed by the lions. They have saved us. Do they not deserve honour in return?'

Athithigva nodded hesitantly. He looked out of the window of his private chambers. The Ganga flowed languidly, cradling the reflection of the Eastern palace on the far bank. Where his beloved sisters Maya led a miserable life, practically imprisoned. He would have loved to challenge the fear of the Nagas in his people. But had always lacked the courage. The fact that the Neelkanth's wife stood by her family, gave him hope. For who would dare to challenge the Neelkanth? Everyone knew how Shiva had abolished one set of unjust laws. So why not the same for the Nagas too?

The King turned back towards Sati. 'Your family can stay, My Lady. I'm sure they will be comfortable in the wing of the Kashi palace allocated to the Lord Neelkanth.'

'I'm sure they will,' replied a smiling Sati. 'Thank you so much, Your Highness.'

— ⊹◎ᘮ⼂⊕ —

Shiva was standing at the head of the ship, Parvateshwar next to him.

'I've doubled the speed of the lead ship, My Lord,' said Parvateshwar.

Shiva had asked Parvateshwar to ensure a quick arrival of their fleet to Kashi. He had been away from his family for more than two years. It was too long a time and he missed them dearly.

'Thank you, General,' smiled Shiva.

Parvateshwar bowed and turned to look at the Ganga again.

Shiva spoke with a hint of a smile on his face. 'So how is married life, General?'

Parvateshwar looked at Shiva with a broad smile. 'Heaven, My Lord. Absolute heaven. A very intense heaven though.'

Shiva smiled. 'Normal rules don't seem to apply, do they?'

Parvateshwar laughed out loud. 'Well, Anandmayi continues to update the rules as each day comes along and I just follow them!'

Shiva laughed loudly as well and patted his friend. 'Follow those rules, my friend, follow those rules. She loves you. You will be happy with her.'

Parvateshwar nodded heartily.

'Anandmayi told me that she has sent a cutter to Ayodhya to inform Emperor Dilipa of your nuptials,' said Shiva.

'Yes, she has,' said Parvateshwar. 'His Highness will be coming to Kashi to receive us. He has promised to hold another, completely extravagant celebration for us in Kashi within ten days of our arrival.'

'That should be fun!'

— ༄☉ᠸ⊕ —

'Yes, My Lord?' asked Nandi.

Nandi and Bhagirath were with Shiva in his cabin.

'When we reach Kashi, stay close to Prince Bhagirath.'

'Why, My Lord?' asked Bhagirath.

Shiva raised his hand. 'Just trust me.'

Bhagirath narrowed his eyes. 'My father's coming to Kashi?'

Shiva nodded.

'I will be the Prince's shadow, My Lord,' said Nandi. 'Nothing will happen to him as long as I am alive.'

Shiva looked up. 'I don't want anything happening to you either, Nandi. Both of you keep your eyes open and remain careful.'

— ⵝ◍Ⴑ⟡⊕ —

'My son!' cried Sati as Kartik ran into her arms.

Kartik was only three, but, due to the Somras, he looked like a six–year–old. He screamed, '*Maa*!'

Sati twirled her son around happily. 'I've missed you so much.'

'I missed you too,' said Kartik softly, still unhappy about his mother leaving him behind.

'I'm sorry I had to go away, my child. But I had very important work to do.'

'Next time, take me with you.'

'I will try.'

Kartik smiled, seemingly mollified. He then pulled his wooden sword out of the scabbard. 'Look at this, *Maa*.'

Sati frowned. 'What's this?'

'I started learning how to fight the day you left. If I was a good soldier, you would have taken me with you, no?'

Sati smiled broadly and plonked Kartik on her lap. 'You are a born soldier, my son.'

Kartik smiled and hugged his mother.

'You know how you always ask me for a brother, Kartik?'

Kartik nodded vigorously. 'Yes! Yes!'

'Well, I've found a wonderful brother for you. An elder brother who will always take care of you.'

Kartik frowned and looked towards the door. He saw a giant of a man enter the chambers. He was wearing a simple white *dhoti* and an *angvastram* was draped loosely across his right shoulder, his immense stomach jiggling with every breath. But it was the face that startled Kartik. The head of an elephant on top of a human body.

Ganesh smiled broadly, his heart beating uncertainly, anxious for Kartik's acceptance. 'How are you, Kartik?'

The normally fearless Kartik hid behind his mother.

'Kartik,' smiled Sati, pointing at his *elder brother* Ganesh. 'Why don't you say hello to your *dada?*'

The boy continued to stare at Ganesh. 'Are you human?'

'Yes. I am your brother,' smiled Ganesh.

Kartik didn't say anything. But Sati had taught Ganesh well. The Naga held out his hand, displaying a succulent mango, Kartik's favourite fruit. The boy was at once delighted and surprised at seeing a mango so late in the year. He inched forward.

'Do you want this, Kartik?' asked Ganesh.

Kartik frowned, drawing out his wooden sword. 'You are not going to make me fight for it, are you?'

Ganesh laughed. 'No, I'm not. But I will charge a hug from you.'

Kartik hesitated and looked at Sati.

Sati nodded and smiled. 'You can trust him.'

Kartik moved slowly and grabbed the mango. Ganesh embraced his little brother, who immediately got busy, biting strongly into his favourite fruit. He looked up at

Ganesh and smiled, whispering between loud slurps. 'Wow... Thank you... dada.'

Ganesh smiled again and patted Kartik lightly on his head.

— 🕉 —

The lead ship docked lightly onto the Dasashwamedh ghat. As the gangway was being drawn, Shiva's eyes desperately sought Sati. He could see Emperor Dilipa and King Athithigva standing at the royal platform, with their families. There was a multitude of Kashi citizens thronging the ghats, but...

'Where is she?'

'I'll find her, My Lord,' said Bhagirath as he disembarked, closely followed by Nandi.

'And, Bhagirath...'

'Yes, My Lord,' said Bhagirath, stopping.

'After all this is over, please take Purvaka to the King's palace. Ensure that he is comfortable in my family's area.'

'Yes, My Lord,' said Bhagirath, as he darted away, ignoring Dilipa, his father and the Emperor of Swadweep. But Nandi was surprised at the changes visible in the Emperor. Dilipa looked at least ten years younger, his face glowing with good health. Nandi frowned, before turning to catch up with Bhagirath.

Shiva stepped off the gangway.

Dilipa directed one long hard stare at the retreating form of his son and shook his head, before turning towards the Neelkanth. He bowed low before Shiva, touching his feet.

'May your dynasty continue to spread prosperity, Your Highness,' said Shiva, himself bowing his head with a namaste to Dilipa.

Veerbhadra, meanwhile, had found Krittika and spun her in his arms. An ecstatic yet embarrassed Krittika tried to free herself, blushing as she asked her husband to restrain his public display of affection.

Athithigva also stepped forward and sought Shiva's blessings. Having completed the formalities, the Neelkanth turned, searching for his family. 'Where is my family, Your Highness?'

'*Baba*!'

Shiva turned with a broad smile. Kartik was running towards him. As he lifted his son into his arms, Shiva said, 'By the holy lake, you have grown really fast, Kartik.'

'I missed you!' whispered Kartik, holding his father tight.

'I missed you too,' said Shiva. His pleasure at seeing his son turned into surprise as he recognised the mouthwatering smell of ripened mangoes. 'Who has been giving you mangoes so late in the season?'

Just then Sati appeared in front of Shiva. A smiling Shiva held Kartik to his right and wrapped his left arm around Sati, holding his world close to him, oblivious to the thousands staring at them. 'I've missed you both so much.'

'And we missed you,' smiled Sati, pulling her head back to glance at her husband.

Shiva pulled her close again, eyes closed, taking pleasure in his family's loving touch, his wife and son resting their heads on his shoulders. 'Let's go home.'

— 𝕚⦿𝕌𝟜⊕ —

The carriage was moving slowly down Kashi's Sacred

Avenue. The Emperor of Ayodhya and the King of Kashi followed in their carriages while the brigade that had travelled with Shiva marched behind. Citizens had lined the streets, to get their first glimpse of their Lord after more than two–and–a–half years. Shiva sat comfortably, Sati next to him and Kartik on his lap, waving to the crowds.

Both Shiva and Sati spoke simultaneously. 'I have something to tell...'

Shiva started laughing. 'You first.'

'No. No. You first,' said Sati.

'I insist. You first.'

Sati swallowed. 'What have you found out about the Nagas, Shiva?'

'Surprising things actually. Maybe I have misjudged them. We need to find out more about them. Maybe they are not all bad. Maybe they just have a few bad apples amongst them, like in all communities.'

Sati sighed deeply, finding some release for the tension coiled inside her like a snake.

'What happened?' asked Shiva, staring hard at his wife.

'Umm, there is something that I have also discovered recently. Something very surprising. Something that was kept hidden from me until now. It is about the Nagas.'

'What?'

'I found... that...'

Shiva was surprised to see Sati so nervous. 'What's the matter, darling?'

'I found out that I'm related to them.'

'What?!'

'Yes.'

'How can that be? Your father hates the Nagas!'

'It could be guilt more than hatred.'

'Guilt?'

'I was not born alone.'

Shiva frowned.

'A twin was born along with me. I have a sister.'

Shiva was shocked. 'Where is she? Who kidnapped her? How did this happen in Meluha?'

'She was not kidnapped,' whispered Sati. 'She was abandoned.'

'Abandoned?' Shiva stared at his wife, at a loss for words.

'Yes, she was born a Naga.'

Shiva held Sati's hand. 'Where did you find her? Is she all right?'

Sati looked up at Shiva, her eyes moist. 'I didn't find her. She found me. She saved my life.'

Shiva smiled, not at all surprised to hear yet another tale of Naga heroism and generosity. 'What's her name?'

'Kali. Queen Kali.'

'Queen?'

'Yes, the Queen of the Nagas.'

Shiva's eyes widened in surprise. Kali may be the one who would help him find Brahaspati's killer. Maybe that's why fate had conspired to bring them together. 'Where is she?'

'Here in Kashi. Outside our palace. Waiting to meet you. Waiting for you to accept her.'

Shiva smiled, shaking his head and pulling Sati close to him. 'She's your family. That makes her my family. Where's the question of my not accepting her?'

Sati smiled slightly, resting her head on Shiva's shoulders. 'But she is not the only Naga waiting for your acceptance.'

Shiva frowned.

'Another, even more tragic secret, was kept from me,' said Sati.

'What?'

'I was told ninety years back that my first child was stillborn. As still as a statue.'

Shiva nodded, as though sensing where this conversation was headed, holding his wife's hand tighter.

'That was a lie,' sobbed Sati. 'He...'

'He was alive?!'

'He is still alive!'

Shiva's jaw dropped in shock. 'You mean... I have another son?'

Sati stared up at Shiva, smiling through her tears.

'By the Holy Lake! I have another son!'

Sati nodded, happy at Shiva's joy.

'Bhadra! Drive quickly. My son waits for me!'

Chapter 19

Rage of the Blue Lord

Shiva's carriage quickly turned into the gates of Athithigva's palace. As it sped along the road around the central garden, an excited Shiva lifted Kartik into his arms and reached for the door. He was off as soon as the vehicle stopped, setting Kartik on the ground, holding his hand and walking quickly ahead. Sati followed.

Shiva stopped in his tracks as he saw Kali, holding a *puja thali,* a *prayer tray,* with a ceremonial lamp and flowers.

'What the...!'

Standing in front of Shiva was a splitting image of Sati. Her eyes, face, build — everything. Except that her skin was a jet black to Sati's bronze. Her hair open, unlike Sati who usually restrained her flowing tresses. The woman was wearing royal clothing and ornaments, a cream and red coloured *angvastram* covered her entire torso. Then he noticed the two extra hands on her shoulders.

A nervous Kali continued to stare at Shiva, unsure. Much to her surprise, Shiva stepped forward and embraced her gently, careful not to disturb the puja thali.

'What a pleasure it is to meet you,' said Shiva, smiling broadly.

Kali smiled tentatively, shocked by Shiva's warm gesture, clearly at a loss for words.

Shiva tapped the puja thali. 'I think you are supposed to move this around my face six or seven times in order to welcome me home.'

Kali laughed. 'I'm sorry. Just that I have been very nervous.'

'Nothing to be nervous about,' grinned Shiva. 'Just circle the thali around, shower flowers on me and be sure not to drop the lamp. Burns are damn painful!'

Kali laughed and completed the ceremony, applying a red *tilak* on Shiva's forehead.

'And now,' said Shiva. 'Where's my other son?'

Kali stepped aside. Shiva saw Ganesh in the distance, atop the stairs leading to Athithigva's main palace.

'That's my dada!' beamed Kartik at his father.

Shiva smiled at Kartik. 'Let's go meet him.'

Holding Kartik's hand, Shiva walked up the flight of stairs, with Sati and Kali in tow. Everyone else waited quietly at the bottom, giving the family its own private moment.

Ganesh, in a red *dhoti* and white *angvastram*, was standing at the entryway of his mother's wing of the palace, almost like a guard. As Shiva reached him, Ganesh bent to touch his father's feet.

Shiva touched Ganesh's head gently, held his shoulders and pulled the Naga up to embrace him, blessing him with a long life. '*Ayushman bhav*, my...'

Shiva suddenly stopped as he stared hard at Ganesh's calm, almond-shaped eyes. His hands were rigid on Ganesh's shoulders, eyes narrowed hard.

Ganesh shut his eyes and cursed his fate silently. He knew he had been recognised.

Shiva's eyes continued to bore into Ganesh.

Sati, looking surprised, whispered, 'What's the matter, Shiva?'

Shiva ignored her. He continued to stare at Ganesh with repressed rage. He reached for his pouch. 'I have something that belongs to you.'

Ganesh kept quiet, continuing to stare at Shiva, his eyes melancholic. He didn't need to look in order to know what Shiva was bringing out of his pouch. The bracelet, whose clasp had been destroyed, belonged to him. He had lost it at Mount Mandar. It was frayed at the edges by flames that had tried to consume it. The embroidered symbol of Aum, in the center, was unblemished. But it wasn't a normal Aum symbol. The representation of the ancient holy word had been constructed from snakes. The serpent

Aum!

Ganesh quietly took his bracelet from Shiva's hand.

Sati looked on with disbelieving eyes. 'Shiva! What is going on?'

Furious rage was pouring out of Shiva's eyes.

'Shiva...,' repeated Sati, as she touched her husband's shoulder anxiously.

Shiva flinched at Sati's touch. 'Your son killed my brother,' he growled.

Sati was shocked. Disbelieving.

Shiva spoke again. This time his voice was hard, furious. 'Your son killed Brahaspati!'

Kali sprung forward. 'But it was an...'

The Queen of the Nagas fell silent at a gesture from Ganesh.

The Naga continued to look straight at Shiva. Offering no explanations. Waiting for the Neelkanth's verdict, his punishment.

Shiva stepped close to Ganesh. Uncomfortably close. Till his fuming breath blew hard on Ganesh. 'You are my wife's son. It's the only reason why I'm not going to kill you.'

Ganesh lowered his eyes. Hands held in supplication. Refusing to say anything.

'Get out of my house,' roared Shiva. 'Get out of this land. Never show your face here again. The next time, I may not be so forgiving.'

'But... But Shiva. He's my son!' begged Sati.

'He killed Brahaspati.'

'Shiva...'

'HE KILLED BRAHASPATI!'

Sati stared blankly, tears flowing down her cheeks. 'Shiva, he's my son. I cannot live without him.'

'Then live without me.'

Sati was stunned. 'Shiva, please don't do this. How can you ask me to make this choice?'

Ganesh finally spoke. 'Father, I...'

Shiva interrupted Ganesh angrily. 'I am not your father!'

Ganesh bowed his head, took a deep breath and spoke up once again. 'O Great Mahadev, you are known for your fairness. Your sense of justice. The crime is mine. Don't punish my mother for my sins.' Ganesh pulled his knife out, the same knife that Sati had flung at him in Ayodhya. 'Take my life. But don't curse my mother with a fate worse than death. She cannot live without you.'

'No!' screamed Sati as she darted in front of Ganesh. 'Please, Shiva. He's my son... He's my son...'

Shiva's anger turned ice cold. 'Looks like you've made your choice.'

He picked up Kartik.

'Shiva...' pleaded Sati. 'Please don't go. Please...'

Shiva looked at Sati, his eyes moist, but voice ice cold. 'This is something I cannot accept, Sati. Brahaspati was like my brother.'

Shiva walked down the steps, carrying Kartik with him

— ᛒ⦿ᚢᛏ⊕ —

as a shocked Kashi citizenry kept deathly silent.

'Shiva doesn't know the entire picture. Why didn't you tell him?' asked an agitated Kali.

Kali and Ganesh were sitting in Sati's chambers in Athithigva's palace. Sati, torn between her love for her long-lost son and her devotion to her husband, had gone to the Branga building, where Shiva had set up temporary quarters. She was trying to reason with him.

'I can't. I have given my word, *Mausi*,' answered Ganesh, his calm voice hiding the deep sadness within.

'But...'

'No, *Mausi*. This remains between you and me. There is only one condition under which the secret behind the attack on Mount Mandar can be revealed. I don't see that happening too soon.'

'But tell your mother at least.'

'A word of honour does not stop at a mother's door.'

'*Didi* is suffering. I thought you'd do anything for her.'

'I will. She can live without me but not without the Mahadev. She's not letting me leave because of her guilt at not being there for me earlier.'

'What are you saying? You will leave? '

'Yes. In another ten days. Once the Meluhan General and the Chandravanshi Princess' wedding celebrations are done. Then father can return home.'

'Your mother will not allow this.'

'It doesn't matter. I will leave. I will not be the reason

— $\dagger \textcircled{0} \overline{U} \, \dagger \circledast$ —

for my parent's separation.'

'Your Highness,' said Kanakhala, the Meluhan Prime Minister. 'It is not advisable for you to leave for Swadweep without a formal invitation. It is against protocol.'

'What nonsense,' said Daksha. 'I am the Emperor of India. I can go wherever I please.'

Kanakhala was a loyal Prime Minister. But she did not want her Emperor to commit any act which would embarrass the Empire. 'But the terms of the Ayodhya treaty are that Swadweep is only our vassal and has direct control over its own territory. Protocol dictates that we seek their permission. They cannot deny permission. You are their Lord. But it's a formality that must be completed.'

'No formalities needed. I'm just a father going to meet his favourite daughter!'

Kanakhala frowned. 'Your Highness, you have only one daughter.'

'Yes. Yes. I know,' said Daksha, waving his hand dismissively. 'Look I am leaving in three weeks. You can send a messenger to Swadweep asking for permission. All right?'

'Your Highness, bird couriers are still not set up in Ayodhya. You know how inefficient those people are. And Ayodhya is further than Kashi. So even if the messenger leaves today, he will reach Ayodhya in a little over three months. You will reach Kashi at the same time.'

Daksha smiled. 'Yes, I will. Go and make the arrangements for my departure.'

— ⵣⵟⵟⵟⵟⵟ —

Kanakhala sighed, bowed and left the chambers.

The Emperor of Swadweep, Dilipa, had planned grand festivities to celebrate the wedding of his daughter Anandmayi with Parvateshwar. But the unexpected bitterness between the Mahadev and his wife had soured the mood. However, the pujas could not be cancelled. It would be an insult to the gods. While all the parties had been put on hold, the pujas to the elemental gods Agni, Vayu, Prithvi, Varun, Surya and Som were to proceed as planned.

The puja for the *Sun god* was being conducted at the *Surya* temple on the Sacred Avenue, just a little South of Assi Ghat. A grand platform had been erected on the road, directly overlooking the temple. Shiva and Sati were seated next to each other on specific thrones designed for them. Unlike their earlier public appearances, they were sitting stiff and apart. Shiva was not even looking at Sati, righteous anger still radiating from every pore in his body. He had only come for the puja and would return to the Branga residence as soon as it was over.

Every citizen of Kashi, who had never seen Shiva's temper, was deeply troubled. But none more than Kartik.

He had been pestering both his parents to get back together. Knowing Kartik would get even more insistent if he saw the both of them together, Shiva had told Krittika to take Kartik to the park adjoining the nearby Sankat Mochan temple.

Next to Shiva on the platform built for the thrones, were Kali, Bhagirath, Dilipa, Athithigva and Ayurvati. Parvateshwar and Anandmayi were at the temple platform, where the Surya Pandit helped them consecrate their love with the purifying blessings of the Sun God.

To avoid an embarrassing situation, Ganesh had wisely declined his invitation to the puja.

While all of Kashi was at the puja, Ganesh sat by himself at the Sankat Mochan temple. He had first gone to the adjoining park to meet his little brother for the first time in ten days, carrying a sack full of mangoes. After a lively thirty minutes, Ganesh had retired to the temple, leaving Kartik to play with Krittika and his five bodyguards. He sat there quietly, gazing at Lord Hanuman, the most ardent devotee of Lord Ram.

Lord Hanuman was called *Sankat Mochan* for a reason. People believed he always *helped his devotees in a crisis*. Ganesh thought that even Lord Hanuman would find it impossible to help him get out of this mess. Neither could he imagine a life without his mother nor could he bear it if he became the reason for his parents living separately. He had decided to leave Kashi the next day. But he knew that he would spend the rest of his life pining for his mother, now that he had experienced her love.

He smiled as he heard the loud cacophony of Kartik's boisterous antics in the park.

The carefree laughter of a soul strongly nourished by his mother's love.

Ganesh sighed, knowing such carefree laughter would never be a part of his destiny. He drew out his sword, pulled a smooth stone and started doing what Kshatriyas usually do when they have nothing else to do: Sharpen their blades.

So lost was Ganesh in his thoughts that he paid heed to his gut instinct quite late. Something strange was happening in the park. He held his breath and listened. And then it hit him. The park had gone absolutely quiet. What had happened to the loud laughter of Kartik, Krittika and his companions?

Ganesh got up quickly, put his sword into his scabbard and started walking towards the park. And then he heard it. A low growl, followed by a deafening roar. The kill was nigh.

Lions!

Ganesh drew his sword and started sprinting. A man was stumbling towards him. One of the Kashi soldiers, who was slashed across his arm. The clear markings of sharp claws.

'How many?' Ganesh was loud enough for the soldier to hear even at a distance.

The Kashi soldier did not respond. He just stumbled forward, shell-shocked.

Ganesh reached him in no time, jolted him hard and repeated again. 'How many?'

'Thr...ee,' said the soldier.

'Get the Mahadev!'

The soldier still looked shocked.

Ganesh shook him again. 'Get the Mahadev! Now!'

The soldier started running towards the Sun temple as

Ganesh turned towards the park.

The Kashi soldier knew what he was running away from and yet his feet were unsteady. Ganesh knew what he was running towards, but his pace was sure and strong.

He used a side stone as leverage to leap over the park fence without a sound.

He landed on the other side, close to a lioness busy crushing the broken neck of a soldier between her jaws, asphyxiating an already dead man. Ganesh slashed at her as he ran by, cutting through a major vein on her shoulder. Blood poured out of the lioness' wound as Ganesh raced towards Krittika, another Kashi soldier and Kartik, who were at the centre of the garden. Two other soldiers were lying dead in a far corner. Judging from their positions, they were probably the first to be killed.

Ganesh dashed to Krittika's side. They were hemmed in from one side by a lioness and a massive liger.

Bhoomidevi be merciful! They have followed us from Icchawar!

The other side was blocked off by the lioness whose shoulder was bleeding profusely after Ganesh's blow.

Kartik, his wooden sword drawn, was ready for battle. Ganesh knew Kartik was childishly brave enough to charge at the liger with just his wooden sword. He stood in front of his brother, with Krittika on one side and the soldier on the other.

'No way out,' whispered Krittika, sword drawn.

Ganesh knew Krittika was not a trained warrior. Her maternal instincts would drive her to protect Kartik, but she probably wouldn't be able to kill any of the cats. The soldier on the other side was shivering. He was unlikely to be much help.

Ganesh nodded towards the bleeding lioness limping

towards them. 'She'll not last too long. I've cut a major vein.'

The liger was circling them while moving towards the front, as the lionesses flanked the humans. Ganesh knew it was only a matter of time. They were preparing for the charge.

'Pull back,' whispered Ganesh. 'Slowly.'

There was a hollow in the main trunk of a banyan tree behind them. Ganesh intended to push Kartik in there and defend it from the lionesses.

'We can't last long,' said Krittika. 'I'll try to distract them. You run with Kartik.'

Ganesh didn't turn towards Krittika, staring hard at the liger. But his admiration for Veerbhadra's wife shot up. She was willing to die for his brother.

'That won't work,' said Ganesh. 'I can't move fast enough with Kartik. The walls are high. Help is on its way. The Mahadev is coming. We just have to hold the lions off for some time.'

Krittika and the soldier followed Ganesh's lead as they edged slowly to the rear, pushing Kartik back. The liger and lionesses crept forward, their blind aggression from just a few moments earlier dissipating at the sight of the giant man holding a blood-stained sword.

A little while later, Kartik had been pushed into the banyan hollow, with the tree's hanging roots tied around it to prevent him from charging out. He was safe. At least for as long as Ganesh stood.

The cats charged. Ganesh was surprised to see the limping lioness bounding forward. Krittika was covering that area.

'Stay low!' shouted Ganesh. He couldn't move to support Krittika since the liger could charge through the opening to attack Kartik. 'Stay low Krittika! She's injured. She can't leap high!'

Krittika had held her sword low, waiting for the wounded lioness to reach her. But to her surprise, the big cat suddenly veered left. As Krittika was about to charge after her, she heard a blood-curdling scream.

The lioness from the other side had used the distraction and crept up to the Kashi soldier. He was screaming in agony as the lioness dragged his body back, slashing at him with her claws. The soldier kept screeching, trying to push the lioness back, hitting her with weak blows from his sword. She kept biting into him, finally getting a choke hold on the convulsing soldier's neck. Moments later he was dead.

The liger remained stationary in front of Ganesh, blocking any escape. The other lioness left the dead Kashi soldier and returned to position.

Ganesh breathed slowly. He marvelled at the intelligent, pack-hunting behaviour these animals were displaying.

'Stay low,' said Ganesh to Krittika. 'I will cover the liger and this lioness. You have to focus on the injured one. I cannot see to all three. These animals hunt as a pack. Whoever gets distracted is dead.'

Krittika nodded as the injured lioness started ambling towards her. The animal was losing too much blood from her shoulder injury. She was slow in her movements. Suddenly, she charged at Krittika.

As the lioness came close, she leapt high. As high as her injured shoulder allowed. It was a weak jump. Krittika bent low, holding her sword up high, brutally stabbing it into the lioness' heart. The beast fell on Krittika and was soon dead.

Ganesh glanced at Krittika out of the corner of his eye.

Before being felled, the lioness had managed to dig her claws into Krittika and rip away a part of her shoulder. Krittika was bleeding profusely, practically immobile under the lioness' corpse which was pinning her down. But she was alive. She had Ganesh in her line of sight.

Ganesh flipped his shield onto his back, pulled out his second shorter sword and stood close to the banyan tree. The short sword had a twin blade, which clipped together as the victim's body moved. It was a fearsome weapon if it was stabbed deep into a body as it would cut again and again.

Ganesh waited, biding time, hoping the Mahadev would arrive before it was too late.

The liger moved to Ganesh's right. The lioness to his left. There was enough distance between the beasts to make it difficult for Ganesh to observe both of them at the same time. Having established a good offensive position, the animals moved forward slowly, in sync.

The lioness suddenly charged. Ganesh lashed out with his left hand. But the shorter sword did not have the reach. The movement forced him to look left. The liger, taking advantage, charged into Ganesh and bit hard into his right leg, at the same spot that Ganesh had been injured in, at Icchawar.

Ganesh screamed in agony and swung hard with his right sword arm, slashing the liger across the face. The liger retreated, but not before he had bitten off a chunk of Ganesh's thigh.

Ganesh was losing blood fast. He stepped back, leaning against the banyan tree. His kid brother was screaming behind him. Shouting to be let out so that he could battle the lions too. Ganesh did not move. And the cats charged again.

This time the liger came first. Seeing a pattern in their attack, Ganesh kept his eyes dead centre, able to now see both the liger and lioness. He held his right sword out to stop the liger from coming in too close. The liger slowed down and the lioness came in faster. Ganesh jabbed hard with his short sword, straight into the lioness' shoulder, but not before she had bitten into Ganesh's limb. The lioness retreated with Ganesh's short, twin bladed sword buried in her shoulder after having left another gaping injury in Ganesh's left arm.

Ganesh knew that he couldn't stand on his feet much longer. He was losing too much blood. He did not want to fall sideways because Kartik would then become vulnerable. He fell back and sat against the tree, covering the hollow with his body. The animals would have to go through him to get to his brother.

Due to the severe loss of blood, Ganesh's vision was beginning to blur. But despite that, he could see that the wound on the lioness had been telling. She was still struggling at a distance from him, trying to lick her shoulder, unable to stand straight. As she moved, the twin-blade cut further into her, hacking tissue away from bone. He saw the liger moving in from the right, edging closer. Once close enough, the liger bounded and lashed out with his paw while Ganesh slashed with his sword at the same time. The liger's claws tore through Ganesh's face, causing a deep gash on his long nose. Simultaneously, Ganesh's blow gouged the liger's left eye. The animal retreated, howling in agony.

But Kartik had seen what Ganesh hadn't. He was trying to reach out with his wooden sword. But he couldn't get far enough. 'Dada! Look out!'

The lioness had used Ganesh's distraction to crawl closer. She lunged forward and bit into Ganesh's chest. Ganesh swung his blade, slashing her face. The lioness retreated, snarling in pain, but not before ripping out a large amount of flesh from Ganesh's torso. The Naga's heart, pumping blood and adrenaline through the body at a furious rate, was now working against him as the numerous wounds leaked blood alarmingly.

Ganesh knew his end was near. He couldn't last much longer. And then he heard a loud war cry.

'HAR HAR MAHADEV!'

A warm, comforting darkness was beckoning Ganesh. He struggled to stay awake.

Nearly fifty furious Suryavanshi soldiers charged into the park. They fell upon the two big cats. The weakened animals did not stand a chance and were soon killed.

Through his rapidly fading vision, Ganesh thought he saw a handsome figure rushing towards him, bloodied sword held to the side. His throat, an iridescent blue. Behind the man, he could barely make out the blurred vision of a bronzed woman racing towards him. A warrior Princess, the blood of the liger splattered all over her.

The Naga smiled, delighted to be the bearer of good news to two of the most important people in his world.

'Don't worry... *baba*,' whispered Ganesh to his *father*. 'Your son is safe... He is hidden... behind me.'

Saying so, Ganesh collapsed. Unconscious.

Chapter 20

Never Alone, My Brother

Ganesh thought he should feel pain. But there was nothing.

He opened his eyes. He could barely distinguish the formidable Ayurvati next to his body.

He shifted his eyes down towards his ravaged body; skin torn asunder, flesh ripped out, blood congealed all over, arm bone sticking out, a gaping hole in his chest, ribs cracked and visible.

Bhoomidevi be merciful. I don't stand a chance.

Ganesh returned to darkness.

— ⵣ◍Ꙋ⵿⊕ —

A sharp sting on his chest. His eyes opened slowly. Barely.

Through the slits, he could see Ayurvati changing his dressing.

He could feel again.

A good thing, right?

He slipped into his dream world once again.

— ⵣ◍Ꙋ⵿⊕ —

A soft caress. Then the hand moved away. A sleeping Ganesh moved his head. He wanted the hand back. It returned to his face, stroking it gently.

Ganesh opened his eyes slightly. Sati was sitting next to him, leaning over, her eyes swollen, red.

Maa.

But Sati didn't respond. Maybe she hadn't heard him.

Ganesh could see outside the window behind Sati. It was raining.

The monsoons? How long have I been unconscious?

Ganesh saw a man leaning next to the window, against the wall. A strong man, whose normally mischievous eyes were expressionless. A man with a blue throat. A man staring intensely at him. Trying to figure him out.

Sleep snatched Ganesh away yet again.

— 𑀲𑀻𑀢𑀸 —

A warm touch on his arm. Someone was gently applying the ointment on him.

The Naga opened his eyes slowly. And was surprised to see the hand applying the medicine so tenderly was not soft and feminine, but strong and masculine.

He turned his eyes slowly to see the kindly doctor. The torso was powerful and muscled. But the neck! It was different. It radiated a divine blue light.

Ganesh was stunned. A gasp escaped his mouth.

The hand applying the medicine froze. Ganesh could feel a pair of eyes boring into him. And then the Neelkanth rose and left the room.

Ganesh shut his eyes again.

— 𑀲𑀻𑀢𑀸 —

Ganesh finally emerged from his sleepy cocoon after a long, long time without the immediate need to slip back into its safety. He could hear the soft pitter-patter of raindrops.

He loved the monsoon. The heavenly whiff of a rejuvenated earth. The melody of falling rain.

He turned his head slightly to his left. It was enough to wake Sati. She immediately rose from her bed at the far end of the room and walked up to Ganesh. She pulled a chair up close and rested her hand on her son's.

'How are you, my son?'

Ganesh smiled softly. He turned his head a little more.

Sati smiled and ran her fingers across her son's face. She knew he liked that.

'Krittika?'

'She's much better,' said Sati. 'She wasn't as badly injured as you. In fact she was out of the ayuralay very quickly. Just two weeks.'

'How long...?'

'How long have you been here?'

Ganesh nodded in reply.

'Sixty days. In and out of consciousness.'

'Rains...'

'The monsoon is almost over. The moisture led to complications, slowing down your healing process.'

Ganesh took a deep breath. He was tired.

'Go to sleep,' said Sati. 'Ayurvati ji says you are well on the road to recovery. You will be out of here soon.'

Ganesh smiled and went back to sleep.

— 𖤍 ⦿ � ⸙ ⊕ —

Ganesh was woken up abruptly by Ayurvati, who was staring at him pointedly.

'How long have I been sleeping?'

'Since the last time you were awake? A few hours. I sent your mother home. She needs to rest.'

Ganesh nodded.

Ayurvati picked some paste she had kneaded. 'Open your mouth.'

Ganesh winced at the foul smelling paste. 'What is this, Ayurvati ji?'

'It will make the pain go away.'

'But I don't feel any pain.'

'You will when I apply the ointment. So open your mouth and keep it under your tongue.'

Ayurvati waited for the medicine to take effect. Then she opened the dressing on Ganesh's chest. His wound had healed dramatically. Flesh had filled up and some scar tissue had formed.

'The skin will smoothen out,' said an aloof Ayurvati.

'I'm a warrior,' smiled Ganesh. 'Scars are more welcome than smooth skin.'

Ayurvati stared at Ganesh, impassive. Then she picked up a bowl.

Ganesh held his breath as Ayurvati started applying the ointment. Despite the anaesthetic, the ointment still stung. She finished applying the paste quickly and covered the wound again with a bandage of neem leaves.

Ayurvati was quick, efficient and sure, qualities that Ganesh admired deeply.

The Lord of the People took a deep breath, gathering some strength. 'I didn't think I would survive. Your reputation is truly deserved, Ayurvati ji.'

Ayurvati frowned. 'Where did you hear of me?'

'I was injured in Icchawar as well. And *Maa* told me that you could have healed me twice as fast. She said that you are the best doctor in the world.'

Ayurvati raised her eyebrows. 'You have a silver tongue. Capable of making anyone smile. Just like the Lord Neelkanth. It's sad you don't have his untainted heart.'

Ganesh kept quiet.

'I admired Brahaspati. He was not just a good man, but a fount of knowledge. The world suffered when he died before his time.'

Ganesh did not respond, his sad eyes looking deep into the doctor's eyes.

'Now, let me look at that arm,' said Ayurvati.

She yanked his bandage open. Hard enough to make it sting, but soft enough to not cause any serious damage.

Ganesh didn't flinch.

— 𑀓𑀇𑀝𑀧𑀒 —

The next day, Ganesh woke up to find his mother and aunt in the room, whispering.

'*Maa, Mausi,*' whispered Ganesh.

Both the sisters turned to him with a smile.

'Do you want something to eat or drink?' asked Sati.

'Yes, *Maa*. But can I also go for a walk today? I've been sleeping for sixty days. This is terrible.'

Kali smiled. 'I'll speak with Ayurvati. For now, stay put.'

As Kali left to find Ayurvati, Sati pulled her chair closer to Ganesh.

'I've got *parathas* for you,' said Sati, opening a small ivory box that she was carrying.

Ganesh beamed. He absolutely loved the stuffed *flat breads* his mother made. But his smile vanished just as quickly when he remembered that so did his step-father, Shiva.

Sati rose to find the mouth rinse Ayurvati had prescribed for Ganesh before he could eat.

'Has father returned to your quarters, *Maa*?'

Sati looked back from the medicine cabinet. 'Now you don't worry about these things.'

'Has he started speaking to you at least?'

'You needn't worry about this,' said Sati as she walked back to Ganesh.

The Naga was staring at the ceiling, guilt gnawing at his heart. He narrowed his eyes. 'Did he...'

'Yes he did,' replied Sati. 'Shiva came to check on you every day. But I don't think he'll be coming from today.'

Ganesh smiled sadly and bit his lip.

Sati patted him on the head. 'Everything will become all right when it is meant to become all right.'

'I wish I could explain what happened at Mount Mandar. I wish I could explain why it happened. I don't know if he would forgive me. But at least he would understand.'

'Kali has told me a little bit. I understand somewhat. But Brahaspati ji? He was a great man. The world lost something when he died. Even I cannot understand completely. And Shiva loved him like a brother. How can we expect him to understand?'

Ganesh looked at Sati with sad eyes.

'But you saved Kartik's life,' said Sati. 'You saved me. I know that's worth a lot to Shiva. Give him time. He will come around.'

Ganesh remained silent, clearly sceptical.

— ⚴ᚺ —

The next day, with Ayurvati's permission, Ganesh left his ayuralay room to take a short walk in the garden next door to Athithigva's grand palace. Ganesh walked slowly, leaning on Kali's shoulder, with a walking stick taking the bulk of his weight. He had wanted to walk alone, but Kali would hear none of it. As they reached the garden, they heard the loud sounds of clashing steel.

Ganesh narrowed his eyes. 'Someone's practicing. Practicing hard!'

Kali smiled. She knew Ganesh liked nothing better than seeing warriors practice. 'Let's go.'

The Naga Queen helped Ganesh to the central area of the garden. Ganesh was, meanwhile, commenting on the quality of the practise, based on the sounds he heard. 'Quick moves. These are steel swords, not meant for practice. Accomplished warriors duel over there.'

Kali simply helped Ganesh through the fence gate.

As they entered, Ganesh recoiled. Kali strengthened her hold on him. 'Relax. He is not in danger.'

At a distance, Kartik was engaged in a furious duel with Parvateshwar. He was moving at a speed that shocked Ganesh. The three-year-old may have been the size of a seven-year-old, but he was still significantly smaller than the gargantuan Parvateshwar. The Meluhan General was swinging hard with his sword. But Kartik was using his size to devastating effect. He bent low, forcing Parvateshwar to sweep lower with his sword, an action that most skilled swordsmen were not good at. Nobody trained to battle midgets. Kartik also had the ability to jab and swing with shattering speed and accuracy, swinging up at Parvateshwar at an angle that any grown man would have found impossible to defend. In just a few minutes,

Kartik had already stopped short of three deathly blows at the Meluhan General, all in the lower torso area.

Ganesh stood gaping.

'He's been practicing every day since you were injured,' said Kali.

Ganesh was even more amazed by something he had seen only a handful of warriors do. 'Kartik uses two swords simultaneously.'

'Yes,' smiled Kali. 'He doesn't use a shield. He strikes with his left hand also. The boy says that offence is better than defence!'

Ganesh heard Sati's voice speak out loudly. 'Stop!'

He turned to see his mother rise from a ledge at the corner.

'Sorry to disturb you, *Pitratulya,*' said Sati to Parvateshwar, the man she respected *like a father*. 'But perhaps Kartik may want to meet his dada.'

Parvateshwar looked up at Ganesh. The Meluhan General did not acknowledge Sati's older son, not even a curt nod. He simply stepped back.

Kartik smiled at seeing Ganesh ambling slowly towards him. Ganesh was shocked at the change in Kartik. His eyes didn't have the innocent look of a little boy anymore. They had steel in them. Pure, unadulterated steel.

'You fight very well, brother,' said Ganesh. 'I didn't know.'

Kartik hugged his brother, holding him tight. The embrace hurt Ganesh's wounds, but he didn't flinch or pull back.

The boy stepped back. 'You will never again fight alone, dada. Never.'

Ganesh smiled and embraced his little brother once again, his eyes moist.

The Naga noticed that Sati and Kali were silent. He

looked up to see Parvateshwar turning towards the gate. Parvateshwar banged his right fist on his chest and bowed low, executing the Meluhan military salute. Ganesh turned in the direction Parvateshwar was facing.

At the gate stood Shiva. Arms crossed across his chest. Expression blank. His hair windswept and clothes fluttering in the breeze. Staring at Ganesh.

Ganesh, with Kartik still in his embrace, bowed low in respect to the Neelkanth. When he straightened up, Shiva was gone.

— 人◎ᚾᚫ⊕ —

'He may not be such a bad man, Shiva,' said Veerbhadra, exhaling the marijuana fumes softly.

Shiva looked up with a deadpan expression. Nandi looked at Veerbhadra in alarm.

But Veerbhadra was adamant. 'We don't know everything about him, Shiva. I spoke to Parshuram. It was Ganesh who assisted him, the one who helped him fight against the injustices he faced. Apparently, Parshuram had been grievously injured when the Brangas first attacked him. Ganesh found the wounded Brahmin on the banks of the Madhumati and rescued him. On hearing Parshuram's terrible story, he also swore to support him in any way that he could.'

Shiva simply took the chillum from Veerbhadra and took a deep drag, not saying a word.

'You know what Krittika said. Ganesh fought like a man possessed to save Kartik, nearly sacrificing his own life in the process. Krittika is a good judge of character. She says that Ganesh has a heart of gold.'

Shiva kept quiet, exhaling smoke.

'I heard from Queen Kali,' continued Veerbhadra, 'that it was Ganesh who arranged for the Naga medicine which saved Kartik's life during his birth.'

Shiva looked up, surprised. He narrowed his eyes. 'He is a strange man. I don't know what to make of him. He has saved my son's life. Twice, if I am to believe you. He saved my wife's life in Icchawar. For all this I must love him. But when I look at him, I hear Brahaspati's desperate cry for help ring in my ears. And then, I want nothing more than to cut off his head.'

Veerbhadra looked down, unhappy.

The Neelkanth shook his head. 'But I know of a man that I definitely want answers from.'

Veerbhadra looked up at him, suspecting his friend's train of thought. 'His Highness?'

'Yes,' said Shiva. 'Kali and Ganesh could not have been abandoned without his consent.'

Nandi piped up for his Emperor. 'But My Lord, Emperor Daksha had no choice. That is the law. Naga children cannot live in Meluha.'

'Well, isn't it also the law that the Naga's mother has to leave society? That the mother should be told the truth about her child?' asked Shiva. 'Laws cannot be applied selectively.'

Nandi kept quiet.

'I don't doubt the love the Emperor has for Sati,' said Shiva. 'But didn't he realise how much he was going to end up hurting Sati by banishing her son?'

Veerbhadra nodded.

'He hid this fact from her all her life. He even hid her twin sister's existence. I always thought the way he examined Kartik's body at birth was strange. Now it makes sense. He acted as though he was almost expecting another Naga.'

'Hmm,' said Veerbhadra.

'And I have a dirty feeling that this is not where the story ends.'

'What do you mean?'

'I suspect that Chandandhwaj did not die naturally.'

'Her first husband?'

'Yes. It is just too convenient that he drowned the day Ganesh was born.'

'My Lord!' Nandi spoke up in shock. 'But that cannot be true. That is a crime. No Suryavanshi ruler will ever stoop so low.'

'I'm not saying that I know for sure, Nandi,' said Shiva. 'It is just a feeling that I have. Remember nobody is good or bad. They are either strong or weak. Strong people stick to their morals, no matter what the trials and tribulations. Weak people, many a times, do not even realise how low they have sunk.'

Nandi kept quiet.

Veerbhadra looked straight at Shiva. 'I will not be surprised if what you suspect is true. It may have been His Highness' twisted way of thinking that he is doing Sati a favour.'

Chapter 21

The Maika Mystery

It had been nearly three months since Ganesh had saved Kartik's life. Though still limping, he had recovered enough to know that he had to go back to Panchavati. He had been conscious for a month now. Each waking moment reminded him of the torment in his mother's heart. The rift between Shiva and Sati was more than he could bear. As far as he knew, the only way out was for him to leave.

'Let's leave tomorrow, *Mausi*,' said Ganesh.

'Have you told your mother?' asked Kali.

'I intend to leave a note for her.'

Kali narrowed her eyes.

'She will not let me go, even though she must.'

Kali took a deep breath. 'So you are just going to forget her?'

Ganesh smiled sadly. 'I have got enough love from her in the past few months to last me a lifetime. I can live on my memories. But she cannot live without the Neelkanth.'

— ☦Ⓐ℧⅄⊕ —

A puzzled Shiva rose to receive Athithigva. The Kashi king had never stepped into the Branga quarters before. He had always waited for the Neelkanth outside.

'What is the matter, Your Highness?'

'My Lord, I just received word that Emperor Daksha is on his way to Kashi.'

Shiva frowned. 'I don't understand the urgency. If you have received word today, I'm sure the Emperor will not be here for another two to three months.'

'No, My Lord. He's coming today. In a few hours. I just received word from an advance party.'

Shiva raised his eyebrows, surprised beyond words.

'My Lord,' said Athithigva, 'I wanted to request you to come to the throne room to take your rightful place so that we may receive the Emperor.'

'I'll come,' said Shiva. 'But please ensure that only you are there. I do not want to receive him along with your courtiers.'

This was unorthodox. Athithigva frowned, but didn't question Shiva's unusual demand. He simply left to carry out the orders.

'Nandi, word may have been sent to Parvateshwar and Bhagirath as well,' said Shiva. 'Please tell them it is my wish that they do not come to the court right now. We will have a ceremonial welcome for His Highness a little later.'

'Yes, My Lord.' Nandi saluted and left.

Veerbhadra whispered to Shiva. 'You think he knows?'

'No. If I know anything about him, he wouldn't have come had he known that Kali and Ganesh were here. He has come in haste, without regard for protocol. It is the action of a father, not an Emperor. He was probably missing Sati and Kartik.'

'What do you want to do? Let it go or discover the truth?'

'No way will I let it go. I want to know the truth.'

Veerbhadra nodded.

'I hope for the sake of Sati,' said Shiva, 'that my suspicions are wrong. That he knew nothing. That the only thing that happened was that Maika's administrators followed the law.'

'But you fear you are right?' asked Veerbhadra.

'Yes.'

'Any idea how we can find out what actually happened that day?'

'Confront him. Catch him by surprise. This is the perfect time.'

Veerbhadra frowned.

'I intend to spring Kali and Ganesh on him,' said Shiva. 'His face will tell me the rest.'

— 人◎ᠧᚭ⊛ —

'What is His Highness doing here?' asked Parvateshwar. 'Nobody told me of his plans. How can Kashi do this? This is a breach of protocol.'

'Nobody knew of this, My Lord,' said Nandi. 'Even King Athithigva got to know of it right now. Meluha sent no intimation earlier.'

Parvateshwar looked flabbergasted. Such slips in Meluhan diplomatic procedures were unheard of.

Bhagirath shrugged his shoulders. 'All kings are alike.'

Parvateshwar ignored the jibe aimed at the ruler of his realm about his lack of etiquette and protocol. He spoke to Nandi. 'Why does the Lord Neelkanth not want us to come to the throne room?'

'I couldn't say, My Lord,' replied Nandi. 'I'm just following orders.'

Parvateshwar nodded. 'All right. We'll stay here till the Lord calls us.'

— ⊼⦿ᘮⴹ⊛ —

'Shiva can have any number of reasons for wanting to meet Kali. But why Ganesh? What's going on?' asked Sati, frowning.

Veerbhadra was stumped. Not only was Ganesh in Kali's chamber, but so was Sati. Considering that Daksha was already in Kashi, he had to get Kali and Ganesh into the throne room as fast as he could. It was entirely possible that Daksha might find out about the presence of his Naga daughter and grandson. Time was of the essence. If their surprise meeting had to work, it had to happen now. Veerbhadra had no choice but to announce Shiva's summons to Kali and Ganesh.

'I'm just following orders, My Lady.'

'Following orders doesn't entail your not knowing what's going on.'

'He wants them to see something.'

'Bhadra,' said Sati. 'My husband is your best friend. You are married to my best friend. I know you. I know that you know more. I am not letting my son go till you tell me.'

Veerbhadra shook his head at Sati's doggedness. He could see what drew Shiva to Sati, despite their temporary estrangement. 'My Lady, your father is here.'

Sati was surprised. Partly at the unannounced appearance of her father, but more so at Shiva summoning Kali and Ganesh to meet Daksha.

Somewhere in his heart, Shiva actually believes that injustice had been done to my sister and son.

'Do you want to go?' Sati asked Kali.

The Naga Queen narrowed her eyes, hand tightening on her sword hilt. 'Yes! Even wild horses couldn't keep me away.'

Sati turned to her son. He didn't want a confrontation. He didn't want the truth to come out. To hurt his mother even more. He shook his head.

Kali spoke up in surprise. 'Why? What are you afraid of?'

'I don't want this, *Mausi*,' replied Ganesh.

'But I do!' said Sati. 'Your existence was hidden from me for ninety years.'

'But those were the rules, *Maa*,' said Ganesh.

'No, the rules are that a Naga child cannot live in Meluha. Hiding the truth from the mother is not part of the rules. Had I known, I would have left Meluha with you.'

'Even if the rule was broken, it's in the past. Please *Maa*, forget it.'

'I will not. I cannot. I want to know how much he knew. And if he did know, why did he lie? To protect his name? So that no one can accuse him of being the progenitor of Nagas? So that he can continue to rule?'

'*Maa*, nothing will come of this,' said Ganesh.

Kali started laughing. Ganesh turned to her in irritation.

'When you were scouring all of India to confront Sati, I had told you this very thing,' said Kali. 'And what had you said? You wanted answers. That you would not be at peace till you knew the truth about your relationship with your mother. That it would complete you. Then why can't your mother want or expect the same from her father?'

'But this is not completion, *Mausi*,' said Ganesh. 'This is only confrontation and pain.'

'Completion is completion, my child,' said Kali. 'Sometimes completion causes happiness and sometimes pain. Your mother has a right to do this.' Saying so, Kali turned to Sati. 'Are you sure you want to do this, *didi*?'

'I want answers,' said Sati.

Veerbhadra gulped. 'My Lady, Shiva only asked for Queen Kali and Lord Ganesh. Not you.'

'I'm coming, Bhadra,' said Sati. 'And you know very well that I must.'

Veerbhadra looked down. Sati was right. She had the right to be there.

'*Maa...*' whispered Ganesh.

'Ganesh, I am going,' said Sati firmly. 'You can either come along or not. That is your choice. But you cannot stop me.'

The Lord of the People took a deep breath, pulled his *angvastram* on his shoulder and said, 'Lead us on, brave Veerbhadra.'

— 人◎Ո྾⊕ —

'What a pleasant surprise to see you, Your Highness,' said Athithigva, bowing to the Emperor of India.

Daksha nodded as he entered the antechamber of the court. 'It is my empire, Athithigva. I think I can throw in a surprise or two!'

Athithigva smiled. Daksha had his wife Veerini in tow. She in turn was trailed by the famed Arishtanemi warriors, Mayashrenik and Vidyunmali. With Parvateshwar's absence from Swadweep, Mayashrenik had been appointed provisional General of Meluha's armed forces.

Daksha was surprised when he entered the main throne room, as the usual courtly nobles and officials were absent. Only Shiva and Nandi were present. Nandi immediately brought his fist up to his chest and bowed low to his Emperor. Daksha smiled at Nandi genially.

Shiva remained seated, joining his hands in a namaste. 'Welcome to Kashi, Your Highness.'

Daksha's smile disappeared. He was the Emperor of all of India. He deserved respect. Even if Shiva was the Neelkanth, protocol demanded that he stand up for the Emperor. In the past, Shiva had always done so. This was an insult.

'How are you, my son-in-law?' said Daksha, trying to keep his anger in check.

'I am well, Your Highness. Why don't you sit next to me?'

Daksha sat. So did Veerini and Athithigva.

Turning to Athithigva, Daksha said, 'For such a noisy city, you seem to run a very quiet court, Athithigva.'

Athithigva smiled. 'No My Lord, it's just that...'

'My apologies for interrupting, Your Highness,' said Shiva to Athithigva, before turning to Daksha. 'I thought it would be a good idea for you to meet your children in private.'

Veerini perked up immediately. 'Where are they, Lord Neelkanth?'

Just then Veerbhadra walked in. Followed by Sati.

'My child!' said a smiling Daksha, forgetting the slight from Shiva. 'Why didn't you bring my grandson along?'

'I have,' said Sati.

Ganesh entered the room. Behind him was Kali.

Shiva was staring hard at Daksha's face. The Meluhan

Emperor's eyes sprung wide open in recognition. His jaw dropped in shock.

He knows!

Then Daksha swallowed hard, straightening up.

He's afraid. He's hiding something.

Shiva also noticed Veerini's expression. Profound sadness. Eyebrows joined together, but her lips curled up slightly in a smile struggling to break through. Her eyes moist.

She knows too. And she loves them.

Daksha turned to Athithigva and blustered. 'How dare you consort with terrorists, King of Kashi?'

'They aren't terrorists,' said Sati. 'Terrorists kill innocents. Kali and Ganesh have never done that.'

'Does Sati speak for the King of Kashi now?'

'Don't speak to him, father,' said Sati. 'Speak to me.'

'What for?' asked Daksha, pointing at Ganesh and Kali. 'What do you have to do with them?'

'Everything! Their place is with me. Should have always been with me.'

'What? Vile Nagas have only one place. South of the Narmada! They are not allowed into the Sapt Sindhu!'

'My sister and son are not vile. They are my blood! Your blood!'

Daksha stood, stepping up to Sati. 'Sister! Son! What nonsense? Don't believe the rubbish these scum tell you. Of course, they hate me. They will say anything to malign me. I am their sworn enemy. I am the ruler of Meluha! Under oath to destroy them!'

Kali reached for her sword. 'I am in the mood to challenge you to an Agnipariksha right now, you repulsive goat!'

'Don't you have any shame?' Daksha shouted at Kali. 'Do penance for your past life sins quietly instead of creating bad blood between a loving father and his daughter! What lies have you told her about me?'

'They haven't said a word, father,' said Sati. 'But their existence says a lot about you.'

'It's not me. They exist because of your mother. Her past life sins have led to this. We never had Nagas in our family before her.'

Sati's jaw fell. She was seeing the levels to which her father could stoop to for the first time.

Veerini was staring at Daksha, silent anger smouldering in her eyes.

'This is not about past lives, father,' said Sati. 'It is about this life. You knew. Yet you didn't tell me.'

'I am your father. I have loved you all my life. I have fought the world for you. Will you trust me or some deformed animals?'

'They are not deformed animals! They are my family!'

'You want to make these people your family? People who lie to you? Who turn you against your own father?'

'They never lied to me!' shouted Sati. 'You did.'

'No, I did not!'

'You said my son was still born.'

Daksha took a deep breath, looked up at the ceiling as though struggling to regain control and then glared at Sati. 'Why don't you understand? I lied for your own good! Do you know what your life would have been like if you had been declared a Naga's mother?'

'I would be with my son!'

'What rubbish. What would you have done? Lived in Panchavati?'

'Yes!'

'You are my daughter!' screamed Daksha. 'I have always loved you more than anyone else. I would never have allowed you to suffer in Panchavati.'

'It wasn't your choice to make.'

An exasperated Daksha turned to Shiva. 'Talk some sense into her, Lord Neelkanth!'

Shiva's eyes were narrowed. He wanted to know how wide this web of deception spread. 'Did you get Chandandhwaj killed, Your Highness?'

Daksha blanched. Fear was written all over his face. He looked sharply at Sati and then quickly back at Shiva.

Oh Lord! He did!

Sati was reeling, shocked into absolute silence. Kali and Ganesh did not seem surprised.

Daksha immediately regained control. He pointed a finger at Shiva, his body shaking. 'You did this. You choreographed this!'

Shiva stayed quiet.

'You have turned my daughter against me,' screamed Daksha. 'Maharishi Bhrigu was right. The evil Vasudevs control you.'

Shiva continued to stare at Daksha, as if actually seeing him for the first time.

Daksha was boiling. 'What were you? A stupid tribal from a barbaric land. I made you the Neelkanth. I gave you power. I gave it to you so that you would bring the Chandravanshis under Meluhan control. So that I could establish peace in India. And you dare to use the power I bestowed upon you against me?'

Shiva remained passive, making Daksha spew even more venom.

'I made you. And, I can destroy you!'

Daksha pulled his knife out and lunged forward.

Nandi jumped in front of Shiva, taking the blow on his shield. His Meluhan training didn't allow him to draw his sword at his monarch. Kali and Ganesh, however, had no such compunctions, drawing their blades rapidly on Daksha. Ganesh jumped in front of Shiva even as Vidyunmali drew his sword. Mayashrenik, a loyal Meluhan who would have fought to the death for his King, was stunned into inaction. He was deeply devoted to Shiva. How could he draw his sword against the Neelkanth?

'Calm down,' said Shiva, raising his hand.

Vidyunmali still had his sword drawn. Daksha's knife had fallen to the ground.

Shiva spoke once again. 'Nandi, Ganesh, Kali, stand down. NOW!'

As Shiva's warriors lowered their swords, Vidyunmali also sheathed his blade.

'Your Highness,' Shiva addressed Daksha.

Daksha's eyes were glued on a teary-eyed Sati, who had her sword inches away from her father's throat. His face exhibited the sense of betrayal and loss he felt. Sati was the only person he had ever truly loved.

'Sati...' whispered Shiva. 'Please. Put it down. He's not worth it.'

Sati's sword inched closer.

Shiva stepped forward slowly. 'Sati...'

Her hands were shaking slightly, rage driving her dangerously close to the edge.

Shiva touched her shoulder lightly. 'Sati, put it down.'

Shiva's touch brought Sati back from the precipice.

She lowered her sword a little. Her eyes narrowed, her breathing heavy, her body stiff.

Daksha continued to stare at Sati.

'I am ashamed that your blood runs in my veins,' said Sati.

Tears began to flow down Daksha's face.

'Get out,' whispered Sati through gritted teeth.

Daksha was deathly still.

'GET OUT!'

Veerini got a jolt from Sati's loud voice. Her expression a mix of sadness and anger, she walked up to Daksha. 'Move.'

Daksha stood paralysed, shocked at this turn of events.

'Come on,' Veerini repeated louder, pulling her husband by his arm. 'Mayashrenik, Vidyunmali, let's leave.'

The Empress of India dragged her husband out of the room.

Sati was shattered. She dropped her sword, tears streaming down her face. Ganesh rushed towards her. But Shiva caught her even as she fell.

Sati was sobbing uncontrollably as Shiva picked her up in his arms.

Chapter 22

Two Sides, Same Coin

'So what are you thinking?' asked Kali.

Ganesh and Kali were in the Naga queen's quarters. After the drama that had unfolded earlier in the day, Shiva had carried Sati over to their room in Athithigva's palace. Daksha, Veerini and their entourage had departed immediately for the Meluhan capital, Devagiri.

'This was unexpected,' said a pensive Ganesh with a slight smile.

Kali raised her eyes. 'Sometimes your stoicism can be very irritating!'

Ganesh smiled. A rare broad smile from one floppy ear to the other, his extended teeth stretching further out.

'Now that's the face I want to see more of,' said Kali. 'You actually look cute.'

Ganesh's face turned serious again. He raised a papyrus scroll. A message from Panchavati. 'I would have been laughing, *Mausi*. But for this.'

'What now?' asked Kali, frowning.

'It's a failure.'

'Again?'

'Yes, again.'

'But I thought...'

'We thought wrong, *Mausi*.'

Kali cursed. Ganesh stared at his aunt. He could feel her frustration. A final solution was so close. Its success would have completed their victory. Now, there was every chance that everything they had done would be lost.

'Do we try again?' asked Kali.

'I think we have to finally accept the truth, *Mausi*. This route is a dead end. We have no choice. The time has come to reveal the secret.'

'Yes,' said Kali. 'The Neelkanth should know.'

'The Neelkanth?' asked Ganesh, surprised at how much had changed in such a short span.

Kali frowned.

'You didn't use his name. You said the Neelkanth. You believe the legend now?'

Kali smiled. 'I don't believe in legends. Never have, never will. But I believe in him.'

How different would my life have been if fate had blessed me with a man like Shiva. Maybe like didi, *all the poison could have been sucked out of my life as well. Perhaps, even I would have found happiness and peace.*

'We have to show him the secret,' said Ganesh, intruding into Kali's thoughts.

'Show him?!'

'I don't think it can be done here, right? He must see for himself.'

'You want to take him to Panchavati?'

'Why not?' asked Ganesh. 'Don't you trust him?'

'Of course, I do. I would trust him with my life. But he doesn't come alone. There are others who come with him. If we take them along, they will know how to get to Panchavati. This will weaken our defences.'

'I think people like Parvateshwar and Bhagirath can be trusted, *Mausi*. I don't think they will ever go against the Neelkanth. They would give their lives for him.'

'If there is one thing I have learnt in life,' said Kali, 'it is that one should not spread one's trust too thin. And, never take things for granted.'

Ganesh frowned. 'If you doubt all his followers, then what about Parshuram? He already knows the way. You know his devotion to the Neelkanth.'

'Remember, I had told you not to bring Parshuram to Panchavati. But you didn't listen.'

'So, now what, *Mausi*?'

'We'll take them through Branga. They will know how to get to Panchavati, but only from Chandraketu's realm. They will never be able to reach us directly from their own kingdoms. The forests of Dandak would consume them if they were to even try! We can trust the Brangas to not let anyone pass without our permission. Even Parshuram doesn't know any other way.'

Ganesh nodded. 'That is a good idea.'

— 人◎ᛌᚦ⊛ —

'Thank the Lord, I didn't do anything rash that I would have regretted later,' said Sati.

Shiva was sitting on a long chair in the balcony of their chambers. Sati was on his lap, her head leaning against his muscular chest, her eyes swollen red. From the heights of the Kashi palace, the Sacred Avenue and the Vishwanath temple were clearly visible. Beyond them flowed the mighty Ganga.

'Your anger was justified, my darling.'

Sati looked up at her husband, breathing slowly. 'Aren't you angry? He actually tried to kill you.'

Shiva stared into his wife's eyes as he ran his hand across her face. 'My anger towards your father is because of what he did to you, not what he tried to do to me.'

'But how dare Vidyunmali draw his sword upon you?' whispered Sati. 'Thank God, Ganesh...'

Sati stopped, afraid that her taking Ganesh's name would ruin this moment.

Shiva gave her a gentle squeeze. 'He's your son.'

Sati kept quiet, body stiff, feeling the intense pain that Shiva felt at Brahaspati's loss.

Shiva held Sati's face and looked straight into her eyes. 'No matter how hard I try, I cannot hate a part of your soul.'

Sati sighed as fresh tears escaped silently from her eyes. She held Shiva tight. Shiva did not want to spoil the moment as he held onto his wife. One thing continued to puzzle him. Who's Bhrigu?

— ⵣ◍ᚒ⳨⊕ —

'The Emperor had got Chandandhwaj killed?' asked a shocked Parvateshwar.

'Yes, General,' said Veerbhadra.

Parvateshwar, numb with shock, looked at Anandmayi and Bhagirath. Then back at Veerbhadra. 'Where is His Highness now?'

'He's on his way back to Meluha, My Lord,' said Veerbhadra.

Parvateshwar held his head. His Emperor had brought

dishonour to Meluha, his motherland. He couldn't even imagine the pain this revelation must have caused to the woman he had always looked upon as the daughter he had never had. 'Where is Sati?'

'She's with Shiva, My Lord.'

Anandmayi looked at Parvateshwar with a smile. At least some good had come out of this sordid episode.

— ∧ⓞℸ⳽⊕ —

The Meluhan royal ship cruised slowly up the Ganga, four ships sailing around it in the standard Suryavanshi defensive naval protocol. Daksha's entourage was on its way home, a day away from Kashi.

Mayashrenik was in the lead boat, maintaining a steady pace. He was still shaken by the incidents at Kashi. He hoped his Emperor Daksha and the Neelkanth would reconcile their differences. He wished to avoid the terrible fate of having to choose between his loyalty to his country and his devotion to his God.

Vidyunmali was in-charge of security on Daksha's ship. He wanted to safeguard against any assassination attempt upon his Emperor by the followers of the Neelkanth. Even though it seemed unlikely, he wanted to take all the possible precautions.

Veerini sat in the royal chambers of the central ship, next to a window, watching the Ganga lap against the ship. She sensed that she had lost all her children now. She turned in anger towards her husband.

Daksha was lying on the bed, eyes forlorn, a lost look on his face. It wasn't the first time he had faced and been overpowered by such terrible circumstances.

Veerini shook her head and turned to look out again.

If only he had listened to me.

Veerini remembered that incident so clearly it was as if it had happened just yesterday. Almost every day, she wondered how her life would have been if things had turned out differently.

It had happened more than a hundred years ago. Sati had just returned from the Maika gurukul, a headstrong, idealistic girl of sixteen. In keeping with her character, she had jumped in to save an immigrant woman from a vicious pack of wild dogs. Parvateshwar and Daksha had rushed in to her rescue. While they had managed to push back the dogs, Daksha had been seriously injured.

Veerini had accompanied Daksha to the ayuralay where the doctors could examine her husband. The most worrying injury was on his left leg, where a dog had ripped out some flesh, cutting through a major blood vessel. The loss of blood had made Daksha lose consciousness.

When he had opened his eyes after a few hours, Daksha's first thought was of his young daughter. 'Sati?'

'She's with Parvateshwar,' said Veerini, as she came closer to her husband and held his hand. 'Don't worry about her.'

'I screamed at her. I didn't mean to.'

'I know. She was only doing her duty. She did the right thing, trying to protect that woman. I'll tell her that...'

'No. No. I still think she shouldn't have risked her life for that woman. I didn't mean to scream at her, that's all.'

Veerini's eyes narrowed to slits. Her husband couldn't be any less Suryavanshi. She was about to say something when the door opened and Brahmanayak walked in.

Brahmanayak, Daksha's father and ruler of Meluha, was

a tall, imposing figure. Long black hair, a well manicured beard, a practically hairless body, a sober crown and understated white clothes could not camouflage the indomitable spirit of the man. He set impossible standards for all those around him with his own great deeds. He was not just respected, but also feared in all of Meluha. Obsessive about the honour and respect that his empire should garner, his son's lack of courage and character was a source of anger and dismay for him.

Veerini immediately arose and stepped back quietly. Brahmanayak never spoke to her unless to give orders. Behind Brahmanayak was the kindly doctor who had stitched up Daksha's leg after the severe mauling it had received.

Brahmanayak, in a matter of fact manner, lifted the sheet to look at his son's leg. There was a bandage of neem leaves tied around it.

The doctor smiled genially. 'Your Highness, your son will be back on his feet in a week or two. I have been very careful. The scars will be minimal.'

Daksha looked for a brief instant at his father. Then, with his chest puffed up, he whispered, 'No doctor. Scars are the pride of any Kshatriya.'

Brahmanayak snorted. 'What would you know about being a Kshatriya?'

Daksha fell silent. Veerini began seething with anger.

'You let some dogs do this to you?' asked Brahmanayak, contemptuously. 'I am the laughing stock of Meluha. Perhaps even the world. My son cannot even kill a dog all by himself.'

Daksha kept staring at his father.

To prevent a further escalation of hostility and to

safeguard the patient's mental health, the doctor cut in, 'Your Highness, I need to discuss something with you. May we talk outside?'

Brahmanayak nodded. 'I haven't finished,' he said, turning to Daksha, before walking out of the chamber.

A livid Veerini stepped up to her husband, who was crying now. 'How long are you going to tolerate this?'

Daksha suddenly turned ferocious. 'He's my father! Speak of him with respect.'

'He does not care about you, Daksha,' said Veerini. 'All that he cares about is his legacy. You don't even want to be King. So what are we doing here?'

'My duty. I have to stay by his side. I am his son.'

'He doesn't think so. You are only someone who would carry forward his name, his legacy. That's all.'

Daksha fell silent.

'He has forced you to give up one daughter. How much more are you going to sacrifice?'

'She's not my daughter!'

'She is! Kali is as much your flesh and blood as Sati is.'

'I am not discussing this again.'

'You have thought about it so many times. For once, have the courage to follow through.'

'What will we do in Panchavati?'

'Doesn't matter. What matters is what we'll be.'

Daksha shook his head. 'And what do you think we'll be?'

'We'll be happy!'

'But I cannot leave Sati behind.'

'Who's asking you to leave her behind? All I want is to unite my family.'

'What?! Why should Sati live in Panchavati? She's not a

Naga. You and I have past life sins that have to be atoned, sins for which we have been punished. Why should she be punished?'

'The real punishment is the separation from her sister. The real punishment is to see her father being humiliated every day.'

Daksha remained silent, wavering.

'Daksha, trust me,' said Veerini. 'We'll be happy in Panchavati. If there was any other place where we could live with both Kali and Sati, I'd suggest that. But there isn't.'

Daksha breathed deeply. 'But how...'

'You leave that to me. I'll make the arrangements. Just say yes. Your father is leaving tomorrow for Karachapa. You are not so badly injured that you can't travel. We'll be in Panchavati before he knows you're gone.'

Daksha stared at Veerini. 'But...'

'Trust me. Please trust me. It will be for all our good. I know you love me. I know you love your daughters. I know you don't care about anything else. Just trust me.'

Daksha nodded.

Veerini smiled, bent closer and kissed her husband. 'I'll make the arrangements.'

A happy Veerini turned and walked out of the room. She had a lot to do.

As she stepped out, she saw Sati and Parvateshwar sitting outside. She patted Sati on her head. 'Go in, my child. Tell your father how much you love him. He needs you. I'll be back soon.'

As Veerini was hurrying away, she saw Brahmanayak walking back towards her husband's chamber.

The Meluhan Queen was jolted back to the present

by some dolphin calls. The more than a century old memory still drew a tear from her eyes. She turned to look at her husband and shook her head. She had never really understood what happened that day. What had Bramhanayak said? All she knew was that when she had gone back to Daksha's chamber the next day with their escape plans, he had refused to leave. He had decided that he wanted to become Emperor.

Your stupid ego and need for approval from your father destroyed our lives!

— ⴵ ⵔ ⵑ ⵖ ⵚ —

'The secret?' asked Shiva, recalling his conversation with Parshuram.

Shiva was sitting with Parshuram, Parvateshwar, Veerbhadra and Nandi. Kali had just entered the chamber. Ganesh, still unsure of his position vis-a-vis Shiva, was standing quietly at the back. Shiva had acknowledged Sati's elder son with a short nod, nothing more.

'Yes, I think you need to know,' said Kali. 'It is India's need that the Neelkanth know the secret the Nagas have been keeping. Thereafter, you can decide whether what we have done is right or wrong. Determine what must be done now.'

'Why can't you tell me here?'

'I need you to trust me. I can't.'

Shiva's eyes bored into Kali's. He could see no malice or deceit in them. He felt he could trust her. 'How many days will it take to reach Panchavati?'

'A little more than a year,' answered Kali.

'A year?!'

'Yes, Lord Neelkanth. We will travel up to Branga by river boats, right down the Madhumati river. Then travel by foot through the *Dandakaranya*. The journey takes time.'

'There is no direct route?'

Kali smiled but refused to be drawn in. She didn't want to reveal the secrets of the *forests of Dandak*. It was the primary defence for her city.

'I'm trusting you. But it appears that you don't trust me.'

'I trust you completely, Lord Neelkanth.'

Shiva smiled, understanding Kali's predicament. She could trust him but not everyone with him. 'All right. Let's go to Panchavati. It is perhaps the route I have to take in order to discharge my duty.'

Shiva turned to Parvateshwar. 'Can you make the arrangements, General?'

'It will be done, My Lord,' said Parvateshwar.

Kali bowed towards Shiva and turned to leave, stretching her hand out to Ganesh.

'And, Kali...' said Shiva.

Kali spun around.

'I prefer Shiva, not Neelkanth. You are my wife's sister. You are family.'

Kali smiled and bowed her head. 'As you wish... Shiva.'

— 大◎ᘮ᚛⊕ —

Shiva and Sati were at the Vishwanath temple. They had come to perform a private puja, seeking Lord Rudra's blessings. Having completed their prayers, they sat against one of the pillars of the temple, looking out towards the idol of Lady Mohini, whose statue was at the back of Lord Rudra's idol.

Shiva reached out for his wife's hand and kissed it lightly. She smiled and rested her head on his shoulder.

'A very intriguing lady,' said Shiva.

Sati looked up at her husband. 'Lady Mohini?'

'Yes. Why isn't she universally accepted as a Vishnu? Why has the number of Vishnus stopped at seven?'

'There may be more Vishnus in the future. But not everyone regards her as a Vishnu.'

'Do you?'

'At one point of time, I didn't. But now, I have come to understand her greatness.'

Shiva frowned.

'It's not easy to understand her,' said Sati. 'There were many things that she did which can be considered unjust. It does not matter that she did those things to the Asuras. They were still unfair. To Suryavanshis, who follow the absolutes of Lord Ram, she is difficult to understand.'

'So what's changed now?'

'I've come to know more of her. About why she did what she did. So I still don't appreciate some of the things that she did, but perhaps I have more compassion for her actions.'

'A Vasudev had once told me that they believe Lord Rudra could not have completed his mission without her support.'

Sati looked at Shiva. 'They may be right. Maybe, just maybe, sometimes, a small sin can lead to a greater good.'

Shiva stared at Sati. He could see where she was going with this.

'If a man has been good all his life despite the unkindness he has faced, if he has helped others, we should try to understand why he committed what appears to be a sin.

We may not be able to forgive him. However, we may be able to understand him.'

Shiva knew Sati was talking about Ganesh. 'Do you understand why he did what he did?'

Sati took a deep breath. 'No.'

Shiva turned his gaze towards Lady Mohini's statue.

Sati pulled Shiva's face back towards her. 'Sometimes it's difficult to understand an event without knowing everything that led up to it.'

Shiva turned his face away. He shut his eyes and breathed deeply. 'He saved your life. He saved Kartik's life. For that I must love him. He has done much to make me think that he is a good man.'

Sati remained silent.

'But...' Shiva took a deep breath. 'But it's not easy for me. Sati... I just can't...'

Sati sighed. *Perhaps going to Panchavati may make everything clear.*

— 入◎Ü♀⊕ —

'My Lord, what are you saying? How can I?' asked a flabbergasted Dilipa.

He was sitting at Maharishi Bhrigu's feet in his private chambers in his palace at Ayodhya. Prime Minister Siamantak had become a past master at keeping Bhrigu's frequent visits to Ayodhya a secret. The Maharishi's medicines were working their magic. Dilipa was looking healthier with every passing day.

'Are you refusing to help, Your Highness?' Bhrigu's voice was menacing, eyes narrowed.

'No, My Lord. Of course not. But this is impossible.'

'I will show you the way.'

'But how can I do it all by myself?'

'You will have allies. I'll guarantee that.'

'But an attack such as this? What if someone finds out? My own people will turn against me.'

'Nobody will find out.'

Dilipa looked disturbed. *What have I got myself into?*

'Why? Why is this needed, Maharishi ji?'

'For the good of India.'

Dilipa remained silent, worry lines on his face.

Bhrigu knew the self-obsessed Dilipa would not particularly care about the larger cause. So he decided to make it very personal. 'You also need to do this, Your Highness, if you want to prevent disease from eating up your body.'

Dilipa stared at Bhrigu. The threat was clear and overt. He bowed his head. 'Tell me how, Maharishi ji.'

— ⸙ ⊚ ᛏ ⹋ ⊕ —

Within two months of the Naga Queen's request to Shiva, Parvateshwar had made arrangements for travelling to Panchavati.

Shiva's entourage had grown considerably since the time he had sailed into the city where the supreme light shines. Accompanying Shiva on the voyage was his entire family, as the Mahadev refused to leave Sati and Kartik behind. Kali and Ganesh obviously had to be there. Veerbhadra and Nandi were fixtures of the Neelkanth's retinue. And Veerbhadra had insisted on his wife Krittika accompanying him this time, not just because they missed each other, but also as he knew she would not be able to bear parting company from Kartik for so long. Ayurvati was the obvious choice for the physician on board. Shiva also wanted Bhagirath and Parshuram with him. And Parvateshwar, his General and security head, could not leave without Anandmayi.

Parvateshwar had arranged for two brigades to travel with them. So two thousand soldiers, both Chandravanshi and Suryavanshi, travelled in a fleet of nine ships along with the royal vessel carrying the Neelkanth and his close aides. Vishwadyumna, the loyal Branga follower of Ganesh, and his platoon, were also commissioned into the Chandravanshi Brigade.

They sailed slowly so they could keep all the ships together. Two months had passed since they had left Kashi when they neared Vaishali.

Remembering his conversation with Gopal, the Chief of the Vasudevs, Shiva turned towards Veerbhadra, Nandi and Parshuram. All of them, except Nandi, were smoking pot on the deck, contemplating the river.

'Apparently Lord Manu had said that Good and Evil are two sides of the same coin,' said Shiva, breaking the silence of the moment, taking the chillum from Parshuram.

Parshuram frowned. 'I have heard this too. But I could never make sense of it.'

Shiva took a deep drag of the marijuana, exhaled and passed the chillum to Veerbhadra. 'What do you make of it, Bhadra?'

'Frankly, a lot of what your Vasudev friends say is mumbo-jumbo!'

Shiva burst out laughing. So did his friends.

'I wouldn't quite say that, brave Veerbhadra.'

A surprised Shiva turned around to find Ganesh behind

them. Shiva fell silent, all traces of humour dropping from him. Parshuram immediately bowed his head to Ganesh, but did not say anything out of fear of angering the Neelkanth.

Veerbhadra, who was growing increasingly fond of the Lord of the People and believed him to be a man of integrity, asked, 'So what would you make of it, Ganesh?'

'I would think it's a clue,' said Ganesh, smiling at Veerbhadra.

'Clue?' asked Shiva, intrigued.

'Maybe for the Neelkanth to understand what he should be searching for?'

'Carry on.'

'Good and Evil are two sides of the same coin. So the Neelkanth has to find one side of a coin, right?'

Shiva frowned.

'Is it possible to find one side of a coin?' asked Ganesh.

Shiva slapped his forehead. 'Of course, search for the whole coin instead!'

Ganesh nodded, smiling.

Shiva stared at Ganesh. A germ of an idea was forming in the Neelkanth's mind.

Search for Good. And you shall find Evil as well. The greater the Good, the greater the Evil.

Veerbhadra held out the chillum to Ganesh. 'Would you like to try some?'

Ganesh had never smoked in his life. He looked at his father and couldn't read what was written in those deep, mysterious eyes. 'I would love to.'

He sat down and took the chillum from Veerbhadra.

'Place it in your mouth like so,' said Veerbhadra, demonstrating by cupping his hands, 'and breathe in deeply.'

Ganesh did as he was told, collapsing in a severe bout of coughing.

Everyone burst out laughing. Except Shiva, who continued to stare at Ganesh, straight-faced.

Veerbhadra stretched out to pat Ganesh on his back and took the chillum away from him. 'Ganesh, you have never been touched by this evil.'

'No. But I'm sure I'll grow to like it,' smiled an embarrassed Ganesh, glancing for a moment at Shiva as he reached out for the chillum again.

Veerbhadra drew it out of reach. 'No, Ganesh. You should remain innocent.'

— 人◎ᵾ⇞⊛ —

The fleet was at the gates of Branga. Parvateshwar, Anandmayi and Bhagirath had transferred into the lead ship to supervise operations.

'I've seen it before, I know,' said Anandmayi, staring at the gates, 'but I still get amazed at their sheer ingenuity!'

Parvateshwar smiled and put his arm around Anandmayi. And almost immediately, much to Anandmayi's annoyance, he turned back to the task at hand. 'Uttanka, the second ship is not high enough. Tell the Brangas to fill more water into the pool.'

Unnoticed by Parvateshwar, Anandmayi raised her eyebrows and shook her head slightly. Then she turned her husband's face and kissed him lightly. Parvateshwar smiled.

'All right, you lovebirds,' said Bhagirath. 'Keep a lid on it.'

Anandmayi laughed and slapped her brother on his wrist.

Parvateshwar smiled and turned towards the gates, to supervise the crossing.

'This crossing will go well, General,' said Bhagirath. 'Relax. We know what the Brangas are doing. There are no surprises here.'

Parvateshwar turned to Bhagirath with a frown. He was surprised the Ayodhyan Prince had used the term 'General'. He could tell his brother-in-law was trying to say something but was being cautious. 'Out with it, Bhagirath. What are you trying to say?'

'We know the path here,' said Bhagirath. 'We know what the Brangas are doing. There will be no surprises. But we have no idea what route the Nagas will lead us on. Only the Almighty knows what surprises they may have in store. Is it wise to trust them so blindly?'

'We're not trusting the Nagas, Bhagirath,' interrupted Anandmayi. 'We are trusting the Neelkanth.'

Parvateshwar remained silent.

'I'm not saying we shouldn't trust the Mahadev,' said Bhagirath. 'How can I? But how much do we know of the Nagas? We're going through the dreaded Dandak forests with the Nagas as our guides. Am I the only one concerned here?'

'Listen,' said an irritated Anandmayi. 'Lord Neelkanth trusts Queen Kali. That means I will trust her. And so will you.'

Bhagirath shook his head. 'What do you say, Parvateshwar?'

'The Lord is My Lord. I will walk into a wall of flames if he orders me to,' said Parvateshwar as he looked towards the banks, where accumulator machines had just been released, pulling their ship forward with tremendous force.

The Meluhan General turned to Bhagirath. 'But how can I forget that Ganesh killed Brahaspati, the greatest scientist of Meluha? That he destroyed the heart of our empire, Mount Mandar. How can I trust him after all this?'

Anandmayi looked at Parvateshwar and then at her brother uncomfortably.

— 人◎Ʊ✝⊕ —

'No, Krittika,' said Ayurvati. 'I am not doing it.'

Krittika and Ayurvati were in the Meluhan doctor's office on the royal ship. The hooks on the sideboards of their ship were being attached onto the machine that would pull it through the gates of Branga. Practically everyone on the vessel was on the deck, to see this marvellous feat of Branga engineering in action. Krittika had used the time to meet Ayurvati without Veerbhadra's knowledge.

'Ayurvatiji, please. You know I need it.'

'No you don't. And I'm sure if your husband knew, he would say no as well.'

'He doesn't need to know.'

'Krittika, I am not doing anything to put your life in danger. Is that clear?'

Ayurvati turned around to prepare a medicine for Kartik. He had cut himself while practicing with Parvateshwar.

Krittika saw her chance. There was a pouch lying on Ayurvati's table. She knew this was the medicine she desperately craved. She slipped it quietly into the folds of her *angvastram*.

'My apologies for disturbing you,' said Krittika.

Ayurvati turned around. 'I'm sorry if I appear rude, Krittika. But it is in your own interests.'

'Please don't tell my husband.'

'Of course not,' said Ayurvati. 'But you should tell Veerbhadra yourself. Right?'

Krittika nodded and was about to leave the room when Ayurvati called out to her. Pointing towards Krittika's *angvastram*, Ayurvati said, 'Please leave it behind.'

Embarrassed, Krittika slowly slipped her hand into her *angvastram*, took the pouch out and left it on the table. She looked up, eyes moist and pleading.

Ayurvati held Krittika's shoulder gently. 'Haven't you learnt anything from the Neelkanth? You are a complete woman exactly the way you are. Your husband loves you for who you are and not for something you can give him.'

Krittika mumbled a soft apology and ran from the room.

Chapter 23

The Secret of All Secrets

The convoy crossed the gates of Branga and sailed into the river's westernmost distributary, the Madhumati. A few weeks later they passed the spot where Shiva had battled with Parshuram.

'This is where we fought Parshuram,' said Shiva, patting the ex-bandit on his back.

Parshuram looked at Shiva and then at Sati. 'Actually, this is where the Lord saved me.'

Sati smiled at Parshuram. She knew what it felt like. Being saved by Shiva. She looked at her husband with love. A man capable of pulling the poison out of the lives of all those around him. And yet, he couldn't pull the poison out of his own memories, still being tortured by his own demons. No matter how hard she tried, she could not get him to forget his past. Perhaps that was his fate.

Sati's musings were interrupted by Parshuram. 'This is where we turn, My Lord.'

Sati looked in the direction the exiled Vasudev pointed. There was nothing there. The river seemed to skirt a large grove of Sundari trees and carry on towards the Eastern Sea.

'Where?' asked Shiva.

'See those *Sundari* trees, My Lord,' said Parshuram, pointing towards a grove with the hook fixed on his amputated left hand. 'They lend their name to this area. The *Sundarban.*'

'*Beautiful forest?*' asked Sati.

'Yes, My lady,' said Parshuram. 'They also hide a beautiful secret.'

On the orders of Kali, the lead ship turned into the grove that Parshuram had pointed towards. From the distance of her own ship, Sati could see the figure of Parvateshwar, also on the deck, looking at Kali and trying to argue with the Naga Queen.

Kali simply ignored him. And the ship continued on a course that appeared to be its doom.

'What are they doing?' asked Sati, panic-stricken. 'They'll run aground.'

To their shock, the lead ship simply pushed the trees aside and sailed through.

'By the holy lake,' whispered an awe-struck Shiva. 'Rootless trees.'

'Not rootless, My Lord,' corrected Parshuram. 'They have roots. But not fixed ones. The roots float in the lagoon.'

'But how can such trees live?' asked Sati.

'That is something I have not understood,' said Parshuram. 'Perhaps it's the magic of the Nagas.'

The other ships, led by the royal ship that carried the Mahadev, glided into the floating grove of Sundari trees and entered a hidden lagoon where the gentle waves of the

Madhumati came to a halt. Shiva looked around in wonder. The area was lush green, alive with raucous bird calls. The vegetation was dense, creating a canopy of leaves over the lagoon which was massive enough to hold ten large ships. It was nearing the end of the second prahar and the sun was at its peak. Within the shaded lagoon however, one could mistakenly think it was evening time.

Parshuram looked at Shiva. 'Very few people know the location of the floating grove. I know of some who have tried to find it and have only run their ships aground.'

The ten ships were quickly anchored into long stakes in the banks after being tied to each other and pulled behind a dense row of floating Sundari trees. The vessels were secure and completely hidden from view.

The path now was on foot. More than two thousand soldiers had to troop through the Dandak forests. They were all asked to assemble on and around the lead ship.

Kali climbed up the main mast, so that all could see her. 'Hear me!'

The crowd quietened down. Kali's voice instantly commanded compliance.

'All of you have heard rumours of the *Dandakaranya*. That the *Dandak forest* is the largest in the world. That it stretches from the Eastern Sea to the Western Sea. That it is so dense that the sun hardly ever cracks through. That it is populated by monstrous animals that will devour those who lose their way. That some trees themselves are poisonous, felling those stupid enough to eat or touch things better left alone.'

The soldiers looked at Kali with concern.

'The rumours are all true, horrifyingly so.'

The soldiers knew the Dandak forests were to the

South of the Narmada, the border mandated by Lord Manu. The border that was never to be crossed. Not only were they violating Lord Manu's orders, but they were also entering the terrifying *Dandakaranya*. None of them wanted to push their luck further by being adventurous in these cursed jungles. Kali's words only sealed their convictions.

'Only Ganesh, Vishwadyumna and I know the path through this death trap. If you want to stay alive, follow our orders and do as we tell you. In turn, I give you my word that you will all reach Panchavati alive.'

The soldiers nodded vigorously.

'For the rest of the day, rest on your ships, eat your fill and get some sleep. We leave tomorrow morning at sunrise. Nobody is to go exploring into the Sundarban by himself tonight. He may discover that these forests are more vicious than beautiful.'

Kali climbed down the mast to find Shiva and Sati below.

'How far is the Dandak forest from here?' asked Sati.

Kali looked around and then back at Sati. 'We are travelling in a large convoy. Normally, the distance should take a month. But I suspect we will take two or three. I don't mind that though. I would rather be slow than dead.'

'You have a way with words, sister.'

Kali smiled with unholy glee.

'Is Panchavati at the centre of the Dandak forest?' asked Shiva.

'No, Shiva. It is more towards the western end.'

'A long way.'

'That's why I said it would take a long time. Once in the *Dandakaranya*, it will take another six months to reach Panchavati.'

'Hmm,' said Shiva. 'We should carry enough food from the ships.'

'No need, Shiva,' said Kali. 'Excess baggage will slow us down. The forests are replete with all the food we need. We just have to be careful that we don't eat something that we shouldn't.'

'But food isn't the only problem. We'll be spending nine months in the forest. There are many other threats.'

Kali eyes lit up. 'Not if you are with me.'

— 人◎� U 午 ⊕ —

Dinner had been served on the deck of the main ship. Shiva had decided to honour the Naga custom of community eating, where many people ate from one humongous plate stitched together from many banana tree leaves.

Shiva, Sati, Kali, Ganesh, Kartik, Parvateshwar, Anandmayi, Bhagirath, Ayurvati, Parshuram, Nandi, Veerbhadra and Krittika sat around the massive plate. Parvateshwar found the custom odd and unhygienic, but as always, followed Shiva's orders.

'What is the reason behind this custom, Your Highness?' asked Bhagirath to Kali.

'We Nagas believe Devi Annapurna, the goddess of food, is one of our collective mothers. After all, doesn't she keep us all alive? What this custom does is that it makes us all receive her blessings together. We eat all our meals, while travelling, in this manner. We are brothers and sisters now. We share the same fate on the journey.'

'That's true,' said Bhagirath, simultaneously thinking that community eating was a good way to hedge against poisoning.

'Is it really that dangerous in Dandak, Your Highness?' asked Parvateshwar. 'Or are these just rumours that ensure discipline?'

'The forest can be abundant and caring like an indulgent mother if we follow her rules. But stray out of line and she can be like a demon who will strike you down. Yes, the rumours help ensure discipline. Nine months is a long time to stick to a fixed path, to not stray. But trust me, those who stray will find that the rumours are not far from hard facts.'

'All right,' said Shiva. 'Enough of this. Let's eat.'

All this while, Ayurvati had been looking at Krittika and Veerbhadra. Between bites, Veerbhadra was pointing towards Kartik and whispering to his wife. They looked at Kartik with loving eyes, almost like he was their own son.

Ayurvati smiled sadly.

— 𝑘⬭⬭⬭ —

'General,' said Veerbhadra.

Parvateshwar was clearly irritated. The two men were on the floating dock next to the lead ship, along with a hundred soldiers. At the lead were Kali and Ganesh. No road was visible. Dense bushes covered the path in every direction.

Seeing Veerbhadra, Parvateshwar calmed down. 'Is the Lord coming?'

'No General, just me.'

Parvateshwar nodded. 'That's all right.' And then, he turned towards Kali. 'Your Highness, I hope you do not expect my men to hack their way through these bushes all the way to Panchavati?'

'Even if I did, I'm sure your Suryavanshi men would be able to do so very easily.'

Parvateshwar's eyes narrowed in irritation. 'My Lady, I am at the end of my tether. You either give me some straight answers or I take my men and sail out of here.'

'I don't know what to do to earn your trust, General. Have I done anything in this journey thus far to hurt your men?' Kali pointed in a westerly direction. 'All I need your men to do now is hack their way through these bushes for a hundred metres in that direction.'

'That's it?'

'That's it.'

Parvateshwar nodded. The soldiers immediately drew their swords and formed a line. Veerbhadra joined them. They moved forward slowly slashing through almost impenetrable bushes. Vishwadyumna and Ganesh were at the two ends of the line, swords drawn, facing outwards. It was obvious from their stance that they were protecting the men from some unknown danger.

A little while later, Veerbhadra and the soldiers were surprised to emerge from the dense undergrowth on to a pathway. It was broad enough for ten horses riding side by side.

'Where, in Lord Ram's name, did this come from?' asked an astonished Parvateshwar.

'The road to heaven,' said Kali. 'But it passes through hell before that.'

Parvateshwar turned back to the Naga Queen.

Kali smiled. 'I told you so. Trust me.'

Veerbhadra walked up and stared in wonder at the road ahead. It ran straight, right into the distance. A stony path, it had been levelled reasonably well. Along the sides, running parallel to the trees, were two continuous hedges of long, thorny creepers.

'Are they poisonous?' asked Parvateshwar, pointing at the twin fences.

'The inside one, on the side of the road, is made of the Nagavalli creeper,' said Kali. 'You can even eat the leaves if you like. But the hedge on the outside, facing the forest, is highly toxic. If you get pricked by its thorns, you will not even have time to say your last prayers.'

Parvateshwar raised his eyebrows. *How did they build all this?*

Veerbhadra turned towards Kali. 'Your Highness, is that it? Is this all we have to do? Uncover this road and keep walking? And we find the city of the Nagas?'

Kali grinned. 'If only life was that simple!'

— ♈◉℧♉⊕ —

The first prahar was just about ending. The sun glimmered over the horizon. Within a few minutes, it would be shining down in all its glory, spreading light and warmth. In the dense Sundarban however, the sun was a shadow of its fiery self. Only a few rays courageously penetrated the heavy foliage to light the pathway for Shiva's convoy.

A company of men had been stationed at the clearing made by hacking the bushes up to the Naga road, with express instructions. Kill anything and everything emerging from the forest.

The foot soldiers marched through the clearing, entering the Naga road with wonder in their eyes. The last thing they had expected was a comfortable and secure road through the forest. The procession was flanked by mounted riders, bearing torches, lighting the way.

Riding a black horse, Vishwadyumna was at the head accompanied by Parvateshwar, Bhagirath and Anandmayi. The Neelkanth's family travelled in the centre, along with Kali, Ayurvati, Krittika and Nandi. Ganesh was at the clearing with Veerbhadra and Parshuram. He would wait till every soldier had passed through. He had a task to do.

'Do we really need a rear guard, Ganesh?' asked Veerbhadra. 'It is almost impossible to find the floating Sundari grove.'

'We are Nagas. Everyone hates us. We can never be too careful.'

'That is the last of the soldiers. What now?'

'Please guard me,' said Ganesh.

Ganesh walked into the clearing bearing a bag of seeds. Veerbhadra and Parshuram walked alongside, their weapons drawn, protecting his right and left flank.

They had been in the clearing for a few moments when a wild boar sauntered in. It was the largest boar Veerbhadra had ever seen. The animal stopped at a distance, staring at the humans, shuffling its front hoof, snorting softly. Parshuram turned to Ganesh. The animal was obviously gearing up to charge. The Naga continued to perform the task of scattering seeds on the ground as he nodded softly. Parshuram lunged and swung hard with his axe, cutting the boar's head off in one clean sweep.

Veerbhadra was edging forward to help Parshuram, when Ganesh stopped him sharply. 'You keep your eyes focussed on the other side, Veerbhadra. Parshuram is capable of handling this.'

Parshuram, meanwhile, continued to hack the beast's

body. He then pulled the fragmented parts of the boar's corpse onto the road.

As Parshuram walked back, he explained to Veerbhadra. 'That carcass will only attract other carnivores.'

Ganesh, meanwhile, had finished scattering all the seeds. He turned and walked back to the road, followed by Parshuram and Veerbhadra.

As soon as they entered the road, Veerbhadra spoke up. 'That was one massive boar.'

'Actually, that one was pretty small since it was young,' said Ganesh. 'Others in its pack would be much larger. You don't want it to be close by when we are defending the road. A sounder of boars in this region can be vicious.'

Veerbhadra turned and looked at the hundred Branga soldiers waiting for them, holding their horses steady. He turned to Ganesh. 'What now?'

'Now we wait,' said Ganesh, drawing his sword, his voice calm. 'We have to protect this gateway till tomorrow morning. Kill everything that tries to enter.'

'Only till tomorrow? Those bushes will not be full grown by then.'

'Oh yes, they will.'

— ⅄◍∇ϙ⊕ —

Veerbhadra was woken up by the loud snarls of a tiger. Some animal, perhaps a deer, had fallen victim to the mighty cat. He looked around. The jungle was waking up. The sun had just risen. Fifty soldiers were sleeping in front of him. Beyond them was the Naga road on which Shiva's entourage had left the previous day.

Veerbhadra pulled his *angvastram* close around himself,

breathing hard onto his hands. It was cold. He saw Parshuram next to him, sleeping soundly, snoring, his mouth slightly open.

Veerbhadra raised himself on his elbows and turned around. The other fifty soldiers were standing guard, their swords drawn. They had taken over from their fellow soldiers at midnight.

'Ganesh?'

'Out here, Veerbhadra,' said Ganesh.

Veerbhadra walked forward as the guards parted to reveal the Lord of the People. Veerbhadra was stunned.

'By the holy lake,' said Veerbhadra. 'The bushes have grown back completely. It's almost as if they had never been cut.'

'The road is protected completely now. We can ride out. Half a day's hard riding and we will catch up with the rest.'

'Then what are we waiting for?'

— ⋏⦿∪�⊕ —

'You should ask him,' said Veerbhadra to Krittika.

It had been a month of uneventful marching through the Sundarban. Despite the mammoth size of the convoy, they were making good progress. Krittika had slipped back from the centre of the convoy to ride with her husband at the rear. She was enjoying her conversations with Ganesh and had grown increasingly fond of the elder son of her mistress.

Ganesh, whose horse was keeping pace with Veerbhadra's and Krittika's, turned. 'Ask me what?'

'Well,' said Krittika. 'Veerbhadra tells me that you weren't too surprised to hear that Emperor Daksha may have killed Lord Chandandhwaj.'

Parshuram pulled his horse up to fall in line with the others. Curious.

'Did you know?' asked Krittika.

'Yes.'

Krittika stared hard at Ganesh's face, trying to glean some traces of hate and anger. There were none. 'Do you not feel the need for vengeance? A sense of injustice?'

'I feel no need for vengeance or justice, Krittika,' said Ganesh. 'Justice exists for the good of the universe. To maintain balance. It does not exist to ignite hatred among humans. Furthermore, I do not have the power to administer justice to the Emperor of Meluha. The universe does. It will deliver justice when it is appropriate. In this life or in the next.'

Parshuram interjected. 'But wouldn't vengeance make you feel better?'

'You got your vengeance, didn't you?' asked Ganesh to Parshuram. 'Did you really feel better?'

Parshuram took a deep breath. He didn't.

'So you don't want anything to be done to Daksha?' asked Veerbhadra.

Ganesh narrowed his eyes. 'I simply don't care.'

Veerbhadra smiled. Parshuram frowned at Veerbhadra's reaction.

'What?' asked Parshuram.

'Nothing much,' said Veerbhadra. 'Just that I have finally understood something Shiva had told me once. That the opposite of love is not hate. Hate is just love gone bad. The actual opposite of love is apathy. When you don't care a damn as to what happens to the other person.'

— 人◎Ʊ무⊕ —

'The food is delicious,' said Shiva, smiling.

It had been two months since Shiva's men had marched out of the floating Sundari grove. They had just entered the dreaded Dandak forests. The road had ended in a giant clearing, capable of accommodating many more than Shiva's band of travelling men. As was the Naga custom, groups of people were eating their dinner together on giant plates.

Kali smiled. 'The forest has everything that we need.'

Sati patted Ganesh on the back. He rode separately from the rest of the family, so Sati enjoyed the common dinners where she got to talk to her elder son. 'Is the food all right?'

'Perfect, *Maa*,' smiled Ganesh.

Ganesh turned to Kartik and slipped a mango to his younger brother. Kartik, who rarely smiled these days, looked at his elder brother with affection. 'Thank you, *dada*.'

Bhagirath looked up at Kali. He couldn't contain himself any longer. 'Your Highness, why are there five roads leading out of this clearing?'

'I was wondering how you had kept yourself from asking that question up until now!'

Everyone turned to Kali.

'Simple. Four of those paths lead you deeper and deeper into the Dandak. To your doom.'

'Which path is the right one?' asked Bhagirath.

'I will tell you tomorrow morning, when we leave.'

'How many such clearings are there, Kali?' asked Shiva.

Kali's lips drew in a broad smile. 'There are five such clearings on the way to Panchavati, Shiva.'

'Lord Ram be merciful,' said Parvateshwar. 'That means

there is only a one in three thousand chance of marching down the right path to Panchavati!'

'Yes,' smiled Kali.

Anandmayi was grinning. 'Well, we better hope you don't forget the right path, Your Highness!'

Kali smiled. 'Trust me, I won't.'

— 🕉 —

Kali looked at Shiva, Sati and Nandi riding a little ahead of her. Shiva had just said something which made Sati and Nandi crack up in laughter. Then the Neelkanth turned to Nandi and winked.

Kali turned to Ayurvati. 'He has the gift.'

They were marching at the centre of the convoy to Panchavati. It had been three months since the march from the Madhumati river. Deep in the Dandak now, the march had been surprisingly uneventful and probably a little tedious. Conversations were the only relief from the boredom.

'What gift?' asked Ayurvati.

'Of bringing peace to people, drawing out their unhappiness,' said Kali.

'That he does,' said Ayurvati. 'But it is one of his many gifts. *Om Namah Shivaiy.*'

Kali was surprised. The Meluhan doctor had just corrupted an old mantra. The words *Om* and *Namah* were only added to the names of the old gods, never living men.

The Queen of the Nagas turned to gaze at Shiva, riding ahead. And smiled. Sometimes, simple faith could lead to profound peace.

Kali repeated Ayurvati's line. '*Om Namah Shivaiy.*'

The universe bows to Lord Shiva. I bow to Lord Shiva.

Ayurvati turned towards Kartik riding a little behind. The boy, a few months older than four, looked like a nine-year-old. He presented a disturbing sight. Scars were visible on his arms and face. Two long swords tied in a cross across his back, no sign of a shield. His eyes were focussed beyond the fence, searching for threats.

Kartik had become withdrawn after the day his elder brother had saved him single-handedly from the lions, nearly dying in the process. He rarely spoke, except to his parents, Krittika and Ganesh. He almost never smiled. He always accompanied hunting parties into the jungle. Many a times, he had brought down animals single-handedly. Awed soldiers had given Ayurvati graphic details of Kartik moving in for the kill: Quiet, focussed and ruthless.

Ayurvati sighed.

Kali, who had developed a strong bond with Ayurvati over the months since they had left Kashi, whispered, 'I think you should be happy he has taken the right lessons from life.'

'He is a child,' said Ayurvati. 'He has many years to go before he grows up.'

'Who are we to decide when it is time for him to grow up,' said Kali. 'The choice belongs to him. He will make all of us proud one day.'

— ᛏ⊚ᚒᚺ⊕ —

It had been eight months since the march from the banks of the Madhumati. The convoy was only a day away from the Naga capital Panchavati. They were camped near the road, next to a mighty river as big as the Saraswati in its early reaches.

Bhagirath thought that this great river must be the fabled Narmada. The border mandated by Lord Manu that was never to be crossed. They were on the northern side of the river.

'This must be the Narmada,' said Bhagirath to Vishwadyumna. 'I guess we'll cross over tomorrow. Lord Manu have mercy on us.'

Parvateshwar spoke up. 'It must be. Narmada is the only river in the southern regions as enormous as the mighty Saraswati.'

Vishwadyumna smiled. They were already far South of the Narmada. 'My Lords, sometimes the mind makes you believe what you want to believe. Look again. There is no need to cross this river.'

Anandmayi's eyes widened in surprise. 'By the great Lord Rudra! This river flows West to East!'

Vishwadyumna nodded. 'That it does, Your Highness.'

This couldn't be the Narmada. That river was known to flow East to West.

'Lord Ram be merciful!' cried Bhagirath. 'How can the existence of such a wide river be a secret?'

'This entire land is a secret, My Lord,' said Vishwadyumna. 'This is the Godavari. And you should see how much bigger it gets by the time it reaches the Eastern Sea.'

Parvateshwar stared in awe. He put his hands together and bowed to the flowing waters.

'The Godavari is not the only one,' said Vishwadyumna. 'I have heard rumours of other such giant rivers further South.'

Bhagirath looked at Vishwadyumna wondering what further surprises lay ahead the next day.

— ⚛ —

'Ganesh,' said Nandi.

'Yes, Major Nandi,' said Ganesh.

Nandi had slipped back to the end of the caravan to relay a message from Kali to Ganesh. 'The Naga outposts will follow their standard practice vis-a-vis the convoy, irrespective of the fact that the Queen and the Lord of the People travel with it.'

Queen Kali, ever cautious when it came to the welfare of her people, was indirectly referring to the fact that the progress of the convoy would now be monitored all the way to the Naga capital so that any potential threats could be neutralised.

Ganesh nodded. 'Thank you, Major.'

Nandi looked back at the small Naga outpost that they had just passed. 'What security can a hundred men provide, Ganesh? They are isolated, a day's journey from the city. The outpost is not even fortified properly. Seeing all the elaborate security measures the Nagas have in place, most of them bordering on genius, this one makes no sense.'

Ganesh smiled. He would normally not have trusted any non-Naga with details of their security. But this was Nandi, Shiva's shadow. Doubting him was like doubting the Neelkanth himself. 'They cannot offer much protection on the road. But if there is such an attack, they trigger an early warning. Their key task then is to set booby traps along the way to Panchavati as they fall back towards the city.'

Nandi frowned. *An outpost just to set booby traps?!*

'But that is not their primary task,' continued Ganesh, pointing with his finger. 'Their key function is to protect us from a river attack.'

Nandi looked at the Godavari. Of course! It must meet

the Eastern Sea somewhere. An opening that could be exploited. The Nagas truly thought of everything.

— 𖤍⦿Ʊ⚶⊕ —

The faint light of the full moon, breaking through the dense foliage intermittently, had lulled the creatures of the Dandak into a false sense of security. All was quiet in Shiva's camp, everyone fast asleep. Most had been awake till late into the night, eagerly discussing the end of their long and surprisingly uneventful journey through the dangerous woods of Sundarban and Dandak. Panchavati was only a day away.

Suddenly, the quiet of the night was broken by the shrill call of a loud conch shell. Actually, many shells.

Kali, at the centre of the huge encampment, was up immediately. As were Shiva, Sati and Kartik.

'What the hell is that?' shouted Shiva, over the din.

Kali was looking towards the river, stunned. This had never happened before. She turned back towards Shiva, teeth bared. 'Your men have betrayed us!'

The entire camp was up as the conch shells kept persistently sounding out their warning.

Ganesh, closest to the blaring conches at the camp end nearest to the river, was making a beeline for it, Nandi, Veerbhadra and Parshuram in tow.

'What is going on?' screamed Veerbhadra, to make himself heard over the din.

'Enemy ships are sailing up the Godavari,' shouted Ganesh. 'They have tripped our river warning system.'

'What now?' yelled Nandi.

'To the outpost! We have devil boats!'

Nandi turned around and relayed out the order to the three hundred men who had already rallied around to face the unknown threat. The soldiers had been following close on the heels of the four men. They doubled back to the outpost, where the hundred Naga men were already pushing out their devil boats.

Meanwhile Vishwadyumna, at the end farthermost from the enemy threat, rapidly controlled his disbelief and started carrying out the standard drill set in place for such an eventuality. A red flame was lit, warning Panchavati in the distance.

Meanwhile, Bhagirath ran up to Vishwadyumna. 'What are your river defences?'

Vishwadyumna glared angrily at Bhagirath, refusing to answer. He was sure the Nagas had been betrayed.

Bhagirath shook his head and ran to Parvateshwar, who was already gathering soldiers and deploying them in defensive formations along the river.

'Any news?' asked Parvateshwar.

'He won't talk, Parvateshwar,' screamed Bhagirath. 'My fears have come true. They have betrayed us. We walked straight into a trap!'

Parvateshwar clenched his fists, looking at the five hundred men arrayed behind him in battle formation. 'Kill everything that emerges from the river!'

And then, the sky lit up, ablaze at a thousand points. Bhagirath looked up. 'Lord Ram be merciful.'

A shower of fiery arrows flew high. They had obviously been fired from a distance, from the battleships racing up the Godavari.

'Shields up!' screamed Parvateshwar.

At the centre, Shiva and Kali had issued similar orders.

Soldiers ducked under their shields, waiting for the onslaught of flaming arrows to stop. But scores of arrows had already found their targets. Setting clothes on fire and piercing through many bodies. Injuring large numbers and killing some unfortunate ones.

There was no respite. The curtain of arrows kept raining down in an almost continuous shower.

One arrow hit Ayurvati's leg. She screamed in pain, folding her leg closer to her body, holding her shield nearer.

The sudden attack and its severity had forced most of Shiva's camp to cower behind their shields. But real fighting was on at the river end of the campsite, within the Godavari itself.

'Quickly!' screamed Ganesh. If the downpour of arrows continued for a few more minutes, the entire camp would be destroyed. He had to move fast.

His soldiers, the Suryavanshis, Chandravanshis and the Nagas, were swimming hard, pushing the hundred small boats towards the five large ships rowing rapidly up the Godavari. The small boats, with dried firewood and a small flint inside, had been covered by a thick cloth. Once in range, the devil boats would be lit and rammed into the ships. Fire was the best way to destroy such large, wooden ships.

The ships were sailing up river rapidly, the flaming arrows still being continuously shot from their decks. Due to the manic speed of the vessels coming towards them, Ganesh's soldiers didn't have to swim too far to reach the enemy battle ships. The devil boats were already in place, aligned to ram into them.

'Light them!' screamed Ganesh.

Soldiers rapidly pulled the cloth off each boat and struck the flints. The boats were aflame almost instantaneously, before the assassins on any ship could react. Ganesh's men pushed the boats into the sides of the ships.

'Hold them in place!' screamed Nandi. 'The ships have to catch fire!'

The lookout assassins on the ships turned their bows onto their attackers in the water. A hailstorm of arrows started tearing into the brave soldiers in the river, maiming and killing many. The fire from the devil boats was also lapping Ganesh's men, but they grimly kept swimming, pushing the boats onto the ships.

All five ships were aflame within moments, but the loss of life till they had caught fire made it seem like an eternity.

'Back to the shore!' screamed Ganesh.

He knew he had to form his line on the Godavari's banks now. As fire spread through the ships, the assassins would jump over or into lifeboats and row up to the shores to resume battle.

Ganesh's soldiers had barely made it to the riverbanks when they heard a deafening blast. They turned around in shock. The first ship of the enemy fleet had just blown up. Within a few moments, the other ships went up in gigantic explosions as well.

Ganesh turned to Parshuram, stunned. '*Daivi astras!*'

Parshuram nodded, shocked out of his wits. Only *divine weapons* could have led to such explosions. But how could anyone lay their hands on such weapons? And that too in such alarming quantities?

Ganesh rallied his men, counting the living. He had lost one hundred of the valiant four hundred who had charged behind him, mostly Nagas — the only ones who knew the drill. The Lord of the People gritted his teeth in anger and marched towards the camp to find Kali and Shiva.

— ⵝⵔⵓⵝ⊛ —

'You led us into a trap!' a livid Parvateshwar screamed. He had lost twenty men in the hail of arrows.

The number of dead in the camp centre was significantly higher. Close to fifty soldiers had been killed. The highest casualties were of course at the end closest to the enemy warships. Three hundred soldiers had died there, including the hundred that were killed while attacking the enemy ships. Ayurvati, with a broken shaft buried in her thigh, was rushing around with her medics, trying to save as many as she could.

'Nonsense!' yelled Kali. 'You betrayed us! Nobody has ever attacked us from the Godavari. Ever!'

'Quiet!' shouted Shiva. He turned to Veerbhadra, Parshuram, Nandi and Ganesh, who had just arrived. 'What were those explosions, Parshuram?'

'*Daivi astras*, My Lord,' said Parshuram. 'The five enemy ships were carrying them. The fires triggered the explosions.'

Shiva breathed deeply, staring into the distance.

'My Lord,' said Bhagirath. 'Turn back now. More traps await us on the way and at Panchavati itself. There are only two Nagas here. Think of what a fifty thousand could do!'

Kali exploded. 'This is your doing! Panchavati has never been attacked. You led your cohorts here. It was lucky that Ganesh led a fight back and decimated your troops. Otherwise we would all have been slaughtered.'

Sati touched Kali lightly. She wanted to point out

that even Suryavanshi and Chandravanshi men fighting alongside Ganesh had been killed.

'Enough!' shouted Shiva. 'Don't any of you get what really happened?'

The Neelkanth turned towards Nandi and Kartik. 'Take a hundred men and go down-river. See if there are any survivors from the enemy ships. I want to know who they were.'

Nandi and Kartik left immediately.

Shiva looked at the people around him, seething. 'We were all betrayed. Whosoever was firing those arrows was not picking and choosing targets. They wanted us all dead.'

'But how did they come up the Godavari?' asked Kali.

Shiva glared at her. 'How the hell should I know? Most people here didn't even know this river wasn't the Narmada!'

'It has to be the Nagas, My Lord,' said Bhagirath. 'They cannot be trusted!'

'Sure!' said Shiva, sarcastically. 'The Nagas sprung this trap to kill their own Queen. And then Ganesh led a counterattack on his own people and blew them up with *daivi astras*. If he had *daivi astras* and wanted us dead, why didn't he just use the weapons on us?'

Pin-drop silence.

'I think the astras were meant to destroy Panchavati. They planned to slaughter us easily from their ships and then sail up to the Naga capital and destroy it as well. What they didn't bet on was the Naga wariness and extensive security measures, including the devil boats. That saved us.'

What the Neelkanth was saying made sense. Ganesh thanked Bhoomidevi silently that the Naga Rajya Sabha had agreed to his proposal of arming the banks of the Godavari outpost with devil boats for any such eventuality.

'Someone wants us all dead,' said Shiva. 'Someone powerful enough to get such a large arsenal of *daivi astras*. Someone who knows about the existence of such a huge river in the South and has the ability to identify its sea route. Someone resourceful enough to get a fleet of ships with enough soldiers to attack us. Who is that person? That is the question.'

The sun was rising slowly over the horizon, spreading light and warmth over the tired camp. A relief party from Panchavati had just arrived with food and medical supplies. Ayurvati had finally relented and was resting in a medical tent, after having been assured that most of the injured were taken care of. The death toll had not risen further as the night had progressed. Even those with nearly fatal injuries had been saved.

Kartik and Nandi trooped into the camp after the night long search along the river and went straight up to Shiva. Kartik spoke first. 'There are no survivors, *baba*.'

'My Lord, we checked both the riverbanks,' Nandi added. 'Went through all the wreckage. Even rowed five kilometres downriver, in case some survivors had been washed off. But we found no one alive.'

Shiva cursed silently. He suspected who the attackers were but wasn't certain. He called Parvateshwar and Bhagirath. 'Both of you recognise the ships in your respective countries. I want you to study the wrecks properly. I want to know if any of those ships were Meluhan or Swadweepan.'

'My Lord,' cried Parvateshwar. 'It cannot be...'

'Parvateshwar, please do this for me,' interrupted Shiva. 'I want an honest answer. Where did those goddamned ships come from?'

Parvateshwar saluted the Neelkanth. 'As you command, My Lord.'

The Meluhan General left, followed by Bhagirath.

— 𝕏⦿ᵾ𝟺⊕ —

'You think it's a coincidence that this attack happened just a day before you were to discover the secret?'

Shiva and Sati were sitting in a semi-secluded area along the river near the camp. It was the last hour of the first prahar. The cremation ceremonies had been completed. Though the injured were in no state to travel, the general consensus was that reaching the safety of Panchavati was imperative. The Naga city offered better protection than an indefensible forest road. The Nagas had arranged carts to carry the injured in the convoy to their capital and were scheduled to leave within the hour.

'I can't say,' said Shiva.

Sati remained quiet, looking into the distance.

'You think... that your father could be...'

Sati sighed. 'After all that I have learned about him recently, I would not put it past him.'

Shiva reached out and held Sati.

'But I don't think he can order an attack of this magnitude all by himself,' continued Sati. 'He doesn't have the capability. Who is the master puppeteer? And why is he doing this?'

Shiva nodded. 'That is the mystery. But first, I need to know this big secret. I have a feeling the answers could be deeply connected with all that is going on in Meluha, Swadweep and Panchavati.'

— ⸱𝄇⟐⎔⬡ —

The sun was high when the entourage, bloodied and tired, marched up the river banks of the Godavari to the Naga capital, *Panchavati*. The *land of the five banyan trees.*

These weren't just any odd five banyans. Their legend had begun more than a thousand years ago. These were the trees under which the seventh Vishnu, Ram, accompanied by his wife Sita and brother Lakshman, had rested during their exile from Ayodhya. They had set up house close to these trees. This was also the unfortunate place from where the demon king Ravan had kidnapped Sita, triggering a war with Ram. That war destroyed Ravan's glittering and obscenely rich kingdom of Lanka.

Panchavati was situated on the north-eastern banks of the Godavari. The river flowed down from the mountains of the Western Ghats towards the Eastern Sea. To the West of Panchavati, the river took a strange ninety degree turn to the South, flowed straight down for a little less than a kilometre and then turned East once again to continue its journey to the sea. This turn of the Godavari allowed the Nagas to build grand canals, and to use this cleared part of the Dandak to meet the agricultural needs of their citizens.

To the surprise of the Suryavanshis, Panchavati was built on a raised platform, much like the cities of Meluha. Strong walls of cut stone rose high, with turrets at regular intervals to defend against invaders. The area around the walls, extending a long distance, was used by Nagas for agricultural purposes. There was also a comfortable colony of guest houses set up for regular Branga visitors. A second wall surrounded these lands. Beyond this second wall, land was again cleared far and wide, to give a clear line of sight of approaching enemies.

Panchavati had been established by Bhoomidevi. The mysterious non-Naga lady had instituted the present way of life of the Nagas. Nobody knew the antecedents of Bhoomidevi. And she had strictly forbidden any image of hers from being recorded. Hence the only memories of the founder of the present Naga civilisation were her laws and statements. The city of Panchavati was the epitome of her way of life, combining the best of the Suryavanshis and the Chandravanshis. It loudly proclaimed her aspiration above the city gates. '*Satyam. Sundaram.*' Truth. Beauty.

Shiva's convoy was allowed entry from the outer gates and led straight to the Branga guest quarters. Each member of the convoy was assigned comfortable rooms.

'Why don't you relax, Shiva,' said Kali. 'I will bring the secret out.'

'I want to go into Panchavati now,' said Shiva.

'Are you sure? Aren't you tired?'

'Of course I'm tired. But I need to see the secret right now.'

'All right.'

— 𝍏 ⦿ ꭂ 𝍩 ⊕ —

While Shiva's company waited outside in the guesthouse, Kali and Ganesh led Shiva and Sati into the city.

The city was nothing like they had expected. It had been laid out in a neat grid-like pattern, much like Meluhan cities. But the Nagas appeared to have taken the Suryavanshi ideal of justice and equality to its logical extreme. Every single house, including that of the Queen, was of exactly the same design and size. There were no poor or rich amongst the fifty thousand Nagas who lived there.

'Everyone lives the same way in Panchavati?' Sati asked Ganesh.

'Of course not, *Maa*. Everyone has a right to decide what they want to do with their lives. But the state provides housing and basic necessities. And in that, there is complete equality.'

Practically all the inhabitants had lined up outside their houses to see the Neelkanth walk by. They had heard of the mysterious attack on the Neelkanth's convoy. The people were thanking Bhoomidevi that nothing had happened to their Queen or the Lord of the People.

Shiva was shocked to see that many people did not have any deformities. He saw many of them cradling Naga babies in their arms.

'What are these non-Nagas doing in Panchavati?' asked Shiva.

'They are parents of Naga children,' said Kali.

'And they live here?'

'Some parents abandon their Naga children,' said Kali. 'And some feel a strong bond with their progeny. Strong enough to overcome their fear of societal prejudices. We give refuge to such people in Panchavati.'

'Who takes care of Naga babies whose parents abandon them?' asked Sati.

'Childless Nagas,' said Kali. 'Nagas cannot have natural

children. So they readily adopt the abandoned children from Meluha and Swadweep and bring them up as their own. With the love and attention that is the birthright of every child.'

They walked in silence to the city centre. It was here, around the five legendary banyan trees, that all the communal buildings were situated. These edifices, to be used by all the residents of Panchavati, had been built in the grand style of Swadweepan buildings. There was a school, a temple dedicated to Lord Rudra and Lady Mohini, a public bath and a stadium for performances, where the fifty thousand citizens met regularly. Music, dance and drama were coveted lifestyle choices and not paths to knowledge.

'Where is the secret?' asked Shiva, getting impatient.

'In here, Lord Neelkanth,' said Ganesh, pointing to the school.

Shiva frowned. A secret in a school? He expected it to be in the spiritual centre of the city, the temple of Lord Rudra. He walked towards the building. The rest followed.

The school had been built in traditional style around an open courtyard. A colonnaded corridor ran along the courtyard with doors leading into the classrooms. At the far end was a large open room. The library. Along the side of the library was another large corridor leading to the playground beyond the main building. On the other side of the ground were the other facilities such as halls and practice laboratories.

'Please keep quiet,' said Kali. 'The classes are still on. We would like to disturb only one class and not all of them.'

'We will disturb none,' said Shiva, walking towards the

library, where he expected the secret of the Nagas to be. Perhaps a book?

'Lord Neelkanth,' said Ganesh, halting Shiva mid-stride.

Shiva stopped. Ganesh pointed to the curtained entrance of a classroom. Shiva frowned. An oddly familiar voice was expounding philosophies. The voice was crystal clear behind the curtain.

'New philosophies today blame desire for everything. Desire is the root cause of all suffering, all destruction, right?'

'Yes, Guruji,' said a student.

'Please explain,' said the teacher.

'Because desire creates attachment. Attachment to this world. And, when you don't get what you want or get what you don't want, it leads to suffering. This leads to anger. And that to violence and wars. Which finally results in destruction.'

'So if you want to avoid destruction and suffering, you should control your desires, right?' asked the teacher. 'Give up *maya*, the *illusion* of this world?'

Shiva, from the other side of the curtain, answered silently. *Yes.*

'But the Rig Veda, one of our main sources of philosophy,' continued the teacher, 'says that in the beginning of time, there was nothing except darkness and a primordial flood. Then out of this darkness, desire was born. Desire was the primal seed, the germ of creation. And from here, we all know that the *Prajapati*, the *Lord of the Creatures*, created the Universe and everything in it. So in a sense, desire is the root of creation as well.'

Shiva was mesmerised by the voice on the other side of the curtain. *Good point.*

'How can desire be the source of creation as well as destruction?'

The students were quiet, stumped for answers.

'Think about this in another way. Is it possible to destroy anything that has not been created?'

'No, Guruji.'

'On the other hand, is it safe to assume that anything that has been created, has to be destroyed at some point in time?'

'Yes,' answered a student.

'That is the purpose of desire. It is for creation and destruction. It is the beginning and the end of a journey. Without desire, there is nothing.'

Shiva smiled. *There must be a Vasudev Pandit in that room!*

The Neelkanth turned to Kali. 'Let's go to the library. I want to read the secret. I will meet Panditji later.'

Kali held Shiva. 'The secret is not a thing. It is a man.'

Shiva was taken aback. His eyes wide with surprise.

Ganesh pointed at the curtained entrance to the classroom. 'And he waits for you in there.'

Shiva stared at Ganesh, immobilised. The Lord of the People gently drew the curtain aside. 'Guruji, please forgive the interruption. Lord Neelkanth is here.'

Then Ganesh stepped aside.

Shiva entered and was immediately stunned by what he saw.

What the hell!

He turned to Ganesh, bewildered. The Lord of the People smiled softly. The Neelkanth turned back to the teacher.

'I have been waiting for you, my friend,' said the teacher. He was smiling, his eyes moist. 'I'd told you. I would go anywhere for you. Even into *Patallok* if it would help you.'

Shiva had rerun this line in his mind again and again. Never fully understanding the reference to the *land of the demons*. Now it all clicked into place.

The beard had been shaved off, replaced by a pencil-thin moustache. The broad shoulders and barrel chest, earlier hidden beneath a slight layer of fat, had been honed through regular exercise. The *janau, the string signifying Brahmin antecedents*, traced a path over newly-developed, rippling muscles. The head remained shaved, but the tuft of hair at the back of his head appeared longer and better oiled. The deep-set eyes had the same serenity that had drawn Shiva to him earlier. It was his long-lost friend. His comrade in arms. His brother.

'Brahaspati!'

...*to be continued.*

Glossary

Agni: God of fire

Agnipariksha: A trial by fire

Angaharas: Movement of limbs or steps in a dance

Ankush: Hook-shaped prods used to control elephants

Annapurna: The Hindu Goddess of food, nourishment and plenty; also believed to be a form of Goddess Parvati

Anshan: Hunger. It also denotes voluntary fasting. In this book, Anshan is the capital of the kingdom of Elam

Apsara: Celestial maidens from the court of the Lord of the Heavens – Indra; akin to Zeus/Jupiter

Arya: Sir

Ashwamedh yagna: Literally, the Horse sacrifice. In ancient times, an ambitious ruler, who wished to expand his territories and display his military prowess, would release a sacrificial horse to roam freely through the length and breadth of any kingdom in India. If any king stopped/captured the horse, the ruler's army would declare war against the challenger, defeat the king and annexe that territory. If an opposing king did not stop the horse, the kingdom would become a vassal of the former

Asura: Demon

Ayuralay:	Hospital
Ayurvedic:	Derived from Ayurved, an ancient Indian form of medicine
Ayushman bhav:	May you have a long life
Baba:	Father
Bhang:	Traditional intoxicant in India; milk mixed with marijuana
Bhiksha:	Alms or donations
Bhojan graham:	Dining room
Brahmacharya:	The vow of celibacy
Brahmastra:	Literally, the weapon of Brahma; spoken of in ancient Hindu scriptures. Many experts claim that the description of a Brahmastra and its effects are eerily similar to that of a nuclear weapon. I have assumed this to be true in the context of my book
Branga:	The ancient name for modern West Bengal, Assam and Bangladesh. Term coined from the conjoint of the two rivers of this land: *Brahmaputra* and *Ganga*
Brangaridai:	Literally, the heart of Branga. The capital of the kingdom of Branga
Chandravanshi:	Descendants of the moon
Chaturanga:	Ancient Indian game that evolved into the modern game of chess
Chillum:	Clay pipe, usually used to smoke marijuana
Choti:	Braid
Construction of Devagiri royal court platform:	The description in the book of the court platform is a possible explanation for the mysterious multiple-column buildings made of baked brick discovered at Indus Valley sites, usually next to the public baths, which many historians suppose could have been granaries
Dada:	Elder brother

Daivi Astra:	Daivi = Divine; Astra = Weapon. A term used in ancient Hindu epics to describe weapons of mass destruction
Dandakaranya:	Aranya = forest. Dandak is the ancient name for modern Maharashtra and parts of Andhra Pradesh, Karnataka, Chhattisgarh and Madhya Pradesh. So Dandakaranya means the forests of Dandak
Deva:	God
Dharma:	Dharma literally translates as religion. But in traditional Hindu belief, it means far more than that. The word encompasses holy, right knowledge, right living, tradition, natural order of the universe and duty. Essentially, dharma refers to everything that can be classified as 'good' in the universe. It is the Law of Life
Dharmayudh:	The holy war
Dhobi:	Washerman
Divyadrishti:	Divine sight
Dumru:	A small, hand-held, hour-glass shaped percussion instrument
Egyptian women:	Historians believe that ancient Egyptians, just like ancient Indians, treated their women with respect. The anti-women attitude attributed to Swuth and the assassins of Aten is fictional. Having said that, like most societies, ancient Egyptians also had some patriarchal segments in their society, which did, regrettably, have an appalling attitude towards women
Fire song:	This is a song sung by Guna warriors to agni (fire). They also had songs dedicated to the other elements viz: *bhūmi* (earth), *jal* (water), *pavan* (air or wind), *vyom* or *shunya* or *akash* (ether or void or sky)

Fravashi: Is the guardian spirit mentioned in the *Avesta*, the sacred writings of the Zoroastrian religion. Although, according to most researchers, there is no physical description of Fravashi, the language grammar of *Avesta* clearly shows it to be feminine. Considering the importance given to fire in ancient Hinduism and Zoroastrianism, I've assumed the Fravashi to be represented by fire. This is, of course, a fictional representation

Ganesh-Kartik relationship: In northern India, traditional myths hold Lord Kartik as older than Lord Ganesh; in large parts of southern India, Lord Ganesh is considered elder. In my story, Ganesh is older than Kartik. What is the truth? Only Lord Shiva knows

Guruji: Teacher; ji is a term of respect, added to a name or title

Gurukul: The family of the guru or the family of the teacher. In ancient times, also used to denote a school

Har Har Mahadev: This is the rallying cry of Lord Shiva's devotees. I believe it means 'All of us are Mahadevs'

Hariyupa: This city is currently known as Harappa. A note on the cities of Meluha (or as we call it in modern times, the Indus Valley Civilisation): historians and researchers have consistently marvelled at the fixation that the Indus Valley Civilisation seemed to have for water and hygiene. In fact historian M Jansen used the term 'wasserluxus' (obsession with water) to describe their magnificent obsession with the physical and symbolic aspects of water, a term Gregory Possehl builds upon in his brilliant book, *The Indus Civilisation — A Contemporary Perspective*. In the book, *The Immortals of Meluha*, the obsession with water is shown to arise due to its cleansing of the toxic sweat and urine triggered by consuming the Somras. Historians have also marvelled at the level of sophisticated standardisation in the Indus Valley Civilisation. One of the examples of this was the bricks, which across the entire civilisation, had similar proportions and specifications

Holi:	Festival of colours
Howdah:	Carriage placed on top of elephants
Indra:	The God of the sky; believed to be the King of the gods
Jai Guru Vishwamitra:	Glory to the teacher Vishwamitra
Jai Guru Vashishta:	Glory to the teacher Vashishta. Only two Suryavanshis were privileged to have had both Guru Vashishta and Guru Vishwamitra as their gurus (teachers) viz. Lord Ram and Lord Lakshman
Jai Shri Brahma:	Glory to Lord Brahma
Jai Shri Ram:	Glory to Lord Ram
Janau:	A ceremonial thread tied from the shoulders, across the torso. It was one of the symbols of knowledge in ancient India. Later, it was corrupted to become a caste symbol to denote those born as Brahmins and not those who'd acquired knowledge through their effort and deeds
Ji:	A suffix added to a name or title as a form of respect
Kajal:	Kohl, or eye liner
Karma:	Duty and deeds; also the sum of a person's actions in this and previous births,

	considered to limit the options of future action and affect future fate
Karmasaathi:	Fellow traveller in karma or duty
Kashi:	The ancient name for modern Varanasi. Kashi means the city where the supreme light shines
Kathak:	A form of traditional Indian dance
Kriyas:	Actions
Kulhads:	Mud cups
Maa:	Mother
Mandal:	Literally, Sanskrit word meaning circle. Mandals are created, as per ancient Hindu and Buddhist tradition, to make a sacred space and help focus the attention of the devotees
Mahadev:	Maha = Great and Dev = God. Hence Mahadev means the greatest God or the God of Gods. I believe that there were many 'destroyers of evil' but a few of them were so great that they would be called 'Mahadev'. Amongst the Mahadevs were Lord Rudra and Lord Shiva
Mahasagar:	Great Ocean; Hind Mahasagar is the Indian Ocean
Mahendra:	Ancient Indian name meaning conqueror of the world
Mahout:	Human handler of elephants
Manu's story:	Those interested in finding out more about the historical validity of the South India origin theory of Manu should read Graham Hancock's pathbreaking book, *Underworld*
Mausi:	Mother's sister, literally translating as maa *si* i.e. like a mother
Maya:	Illusion
Mehragarh:	Modern archaeologists believe that Mehragarh is the progenitor of the Indus

	Valley civilisation. Mehragarh represents a sudden burst of civilised living, without any archaeological evidence of a gradual progression to that level. Hence, those who established Mehragarh were either immigrants or refugees
Meluha:	The land of pure life. This is the land ruled by the Suryavanshi kings. It is the area that we in the modern world call the Indus Valley Civilisation
Meluhans:	People of Meluha
Mudras:	Gestures
Naga:	Serpent people
Namaste:	An ancient Indian greeting. Spoken along with the hand gesture of open palms of both the hands joined together. Conjoin of three words. 'Namah', 'Astu' and 'Te' – meaning 'I bow to the godhood in you'. Namaste can be used as both 'hello' and 'goodbye'
Nirvana:	Enlightenment; freedom from the cycle of rebirths
Oxygen/ anti-oxidants theory:	Modern research backs this theory. Interested readers can read the article 'Radical Proposal' by Kathryn Brown in the *Scientific American*
Panchavati:	The land of the five banyan trees
Pandit:	Priest
Paradaeza:	An ancient Persian word which means 'the walled place of harmony'; the root of the English word, Paradise
Pariha:	The land of fairies. Refers to modern Persia/Iran. I believe Lord Rudra came from this land
Parmatma:	The ultimate soul or the sum of all souls

**Parsee immigration
to India:** Groups of Zoroastrian refugees immigrated to India perhaps between the 8th and 10th century AD to escape religious persecution. They landed in Gujarat, and the local ruler Jadav Rana gave them refuge

Pashupatiastra: Literally, the weapon of the Lord of the Animals. The descriptions of the effects of the Pashupatiastra in Hindu scriptures are quite similar to that of nuclear weapons. In modern nuclear technology, weapons have been built primarily on the concept of nuclear fission. While fusion-boosted fission weapons have been invented, pure fusion weapons have not been invented as yet. Scientists hold that a pure nuclear fusion weapon has far less radioactive fallout and can theoretically serve as a more targeted weapon. In this trilogy, I have assumed that the Pashupatiastra is one such weapon

Patallok: The underworld

Pawan Dev: God of the winds

Pitratulya: The term for a man who is 'like a father'

Prahar: Four slots of six hours each into which the day was divided by the ancient Hindus; the first prahar began at twelve midnight

Prithvi: Earth

Prakrati: Nature

Puja: Prayer

Puja thali: Prayer tray

Raj dharma: Literally, the royal duties of a king or ruler. In ancient India, this term embodied pious and just administration of the king's royal duties

Raj guru: Royal sage

Rajat:	Silver
Rajya Sabha:	The royal council
Rakshabandhan:	Raksha = Protection; Bandhan = thread/tie. An ancient Indian festival in which a sister ties a sacred thread on her brother's wrist, seeking his protection
Ram Chandra:	Ram = Face; Chandra = Moon. Hence Ram Chandra is 'the face of the moon'
Ram Rajya:	The rule of Ram
Rangbhoomi:	Literally, the ground of colour. Stadia in ancient times where sports, performances and public functions would be staged
Rangoli:	Traditional colourful and geometric designs made with coloured powders or flowers as a sign of welcome
Rishi:	Man of knowledge
Sankat Mochan:	Literally, reliever from troubles. One of the names of Lord Hanuman
Sangam:	A confluence of two rivers
Sanyasi:	A person who renounces all his worldly possessions and desires to retreat to remote locations and devote his time to the pursuit of god and spirituality. In ancient India, it was common for people to take sanyas at an old age, once they had completed all their life's duties
Sapt Sindhu:	Land of the seven rivers – Indus, Saraswati, Yamuna, Ganga, Sarayu, Brahmaputra and Narmada. This was the ancient name of North India
Saptrishi:	One of the 'Group of seven Rishis'
Saptrishi Uttradhikari:	Successors of the Saptrishis
Shakti Devi:	Mother Goddess; also Goddess of power and energy
Shamiana:	Canopy
Shloka:	Couplet
Shudhikaran:	The purification ceremony

Sindhu:	The first river
Somras:	Drink of the gods
Sundarban:	Sundar = beautiful; ban = forest. Hence, Sundarban means beautiful forest
Svarna:	Gold
Swadweep:	The Island of the individual. This is the land ruled by the Chandravanshi kings
Swadweepans:	People of Swadweep
Swaha:	Legend has it that Lord Agni's wife is named Swaha. Hence it pleases Lord Agni, the God of Fire, if a disciple takes his wife's name while worshipping the sacred fire. Another interpretation of Swaha is that it means offering of self
Tamra:	Bronze
Thali:	Plate
Varjish graha:	The exercise hall
Varun:	God of the water and the seas
Vijayibhav:	May you be victorious
Vikarma:	Carrier of bad fate
Vishnu:	The protector of the world and propagator of good. I believe that it is an ancient Hindu title for the greatest of leaders who would be remembered as the mightiest of gods
Vishwanath:	Literally, the Lord of the World. Usually refers to Lord Shiva, also known as Lord Rudra in his angry avatar. I believe Lord Rudra was a different individual from Lord Shiva. In this trilogy, I have used the term Vishwanath to refer to Lord Rudra
Yagna:	Sacrificial fire ceremony

Amish is a 1974-born, IIM (Kolkata)-educated, boring banker turned happy author. The success of his debut book, *The Immortals of Meluha* (Book 1 of the Shiva Trilogy), encouraged him to give up a fourteen-year-old career in financial services to focus on writing. He is passionate about history, mythology and philosophy, finding beauty and meaning in all world religions.

Amish lives in Mumbai with his wife Preeti and son Neel.

www.authoramish.com
www.facebook.com/authoramish
www.twitter.com/authoramish